Shadrach Tompkins was lured from the coal mines of England by the promise of a rich new life in America, but instead he found an unfriendly wilderness and a desperate people in search of a home for their beliefs.

SPOKEN IN WHISPERS . . .

Sarah Putnam fell in love with the handsome Shadrach, but she would have to overcome jealousy and envy in order to share her bed and her man with other women, unlike her in every way except for their passion for Shadrach.

CARVED IN STONE . . .

A powerful story of proud pioneers, escaping murder, starvation and persecution—an epic saga of a passionate people who scratched an unlikely empire from the alkaline wastes of the Great Utah Basin. It was their Zion, where they would obey no laws but God's, and it would be called . . .

DESERET!

DESERET

ERIC ALTER

PINNACLE BOOKS  **NEW YORK**

DESERET

Copyright © 1983 by Eric Alter

An original Pinnacle Books edition, published for the first time anywhere.

First printing, May 1983

ISBN: 0-523-41483-8

Cover illustration by John Solie

Printed in the United States of America

PINNACLE BOOKS, INC.
1430 Broadway
New York, New York 10018

Tompkins Family Tree

Nicholas Tompkins (1791–1829) — Martha Morrison (1800–1832)

Children:
- Shadrach Tompkins (1818–)
- Lemuel Tompkins (1825–1835)

Sarah Putnam (1820–) m. 1838	Rachel Putnam (1817–) m. 1844	Polly Halloran (1826–) m. 1847	Mariah (Kaleesh) (?–1855) m. 1851	Theresa Gluck (1831–) (m. 1862)	Wamoa (?–) m. 1867	Lilly Lamont (1854–) m. 1872
Ham	Rebbecca	Finnegan	Walker	Ilsa	Aaron	
Zina	John	Brian Boru		Bernard	Bethany	
Orson	Nathan	Wolf Tone		Karl	Meeshach	
Lehi	Eliza	Erin		Gertrude	Abednigo	
Martha	Lemuel	Craig		Johanna	Cynthia	
Samuel	Ebeneezer	Molly		Nicholas	Joseph	
Katherine	Eli	Gerard		Alexander	Sharon	
	Charles			Joachim	James	
	Mathew				John	
					Bea	
					Peter	

The founding of Deseret, later to become Utah, was one of the most heroic chapters of the American saga. But because of the controversy surrounding the era, it has been neglected by historians.

This novel chronicles the unparalleled courage, the suffering, the brilliant dreams and great accomplishments of a unique people.

It is to these powerful men and brave women that this book is dedicated.

DESERET

Chapter One

In lower Utah, the earth is as rumpled as a giant's unmade bed. The land flashes with patterns of bright colors like a patchwork quilt covering that bed. The restless landscape was created when the mountains of Utah were pushed off into a corner by themselves. Ignored by the rest of the world, they became as wrinkled and angry as an old woman's brow.

Crumbling rock fortresses block the way of any traveler. The only easy entrance to this land was created by a few rivers that leave tracks like muddy sidewinders. The silence of the canyons is scarcely disturbed by a puff of wind, a sprinkling of snow or the tinkle of falling rock. Only the cry of a raven disturbs ten thousand square miles of weathered sandstone.

It is a heroic land, made for heroic people. . . .

Late in the summer of 1911, the gorge of the Kanaputs echoed with the popping exhaust of a Model-T Ford which churned axle deep through the sand of a dry river bottom. The driver of the car was a blond-haired young man named George Armstrong who had managed to stay clean-shaven even in the middle of the wilderness. The temperature under the black canvas top of the Ford reached one hundred and thirty degrees. The salt in his own sweat stung his eyes, but Armstrong refused to loosen the black tie which held together the collar points of his starched white shirt.

When the wheels of the Model-T spun helplessly in the coarse sand, the car bogged down. A local person would have loudly cursed his luck, kicked the car, and hiked back to the nearest ranch for a team of mules to pull him free. Instead, Armstrong picked a black briefcase from the Ford and continued up the canyon, slogging through the sand on foot.

The ochre sandstone walls of the narrow gorge rose one thousand feet above his head as he traveled toward Anvil

Butte. He clamored over slick rock worn smooth by eons of floods. He passed by fossils left by ancient oceans. He walked under carvings left by prehistoric hunters.

Armstrong spent the night in Kanaputs Gorge, shivering on the ice cold rock wondering how it could have been so hot in the daytime. In the slit of sky squeezed between the overhead cliffs, the black night was freckled with billions of stars.

The next day, Armstrong ascended Anvil Butte, a flat-topped mountain which looked as solid as a safe in the Deseret Bank. The only trail was a narrow rim of rock which led up the sheer face of the mountain. The sun poured down on him like rifle fire and he had to steady himself against the burning face of the mountain to keep from falling dizzily into the abyss.

The afternoon sun had fallen below the next ridge when Armstrong neared the top of the butte. Ahead of him in the shadows of an overhang, the grey stone ruins of an Indian dwelling stood hidden by the cliff. The sudden loss of sunlight removed the last friendliness from the cliff face and it now took on a more sinister feeling.

His own labored breathing and the rustle of falling pebbles were the only sounds for one hundred miles.

He quickened his pace, anxious to reach the top of the Butte by sundown. To his surprise, the trail narrowed and then dwindled away to nothing, fading into the sheer face of the cliff. Armstrong was left with no way to reach the top of the butte. Moreover, he now faced a long trek down the steep trail at night.

For the first time, he loosened his collar. He was sweating now, not from the heat but from the danger. It suddenly crossed his mind that he stood a chance of dying on the side of that mountain.

"Lose your way, sonny?"

Armstrong jumped as a dry voice snapped from the cliff above him. Searching the lip of the butte he saw an old man crouching on the edge staring down at him. The man had a long white beard and a tanned face as creased as an old pair of boots. He wore homespun clothes which were covered with patches and a weatherbeaten broad-brimmed hat.

"I'm looking for Brother Shadrach Tompkins," Armstrong called. "I came all the way from Salt Lake."

"Why do you want him? Are you a dep?"

"No, I'm not a deputy marshal. I'm from the church historians office."

The old man laughed at this and threw a coil of rope over the clifftop. The rope arced down, falling neatly beside Armstrong. "I should have known. Only a church official would be bull-headed enough to come all this way. They must have found out I was behind on my tithing."

The white-beard appeared old, but he pulled the younger man up the cliff face like he might pull a goat out of a ditch. Standing beside him Armstrong looked up at a man who stood well over six feet and was unbowed with age. His handshake was the calloused, powerful grip of one who has spent his life outdoors.

"I'm Shadrach Tompkins. Follow me."

He abruptly led Armstrong along the top of the butte as the younger man looked at a world much different from the arid land below. An ocean of pine trees carpeted the top of the mountain and the air was sweet from the smell of resin. Blue jays and crows watched their progress through the forest. Deer and bushy topped squirrels foraged unafraid.

Tompkins moved quickly, leading the visitor through a large garden where the sun sparkled on the tassels of corn silk. The garden spread out over several acres of cleared land, watered by an irrigation ditch leading from a spring, and lovingly tended by people whose survival depended on its harvest.

Not far from the garden, a rambling house had been built of tan adobe bricks. The lines of the two-story house were as plumb and neat as any in the valley, but the lintels of the doors and the pine shakes of the roof all bore the marks of a carpenter's adz. Behind the house, where chickens and geese competed for their attention, Shadrach dipped a wooden dipper into a well bucket and watched as his guest poured the chilled water down his throat.

Armstrong was too busy slaking his thirst to notice the appearance of five women who eased out on the porch to stare at the stranger in their midst. The women were as lean and alert as his host. They ranged in age from a severe, white-haired woman in her eighties to a dark-skinned Polynesian woman who appeared to be in her sixties. All the women wore faded dresses in a style that had been popular in the 1890s.

"George Armstrong, these are my wives," Shadrach said

in introduction. "Sarah, Rachel, Polly, Theresa and Wamoa Tompkins. This young man is from the church historians office."

The eldest woman stared at him through her much-repaired wire-rimmed glasses.

"I thought we had been forgotten about up here," Rachel said suspiciously. "What brings you all the way from Salt Lake?"

"The church is interested in preserving the life histories of the founders of Deseret," Armstrong said. "As pioneers you can add an important chapter to the story of Deseret."

"They weren't half as interested in us twenty years ago," Polly said. "We've made a peaceful life up here. We don't want it disturbed."

"There will be no disturbance, I assure you. I simply want to encourage you to write your memoirs."

"I'm sorry, sonny," Shadrach said, grinning mischievously at his wives. "That's impossible."

"May I inquire your reasons for refusing?" Armstrong asked cautiously. It was dangerous to press some of these Plurals living underground too hard.

"Because I can't write!" Shadrach said as though he had been waiting to pop the punchline for a joke.

Wamoa, the Polynesian wife, had skin as soft and unlined as a girl's. She leaned forward and threw another knot of piñon wood on the fire. The blaze leapt up illuminating the low-ceilinged room of the ranchhouse.

Armstrong could not help from staring at the scene before him. It was if he had been transported back fifty years to the earliest days of Deseret. One hundred miles from the nearest settlement, these six people lived a self-sufficent life.

The dishes had been cleared from the pine table and as the coyotes jabbered like children outside, they sat before the fireplace. Sarah Tompkins sat at a small loom, passing the niddy-noddy back through the strands of fabric. Theresa sipped a catwillow tea to calm a stomach which had been troubling her for weeks. Shadrach sat in front of the fire, crunching on resinous pine nuts and spitting the husks into the fire.

"Tell me where you come from, Brother Tompkins?"

Armstrong asked breezily, trying to get the recalcitrant man into a conversation.

"He comes from Wallsend, England," Polly prompted. "He was born there in 1818. His father was a miner. His mother was a washerwoman."

"He was the strongest boy in the village," Sarah said proudly. "He had more talents between his shoulders than he had between his ears. I don't think he ever saw the inside of a schoolhouse."

"Was his family religious?"

"His father was a drunk. His mother was too busy looking after the family to follow a religion," Rachel sniffed.

"Ladies, allow me to tell my own story," Shadrach said, returning the pine nuts to the wicker basket he kept them in.

He looked at his wives to see if they were listening.

"Wallsend coal is the finest in the whole world, hard as diamonds and blacker than six feet down a mule's throat," he said grandly. "I was the son of a miner and he was a miner's son. When I was seven years old I went into the pits with the rest of the men. I picked slate with the boys and then became a mucker, hauling the coal from the tunnel shafts in a hand cart. My younger brother Lemuel followed me into the mines."

Shadrach's face clouded over as a painful memory was passing through. "In 1836, we were both working underground late in the shift. The men had already gone aloft when an explosion ripped through the mine. I lay buried in the bottom of the earth for three days. My brother's body was found a week later."

Shadrach paused and passed the basket of pine nuts to Armstrong who politely took some.

"Seventy lads died in the explosion of the coal damp. I, myself, could not be forced to go back into the pits. For a year I wandered the countryside with a bottle as my companion. There was a general depression in the country and the roads were full of lads like me. One morning I awoke on the side of a running stream in Northumberland. As my friends and I watched, we were surprised to see a man in a white shirt trying to drown a young woman in the stream! He was yelling at the top of his lungs and pushing her under water while she cried.

My mates and I ran to the stream to save the woman. Only after we saw a crowd of people watching this murder take place did we realize what it was."

"A baptism?"

Shadrach looked piqued that his visitor had guessed the secret.

"It was. A whole flock of people being baptized. We sat on the bank listening to the preacher barking at them. He was telling of the miracle in America, where Joseph Smith had been revealed as to the existence of Golden Tablets. About the new Zion that was being built in a place called Missouri. The minister told about how the world had fallen away from the true Church. Now, as the Millenium approached, the church was being restored in America. Before the Babylon of western civilization fell, the faithful would be gathered to Zion."

Shadrach paused, lost in his memories of that morning.

"What most appealed to you about the church?" Armstrong asked, prodding his host's memory.

"It was the work of being baptized for those who had gone on before us," Shadrach said. "My younger brother Lemuel had been killed without the benefit of being baptized. I was determined to undertake his baptism for him to save his soul for eternity."

"Were you yourself baptized in that stream?"

"No. Some of my friends began throwing stones at the brethren. I had to crack some skulls to teach them respect. I followed that preacher on his travels and when I reached Liverpool I was baptized."

"What was the status of the British mission at that time?"

"I can scarcely tell you. A short time after my baptism I prepared myself to journey to America. I had never thought of leaving England, but the opportunity of participating in the building of Zion captivated me. There was a general excitement among all the Saints at that time. It was feared the Millenium would arrive and we would be stranded in Liverpool."

"How did you afford passage to America?"

"Afford? At that time I didn't have two shillings to rub together," Shadrach laughed. "A wealthy Saint was willing to pay my passage to New Orleans. It cost five pounds in those days. I sailed aboard the *Hotspur* in March of 1838."

Shadrach looked around to see if the ladies were still awake.

"That was a hell of a long time ago! 1838! We're all lucky we're still alive and kicking!"

"What prompted your eagerness to come to America?" Armstrong pressed.

Shadrach looked at him as if he were being addressed by a fool.

"Why, for what other reason?" the old man demanded. "I was ready to become a Saint!"

THE GATHERING
1838

Chapter Two

Accustomed to the bashful sun of his native England, the pale skin on the face of Shadrach Tompkins had burned three times and peeled off in snowflakes of skin by the time he was halfway across Missouri. The scorching sun of July, 1838, blinded the man who had labored in the coal mines of Northumberland for most of his twenty years. Since he had been seven years old he had hardly seen the sun, for he had descended into the pits before daylight and emerged after dark.

Now he stood defenseless on a rutted wagon road, blasted by the light and heat. The flaxen shirt and broadcloth pants, which hung on his large frame, were soaked with sweat. Worse, the wide-rimmed black felt hat drew the heat to him like a magnet, cooking the juices out of his curly black hair and sending them splashing.

"Damnation! It's hotter than the doorknockers on Hell's Gates!" he roared to the deserted countryside, perhaps hoping for an answering sign of human life.

Only the cawing of a startled crow emerged from the forests on either side of the frontier road. He swung his canvas bag over his shoulder and began plodding toward the next hill. Perhaps from there he could catch a glimpse of Zion.

"A hell of a place to build the city of Heaven!" he muttered. "The world could come to an end this afternoon and I'd be lost in the middle of this cursed wilderness!"

He looked guiltily around. If he was ever to find perfection, he was going to have to leave this blasphemous language behind. But it was hard to change the way he had learned to talk in the colliery, where the youngest slate picker could curl the ears of a Royal Marine. He had given up smoking and drinking, but cursing was a harder nut to crack.

He redoubled the pace of his walk, hoping that the soles of

his feet could do penance for the soul of his tongue. He had been walking for more than two weeks, worried about missing the coming of the Millenium as others might worry about missing a train. He was afraid to be left behind in the Babylon of America.

The towering clouds of evening caught the brilliant orange colors of the setting sun, reminding Shadrach of the engravings he had seen about the Great Fire of London. He trudged to the crest of the hill where he stood marveling at the billowing fires within the tall clouds.

"Cities on fire! That's for sure!" he said outloud. "A revelation about Sodom and Gommorah being destroyed by brimstone!"

No Zion was in sight from his vantage point. But he could see a tiny village tucked in the shadow of the valley, hard beside a winding creek. He could count half a dozen dwellings in the village. He began whistling as he descended the hill. Perhaps he could find some friends here.

Five of the buildings in the settlement were made of logs cut from the surrounding forest. The sixth was a new, two-story stone house which dominated the center of the village. It was from the saddle of its rafters that the notes of hammers echoed across the valley, as roofers worked to finish the wood shakes. One of these workers was boiling a pot of pine waterproofing tar when he spied a stranger coming down the hill.

"Someone's on the road!" he sang out as he scrambled to get off the exposed roof.

This alarm caused a flurry of activity in the quiet village as men stopped work and women shepherded the children into the cabins. The crumbs of early suppers were brushed from the beards of farmers who gathered on the road. Their stern eyes watched the hills while their reddened hands held muskets.

As he made his way down the hill, the settlers took Shadrach's measure. The could see he was a large man, who walked with a bouncing stoop learned in the low-ceilinged mineshafts. They noted his wide shoulders and powerful arms tempered by tens of thousands of swings of a pick handle. As he drew hear, he took off his hat and they could see his broad dimpled face and a gap-toothed smile. His curly hair and long sideburns couldn't quite conceal a blue scar which snaked across his forehead like a vein.

Shadrach, in turn, was studying the ragged score of men who suspiciously waited on the road, like the crows who had been following his journey from St. Louis.

"Good evening to you brothers!" he said in a thick English accent as he drew up before them. "Perhaps we'll get some relief from the heat now that the sun is setting?"

None of the men returned his greeting. Instead, they continued to stare at him. They were joined by a heavy-set man who walked from the front porch of the stone house pulling a napkin from the collar of his frock coat.

"Where might you be bound for?" he gruffly demanded without a word of introduction.

Shadrach studied the man who the others had deferred to. Their leader had long, greasy hair and a terribly pocked face, the legacy of near-fatal disease. The man kept his face clean-shaven, perhaps to show what he had survived.

"For a village called Far West where I have friends," Shadrach said clearly. "Perhaps you can direct me there?"

The name "Far West" sent a murmur through the crowd.

"I can not, and shall not direct you there, sir!" the poxed man said, "For it is a nest of blasphemers and thieves!"

Shadrach's eyes widened at this unexpected hostility, but the smile never left his face. "I've rubbed shoulders with blasphemers before," he said easily, "and come out none the worse for it."

"And what might your faith be that you can be so bold?"

The smile on Shadrach's face began to come unglued.

"What a question?"

"Then answer it!"

"Why, a Christian, of course," Shadrach said nervously. "True and simple."

"In whose church?"

Shadrach throught it wise not to answer that question and he began to take a step backward with the idea of running. Strong hands behind him gripped his arms, freezing him to his spot. A tow-headed boy opened his sack and dumped his valuables, such as they were, on the ground. The only book in the bag tumbled into the dust. It was a leather-bound Book of Mormon.

"So? A follower of old Peepstone Joe, himself?" the poxed man growled. "One of Joe Smith's Mormons?"

"I can't deny it," Shadrach said.

"Then you must turn around and go back to where you began," the man threatened. "For it will mean your life to try to go farther."

"I obey a higher order," Shadrach said quietly. "I've been called to the gathering and nothing is going to stop me."

As if to prove him wrong, a musket butt struck him on the back of the neck sending him to his knees. A dozen boots kicked him in the ribs as he crawled along the road, desperately seeking an escape. He was dragged to his feet and a hand grasped a hank of his black hair, pulling his face up to the level of the poxed man's.

"We've run out of patience with you Mormons. You're like a pestilence on this state," the man roared, as if to rally his neighbors. "And a plague must be burned out."

He held Shadrach's book up in front of his face.

"Spit on it!"

Shadrach shook his head. He balled his fists, ready to fight for the first time, but strong hands bound his arms.

"Spit on it, and go free!"

"I can't. My mouth won't pucker to it."

The poxed man nodded and ducked as a Missourian thrust a musket butt, cracking Shadrach's teeth to splinters. Still, he shook his head.

"Take your time. We have more wood than you have teeth," the man said.

As if to prevent Shadrach from refusing again, the man held the book under Shadrach's chin as a trickle of blood dripped down. Satisfied that his order was obeyed, the man turned to the mob.

"Let's rebaptize this fellow and send him back to St. Louis!" he shouted.

Lifting Shadrach off the ground, the mob pressed forward, carrying him to the front porch of the stone house. He limply let them carry him, refusing to resist them any longer. But he stiffened again when he saw a kettle of steaming pitch being lowered from the roof.

The white linen shirt that he had paid so much for in Liverpool was torn off his back, and the crowd cheered as the hot pitch was poured over his scalp. It coursed down over his shoulders and chest like a hot knife cutting through him as his voice rebelled and roared a painful oath.

"See! The devil is being scalded out of him," the poxed man said in glee, as Shadrach cursed the mob.

His screams brought a young woman out of the house. Peeking through the mob, she stared pityingly at him, clutching a comforter to her chest. Shadrach stared at her, the only person with mercy in her eyes.

"What are you doing to that poor fellow?" she asked, tucking back her coiled hair.

"We're baptizing this heathen so we can send him on his way with a clean conscience," the poxed man informed her.

"Well, you don't want to send him half naked into the night," the woman said, tearing open the comforter. Standing over Shadrach she emptied the ticking over his head. A cloud of feathers poured out, sticking to the tar that had covered his hair and torso.

She broke out into a laugh, flashing her blackened teeth at the crowd who followed her example. They whisked Shadrach onto their shoulders and carried him to the edge of town like a triumphant politician. There, he was launched into the air and landed with a splash in the creek where a shower of stones quickly encouraged him to stumble back up the hill.

Sarah Putnam walked carefully through the Missouri woods keeping one eye on the ground and one eye on the path ahead of her. Ahead, her brother, Nathan, and sister, Rachel, were watching for the enemy, leaving Sarah free to search for the secret herbs that could cure her mother's sickness.

Their mother had fallen sick on the journey from Boston and had never forgiven her husband for following his new religion to the western frontier. Sarah, on the other hand, was always thankful they had left the noise and confusion of the East to seek a purer way of life in the wilderness.

People belonged close to the earth, she believed. Close to the herbs and flowers, close to the food they grew and the animals they tended. When men and women were in closer harmony with the natural world, they were less tempted to meanness and bad habits.

She devoted her life to the attendance of the meetings where the bishops spoke of the words of Joseph Smith and his revelations. She was truly happy, if a bit lonely, in the wilderness.

Suddenly, her brother froze in his tracks and held up his hand to halt them. Pulling a pistol from his belt, Nathan cocked it and crept forward. Sarah peered to see what he was looking at, and gasped. A body lay right in their path.

At first she thought the body had decomposed, but as she got closer she could see the corpse was covered with feathers.

Suddenly the corpse began to snore.

"What is it?" she whispered.

"A man," Nathan observed, still holding the gun. "Tarred and feathered. He looks like a big bird. You, sir! What kind of a bird are you?"

Shadrach opened his eyes and the blinding sun reminded him of where he was. He felt the toe of a boot nudging his sensitive ribs. Carefully turning his head, he found himself peering into the gaping muzzle of a horse pistol. The pistol was held by the steady hand of a young man about Shadrach's age who was dressed in the patched clothing of a poor dirt farmer. Behind the man were two young women who peeked at Shadrach with a fear that was losing to curiosity.

"Are you a Saint or are you a Puke?" Nathan asked.

"Oh, lordy, not again," Shadrach groaned.

"Speak up, rooster!" the boy said. "This piece is primed and ready to spark."

Although he wasn't familiar with the other word, Shadrach was encouraged by the man's use of the word *Saint*.

"A Saint," Shadrach answered firmly. "And proud of it."

"I knew he was a Saint," the younger of the women, a kindly faced girl with plain features and severely parted brown hair, volunteered. She stepped around him until her faded gingham dress almost touched his face.

"He's a liar. It's Satan tempting us," the older girl said.

Shadrach stared at her. She was perhaps seventeen years old, much more striking than the other girl. Her face was pinched, but finely featured and her hair was a richer brown, hanging defiantly on her shoulders. She carried herself with a more graceful carriage, almost fiercely.

"If you're a Saint," the man asked suspiciously, "where were you baptized?"

"In Liverpool. By Elder Caleb Waters," Shadrach said, trying to inch backwards away from the muzzle which stared at him like an angry dog.

"Don't take the sights from him," the older woman warned.

"Madam, I just received a set of feathers from a mob of Gentiles last night," Shadrach said, boldly trying a new tack. "Now do I presume I'm about to be plucked by a group of fellow Saints?"

"If you're a Saint, then you should know 'Gather to Zion,' " the younger woman observed.

All three looked expectantly at him and Shadrach licked his swollen lips. With a quavering voice he began to sing . . .

"Gather . . . Gather to Zion . . . For heaven's calling you . . .

Gather . . . Gather to. . . ."

"Enough!" the younger woman said, looking at the others. "Only a Saint could have the courage to sing with a voice like that."

The man uncocked his pistol, but didn't put it in his belt. He watched as the younger woman helped Shadrach to his feet and steadied the Englishman. The older woman still watched him with visible suspicion.

"Pray tell what you're doing out on the roads alone?" she asked. "Don't you know of the conditions in this country?"

"I landed not six weeks ago with a party of English Saints under the guidance of Brother Wheelock. In New Orleans I was stricken with the yellow jaundice. Fortunately I was spared but I was left by my brethren who traveled ahead of me. While I waited in St. Louis for another party to form, my impatience got the better of me and, against the advice of the others, I decided to seek the Holy City before the end came. This is the state in which you find me."

"Your impatience has rewarded you with a new suit of feathers," the young woman pointed out. "From now on you should obey the words of the elders and bide your time."

"But what of the building of Zion?" Shadrach asked impatiently. "How goes it?"

The three looked at each other with the frowns that accompany bad news before they turned to Shadrach.

"Times are hard, brother," the young man said gravely. "The Pukes are intent on driving us from Missouri. We are holding on by our fingernails here, much less making progress on the building of Zion."

"The Pukes?"

"The Gentiles. The same ones who gave you a new set of feathers. They've formed an army and are riding against us. Fields are put to the torch and animals driven off. Homes are plundered. Women are violated. Men are murdered if they resist. We all fear for our lives."

This news affected Shadrach worse than his beating of the

night before. He stood in confusion, afraid to believe what he was hearing.

"But what do the Gentiles fear that they should treat us so hard? This land could be an Eden with plenty for all."

The man and women he faced were at a loss for an explanation.

"The Missourians are slaveholders. They fear that we bring abolitionist sentiments with us," the young man offered. "They fear that our increasing numbers will allow us to take control of the state."

"They fear our industry and spirit of cooperation," the older girl speculated. "Already our farms are producing twice what the average Puke can grow. As soon as we set up our full system, the old settlers will envy our thrift."

"I suspect that Satan is working through the personage of Governor Lilburn Boggs," the younger woman said, "and that we are battling not the Missourians but rather the forces of evil incarnate."

The idea of this challenge brightened Shadrach. He slapped his hands together as if to show that he was ready for the battle in spite of his recent setback.

"Surely it is a test of our resolve then," he said cheerfully. "And these things shall pass as surely as night fades into day!"

In whispered fragments of conversation, Shadrach discovered he was in the company of the children of the Putnam family. Nathan, the eldest, was their guide. The two girls, Rachel and Sarah, steadied him with pale white hands as they walked along.

Through the talkativeness of Sarah, the younger of the two, he discovered that she was fifteen years old, her sister, sixteen. They had been gathering a herb that grew only on a hill uncomfortably close to the Gentile village. The plant, called Fiddle Root, would be used to treat their mother's infirmity of the chest.

Shadrach was happy for the conversation of the plain sister, although he kept hoping for more engagement from Rachel, she studiously avoiding his eyes. The farther they traveled from the main road, the more talkative Sarah became.

"What was your trade in England?"

"I hewed coal in the Wallsend mine, outside Newcastle. The finest coal and the heartiest men who ever held picks."

"A coal miner? Precious little good will that do us here," Sarah laughed. "How did you come to leave the mines?"

"A fearsome explosion trapped me underground. Killed seventy brave lads, my brother among them. After that, I swore never to go below again."

"A terrible business," Sarah agreed. "The digging of minerals was not meant for mankind. The tilling of the soil is sufficient for our sustenance."

"The Depression of 1835 drove me to the cities. . . ."

"And the lack of money drove you into the church?" Rachel quipped.

"I should say that I would be wed to Mother Gin if it weren't for the church," Shadrach said good-naturedly, "but the passage to America took my last five pounds."

"And you're better for it. All the gold in Babylon won't save you on the day of reckoning," Sarah said.

"And what of your past?" Shadrach asked.

"Our family is from Boston. Two years ago father consecrated all his wealth to the church, much to the displeasure of our mother, and moved the family to Missouri. Our life has seen its share of hardship since then, but we have dedicated ourselves to the building of the land of milk and honey so our hearts are glad."

"Your heart is glad," Rachel said, acidly, "but others beat with less enthusiasm."

Like oil being poured on troubled waters, the momentary tension between the two sisters was broken when Nathan charged up the hillside and stood boldly on the crest. He waited for the trio to catch up to them and then he pointed into a small valley.

"There it is. Haun's Mill," he announced.

Below them, a neat village sat as naturally by a stream as a cat sits in an old woman's lap. A small mill formed the centerpiece of the community and was surrounded by a score of smaller cabins and outbuildings. Wisps of smoke curled from the chimneys, scenting the air with the smell of hickory.

On all sides the village was surrounded by fields of barley and corn grown tall in the August sun. Shadrach could make out the figures of the farmers who were almost swallowed up by the stalks of corn. The barking of a dog signaled the advance of a group of small children squealing through a vacant lot near a hewn log schoolhouse. A group of young men were dragging a hog out of the cornfield back into its pen with a rope tied around the left rear leg of the protesting animal.

As if to gild this perfect scene, a family of swallows swooped past the hillside and with a twisting flight dived toward the fields. The three Putnams stood to the side like proud owners of a painting, to allow their guest to look. The sight before him fulfilled every hope of Shadrach's for a bucolic paradise and he sank reverently to the soft earth and held out his hands, each of which was taken in the warm grip of the Putnam girls.

Chapter Three

The news of Shadrach's arrival flashed through the village like a fire alarm and soon he was besieged with concerned villagers who gathered around him, forsaking the fields to see the newcomer from England. Before he had reached the Putnam cabin, he had repeated the story of his torment at the hands of the Pukes ten times, and would have been asked for more had he not been pushed inside the small house.

The Putnams, like the rest of the people in Haun's Mill, lived in a crude hut which had been hastily constructed of dove-tailed logs. The finishing of the hut seemed to be an afterthought. The openings of the greased paper windows were at skewed angles; the mud mortar was chinked crudely; the fireplace which supported the right wall of the house had stones crumbling from it.

The house was furnished with the remnants of a once prosperous home, what might have been salvaged had the family washed up on the shores of a desert island. An oak table with often-mended pine chairs was set with pewter cups and china dishes. A well-constructed highboy and a finely crafted pine chest of drawers stood like the survivors of an elegant collection at one end of the hut. The rest of the furniture was the product of frontier workshops, the hand-shaved pine benches and chair still were blond with the blemishes of pioneer carpenters.

In the corner of the hut, surrounded by the carding combs and spinning jenneys that awaited her recovery, Mrs. Putnam reclined on a rope bed, covered with a patched quilt.

With only a word of civil greeting, Shadrach passed through the house and was hustled into the small backyard of the house where the dirty chickens scattered for the crowd.

As the villagers watched from outside the yard, Shadrach sat on a bench while the Putnam girls started his renewal.

"Now I know how the chicken feels," he complained as

the remaining feathers were pulled from his back and chest by his laughing companions.

Next, a stubby pair of sheep shears were produced as Sarah gathered up his tar-encrusted hair and lopped it off, narrowly saving his ears in the process.

"I wish our home was more presentable," she said as she cut. "This was our first attempt at a house raising and I'm afraid it suffered for it. Father's planning to build a new one next spring."

"It's a palace compared to my accomodations last night," he said as he watched the mats of his own hair fall into his lap. When the top of his head had been reduced to a stubble as bare as a December wheatfield, Nathan returned, bearing a handful of sand. At first it flattered Shadrach to have the blushing girls rubbing the coarse sand across the broad flat muscles of his back and chest. He was proud of the powerful build of his limbs. At Wallsend, he was known for his skill at the rough wrestling matches, which would break out where-ever the miners would drink, and he was grateful that his body had emerged intact from the pits. His enjoyment of this diversion ended, however, as the girls scrubbed harder in an effort to remove the tenacious tar. His back was soon scoured with the traces of the sand and his chest had been reddened with this rash.

When she was finished, Sarah handed him a small bar of lye soap and sent him down to the creek to try to remove the remaining spots.

The Putnam cabin was the most crowded in the village that evening as Shadrach tried to eat a meal of cabbage and fried corn cakes. The elders of the village gathered around him, pressing him time and time again for the details of his adventure. Who were the leaders of the Pukes? How did they command their followings? Were there further threats against the Saints?

Looking at the window, where the other villagers pressed up against the greased paper for a look at the stranger, Shadrach answered all their questions patiently. The Saints had taken him in immediately, providing a patched cotton shirt and a worn coat from their meager supplies.

"That blue scar above your eye," an elder asked him, "is that new?"

Shadrach felt his forehead where his haircut had revealed the sole reminder of his life in the mines.

"That's a tatoo left by a falling roof of slate," he told them, "but I'm more concerned about the tatoo that seems to be scarring this countryside."

His host, Thomas Putnam, was a stern man who had lost his eye in the War of 1812. His patch and short hair gave him a rough appearance and Shadrach could understand why his daughters shrank to the hearth when the others were around.

"They drove us from Jackson County in '33 and forced us to the wildest parts of the state," Putnam said to the nods of the other men around the table. "Now they see we have settled this land well, they will drive us from here unless we protect ourselves. I still have the sword I carried when the British were tempted to trifle with us before. That same sword should now be put to use."

"They say the Saints in Far West have an armory working day and night to forge weapons," another man observed. "We might be wise to do the same."

"I came to Missouri to escape the bloodletting that is sure to come," Shadrach said. "Pity's the time when I have to pick up a sword in Zion."

"That time may not be far off, friend," an elder said grimly. "The persecutors are laying plans already."

"I shall refuse to let blood flow," Shadrach said adamantly, "in preparation for the day when the Lion shall lie down with the Lamb."

"And the lion shall have mutton for dinner," Rachel countered.

"Brethren, there's time for these plans later," Thomas Putnam said, standing up. "In the meantime, the corn doesn't care whether it is tended by a Gentile's hand or a Saint's, so I propose we retire and begin our work early."

The Latter Day Saints had been called to the frontier by their leader Joseph Smith who had received a revelation commanding him to gather his people on the western borders of the state of Missouri. There they would live in harmony, awaiting the Millenium, which would soon destroy the rest of the corrupt world. Striving for perfection, the Saints hoped to be prepared for the Kingdom of Heaven by having duplicated it on earth.

Far from the machines and decadence of the modern world,

the Saints hoped to build an Eden where life could be lived as it was meant to be.

For those who didn't believe in miracles, Joseph Smith, the prophet of the Saints, was a puzzling man. As a young man in upstate New York, he had a revelation in which an angel revealed the existence of a set of golden tablets buried since ancient times. When Smith translated the tablets he found an account of a group of Israelites who had fled the Old World before the birth of Christ to come to the New World. Here, they had founded a civilization which had flourished, waned and then was destroyed when fighting broke out between two of its groups, the Nephites and the Lamanites. Only the Lamanites survived to become the ancestors of the American Indians.

The translation of the tablets became the Book of Mormon, named after Mormon, a general of the Nephites. The Book of Mormon, along with the Bible, served the new religion. Begun by Joseph Smith and several of his witnesses in 1830, The Church of Jesus Christ of Latter Day Saints spread rapidly, as hundreds of converts joined. The followers of the new religion moved from New York and New England first to Kirtland, Ohio, then to Missouri. Unlike many religions, the Saints believed in concentrating their numbers in one place, not spreading out across the land.

The Saints believed in the restoration of the original purity and organization of the primitive church and took their inspiration from the Israelites. Theirs was a religious society, and everyone was able to participate in it. The priesthood was not reserved for a few but was open to all males who had received the proper instruction.

Life in the villages settled by the Saints revolved around the natural world and around their religion. The tending of the fields and the attendance of prayer meetings occupied the people who, in the latter days of the world, were seeking saintliness.

Life in paradise began very early, Shadrach discovered the morning after he arrived when the pounding on the stairway to his sleeping loft awakened him.

"Those who don't work don't eat," Thomas Putnam yelled from below.

It was still dark outside as he shared the family's breakfast of cold barley soup and then joined the father and son as they trudged to the fields. There, they cleared turtle-sized rocks from land for next season's planting. He discovered that the long journey to America had sapped his strength, for the sweat poured from his brow, salting his eyes.

Sledge after sledge of rocks, half-covered with moist mud, was dragged from the field by the lowing oxen who responded to the plaited whip of Nathan Putnam. As the men breathed the rich smell of the soil, they talked more easily and Shadrach could feel some of the elder Putnam's suspicions dissolving.

The one-eyed farmer began the Englishman's education in the flora of his new home. The first lesson was that the tall stalks of tassled grain which Shadrach called "corn," were called "wheat" by Americans. The green shoots bearing the yellow pods of grain, which the English called "maize," were what the Yankees called "corn." Thus confusing his guest, Putnam began to point out the trees and plants that bordered the fields, announcing the name of each in his sharp New England accent.

The oaks, hickory trees and walnuts were already familiar to Shadrach. More exotic were the locust trees, the ironwoods, and pecan trees which he had never seen before. Most peculiar was the persimmon tree, home of the strange opposum. Comforting to him were the fruit trees the Saints were husbanding in groves around the village.

As the sun signaled a few minutes of rest by hanging directly overhead, the three men sat in the shade of a willow that hung over the banks of the creek.

"Do you think it possible that some day I would have a field like that?" Shadrach asked as he scraped the black mud from his boot soles.

"Take that one this afternoon," Putnam said, pointing to a rocky field on the western edge of the village."

"To own?"

"To act as steward of," Putnam said sternly. "The ownership of land is an affront to the Lord. We follow the United Order of Enoch."

"But you own the land, don't you?" Shadrach asked.

"In common with a number of my brethren in the village," he answered. "We share the labor together, believing that if we are equal on earth, we'll be equal in heaven."

Shadrach's face mirrored the disappointment he felt over this news. "I had hoped to buy my own farm here in America," he said "of course with the promise of the tithe to the church."

Putnam laughed out loud at the consternation of the young man.

"I'm sure if you desire badly enough to pay for the air that you can breathe for free, someone will be willing to sell it to you! You can enjoy the ownership of that chestful of air, and I wish you a handsome profit when you breathe it out."

"Profit is not my intent," Shadrach protested, "I see the land as no more important than the ownership of one's clothes."

"Clothes lead to a clothes chest, and a chest leads to a lock," Putnam said, standing to return to the fields. Just remember that it is easier for an ox to squeeze into a whalebone corset than it is for a rich man to enter heaven!"

The threadbare life in Haun's Mill had not dampened the spirits of its residents, Shadrach found after his first few days in the village. Although the food was limited to what the gardens could produce, and the clothes and tools of the villagers had been patched beyond any reasonable life expectancy, there was a sense of common purpose about them that surprised a man coming from a glum mining community.

The testimonies from elderly Saints at the assemblies held in the packed schoolhouse, or the dances held on Saturday nights by the old mill, were always charged with a power that transcended the poverty of the community.

Shadrach had been moved from the loft of the Putnam home to the cabin of an elderly Saint whose wife had passed away. The move was a way of keeping a handsome bachelor away from the impropriety of living under the same roof with two young women, or, as Shadrach's new housemate put it, "to keep the hog out of the buttery."

His removal from the buttery didn't deter Shadrach from his pursuit, as he hunted Rachel. The day's work prevented him from catching more than a glimpse of the tall young woman, but at the Saturday night dances he arrived early and stayed late in order to chance a meeting with her.

The old man Shadrach lived with, Brother McBride, reigned at the dances, sawing out "Old Zip Coon" on a fiddle as patched and worn as the clothes of the dancers. Whatever other instruments would show up accompanied the man as the villagers stomped around in spirited schottisches under the flicker of pine torches.

Try as he might, Shadrach could never separate Rachel Putnam from the Elders she preferred to dance with as she ignored his smiles and hopeful nods. Sarah, on the other hand, was always in his vicinity and he would often spin her around the line to hide his disappointment over her sister's coldness.

"I can't understand why Rachel spurns me?" he complained as he clomped beside her.

"I fear my sister still harbors a grudge against the life we chose over our home in Boston and is being contrary because of it," Sarah whispered out of earshot of the rest of the Saints. "I pray that she will leave her pride behind."

"Surely I could not remind her of part of that?"

"Not at all. I suspect she admires you, in fact she has so told me. But nonetheless she pulls sometimes when she should be pushing."

"I must admit I am sorely vexed by her behavior. Perhaps you could say a good word for me?"

"The good word I would say to you is *patience*. Apart from that I cannot carry messages in the house in which I live."

He angrily pulled away from her and stalked out of the line of dancers. Undaunted, Sarah followed him to where he was leaning against a maple tree watching the dancers.

"I think the contrariness in your family runs deeper than just one member," he said. "I think it is a widespread infirmity."

"Pride, Brother Tompkins. You are a good man but prideful," she said softly. "And pride can grind a man's soul the way corn is ground in a mortar."

"You are quite right, Sister Putnam," Shadrach said, unconvincingly. "My own vanity caused my outburst. I offer my apologies."

"There is no need for that. I understand the provocations of my sister's willfulness."

"You both must have left much behind when you moved here to the frontier."

"But we gained so much more. What we lost was in the temporal world. What we gained will last forever."

As they talked, Shadrach noticed Rachel watching them. She pulled her partner wide out of the line and danced over to them.

"No sparking permitted here in the shadows," she chided mischievously and then flounced back into the line.

"Sparking? My word, what an idea?" Sarah cried, blushing.

Shadrach stood self-consciously and then took his partner's hand and clomped back into the dance.

The shine of life in Eden began to tarnish in the summer heat as surely as the surface of a copper mirror. After several weeks of back-breaking labor, Shadrach felt his enthusiasm for Zion was not quite as strong as it once was. Somehow the joy and ecstacy he had expected to experience was crowded out by the toil and hardship of preparing the village for the harvest.

So the promise of a holiday on August 6, the election day for the state was a welcome revival of his spirits. At dawn a wagon bearing a dozen of the men in the village was waiting for Shadrach as he clamored sleepily in for the ride to Gallatin, the seat of nearby Davies County. Once in the wagon, Shadrach was handed a slip of paper by one of the Elders.

"What's this?" he asked.

"The name of the fellow you're going to vote for," he was told. "Just memorize it and pass it around. He's not an enemy of the Church."

"But I've only been in this country a couple of months. Will they allow me to vote?"

"How are they going to know how long you've been here?" Putnam asked him. "If they protest, just tell them to ask us."

"I'm not sure a Saint should be party to the politics of Babylon," Shadrach grumbled. "A vote is an admittance that the government will be around long enough to survive the Millenium."

"Judge Morin has advised John D. Lee that all Saints should vote," the Elder said, "for that will give the Pukes the notice that we intend to be around for a while."

"I heard they was going to prevent us from entering the polling place," Nathan said. "We may have a fight on our hands."

"So be it," his father chorused to the nods of the rest. "If the Mobocrats show their true colors today, we'll trade them blow for blow."

"I'll vote but not fight," Shadrach said. "I shall not enter the Kingdom minus the skin on my knuckles."

The village of Gallatin had the outward appearance of a fair when the wagon bearing the Haun's Mill Saints rolled in at noon. The center of this Maypole was the brick courthouse which had attracted a large crowd the way a cheese cover draws ants. Leaving one of the boys to watch their wagon in the grove of trees, the Saints warily checked the lay of the land, bunching together in case of trouble. The edge of the village was taken up with peddlers who had spread their merchandise out on the back of their wagons or on blankets. They sang out to the passersby in praise of their rifle flints, ironware, milled calicoes and other trade goods.

It was quickly apparent how the hair of the population was parted. The Gentiles had thrown up a cordon around the table holding the polling box near the front door of the courthouse. The larger members of the Missourians strutted threateningly back and forth like banty roosters protecting their yards. Shadrach and his friends stood with their thumbs in their belts dolefully watching as a bearded Puke harangued the crowd from atop the polling table.

"Rights? What rights can the Mormons claim?" he asked of the crowd in a shrill voice. "What rights can a counterfeiter claim? What rights can a liar claim? Liars? What else can you call those who profess to heal the sick and cast out devils with their bare hands? And we all know that to be a lie! Just as their claim for suffrage is a lie!"

"That's William Peniston, as mad a dog as ever lifted his fourth leg off the ground," Nathan whispered to Shadrach. "We'd all live in peace were it not for a handful like him."

The speech had polarized the crowd and it was not difficult to spot the Saints. They had gathered in a protective knot around an oak tree a discreet distance from the line of patrolling Gentiles. As of yet they had made no move to approach the polling place, preferring to gather in whispered counsel. Shadrach's party stood on the perimeter of this group.

"I think this is the wrong time to confront the Gentiles over an issue that won't amount to a handful of beans," one man whispered nervously. "They are spoiling for a fight. If we sow the wind here, we may reap the whirlwind."

"Then we better harvest with our hats firmly on our heads," another man whispered. "We can't very well leave now with our tails between our legs."

"I heard they have a mounted army outside of the village," the first whispered, "and boxloads of rifles in the courthouse, hoping for a reason to use them."

"Talk. Just talk. But if they see they can chase us away from here without a fight, then what can they do when they do ride against us?"

While this debate was raging, Shadrach noticed a wagon where a stout man was dispensing whiskey from a stone crock. He licked his lips, and returned his attention to the argument at hand, but his eyes involuntarily began measuring the distance from the crock to where he was standing. The wagon seemed to occupy a neutral place in the village, and with the activity centered around the courthouse, no one would notice his sponsorship of a glass or two.

He reached into his pocket and felt the light weight of his last coins floating loosely in his purse. They were surely not enough to purchase anything of value and would probably be lost in the fields if he kept them much longer. Perhaps this was his chance to celebrate his separation from two vices, money and drinking.

He crabbed sideways, backing out of the ring of Saints. Walking straight backwards, he looped around the grove of trees until he passed the wagon of the brewmaster. Looking up, he seemed surprised to see the wagon and he stopped before it.

"Hot day," he said to the merchant who held the gray earthenware jug in his hand.

"Aye and promising to get hotter," the merchant said, nodding at the crowd.

"Perhaps I'll have a drop of your poteen, there, to wet my whistle then," Shadrach said nodding at the jug.

"None finer in Missouri," the merchant said, filling

a cow's horn cup with the clear liquid. "That'll be one bit."

Shadrach pressed two bits into the man's hand and the merchant kept pouring. As he did so, Shadrach was jostled by a group of Missourians who pressed around the wagon, their own cups outstretched.

"Some more liquid courage," the leader of the men ordered. "For it runs out of my body before this matter is resolved."

"A good business to be in on a day like this," the bartender said. "A pity the Mormons don't drink."

Shadrach, who had been drinking with his back to the Saints now tried to escape the stares of the Missourians. As he could feel their interest in him growing, he upended his cup and rasped as the juice brought the tears to his eyes.

Sliding away from the wagon as the eyes of the other drinkers became fixed upon him, he walked back toward the protective circle of Saints, hoping the crowd would not stand downwind from his breath.

But before he reached the oak tree, the Saints had begun to move in the direction of the polling place, bringing the crowd of Gentiles to a peak like the head on a boil. One Saint, a short man in a blue plaid shirt made an attempt to reach the courthouse.

"No niggers or Mormons allowed to vote!" a burly man in a drooping felt hat said, blocking the Saint's way.

"Let us pass," the man said. "You cannot stop us from voting."

To prove him wrong, the burly man put his hand on the Saint's chest and pushed backward to the approval of the crowd. The Saint pushed back and in an instant he was wrestled to the ground by his opponent. Half a dozen other Gentiles swarmed on, kicking and pummeling the helpless man who thrashed in the dust.

The other Saints hung back, undecided about what to do. But a shrill, level whistle cut through the air. Instantly a dozen men burst out of the company of the Mormons and pushed their way to the rescue of their brother.

As Shadrach watched unsteadily, the fight turned into a general melee in front of the courthouse as the two camps melted into one seething throng. The gin had collided with his brain, rendering him helpless to decide what his action should be.

"Help me, Shadrach! For God's sake!" he heard Nathan call as a clump of Gentiles swallowed him up.

Shadrach waded into their midst, pulling the men apart as he might pull dogs out of a fight. Nathan leapt to his feet as though the victory was his, squaring off for the next engagement.

"The Pukes are winning," Nathan cried, almost in tears.

Shadrach pulled Nathan to a merchant whose oak axe handles had caused his attention: The vendor was behind his wagon as Shadrach scooped up an armful of axe handles and hurried toward the fight. Distributing them to the men around him, he took one in his own hand. Swinging it around his head, he felt its power the way he used to feel the power of his pick in the mines.

"Sons of Israel, follow me!" he roared, wading into the pile of Gentiles without once looking behind him.

As the axe handles rose and fell in the country square, shattering jaws and cracking ribs, the Saints quickly carved out a sanctuary around their fallen leaders. The Gentiles backed away from the polling place. Sam Brown, the Saint who had been the first to try the line, was helped to his feet. He angrily led the way as they gathered before the frightened registrar, their oak handles still clasped in their hands.

"Whig or Democrat?" the registrar asked Brown, whose face was now beginning to swell from the beating he had received. "Or any other affiliation you prefer."

"Mormon," Brown said, grasping his ballot.

Chapter Four

Under the threatening skies of early October, the Saints of Haun's Mill hurried to gather in their harvest. The small valley echoed to the sound of whetstones being drawn across the iron blades of scythes as the grain fattened on the ends of the stalks.

Shadrach moved in a line with a dozen other men of the village. He swept his sharp scythe through the barley, toppling the slender stalks in a pile which balanced on the stubble of his last sweep. The other men in his line were moving methodically through the field, while an Elder sang a hymn which timed out their movement.

His arms weighed as heavily as millstones on his knotted shoulders and as he tried to shake life into them, he looked at the women who gathered up the fallen grain. Behind him, Sarah threw him a smile as she held a sheaf of the brownish grain in her arms.

"Cut by Brother Shadrach?" Rachel teased her, as they both hurried to the edge of the field.

"I don't know. It could have been," Sarah said.

"Could have been?" she laughed. "You were following him so closely he almost tripped over you on several occasions!"

"What were you watching so closely for?"

"Only the blind could not have noticed."

"If I was following Brother Shadrach, it was only because he cuts more grain than two others," Sarah said walking faster than her sister. "And we must complete the harvest before the frost!"

She carried her grain to an area where the earth had been cleared. There, the kernel was beaten from the chaff by some of the older women who wielded oak flails, long jointed staffs, which pounded the germ from the stalks.

While the girls rested, they could see the children of

the village crawling through the stubble of the fields, gleaning any remaining grain before the birds could make off with it.

The urgency of this harvest was prompted by the thunder cloud hanging over the troubled state. The election day brawl at Gallatin had curdled relations between the Gentiles and Saints. The Missourians were busily raising an army to suppress the supporters of Joseph Smith. Mormon homes were burned by nightriders taking advantage of the bitter feelings.

Alarmed by the violence of the Missourians, many Saints began to quietly organize for their defense. Arms were smuggled from more peaceful settlements in Ohio and Illinois. Mormon blacksmiths sweated over roaring forges, fashioning swords and crude firearms from the iron of more peaceful implements.

At all hours of the night, riders thundered across the state, bearing news of fresh troubles.

As Shadrach walked from the fields one evening, bone weary, he came upon a couple of horsemen who were watering their mounts from the creek outside the village. They were talking to Nathan Putnam, who called Shadrach over to meet them.

The men wore thick beards and wide-brimmed felt hats. Shadrach was surprised to see that the men wore sabers and carried pistols in their belts.

"What news, Nathan?" Shadrach asked warily. "Is there trouble?"

"This is Brother John D. Lee and Brother Thomas Morse," Nathan said.

"A great scourge is on the land," John D. Lee pronounced.

"Governor Boggs is raising two armies to ride against us. Seven thousand men have sworn to drive us from this land."

"Seven thousand?" Shadrach said, staggered by the news. "Then I fear we are lost!"

"Not if we resist them with all our might," Lee replied.

"But seven thousand? We do not number that many with our women."

"I did not see you counting the odds that day in Gallatin when you waded through a dozen Pukes with your axe handle," Thomas Morse interjected. "We need a man like you now."

"We?"

"Those of us who will fight fire with fire. Those of us who refuse to stand by while the Pukes drive us from our homes."

"I believe that willingly," Shadrach said. "But can we fight seven thousand?"

"Three hundred Athenians defeated ten thousand Persians," John D. Lee pointed out. "With the Lord on our side, we don't count the enemy!"

"Whatever you need done, I will do," Shadrach said. "What do you call yourselves?"

"We call ourselves the Sons of Dan," the man whispered, "after the serpent Dan, the avenger. But it is of no matter what we are called. It is what we shall do that is important. We shall pick up steel when the forces of Satan call us out for final battle."

"And the prophet? He knows and approves of these Sons of Dan?"

"He does. Though if questioned he would deny all knowledge as would we all."

"Say no more, for I am with you," Shadrach said, offering his hand.

The leader of the riders took his hand and turned it right side up. He locked the first knuckle of his own hand around Shadrach's and wrapped his thumb around the Englishman's. The others did the same.

"This is our grip, that you may know us in the future," the man said. "And our sign is 'God and Liberty!' "

" 'God and Liberty,' " Shadrach repeated. "I am ready!"

The three men mounted their horses leaving Shadrach and Nathan standing by the creek.

"Arm yourselves and wait our signal," the leader said. "He then pulled his broad-bladed knife an inch from its sheath so the men could see the gleam of metal before he returned it to his scabbard. "Keep your lips sealed to the grave about what you have done and said here. If your tongue recounts these proceedings, we will know it and dawn will never strike your face again."

Holding a bundle of cloth against her chest, Sarah Putnam ran through the small village. She was the only person in the community in a hurry that cloudy afternoon. The harvest had been gathered in, the barley buried in trenches dug from the earth, the corn stored in thick sacks in a log warehouse. With this work completed, the pace slowed from the frantic activity of the past few weeks as the people rested.

Anyone energetic enough to notice would have seen the younger Putnam girl had her hair down on her shoulders for the first time in memory, and there was a look of excitement on her face that flushed her cheeks more than the nippy weather.

On the edge of the village, a group of the men were standing around while they watched the progress of a small fire which was burning out the stubble of the fields. Shadrach turned as he heard his name being called from the distance.

"I have a surprise for you," she panted, when the Englishman walked over to her.

Shadrach glanced at her freckled face and at the fabric she held. "A blanket?"

"I'm going to make you a coat so you can stand the Missouri winter," she said, throwing the material over his shoulder. "I traded an old mirror to Abigail Smathers for this."

Flattered by this attention, Shadrach allowed himself to be led to the Putnam home where Sarah stood on a small stool while she draped the wool across his back, measuring for the cut of the cloth. She lovingly smoothed the cloth across his back, pressing against him as she did so. Noticing that her mother was watching them quietly from the bed, Shadrach felt a bit embarrassed by the attention.

"I hope some day to repay you for your kindness," he said staring straight ahead as she pinned the blanket. "You have shown me more consideration than I can ever deserve."

"Nonsense. We are all brothers and sisters here," she said through lips holding a dozen pins. "My mirror was an object inspiring vanity, but this blanket will be useful."

"You are very fair of face, both you and your sister. I hope you will not miss your mirror."

He could not see Sarah blushing. "It was a waste of my time and an offense to the Lord," she said.

"I am in earnest about repaying your generosity. If I have some material return for my labor, I shall buy you a new mirror."

"Then you are planning to stay around here?"

"I could think of no better place. Nor better people."

"Your establishment in this community would be ample repayment for me."

"It will take me a good long time before I become truly established here," he sighed. "You yourself found me without a shirt on my back."

"Your first order of business should be finding a good wife," she said, nervously. "God frowns on single men."

"Yes. I suppose a proper helpmate would be the best adjunct I could have. But what woman would marry a poor man?"

"A woman who could have an eye for possibilities."

"Perhaps now that Abigail Smathers has a mirror, it will improve her countenance?"

"She thinks too often of herself," Sarah said quickly. "She is an idler and a time waster. She would be of little help to you."

"Or Alice Nelson? What do you think of her?"

"They say there is a mental infirmity that runs in her family," she said in a lowered voice. "Beware of any children she might bear."

"Well, what of your sister? Do you suppose her loins would yield healthy offspring?"

With a howl, Shadrach leaped forward as the pins punctured his back. "Have mercy on me, woman!" he cried. "I want to *wear* that coat, not have it stitched to my body!"

Chapter Five

The roll of horses hooves brought the residents of Haun's Mill from their homes as surely as drum beats. In the weeks following the brawl at Gallatin courthouse, every rider seemed to bring worse news than the one before. A permanent quorum of worried Saints occupied the small schoolhouse as they desperately sought a dam to stop the flood of war rising around them.

Shadrach had stopped meeting every rider coming to the village. The events in the rest of the state, the burning of Mormon farms, the murders of their owners, had become too much for him to bear. But something drew him to an exhausted courier who had ridden in on a staggering horse.

The crowd flowed out of the schoolhouse by the time he arrived, but Shadrach could hear a curious wailing from within. As he watched, Thomas Putnam walked past him, his face as white and empty as his milky eye. Shadrach followed the man a short distance and spun him around, trying to find out what had drained the life from his friend.

It's over. It's all over," Putnam said wearily. "We're finished!"

"What's over? Who's finished?"

The tears were streaming down the man's face, even from his bad eye. "Everything is finished. The church. Our village. The Saints in Missouri."

"That cannot be."

"The serpent, Governor Boggs, has written calling for our expulsion on pain of extermination. We face certain death. At this moment Far West is surrounded by thousands of Pukes. Farms are being burned. Surely we are through."

"I refuse to believe it. Surely our leaders will fight!"

Putnam shook his head. "The prophet has given his word to abandon our homes and flee to Illinois."

Speechless, Shadrach released the man and returned to the

schoolhouse. Pushing his way inside, he overheard the hoarse courier who was rereading a crumpled message.

". . . the Mormons must be treated as enemies and exterminated or driven from the state if necessary," the messenger read. "Their outrages are beyond description! Signed, Governor Lilburn Boggs!"

As he finished the sentence, the women in the schoolhouse began an unearthly wailing the like of which, Shadrach had heard only once before, in the caved-in mineshaft.

"Oh, Lord! Who will protect my children?" a woman wailed. "Extermination? What a cruel fate! What have we done to deserve this?"

"It's men like him, and their brawls that have brought this down upon our heads!" a woman said, pointing at the dumbfounded Englishman. "The Sons of Dan were the straw that broke the camel's back!"

"Surely the Twelve will be able to effect a compromise," a man said referring to the twelve apostles who counciled Joseph Smith. "I can't believe the hearts of the Missourians could be so black!"

"We can not compromise with Satan," a woman said. "We must obey the prophet and flee this land!"

"Flee where? How? Woman, don't you know winter is coming on. Our houses are built. Our grain is buried. How long will your children last in a tent in the Illinois snows? We must stay here at least until spring. . . ."

Heartsick by the panicked arguing of the Saints, Shadrach turned from the schoolhouse.

The air on the ridge above the village was as crisp and dry as the leaves that crackled under his boots as Shadrach walked along, lost in thought. The brilliant reds of the autumn maple trees and the yellows of the locusts were splattered across the brown background of the oak leaves, but the cheerful colors were lost to his despair. He was so enveloped in his own thoughts that the sound of a voice behind him caused him to jump.

"From here the village looks so peaceful," Sarah said. "It's hard to believe there's trouble afoot. Perhaps this is what the world looks like to those in Heaven?"

Shadrach turned to look at her. Sarah's breath was steaming in the cold. She had wrapped a heavy shawl around her dark coarsespun dress, but she still was blowing on her pink fingers to keep them warm.

"I have reason to doubt whether those in Heaven can even have this close a view,' Shadrach said heavily. "In my short lifetime I've been witness to the sacrifice of a mine full of young lads, and now it appears a worse calumny is about to unfold here."

"Bite your tongue!" she chided him. "I'm sure the Lord is very clear in his mind what the future holds for us."

"And I wager that future's not a bright one. I had a dream last night. I dreamt that I was back at the hog slaughtering. But instead of the hog, I was trussed in the tree. I don't need a seer to interpret this premonition."

"Surely this is not a sign of our doom, but merely a test of our faith and resolve."

They both turned as a flock of birds flew over the valley. Hundreds of dark silhouettes wheeled and plunged as the birds gathered to begin their winter's journey south.

"I feel we should be following their example," Shadrach observed. "When the climate changes, we should find a more comfortable one. I fear we are approaching the winter of our lives."

"The prophesy about the coming of the Millenium," Sarah said distantly. "We always thought that Babylon would be destroyed and we would be left. Perhaps we will be destroyed first and Babylon afterwards."

"Then this is the end of the world?"

"Perhaps we are going to our reward ahead of the crowds."

Shadrach chuckled and took her cold hands in his large palms. "Gentle Sarah," he said, rubbing her fingers. "Always seeing the bright side, even to the end of the world."

"I have only one regret in passing," she said softly, "and that is that I depart this life not having tasted the fruits of matrimony."

"A regret I share, myself. They say an unmarried man shall not find his ultimate reward in heaven."

"It shall certainly be lonely. Spending one's time in solitary pursuits throughout eternity."

"Perhaps there will be sparking and coupling in heaven as well as earth," Shadrach suggested hopefully.

"Perhaps. If not I shall be doomed to remain a spinster throughout time everlasting."

Their eyes warily met and they broke out into shy smiles.

Shadrach moved his hands up her arms until he was pressing her against his chest. Perhaps it was the madness of the times, or perhaps it was the feeling of her next to him, but he left all caution behind him.

He bent over and placed his lips against hers. She averted her eyes from him and moved her face to the side, but not enough to separate their lips. He could smell the sweetness of her breath break into shallow drafts as he pressed more firmly on her mouth. Now, she pressed back, and her lips loosened and yielded to him. Her breast was heaving next to his and his hands worked their way under her shawl.

"Brother Tompkins, such carnality!" she whispered hoarsely.

"Forgive my forwardness, but we have such little time left to us," Shadrach said in a burst of emotion that surprised even himself. "Would you consent to be mine and to spend all eternity in my company?"

Sarah recoiled slightly from this proposition, but Shadrach still held her in his grip. She put her fingers to her forehead as if trying to dispell a dizziness. "Sir, what an awkward position you put me in."

"Follow your natural inclination."

"But if I did that, would it be Love calling, or the confusion of the times?"

"Don't question the motivation of the call. Just follow it. I want you for my wife, on earth and in the heaven we surely shall see in a short while!"

"Then I will be so, and gladly," Sarah said with a impetuousness that matched his own.

The Englishman crushed the blushing girl in a sheltering embrace. "This may appear to be an act of rashness, but in my mind I have rehearsed these words one thousand times."

"And I have silently answered them in my mind an equal number of times."

What might have shocked the Putnam family in normal times, now was smoothed by the topsy-turvy nature of their circumstances. When Shadrach and Sarah had gathered the family in the late afternoon, Putnam blanched when he put his arm around his daughter and spoke in official tones.

"Mr. Putnam, I shall always be in your debt for your generosity shown to me when I first came to this region, and I would add that nothing that I did while under your roof ever took advantage of that hospitality. In the teeth of the approaching gale, your daughter and I feel it would be appropriate to pledge our everlasting loyalty to each other. I wish to ask you for her hand in marriage?''

Rachel uttered a slight gasp and put her knuckles over her lips. Thomas Putnam sat heavily on the bench by the table and stared at them. Nathan Putnam stepped forward and shook Shadrach's hand in a firm grip.

"What did he say?" Mrs. Putnam called from her bed. "I can't hear a thing back here."

"He said he wants to marry Sarah!" Putnam snapped.

"Mary Stuart? Who's she?"

"MARRY SARAH! He wants to marry your daughter," the man roared.

"When?"

"Now. Today," Shadrach said. "TODAY MADAM! IF YOU PLEASE!"

"Never! I refuse to hear of it!" the woman said weakly. "She's much too young. And not without the proper betrothal."

Sarah began to protest, but she was silenced by her father who rose and stood between them and his wife. Taking the couple by the arm and leading them to the doorway, he stepped out into the chill of the afternoon and shut the door behind them.

"If you wish to wed, I object to it, but I shan't bar your way," he said briefly. "Your mother doesn't understand our desperate situation here. I have not told her the news. If you wish to become as one in this dark hour, I can't see the harm in it."

He held out his hand in a strong shake for Shadrach who mumbled his thanks. His daughter embraced him and he winked his good eye at his prospective son-in-law.

"Besides. We may need to produce a lot more Saints than we have now."

To the villagers, nearly hysterical from the news coming from the rest of the country, the whispered announcement of the hasty wedding was like the pouring of oil on stormy waters. Somehow, the idea that a small bit of normalcy could be taking place during the turbulent days seemed to reduce the fears of the Saints. The ceremony was accepted, not as a bulwark against coming doom, but as an affirmation of the future. Like births and baptisms, weddings seemed to proclaim a healthy confidence that all was right with the world.

The wedding took place that evening with a minimum of fuss. The guests assembled in the school house, more out of curiosity than ceremony. There were some whispers and suspicious glances from the women in the group, but the general attitude of the villagers was one of acceptance in view of their extraordinary circumstances.

Brother McBride performed the brief ceremony, reading from his worn book. Nathan stood at Shadrach's side, and Rachel at her sister's, although she never looked her new brother-in-law in the eye during the entire ceremony. And during the wedding feast following the ceremony, Shadrach looked in vain for his new sister-in-law.

Later in the evening, Shadrach opened the door to the cabin Mister McBride had so thoughtfully vacated for the evening, and showed his new bride into their chambers. Sarah was still wearing the same homespun dress she had worn that afternoon when he proposed.

"Well, Mrs. I'm now prepared for the Millenium," he said taking off his boots.

"I'm well prepared for the Millenium," Sarah said nervously as she remained standing by the bed, "but I'm not so sure if I'm prepared for tonight."

Shadrach looked up at her in surprise. "Don't be concerned about your preparations," he assured her. "I'm experienced in these matters."

"Oh! And where might you have come by this expertise?"

"A mining town is no monastery," he said matter-of-factly as he shook off his trousers. "There is plenty of that business afoot."

"And were you much of a businessman?"

"Never you mind about that. Now get into bed with your husband and let's do the deed!"

He leaned over and blew out the candle by the bed. She stood in the dim light of the cabin, and then slowly unhooked her dress and pulled the coarse material over her head with the same distaste with which she might empty a bag of spoiled potatoes. She stood in the dim light of the cabin wearing nothing but her white cotton underskirt until her new husband prompted her by thumping on the tick with the flat of his hand.

Dropping to her knees, she clasped her hands together and froze in silent prayer for, as it seemed to Shadrach, an inordinately long time. Then, still wearing the underskirt, she slid into bed beside him and pulled the scratchy wool blanket up to her neck.

"You may begin, sir!" she whispered tightly.

Needing little encouragement, Shadrach rolled his large frame on top of the young woman and began pecking her cheeks with his grizzled chin, while he removed his shirt, the only article of clothing he was wearing. When he had taken care of himself, he roughly began pulling up her cotton dress until he brought it over her breasts where she resisted its complete removal.

This done, he lay full-length on his wife and tried to force her legs apart with his toes.

"Slowly. Patiently!" she commanded in a whisper. "This moment comes but once in a lifetime, so I pray you not to race through."

Following these instructions, he tried to rub some warmth into the chill that was still in his wife's arms. He squeezed her arms from shoulder to wrist until they limbered up and then admired the smoothness of her thighs and firm calves as he passed his rough palms over them. Her breasts, in particular, seemed cold and he devoted much time to warming them up. They were as firm and muscular as the rest of her body, but with a generous attention paid to them they soon became supple. The poor woman must have been suffering chronically from the cold, for she responded enthusiastically when Shadrach rested his flushed cheeks against her bosom, rubbing them to better kindle the heat. So well did she respond to this attention that he repeated the procedure with noticeable appreciation wherever he rubbed.

But finally the time came when he felt the marriage must be consummated and he indicated as such.

"Thread the needle carefully," she pleaded with him, "and be economical with your energy."

"Hold tight the thread that I might more steadily guide it," he whispered back.

She did so and not long afterwards the act was finished with Shadrach collapsed by her side.

"I am spent," he said. "I had no idea sewing was such hard work."

"Practice is the key to ease," she whispered back. "Perhaps you can try again when the thread dries out."

They lay in bed, holding tight to the heat of the other's

body. Suddenly, a crash on the front door of the cabin brought Shadrach jumping out of bed.

"My God! What is that?" he shouted. "Are we attacked by Pukes?"

Sarah laughed outloud and covered her teeth with her hand.

"Calm yourself, husband!" she called. "It's just the boys of the village pranking us by throwing rocks against the door of the newlyweds!"

Shadrach wiped the crumbs of the wedding breakfast from his lips, noting ruefully that it would be some time before he would see another meal served with sorghum and wetted with buttermilk. Whether it was the afterglow of the meal or the memory of the warmth of the night's sleep he did not know, but he felt a great improvement of disposition from the days before.

"I feel much better about our circumstances than I have for some time," he announced to Sarah. "I truly believe that the single state is a cursed one."

Sarah grinned at him. "I believe our troubles were a divine encouragement to marry. Just as we found the warmth on the coldest night, I believe these hard times will give us a new spirit."

Shadrach smiled and rubbed his matted hair. "I think my bachelorhood had pulled the blinders over my eyes," he admitted. "Now that I'm graced by marriage, I'm wondering if the end of the world is as close to hand as I feared."

"If it is not, then our union will make my anticipation of heaven more sweet."

"But if the end doesn't come, you have been saddled with a husband as poor as a churchmouse. . . ."

"If the end doesn't come, that will be reward in itself!"

The conversation was disturbed by the rumble of hooves.

"An army of Pukes! An army of Pukes!" someone outside the cabin called.

The couple immediately joined the rest of the village in the common where Nathan Putnam reigned in his horse to the alarm of the village. A woman bellowed for her children and the elders came running from every direction to hear the news.

"Two hundred riders, not three miles outside of town," Nathan shouted. "Pukes and Indians in the same group! All armed!"

"My God! What can that mean? Have you parleyed with them?"

"I fear they have not come to parley!"

"Perhaps they will not pass this way?"

The confusion in the village ended as all eyes turned toward the hill on the western end of town. On the very spot where Shadrach had contemplated the brilliance of the autumn colors, another color showed itself.

A single rider galloped over the hill, carrying a blood red banner in his hand. He paused on the crest of the ridge, then waved the flag. From the forest behind him, a legion of mounted men walked their horses to the side. From where he was standing, Shadrach could court at least two hundred men with rifles. Some wore slouch hats of the Missourians, others the feathers of the neighboring Indian tribes.

This sight released pandemonium in the village. A woman began wailing a hymn as others fell on their knees to pray for deliverance. Some of the elders brought out their fowling pieces and tried to form a military square.

"Stay your arms!" Nathan shouted. "What good are a dozen locks against two hundred."

"They have massacre on their minds!"

"Then don't give them the gift of righteousness by firing on them! We must throw ourselves on their mercy."

Nathan spurred his horse and galloped toward the hill. Shadrach began pulling Sarah toward the forest in the opposite direction. She resisted his movement.

"We must consecrate the others into the hands of the Lord and save ourselves," he hissed. "I've no faith in the mercies of the Pukes."

Sarah refused to leave the common as she followed her brother's progress up the hill.

"Brothers! A word with you," she heard him call out.

A puff of smoke from the hilltop and her brother was pulled backwards out of his saddle as quickly as if roped. He fell to the earth and lay motionless as the riders on the hilltop spurred forward.

"Nathan!" Sarah screamed and tore out of her husband's grip. Before he could stop her, she sprang forward toward the attacking Gentiles.

As Shadrach watched in horror, his wife was engulfed by the tide of riders. As they approached the village, they discharged their weapons at one time and two hundred musket balls rained down on the common.

What happened afterwards would never be fully remembered by Shadrach, who had attempted to rescue Sarah, his last thought. Thomas Putnam pushed past him, carrying his old sword as the townspeople scattered to the four points of the compass.

"A musket! Someone fetch my musket," the father called.

The riders broke over the village like the tide on the Liverpool breakwater. They criss-crossed the village, shooting randomly at the fleeing Saints, slashing at others with swords and hatchets, whooping and screaming with the same energy as their victims.

A number of the villagers had barricaded themselves inside the smithy, hoping the thick log walls would offer them a refuge. This improvised fortress became a target of challenge to the attacking Missourians who wheeled their horses around the smithy in a cloud of dust.

"Fire through the chinks!" their leader yelled as he kicked his horse to the wall of the building and poked the muzzle through the mud between the beams. "Rats in a barrel!"

He pressed the trigger and his pan flashed. The gun roared inside the building as the defenseless Saints screamed. This became a sport as rider upon rider thrust the muzzle of his musket through the logs, and sparked his piece.

Hoping to save himself, Shadrach raced through the cabins to the other side of the village, only to discover a party of Indians tying their horses in order to fight on foot.

"Here's one! Get 'im!" one shouted as two others drew hatchets from their belts and gave chase.

The only weapon at hand was a scythe which Shadrach siezed and whipped about him as his pursuers danced backwards. Their leader confronted him. A pock-marked face! Reddish hair! He had seen that man before!

"You're no Indian!" Shadrach snarled as he whipped the scythe in the man's direction.

He could see now the man wore only the feathers and paint in a crude imitation of the Indians. From the neck on down they were pure Puke. They circled Shadrach like dogs and only his violent spins with the scythe kept them from him. As he danced, they taunted him with whoops and curses.

"Nehemiah! Finish him!" someone shouted.

Shadrach spun to fend off his attacker. Instead he faced a

man leveling a musket, some twenty paces distant. Before he could move, fire belched from the muzzle of the gun and he was stuck in the face by a blow of such force he was knocked from his feet. Sprawled in the dust, he felt a dull throbbing in his face, like he had been struck by a rock, but little else. How long he lay there, he couldn't tell, but he was able to stagger to his feet to complete his escape.

As he stumbled from the common, he beheld the sight of old Mr. McBride, at least the body wore the vest and breeches of McBride. But his face had been so horribly mutilated with the stained corn chopper lying at the man's side that Shadrach couldn't recognize him. The sound of more firing urged him onwards and he stumbled to the safety of the trees on the edge of the village. The sound of laughter caused him to look backwards. Rachel Putnam was being pulled by her chestnut hair through the village by one man, while two others held her arms to the sides. They led her into the schoolhouse and the laughter grew louder.

Shadrach tried to call her name. He could make a groaning sound but his jaw would not move, his mouth would not form the words.

He sat up dumbly. Had he been shot in the brain? He tried to command his legs to walk, tried to command his arms to pick up the scythe which lay at his side. The Pukes had cut down his family and he wanted to even the score.

In desperation, he prayed that his limbs would obey him, that he would rise and walk among their hosts like a vengeful reaper.

Instead, he sat on his useless legs, like a broken doll. His body was numb and he was only conscious of the destruction around him. He was aware of a thunder in the distance. Were his prayers being answered?

A dozen horsemen galloped around the cabin. They were Pukes, their faces smeared with warpaint, feathers in their hair. Shadrach sat helplessly as they rode their horses over him, spinning him in the dust.

Then, mercifully, everything was dark.

Chapter Six

The dirt roads of Missouri were frozen as hard as Rachel's heart as the wagon bumped along toward the east. She lay motionless, her head in her sister's warm lap, her hollow eyes staring at the November landscape which they passed on their way from this hateful state.

The breath of the two oxen pulling the wagon steamed from their flaring nostrils. The huge brownish purple beasts seemed pleased with their loads for the wagons were much lighter than they had been when first they came to Missouri. The Saints had been routed by the Pukes and had been given a short time to leave the state. Anxious to flee before more murders were visited upon them, the Saints left their farms and possessions behind to fall into the hands of their enemies. Those Saints who were tempted to burn their houses were stayed by the leadership who wanted the exodus carried out peacefully.

Only the careful organization of the church prevented a panic. Joseph Smith and his closest aides had been thrown into a prison, and the rumor held that he would be murdered by his jailers. The church property had been seized by the Missourians as reparations. Only the steady leadership of the Apostle Brigham Young enabled the Saints to organize caravans of wagons which removed the people to the friendlier lands of Illinois, east across the Mississippi River.

Rachel had no way of knowing of the flight of the thousands of Saints who were being driven from their homes on the frontier. Her mind was occupied with seeing and re-seeing the events which left seventeen of the citizens of Haun's Mill dead, her father and brother buried with the others in the newly dug well shaft, her brother-in-law cruelly wounded, her mother still very ill, unable to comprehend what was going on around her, and herself violated by the Pukes.

The only time she closed her eyes was when she remembered the whiskey smell of the men who carried her into the schoolhouse threw her down on a long oak bench and made sure that she was no longer a maiden.

What paralyzed her now as she rested in the wagon was not fear or self-pity, but a towering, uncontrollable rage which was shared by many of her neighbors. They had been promised a Zion and had been delivered into hell. And now they promised themselves to return to Missouri and drive the devils out.

And as Rachel bounced along, one passage circled through her mind, a thought which would never leave her: "Vengeance shall be mine, sayeth the Lord."

The groans from Shadrach became so horrible that Sarah was forced to pull the wagon to a halt. She turned to look. Beside her mother in the wagon box, her husband lay under a thick wool blanket.

"What's the matter, Sister Tompkins?" the man driving the team behind them called as twenty wagons were held up.

"It's my husband, I fear he is at Death's door."

While the other travelers waited patiently, several of the company gathered in the Tompkin's wagon to view Shadrach's condition. The Englishman's head was wrapped in a cotton bandage; he appeared weak and pale. They gingerly unwrapped the bandage and the odor which escaped from the wound made Sarah gag. The ball from the Puke's pistol had entered Shadrach's right cheek, breaking his bones and shattering a number of his teeth; and had not been removed. The wound had first turned blue and now was turning yellow.

Brother Cullen bent over his face. "His wound is putrefying. The ball has caused the flesh to fester. We must find a surgeon."

"Where can we find a surgeon in this country?" Sarah lamented. "We must drain the wound ourselves."

Cradling her husband's head in her lap, Sarah took a long knife and began probing the wound, as Brother Cullen held a lantern over her. It took all the strength of the men in the wagon to hold the Englishman down as he cried out, and it took all Sarah's strength to continue to probe past his strangled screams. With more determination than skill, she rooted out the flattened lead ball and extricated it. Mopping out the wound, she dressed the raw flesh with the a preparation of cloves and pepper.

The other Saints gathered around him, praying and calling out. Brother Cullen placed his hands on Shadrach's forehead calling for his deliverance from death. A bishop was summoned and annointed Shadrach's head with oil. He put his hands on the wound and added his prayers to the rest.

"Lay your hands on, boys, and let our power fill this man," the Bishop said sternly.

The rest joined in and Sarah began to fear that her husband would be pressed to death by the zealousness of his healers. But as the Bishop looked up through the tarp of the wagon at the heavens, a slight smile of satisfaction came over his face and he removed his hands and packed up his bag.

"I just felt the life force begin to flow strongly in him. He will recover in time to help us build anew," he announced matter-of-factly. "Now let's get this wagon moving. I want to put some distance between myself and Missouri!"

Shadrach's head was indeed harder than the ball which penetrated it and he recovered to witness the dispersion of the Saints. The Tompkins family had been sent to winter in the Iowa wilderness, north of the Missouri line with a group of Saints who were farming the land. The family found shelter from the winter storms in a earthern duggout, which had been a root cellar, hastily converted to a home for the refugees. It was in this cellar on a freezing January night that the long-suffering Mrs. Putnam died, never knowing her son and husband had been murdered.

Isolated in the middle of snowy horizons, Shadrach, Sarah and Rachel found a refuge from the tormenting thoughts of the past. The faith of the Iowa Saints was strong and it nourished them through the bitterness of their memories. Sarah, who though trampled by the onslaught of the attacking Missourians, had been able to save herself from harm in Haun's Mill by escaping into the brush. It was her fortitude and faith in the future that made her able to cheer her family out of their preoccupation with the tragedies of the past and their great personal losses.

Her own pregnancy coincided with the coming of spring to the rolling prairies of Iowa. As the trees blossomed and the fields bloomed around them, her own swelling was a physical reassurance of the promise of the future.

"This is a child who will make up for those that we lost in Missouri," she proudly announced. "And when we have this one we will have another until we have had enough to replace all the dead of that village. Our children will live with the promise of seeing Zion."

"We will never go back there," Shadrach said bluntly. "Once bitten, twice shy."

"Don't talk nonsense," Sarah said firmly. "When we have raised a host we will repopulate that state with Saints."

"And no one will dare oppose us," Rachel said sharply.

The summer sun renewed their strength and they used it to bring in the harvest. The times were quiet, a relief from the danger in Missouri and the family used this period of peace to rest. The Iowans shared their homes willingly and the Tompkins shared the work. And as the harvest was brought in, Sarah brought forth a son to begin the repopulation. He was named Ham, after the general in the Book of Mormon. At his birth he promised to rival his father for size. The Tompkins son had grown strong and healthy as the rest of his family while carried in his mother's womb in the Iowa sunshine.

The diaspora forced upon the Saints threatened to blunt their drive to create a Zion in the wilderness. Scattered up and down the Mississippi shores they were hard pressed to gather again. In fact, many of them argued that the Saints should remain scattered, practicing their religion in small groups. It had been a mistake to bring so many together in one place, these people maintained, for it called attention to the Saints and brought the wrath of their neighbors against them.

But other Saints feared that if the tribe was not brought back together soon, they would drift apart. Rather than blending into the Gentile population they should concentrate their numbers in one area and resist the kind of persecution they experienced before. Pacifism of the sort practiced in Missouri was replaced by a practical sight of Saints carrying rifles.

In their remote haven in the wilderness, the Tompkins heard the good news that the prophet, Joseph Smith, had finally escaped from the Missourians and had fled to Illinois. There, safe from extradition, he had chosen to rebuild the city of the Saints at a bend in the Mississippi River. The site he had chosen he named Nauvoo, after the Hebrew word for beautiful.

Every passing Saint brought some more news of this city where all the people rallied around their prophet. The time on the Iowa frontier had been quite enough for Shadrach so when the sisters begged him to move the family to the new city, he needed little encouragement. With their supplies replenished from the Iowa Saints, they loaded their wagon, yoked their oxen and set out for Illinois.

The ice was still new on the Mississippi River as the family drew up on the western bank. Across the river was the bend where the city was being built, but to reach it they had to cross an impossibly wide expanse of white ice which had a suspiciously peaceful look. The sun was rising in the east, bathing the family in a golden glow as they contemplated the shiny tablet which creaked in the frost of the morning.

Shadrach looked with reluctance at Sarah, who held their child on her breast. "Perhaps we should go upstream and take the ferry," he suggested.

"No, the morning sky is red. There is a storm building," Rachel said, nodding toward the horizon. "If we do not cross now, we may be trapped."

Shadrach dismounted from the wagon and took the long whip with him. Using it on the rumps of the two oxen, he urged them onto the ice.

"Ho, Castor! Up Pollux!" he shouted, trying to build everyone's courage.

The lumbering beasts stepped as gingerly as a thousand-pound animal can onto the ice. Their iron shoes clacked on the thick glasslike surface and the animals stopped, afraid of the new sensation.

"Move! Damn you!" Shadrach shouted, putting his muscle behind the whip.

The two oxen snorted and lurched ahead, carefully treading out onto the glazed river.

"It will be high time we will be getting back into the community of Saints," Sarah scolded him. "Your language is sliding away faster than your beliefs."

"Did you hear a crack?" Shadrach asked, freezing in his steps the way the wind had frozen his words.

The wagon came to an abrupt halt, with even the oxen straining to listen. Sure enough, a singing, whining richochet of a crack in the ice rippled under their feet. It sounded like a piano wire coming loose.

"This was a misbegotten idea to cross the river like this," Shadrach said woefully. "I don't relish the idea of dying in this frozen river."

"Then keep on moving!" Rachel snapped. "Just because your stomach growls doesn't mean that it's going to cave in."

Stung by her words like the rump of his oxen, Shadrach set off, leading the team by a leather throng through their nose rings. He moved quickly, ignoring the incessant groans and complaints of the ice.

As he tried to hide his fear, he looked around him. The river had looked wide when they were standing on the bank, but out in the middle it appeared that they were on the ocean. Both banks seemed to be distant lines on the horizon and the peculiar nature of the ice magnified the clicking of the oxen's feet and the grinding of the wheels into a strange song.

As the wheels ground round and round, Shadrach was reminded of a tune he had heard sung in Wallsend by the old women of the town and he began to sing out loud:

Babylon is falling,

Babylon is falling,

Babylon is falling.

To rise no more. . . .

As he sung the verses, the women began to pick up the refrain. The Illinois bank slowly began to become more defined. Even their child Ham, began to chuckle in imitation as the verses skidded away across the ice . . .

"Babylon is falling to rise no more."

After they coaxed their oxen onto the frozen banks of Illinois, their relief quickly turned to perplexity. The wild countryside revealed no great city being built, and no path to find it. They turned south, more to face the afternoon sun than with any course in mind. Shadrach silently cursed the people who had given him directions. He was concerned about the health of his child if they had to spend the night in the cold.

Heading inland they picked up a rutted road and followed it several miles when they saw a number of riders approaching them.

"Pukes!" Rachel hissed urgently. "Get out your gun."

Shadrach squinted at the riders; there was something familiar about the way several of them rode.

"God and Liberty!" he shouted, giving the old Danite sign.

"God and Liberty!" came the reply and Shadrach relaxed. The men were friends.

Several riders dismounted on the gallop to slap their old friend on the back. Shadrach recognized most of them as comrades from the Sons of Dan. He recognized Porter Rockwell, the mean eyed sharpshooter of the group, and John D. Lee, the affable organizer of the riders. But the Englishman stared suspiciously at a tall, handsome man who was riding with them. The man's brown hair was brushed back over a sculpted face that beamed with self-confidence. The man wore a blue tunic like a military officer's and while the other men dismounted, he remained astride his well-bred horse. Shadrach immediately suspected the man of being a new convert, probably a rich man from the east.

"What happened, Shadrach? Did you get lost coming from Missouri?" John D. Lee said, "We had given you up for an apostate."

"We heard you received a musket ball in the head and we were worried that your face had flattened the ball too badly to be used again," another laughed.

"It takes more than a ball in the face to put me down," Shadrach boasted as he displayed his scarred cheek and his missing side teeth.

"And you're coming now to join us in Nauvoo?"

"God willing. I am here to help build the temple and make up for what we lost in Missouri."

"Don't tell me you have been taken in by Old Peepstone Joe?" a mocking voice rang out, "You don't believe his tales do you."

Shadrach turned to see where the voice came from. The handsome stranger was staring at him, a grin on his face. The name "Peepstone Joe" referred to Joseph Smith who supposedly had used a crystal divining stone to search for treasures in his younger days. Shadrach ignored this insult and turned to his old friends.

"Am I on the right route to the city? How far a journey is it for I wish to arrive before nightfall?"

"You must have been out in the country longer than you

realize if you're going to follow old Holy Joe," the mocking voice rang out. "Do you actually believe he's a prophet?"

Shadrach turned, his anger building. After all his troubles, he wasn't in the mood to be mocked by some greenhorn from the East.

"I believe in the divinity of his revelations," Shadrach said evenly.

"But the man is such a scoundrel! What if he reveals that you should lend him your money for one of his real estate schemes?"

Shadrach looked around him. The ex-Danites were grinning at his befuddlement. Could it be possible that these good men had turned apostates and were living as renegades?

"If the Prophet asks for all my money I would give it to him willingly. And in my presence, do not refer to him as a scoundrel, sir."

The greenhorn grinned his calculating smile and slid from his saddle. "Oh, what a stalwart fellow!" he said. "And what if I was to call him a scoundrel in your presence?"

Shadrach eyed the man. Well-built and muscular, he was still a nose shorter than the Englishman. "I would give you then the drubbing you richly deserve."

He heard Sarah call his name but didn't take his eyes off his opponent.

"Then you consider yourself quite a fighter?"

"For the best cause, the best fighter. My brothers here can tell you of the engagements I've been in."

"Then perhaps you would care to wrestle me?" the stranger said, "for the championship of . . . the highway."

An evil grin spread over Shadrach's face. What he lacked as a debater, he more than made up for as a wrestler. He couldn't conceal his delight in luring this greenhorn into a fight. He would whale the tar out of him.

"It will pleasure me to teach you the ways of the frontier," Shadrach said.

He spit gleefully into his hands and ducked into a crouch. His face was flushed, his eyes alive as he warily circled the stranger who stood upright, his own eyes bemused.

Like an enraged bear, he sprang at the man, but his charge was nimbly side-stepped by the greenhorn who pushed him into the arms of his Danite brothers.

Circling more cautiously, Shadrach moved in, pawing the air with his huge hands. Feigning a move, he caught the man in a bear hug squeezing him with the power that would have crushed the life out of a smaller man. To his surprise, the greenhorn wiped his arms from around him with a powerful sweep and pushed the astonished Shadrach to the ground.

"Don't let that Puke humiliate you!" Rachel cried, angry as his performance.

Shadrach jumped to his feet and waded toward the stranger. Pretending to grapple, he instead launched a powerful fist that had staggered many a Wallsend miner. The stranger picked it out of midair and with a crushing grip of his own brought the Englishman to the ground, threatening to break his arm.

"Cry 'Uncle,' " the man chided.

"Never!" Shadrach said through gritted teeth.

"Cry 'Uncle' or lose the arm! 'Uncle Peepstone!' "

"Enough! 'Uncle! Uncle!' And be damned!"

Shadrach shook his arm out when the stranger let him go. He was on the verge of tears, not from the pain but from the embarrassment at being humiliated in front of his friends and family. The greenhorn swung into his saddle and turned for a parting shot.

"Don't forget what I told you about Peepstone Joe."

As the man spurred his horse and galloped off down the road, Shadrach turned accusingly to his friends. They were laughing at his expense.

"How can you boys keep company with such a blackguard?" he demanded. "After all we suffered in Missouri."

"Don't you know who that was?" Lee asked.

"Someone I am going to take a cudgel to the next time I see him," Shadrach said bitterly.

"Then you will be caning the prophet," Lee informed him with a grin. "You just lost a match to Joseph Smith himself!"

NAUVOO

1840

Chapter Seven

From atop the hill overlooking Nauvoo, Shadrach surveyed the activity around him. Huge grey blocks of limestone lay like a child's toys, scattered in confusion. Straining oxen were moving up the hill dragging sledges with still more blocks as the teamster's whips cracked in the air and boys ran before the sledges lubricating the ground with spoiled milk.

At the crest of the hill, stonemasons wearing leather aprons shaped the blocks of stone into usable shapes, their mauls and chisels sounding like the chirping of iron crickets. Grunting laborers jinked the stones into place using a wooden derrick and their own bulging muscles.

All this activity was being thrown into the building of the Nauvoo Temple, the greatest work the Saints had undertaken. The temple was Joseph Smith's signal to the world that the Saints were here to stay in Illinois. When finished, it would be the largest building on the western frontier. Commanding a view of the Mississippi River below it, the temple would be visible for many miles to the steamboats coming up the river. It made Nauvoo, only in its first few years of existence, a substantial city unlike the frontier backwater towns of Carthage or Chicago. Visitors from all over the world stopped to marvel at the industriousness of the Saints.

The original inspiration had come from the tribes of Israel who had constructed temples where ever they settled. For the Saints, the temple would be more than a place of worship, it would be a place to carry out the baptisms and other work of the church. The regular services and meetings could be held in the halls in Nauvoo.

The temple also served as a beacon for the thousands of Saints on the eastern coast of the United States and in Europe. Contributions poured in providing money for the impoverished Saints to buy the Wisconsin pine for the scaffolding and to pay the stone cutters who quarried the limestone behind the temple hill.

As Shadrach looked around, he could see evidence of the hundreds of Saints arriving every month from New York and from England. The city could not provide jobs for the New Englanders and Welchmen who flooded in, so the unemployed were given jobs on the temple. All Saints contributed to the welfare of the church in the form of a tithe. Those with money, gave cash. Those with little money contributed food and tools to the project or housed the laborers. Those without money contributed their sweat and callouses.

Shadrach had been fortunate that his Danite brothers formed a powerful faction in the community. They had gotten him the job of a foreman on the temple, designed by architect William Weeks to resemble nothing that had ever been built before. With a a steeple over one hundred and sixty feet high; the vertical walls themselves would be sixty feet high, lined with pilasters, or false columns crowned by the sun and moon symbols. The design itself was influenced by a vision of Joseph Smith's to create what they might expect to see in heaven once the Millenium came. When finished, its white walls would gleam in the sun.

Shadrach walked to the keg of water and dipped the ladle into the cask, pulling out a cool drink of the water which had flowed from the temple spring. He swallowed it and handed the dipper to a sweating carpenter who had just arrived from England.

"Is it always this bloody hot here in the summertime?" the man said, pouring the water over his bald head and letting it run over his gingham shirt.

"That it is, mate," Shadrach answered, grateful to hear the familiar accents of his native land.

The carpenter lowered his voice and glanced at Shadrach.

"They say we're building a temple, but have you seen the walls on this thing? They must be five feet thick. Solid stone! This place could be a flaming fortress!"

Shadrach laughed at this. "Why, this building shall last one thousand years! We're building it to stand the siege of time!"

The carpenter went away shaking his head, but Shadrach knew his eyes were keen. The thick stone walls of the temple could, if the need arose, stand off the most powerful cannons in the country. And the spring which flowed up through the temple floor could provide any besieged defenders with drinking water for a long time. The Saints were taking no chances on the tender mercies of the Pukes.

Suddenly, a shout rang out and the confusion of an accident began. Men ran in all direction as the cables supporting the derrick parted and the wooden structure swayed crazily. The stone being hoisted on the wall slowly drifted over the edge of the building and dropped out of its sling. A party of stone masons shouted in panic and ran, but the stone fell among them pinning one man to the ground.

The man was screaming in terror when Shadrach reached him. His legs were trapped under the stone and the Englishman winced as he imagined the damage the limestone had done to the sinew.

"Get me a maul and some wedges!" Shadrach bellowed over the screams of the victim.

A large mallet made from a section of a pine trunk and some stout wedges made of oak were rushed to the site. Workers held the injured man as Shadrach drove the wedges under the rock with powerful strokes of the mallet. The rest of the men heaved at the stone until they had levered it enough to pull the stonemason from under the block.

'You are lucky it rained last night," Shadrach said, examining the man. "The earth was so wet the weight of the stone drove your legs into the ground. They may be broken but at least they're not crushed."

As Sarah hurried up Mulholland Street with her shopping basket she could hear the shrill moan of the steamboat whistle calling the stevedores at the landing to ready the lines. Another crowd of Saints coming up the river from St. Louis would be disgorging at the dock.

The thought of more Saints troubled her. She was happy to have as many of them as possible, but the town was already so crowded she was worried where they would put them all. It was the summer of 1842 and the city, not even four years old, was bursting at the seams with immigrants. Sarah quickened her pace, pulling up the tattered hem of her calico skirt. With more newcomers, the farmers who ran the market at the outskirts of town would be tempted to raise their prices even more.

Nauvoo had been built on a piece of land which bulged into the Mississippi. Joseph Smith and other Saints had bought up

as much land as they could in order to stake out a territory for
the beleaguered people. Instead of scattering across the countryside, they would build a city where they could concentrate
their numbers. The concentration of the people was easily
accomplished but feeding them was another matter. The Saints
began farming all the land around the town with the skills
they had learned in Missouri. However, the new arrivals
coming from England were anything but farmers. They were
mechanics and factory workers, miners and tradesmen who
had escaped the industrial slums of the cities. The skills of
these newcomers were put to work in a tannery, a pottery
factory, and a flour mill, but there was not enough work to go
around.

The move to Nauvoo had pleased Sarah. In Missouri, she
and her sister had longed for their old life in Boston—the
parties, the dances, the Sunday promenades where the society
of the city looked each other over. Now this small town on
the frontier promised someday to have the same way of life.

Already the women took an almost sinful interest in the
newest fashions from New York and the women fresh off the
riverboat were always appraised by jealous eyes. The dances
held outdoors in the summertime were always well-attended
and provided the gossip for the next week's quilting parties.

After the privations of the countryside, the town was a
blessing. The Tompkins lived in a small cabin Shadrach had
built from the extra pine not used for the temple. It was a
crude, one-room home with a loft for sleeping but it would
serve them until they could build a more substantial brick
home like many of the other more affluent Saints. The house
had a small plot of land on which Sarah had cultivated a
garden which took up every inch of it. Their house had been
the only one in their section of Nauvoo when they built it, but
now it was surrounded by the homes of newcomers. Sarah
felt more secure with neighbors around and was grateful for
the help they gave in bringing up her small son.

Most of all, the town afforded the luxury of having several
general stores where she could buy a needle or a ready made
candle when she needed it. The Tompkins had very little
money and the store owned by Joseph Smith was tight on its
credit, but a mercantile owned by some Gentiles was always
willing to carry their account until they could pay.

Now Sarah was hurrying to the section of town where the
farmers would tie up their wagons filled with produce. The

opening of the town had proved a bonanza for them and they took advantage of it. With Ham tugging at her skirts, Sarah walked between the wagons, looking indifferently at the contents. The farmers nodded and smiled at her and she returned a polite nod while sneering at their products. She was hoping to get a bargain on the produce left over at the end of the day.

"My parsnips haven't come up yet and yours look rather scrawny," she said, stopping at one wagon.

"Can't eat what's in the ground," the famrer said, sparring with her. "You can eat mine for three cents a pound."

"I assume that's morning prices. They look a little wilted now."

"They're sun-dried. They'll keep fresh longer now."

"I only have a penny to spend," Sarah said firmly.

"Then I can sell only a third of a pound. . . ."

At once, Sarah became conscious of a conversation going on in the next wagon.

"What did you say about an accident at the temple?" she said quickly.

The three women at the next wagon were pleased that their news was so appreciated by the eavesdropper.

"Some poor man had his legs broken by a falling stone from the temple wall."

"Who was he?"

"Some Englishman, poor fellow. I don't know the name."

Abandoning her bargaining, Sarah picked up her child and rushed from the market. She ran through the same streets she had come so leisurely on, mouthing a silent prayer. Her experience in life gave her no reason for optismism and she feared the worst. It would be her luck that now that they had settled in a liveable place, disaster would strike again.

It wasn't enough that her sister had lain abed for several weeks now, a victim of the swamp fever which bred in the lowland marshes around Nauvoo. Now she feared that the giant body of her husband, upon whom she had depended on for her own strength, would be crippled. She didn't know if she would be able to carry on under such adversity.

Her sister Rachel had not been right since the horror of Haun's Mill. Withdrawn and melancholy, she had shunned all contact with others and had especially been suspicious of the company of men. Although there were many young men who were attracted to her, she ignored their compliments. Her aloofness, combined with her physical beauty, had given all prospective suitors the indication that she thought herself too good for them.

Sarah had observed that there was only one man who Rachel trusted. Her own husband, Shadrach. At first Sarah had encouraged her sister's attention to him, for she felt it did her good to regain her trust in men. But when Rachel confined her companionship to him, Sarah grew slightly nervous about the depth of her sister's interest. Remembering the attention the Englishman had shown in her sister before their marriage, Sarah wondered if it wasn't time for Rachel to find lodging elsewhere. The familiarity of all three of them living in the same household had been advantageous in the wilderness of Iowa, but in the town perhaps it was too much of a temptation.

Sarah shook these thoughts out of her head as she ran. Her troubles had caused her to stray into suspicious ways, she reasoned. She was upset about her husband and the devil had used her perturbance to sow dissension in her mind.

She looked up and down the dirt road which led to their small cabin. The workers from the temple were beginning to straggle home through the dust of the hot July afternoon. Should she try to run to the temple or should she await word at home?

The irritability of her young son, annoyed at being bounced in her arms made her decide to go to the cabin. She hurried anxiously toward it, glancing to see if any of Shadrach's fellow workers were waiting.

No one was outside and when she pushed the door open she was surprised to see the hulking back of her husband hunched over the dinner table. Shadrach turned, tearing a hunk of bread off in his mouth.

"This milk has gone sour," he said, his mouth full of bread. "I thought I told you to keep it in a cool place during the heat of the afternoon?"

All of Sarah's anxiety turned to rage as she picked up the crock of milk. The sweat from the run was pouring down her neck and the veins stood out of the pale skin on her forehead.

"How dare you think you can order me about like one of your stonecutters?" Sarah demanded, ready to break the crock over her husband's thick head. "You had better leave your high and mighty ways on the doorstep with your boots or not enter this house, sir!"

Shadrach protected his head with his hands, staring in

amazement as his wife stomped up the steep narrow steps to the loft.

Despite the heat and humidity of the July night, Rachel trembled from the chill which shook her body. Her face was more pale and drawn than normal. She had hardly reacted to the candle which Sarah held over her as she tucked the wool blankets around her neck. She had watched her sister lie in the throes of a fever, day after day, with no recovery in sight. The prayers said over her bed had no effect and when the fever turned to chills she had become so frightened that she had finally convinced her husband to send for a doctor.

Shadrach had resisted the idea of inviting the medical profession into his home, but finally relented and summoned the man who was not only Joseph Smith's personal physician, but his confidant as well.

Doctor John Bennet had arrived in Nauvoo only a short time earlier, a recent convert to the Church. A handsome and personable man he had quickly insinuated himself into the inner circles of the leadership. An eloquent and persuasive man, he wrote many articles for the Nauvoo newspaper, *The Times and Seasons*, under the pen name, "Joab, General in Israel."

He indeed had been appointed a general of the Nauvoo Legion, a volunteer militia made up of all the able-bodied men of the city, and he cut a resplendent sight in his uniform. Shadrach had been pleased that the doctor had responded to his call.

A knock on the door and Bennet entered, formally dressed in a frock coat and waistcoat, his curly black hair concealed by a high beaver hat. He was an agile and well-formed man and his charisma was apparent.

"Brother Tompkins? I understand a member of your household is suffering from the miasma? Allow me to perform the services of my profession."

Shadrach led him to the bedside where he sat beside the stricken woman, lightly taking her arm by the wrist and placing his other hand on her brow. Rachel opened her eyes and tried to force her cracked lips into a smile.

"A fever of the most common type. Well advanced in its progress," Bennett said in a reassuring voice. "This climate is fertile ground for growing fevers. The sooner we drain these swamps, the sooner our young women will regain the color of their cheeks."

Rachel smiled weakly. "How much longer will I have to suffer," she whispered.

"But a few days more, if you follow my prescriptions," the handsome doctor said.

He reached into the silk pocket of his waistcoat and drew out a thin brass cylinder. He removed a tiny white pill and placed one of them on his patient's tongue. The rest he handed to Sarah.

"Herbal pills with a trace of arsenic will cure what ails her," he said cheerfully. "I have studied the most advanced secrets of homeopathy and I predict a speedy recovery."

He loosened the wool covers around her neck and pulled them from the bed. "Never contradict what nature is telling you," he said, not unaware of Rachel's white skin. "Allow the chills to take their course and healing will be prompted. Feed her only cold soups and foods. And keep the air circulating around her. I will see her on a daily basis to monitor her progress."

If the herbal pills, the cold baths and purgatives didn't contribute to Rachel's recovery, the daily visits from Bennett certainly did. In two days she was able to dress and receive her handsome caller in the main room of the house where, after a brief examination the doctor could always be prevailed upon to stay for tea. Before long, the sound of laughter issued from Rachel's lips which were reddened from her pinching. And Shadrach would be surprised to find the doctor still in attendance when he returned home after work at the temple.

Not long after the doctor had pronounced her fit, Rachel began accompanying him to functions in the town. Sunday services in the oak grove near the foot of the temple hill, the dances on Saturday night, and the promenades by the river dock were soon graced by this new couple. The leaders of the community made a special point of entertaining visitors from the east, for the Saints needed as many sympathizers as they could muster in the legislatures of the various states and in Washington. Rachel became the companion of Bennett for many of these dinner parties and her hours became later and later as the weeks progressed.

Shadrach stood by the door of the cabin, looking out into the darkness of the August night. The fireflies had highlighted the summer and were now scarce in the fields nearby. The crickets and frogs not quite so voiciferous as they had been before. The loudest noise was the *snickety-snack* of Sarah's needles as she hunched by the candle, repairing Shadrach's pants.

"The ruckus from the frogs seems to be dying down," she observed, breaking the stillness.

"They're not so loud in their mating calls," Shadrach snorted, "Unlike some people I know."

"Don't talk nonsense," Sarah chided him. "Bennett is a fine man and I'm sure no sparking is going on between them."

"Humh! Bennett is a notorious lady's man and seducer. I understand his intentions, even if you are blind to it."

"I can see is a marvelous improvement in my sister's disposition. The way she has been taking an interest in life again is nothing short of miraculous. If it takes a lady's man to bring her out, so be it. After all the hardship she has been through, I'm grateful that a man of Bennett's caliber can be found on the frontier."

"Bennett's caliber? Why, it's common knowledge that the man abandoned a wife and child when he moved from Ohio."

"You seemed very pleased to have a man of his influence with the prophet as a visitor to your household."

"On a social level, yes. But to have him gallavanting around with my sister-in-law after dark is unseemly. You know how easily idle talk flows in this town."

"Then you can cease your idle talk, sir," Sarah said testily putting her darning to the side. "I will not have you defaming my sister without reason."

Shadrach drew his nickle-plated watch out of his pocket and held it up to her. "Here is my reason. Nine-thirty in the night is reason enough."

Sarah blew the candle on the table into a glowing char, plunging the room into darkness. "We abandoned many conventions when we began this venture," she said pulling her husband into the house, "and my sister's lifted spirits are reason enough for almost anything!"

Chapter Eight

Joseph Smith stood on the heights, looking out over the Mississippi River the way the captain of a great ship might look out over a troubled ocean. He was standing atop a great mound of earth which lay some miles outside Nauvoo. The mound was a gracefully curving hummock of land that might have been mistaken for a natural hillside. The presence of prehistoric tools and the bones of an ancient people had evidenced that the hill was a giant burial mound, created many years past by a vanished civilization.

"Here is our proof that the descendants of the Lamanites built a flourishing civilization, that our words in the book are correct," Smith said, referring to the tribe in the Book of Mormon. "For what tribe of Indians today could ever build such a structure? Only those who dimly remembered the great Temple of Solomon could have carried the skills of the Israelites to the New World.

Smith's steps were followed by a score of his associates. Shadrach, armed with several pistols, walked among them. He was among a number of the Sons of Dan who always accompanied the prophet wherever he went. The Missourians had never rested in their attempts to return the prophet to the state for trial. Several attempts had been made on his life, including a kidnapping which succeeded in returning Smith to the western side of the Mississippi before his followers rescued him. Missouri sheriffs, hungry for the reward on his head, prowled the Illinois countryside hoping to get a shot at him.

Shadrach was always honored to be included in Smith's bodyguard. He was fascinated to watch the prophet's many moods; from fun-loving and mischievous, reminding Shadrach of the time he had bested him at wrestling; to serious and spiritual as he weighed the future of his people and made the decisions governing them. At all times, however, he was a man of such charisma and magnetism that Shadrach marveled at how he was able to continually project such personal appeal. Even the most skeptical visitor from the East, or the most implacable foe of the Saints came away from a meeting with Joseph Smith with an entirely new perspective on the remarkable leader.

On this day, as Smith walked along the crest of the mound, one of his favorite places in the vicinity, he seemed troubled.

"This mound represents the passing of a great civilization," he announced to no one in particular. "How trivial it makes the fragile civilization in which we live today."

A murmur of agreement came from the group following him.

"I had a dream last night that a mighty earthquake destroyed the temple, pulling down the walls but sparing the lives of the people inside of it," Smith said. "A great flood had sent the waters of the Mississippi over our fair city trapping them on the temple hill. Boats were brought fourth and our people crossed the river to the West. The boats were turned into wagons and they journeyed across a range of great mountains in the distance. I view that as a sign that Nauvoo is but a temporary place of rest for us and that our true destiny lies across the Rocky Mountains. Where no Puke can ever find us."

The men in the party shifted uneasily and avoided looking at the prophet. He had been melancholy lately as the burdens of managing such a large city weighed heavily on him. It was best not to encourage him when he was morose.

"But the strange part of the dream was that I watched the Saints depart from this side of the river," Smith said cheerfully. "I take it as a sign that I will not be making the journey."

"Of course you will, Joseph," one of his aides said, but the Prophet was beyond reassurance.

"We've been through so much, and we have so much more to endure. I wonder if we can all remain together through our ordeals?"

He stopped in front of Shadrach and placed his hands on the Englishman's square shoulders.

"What about you, Brother Tompkins? Can your shoulders bear up under the weight you'll have to carry. Can you continue to pull not only your own load but that of your brothers' and sisters'?"

"You will always be able to count me among those you can rely on, Joseph," Shadrach said, a catch in his throat.

"What about all the doubts you will have along the way? When Satan himself jumps on your back and won't let go?"

"I'll throw him right off. I'm a better believer than I am a wrestler!"

"I know you are, Shadrach," Smith said, slapping him on the collarbone with such force that tears came into his eyes. "And as long as the Saints have stalwarts like you, no one on earth can stop us. I forsee a day when Zion will rise as in prophesy and those who participated in its building will scarcely believe their own deeds. They will look upon a great city and a great people and remember the straws with which they built such a creation. They will marvel at their works and recall the days during which they doubted themselves."

"I will be one of them, Joseph," Shadrach said. "I will always remain in the faith."

By the summer of 1843, Nauvoo could claim to be the most thriving metropolis on the frontier, busier even than St. Louis. It boasted of several hotels, a thriving theatre where acts from New York were presented, and a number of growing businesses. Two newspapers touted the growth of the city, and Nauvoo had representatives in Washington.

In Illinois the Saints had been careful to stay on the good side of the local politicians. They had supported the governor of the state in his re-election and had helped congressman Stephen Douglas defeat his challenger, an unknown named Abraham Lincoln.

Troubles still hung over the city like rain clouds on a hot day. In Missouri, Lilburn Boggs, the tormentor of the Saints, had been the victim of an attempted assassination. Mormon marksman Porter Rockwell was accused of the deed and his close relationship with the Prophet brought a new call for Smith's arrest. Rabidly anti-Mormon newspapers in Illinois and Missouri stirred up hatreds by accusing the Saints of everything from counterfeiting to horse thievery.

The neighboring citizens of Illinois watched uneasily as Joseph Smith drilled his army and declared Nauvoo to have a veto over the laws of other counties when they affected the citizens of the city. The harmony which had existed between Saint and Gentile began to fray like a worn rope.

Mobs of Gentiles began to demand the ouster of Smith and

the Saints from Illinois. The stirrings were not violent yet, but to those who had lived through the persecutions of Missouri, they had an ominous ring.

These troubles passed unnoticed by most of the Nauvoo Saints who lived their lives in optimistic expectation that they would be left in peace. The city was experiencing normal growing pains and the intolerance of outsiders was nothing new.

The symbol of the stability of Nauvoo, the temple, was rising on schedule on the hill above the town. The thick walls were almost completed and work had begun on the steeple. The sight of a nearly finished exterior rising above the town was a great reassurance to the people. It forecast an eternity of service that made their temporary problems unimportant.

Inside the temple, the workmen hurried to complete the two assembly halls. The flooring had been laid and the carpenters worked on the ranks of pews which filled the gallery.

Downstairs in the cool basement, the work of the church had already begun. It gave Shadrach great pride to bring his family to the temple he had helped construct to be baptized. The family changed their clothes in the chambers in the basement, pulling on the white gownlike vestments for the baptism. Sarah's long hair hung down the back of her gown, and the herringbone brick basement floor felt cool to her feet.

Ham looked like a curly headed seraphim in his gown, but Shadrach looked amusing. His gown was too short for his large frame and his chest looked ready to explode it. He had recently grown a beard in order to gain more respect from the older men and he looked like the pictures of the mythological Zeus.

The baptismal font, a large pool hewn out of solid stone, was the pride of Nauvoo and the marvel of all visitors to the city. It had been copied after a font in the Temple of Solomon in Jerusalem. The pool was four feet deep and had stairs leading in and out of it. The font was supported on the backs of twelve life-sized oxen carved from solid stone representing the twelve tribes of Israel.

Sarah felt a thrill as she approached the font. Surely, this must be what heaven was going to be like! Around them the bare feet of other gown-clad Saints kissed the floor. The only sound breaking the silence of the chamber was the singing of water dripping from the baptized, and the blessings of the bishop doing the baptizing.

Shadrach lifted the four-year-old Ham to the top of the font stairs to watch his mother being dipped in the pool. Sarah walked into the pool, pulling down her gown as it started to float up. The bishop took her in his hands and dipped her beneath the surface of the water. She felt strangely renewed as she came to the surface, feeling the way a dirty shirt must feel after it comes out of a tub of lye. She turned to watch the baptism of her son. Ham had begun to cry and clung to his father as he viewed the water with terrified eyes. His pleas to escape the baptism did him no good as Shadrach handed him bodily to the bishop for the ceremony. The boy then went under the water, coming up choking and sputtering as he was passed to his mother.

The large bulk of Shadrach raised the water level in the font as he went under, then dipped again, as he scrambled up the other side. He hugged his family as they padded soggily back to the dressing chambers. They had been baptized in the temple.

Rachel Putnam pulled her sunbonnet tighter around her face as she walked toward the drill field. July 4, 1843, was a steaming hot day and she was afraid she would sweat into the material on her new chintz dress she had spent her last few dollars on. The sun had not deterred one of the largest crowds in the history of Nauvoo from gathering on the flat plain on the outskirts of town where Major General Joseph Smith would review his troops. Over ten thousand people had gathered to see the spectacle. Not only had Saints and Gentiles from all over the region gathered, but half of the Illinois government was represented, as well as newspapermen from every major sheet on the East Coast.

So many rumors about trouble within and without Nauvoo had been floating around that the prophet had chosen July 4 to put on a show of strength to quash the gossip. He had invited the powerful from around the country to witness the miracle he had created on the shores of the Mississippi.

From a nearby hilltop, artillerymen of the Nauvoo legion fired "The Old Sow," the legion's cannon, to gather the crowd. The thousands of civilians moved in a mass toward the field. All were dressed in their Sunday finest, the women in wide-hooped skirts and bonnets, the men in top hats and frock coats when they could afford them, white shirts and polished shoes when they couldn't. Hawkers selling apples, crew beans, and confections to the children were growing rich. The Nauvoo police force kept an eye on the musicians and performers who had come to town to take advantage of the crowds.

Rachel pushed her way through the good-natured crowds. The parade had already started and she could hear the high-pitched trilling of the fifes and the rattle of the drums which preceded the troops.

By persistence she reached the front ranks of spectators and stood scanning the hillside. A cloud of dust was being raised by the troops who passed in review. The Nauvoo Legion, some four thousand strong, was marching by in full dress. A bugle blew and the cavalry thundered by, their sabers drawn, shouting as they charged. Rachel put her fingers in her ears and turned away, frightened to think of facing such a charge. Before the dust from the horses settled, the infantry marched by in formation.

The front ranks of the infantry wore the familiar blue tunics and broad-brimmed black hats of the Legion. These were the men who could afford to buy nice uniforms and carry the latest rifles, some made by gunsmiths in Nauvoo. The ranks following them showed a less standard form of outfitting. Some wore blue shirts, others marched with their regular work clothes on, for it was beyond the budgets of many to pay for uniforms. Many of the men were armed with rifles and pistols, but some carried shovels and pick axes.

Sarah was looking past the troops scanning the hillside where the dignitaries overlooked the field. She could see Ford, the governor of Illinois, sitting beside a reporter from the *New York Herald*. Both men were visibly impressed with what they were seeing. Farther along, she could see Shadrach splendidly dressed in the white uniform of the Avenging Angels, the personal bodyguard of Joseph Smith. The prophet himself, resplendent in his magnificent uniform and plumed hat, was mounted on his horse, Charley. Rachel strained to get a better view, desperately seeking one face among the rest. Her lover, Doctor John Bennett, a general of the legion, should have been at the right arm of his commander.

But Bennett was nowhere to be seen. When the dust settled, she could see that Bennett was neither at the side of the prophet, nor anywhere in evidence on the reviewing field. A terrible dizziness came over Rachel. The worst had happened.

She fled from the pomp of the drill field as the tears ran uncontrollably down her cheeks. From the first moment she had set her fevered eyes on the debonair doctor, he had been the object of all her desire. She developed a strange condition. Nothing in her life was as important as a fleeting glimpse of John Bennett. His continued visits to their house after her recovery had been the happiest in her life; his escorting her on daily walks the most delirious.

It was as if everything she had admired in the handsome young men of Boston—their urbanity, polish, knowledge of the world—was given to her on the frontier. Bennett was not only handsome, but considerate and well-spoken, able to joke one moment and philosophize the next. After the deprivations of the backwoods and the dull people interested only in survival on the frontier, the company of the cosmopolitan doctor gave her renewed hope for an exciting life.

They had made such a handsome couple, the slender doctor and the patrician woman who was always elegant, even in her patched dresses. It pleased her that other people commented on how they looked together. And more that the doctor requested her company more often at ceremonies and dinners where the visitors to Nauvoo were hosted by the leaders of the Church. Any woman could take a man's arm on an afternoon stroll but it took a certain amount of breeding to make conversation with a congressman from Washington.

So natural did their liaison seem that she welcomed his first embrace, desired his first kiss and passionately spent a night in his bed. The ideal of romantic love upon which she had first dreamed of as a girl, had a surprise rennaisance to this twenty-year-old virgin. Romantic love had been frowned on by the religious people as frivolous, and on the grim frontier perhaps it was.

The love that had been dormant in her during the hard years on the frontier burst into bloom when touched by the magic of the dashing doctor and she gave herself to him completely. She saw him whenever she could. Her years of pent-up emotions were atoned for in a flood of passion.

Despite her sister's initial objections to the affair, she kept on seeing the doctor. Despite the obvious disapproval of the other women in Nauvoo, who quickly had learned of her tryst, she was not ashamed. In fact, her lack of guilt about this unsanctioned lovemaking surprised even her and she regarded this happiness and delight in free love as a reward for her stoic patience on the frontier.

So deeply in love with this desirable man was she that the fact that he was seeing other women troubled her only a little. A man of his eligibility and his power in the community would naturally attract the attention of women, but his promises of true love satisfied Rachel's need for fidelity.

Then, her world began to unravel like a newly woven shawl tested by a hard season. The strain developed, not between Rachel and Bennett, but between Bennett and his own ambition. His rapid rise in the leadership of Nauvoo had been due to his close connections with Joseph Smith. Unexplicably, Smith began to cool in his enthusiasm for the charismatic doctor and carefully began to relieve him of his civic duties. The gossips in Nauvoo claimed that Bennett had risen too high, too fast, and now the prophet might be jealous of his power. There could be only one true leader in the movement and that leader was Joseph.

Bennett at first had been deeply hurt by his benefactor's loss of confidence. Hurt turned to anger in the prideful man. He began to speak critically of the prophet's ability to manage the town, to cast doubts on his business talents. As Bennett became more beligerant, his relationship with Rachel suffered. His own problems preoccupied him and she was left in the shadows.

Her efforts to rekindle their romance resulted only in his diatribes against his enemies in the town. He promised his revenge on them and revealed his weapon to be a bit of knowledge he called the "Principle." Rachel had never heard the word before and asked him to explain the *Principle* to her. . . .

Sarah returned to the Tompkin's cabin, exhausted from a day at the review. Ham had become lost in the throng and she had spent hours looking for him until she found him being spoiled by a group of the sisters who were feeding him enough molasses sugar babies to ruin his appetite for a week.

As soon as she had opened the door, Sarah knew something inside the house was amiss. Trouble had a way of dampening the spirit of a house as noticeably as rain and she began searching the cabin for the source of this spirit. Her ears quickly picked up the racking sobs of Rachel and she followed the sound to the loft. Rachel was stretched out on her low slung rope bed, her face buried in the quilt, racked with choking breaths.

"Rachel? What is wrong? Has something happened?"

Sarah rushed to her sister's side but at her touch Rachel froze, burying her head ostrichlike in the feather mattress.

This caused Sarah, who had been dealing with her son's tears all day, to temper her compassion with impatience. "Tell me what's wrong?" she demanded. "Tell me now."

"It's over. It's all over," Rachel moaned hoarsely.

Touched, Sarah gently rolled her sister over on the bed. She loosened the ribbons holding Rachel's bonnet on her head and wiped the tears from her reddened cheeks. Rachel stared up her large eyes filling like a lake in a storm.

"Tell me what's all over," Sarah asked softly. "You and John?"

"No, the Saints are all over, The church is finished," Rachel said. "John and I are over, it's true, but Nauvoo is doomed."

"What?" Sarah was surprised at this answer. She shook her head uncomprehendingly.

"It's true. Our beautiful experiment has ended! There is a plague about to descend on our houses."

"Where is John, now?" Sarah prodded, treating her sister like a woman possessed.

"Gone. Driven out in disgrace. Dishonored."

Sarah nodded. She had heard rumors of the rift between the prophet and his friend. Bennett had left town abruptly and she believed her sister upset because of his abandonment of her.

"And it will not be a few years hence that we will be driven out also. As soon as the Pukes learn about the Principle they will have no mercy on us."

"The Principle? Pray, what is the Principle?" Sarah said quizzically. This was a word with which she was unfamiliar.

"The Principle of Celestial Wives and Plural Marriage."

Sarah's face flushed with a sudden and terrible anger unlike anything Rachel had ever seen before. She had comforted her sister before; she now struck her in the face with her hand.

"Liar!" she screamed, hitting Rachel again and again. "Liar! Liar! Liar!"

The older sister did nothing to protect herself from the blows.

"It's true," she said calmly when Sarah's energy was spent. "John told me himself before he left."

"And you took the word of an apostate who has fled the city? Who is spreading the basest lies about the prophet? Don't you realize that rumors of polygamy have always dogged him?"

Rachel nodded. "This knowledge is no longer rumor. The prophet himself will announce the Principle in the next few weeks."

"This cannot be so. Emma would never stand for it," Sarah said, speaking of the wife of Joseph Smith. "I know her too well to believe she would cooperate with this."

"John said that when the prophet first revealed the existence of the Principle to his wife, she threw the offending document into the fire. But he has persisted."

The truthfulness of this news was beginning to strike home to Sarah but she didn't want to admit her concern. "Perhaps the prophet was referring to plural marriage in heaven, where a man and several women may be joined for all eternity?"

"No. This is a temporal affair."

The two women stared at each other, trying to cope with the enormous consequences of this news. It had long been rumored that Joseph Smith advocated the taking of more than one wife, that he wanted to imitate the ancient tribes of Israel where, by some accounts, polygamy was practiced. This rumor had been so often repeated by Smith's enemies in the Gentile press that most Saints had discounted the reports as scurrilous lies. The prophet did have a roving eye, and was an appreciator of feminine beauty. The Saints overlooked this habit for it made him a more believable human being in their eyes. But if the rumors proved true, then every lie ever printed by the Gentiles would be dragged out and dusted off. There would be no refuge for the Saints.

"Perhaps it is just a test of our faith," Sarah said, regaining her optimistic aplomb.

"And if it is not?"

Sarah embraced her sister, patting her tenderly on the back. "Then we will persevere in the face of this new test," she said. "We have come through so many others that I do not see how we could fail to be rewarded."

Chapter Nine

The new newspaper published in Nauvoo, the *Expositor*, trembled in Shadrach's hands. He was unable to read and moreover did not want to read the headlines, for the words printed in the *Expositor* were so libelous that they could provoke civil war within the community of Saints.

The date was July of 1844, and ever since Dr. John Bennett had fled the city to publish attacks on them, the fortunes of Nauvoo had fallen dangerously. Bennett's widely published revelations of Joseph Smith's avowal of polygamy had been the spark which kindled the fire of Gentile hatred against the Saints. The Pukes needed little excuse to renew their attacks against the assembled people of Nauvoo and the polygamy issue unleashed the hatred anew. Editors of every Gentile newspaper on the frontier found their subscriptions jumped with every inflammatory attack upon Holy Joe. They gleefully advocated bringing the Mormon Prophet to his knees.

This ignited the rest of the Gentile population as militias were mobilized against the Mormons and vigilantes rode in the countryside reawakening the ugly memories of Missouri.

Boldly preferring to attack, Joseph Smith declared himself to be a candidate for the President of the United States in 1844. He hoped to draw national atttention in order to gain credibility and power. He only succeeded in alarming the rest of the country about his ambitions. Now the Pukes could gloat that their predictions about the Prophet's desire to rule the world were also coming true.

Besieged from the outside, Smith now found himself attacked from within. The population of Nauvoo, which had so patiently put up with the anxiety of Gentile harassment, was now growing restive. The Saints who had undergone the deprivations of Missouri were staunchly behind the prophet, but many of the newcomers found it more difficult to bear up under the pressure.

A number of rebellious groups within the city chafed under the leadership of Smith. While they embraced his religion, they feared his mismanagement of the government and advocated his resignation. Matters had gotten so out of hand by 1844 that one group had formed a newspaper to carry their message to the public.

The Nauvoo *Expositor* had been started by the Law brothers, two prosperous Saints who owned the local sawmill. They had been close associates of the Prophet but had fallen away from his leadership. Rallying other disaffected members of their cause, they published a premier issue of the paper advocating Smith's removal from the presidency of the church and attacking his stand on polygamy.

Now Shadrach stood in the middle of Mulholland street, holding the offending paper. Five-year-old Ham stood at his side.

He turned to find a number of his friends approaching him on the street. Porter Rockwell was at their head. Rockwell obeyed a prophesy of Smith's that as long as he wore his hair long, no man could harm him. His hair had grown to his shoulders, and although he was not a large man his fierce eyes and reputation as a fighter made everyone more respectful in his presense.

"Brother Tompkins! What do you make of that rag which you hold in your hands?" Rockwell demanded.

"A sorry bit of treason," Shadrach answered. "At a time when all Saints need to hang together, this will surely rip them apart."

"Then join us while we pay a visit to the Law brothers," Rockwell invited and Shadrach joined the group of men who marched down Mulholland street, gathering others as a flood gathers debris. Some people joined out of outrage at the Law brothers, others joined out of curiosity about what was going on. The crowd crystallized when they passed the house of the prophet and he joined them. He was fresh from Sunday breakfast and he pulled the napkin from his neck and took up the lead of the procession.

By the time they reached the upper part of Nauvoo where the press of the *Expositor* has been set up, the crowd had made the transition from a peaceful parade to a full-fledged mob.

"Bring out the Laws!" an angry man shouted. "Show us

the men who would tear this city apart and put brother against brother!''

The press was housed in a two-story brick commercial building which stood near the foot of the Temple. The building was locked up tightly and the Laws wisely were no place to be seen. The longer the mob waited in the street, the uglier they became.

''Agents of the Pukes or instruments of Satan, we cannot allow this sheet to remain published in the city,'' someone yelled.

Shadrach noticed the Prophet was not leading the mob. Rather, he was being carried by it like the rest of them. The anger of the citizens was too great to tamper with. Shadrach held tight to his son's hand and stood back from the crowd. A rock from the street broke the window of the building and brought out a watchman who had been inside to protect the press. Shadrach recognized the man as a member of the Nauvoo legion who was obviously frightened at the crowd he faced.

''The Laws ain't around,'' he shouted to the assembled crowd.

''You're right about that! They're probably fifty miles away and riding hard,'' someone shouted, bringing the first laughter from the crowd.

''We don't want you! We want the press!'' Rockwell shouted at the watchman. ''Stand aside or be held accountable!''

For some reason, the watchman remained faithful to his post until he was pitched off the porch by the Prophet himself. This unleashed the mob who attacked the front door of the building until it was splintered from its jambs. A number of men rushed in and quickly returned carrying large wooden trays of type which they scattered in front of the mob like a farmer's wife scattering feed to hungry chickens. Moments later more men emerged from the building carrying pieces of the press. Rockwell came from the building carrying a keg of the solvent used to clean the plates and this he threw on the parts of the press and set it on fire. A cheer went up from the crowd as the flames caught the wooden type trays.

Although Shadrach agreed with the crowd, a shudder of fear and dismay overwhelmed him. Had things become as bad as this? He looked for his son. He didn't want the five-year-old boy watching such a spectacle. It would be hard enough for an adult to make sense out of these happenings.

The young boy was scrambling in the dust around the perimeter of the mob when he heard his father's deep voice calling his name. Shadrach rarely raised his voice to his family, so Ham knew that he should hurry to him.

Shadrach was standing in the middle of Mulholland Street when the boy caught up to him. Ham offered him his hand and together they walked home. Ham tried to keep up with his father's long strides. He hoped the pieces of type he held in his right hand would not get ink on his Sunday clothes.

The Female Relief Society had been organized in Nauvoo to enable the women of the church to share the responsibilities of administering to the people of the city. The women, who could not participate in the priesthood of the church, had successfully begun the relief society to care for the brothers and sisters who needed help. Rachel Putnam and her sister had been prime members of the society from its beginning.

The society used as its headquarters the second floor of the Masonic Lodge in the center of Nauvoo. A kitchen and a dormitory had been established to house any Saints who might have fallen on bad times. The society nursed those who were sick and cared for the families of men who were called away to take missions for the church.

Rachel held the fragile head of an elderly man from Vermont who had taken it upon himself to come to Nauvoo at the age of eighty-eight years. The man had no money and no prospect of getting a job, but his happiness in being in the city of the Saints had compensated for this. He had contracted the swamp fever, which seemed to strike all the newcomers, and the ladies of the society had taken him in.

As she spooned the broth into the mouth of the old man, Rachel noticed Eliza Snow entering the hall. Eliza was a beautiful woman, thin and graceful, with a delicately shaped face which belied her forceful manner. She was a poet, a writer of church hymns and one of the most well-known of all the women in Nauvoo. She was also one of the plural wives of Joseph Smith.

Rachel was pleased when Eliza recognized her as she carried her broth back to the kitchen.

"You seem to be spending a great deal of time here, Sister Putnam," Eliza remarked in an interested manner when she saw her.

"I am grateful for the opportunity to do something for the

church," Rachel admitted. "I felt that since I was not admitted to the priesthood, I could serve the order in any way I can."

"But can you serve the church if you are not serving yourself?"

"What do you mean?"

"I rarely see you in the company of a gentleman, Sister Putnam. Anyone as comely as yourself should not be alone in a town with as many bachelors as Nauvoo."

Rachel stiffened at this usurpation of her privacy. She glanced around, looking for a way to get out of the conversation, but the cool eyes of Eliza remained on her.

"I'm afraid I am damaged goods, sister," Rachel stammered. "I was violated against my will in Missouri and tainted by association with Bennett here in Nauvoo. My notoriety precludes normal relations for me."

The understanding eyes of Eliza still remained fixed on her.

"Nonsense! We are talking about eternity, sister. What difference does a few years make?"

"Quite a bit of difference when the few years are recently accomplished."

"Surely there are men who would not care about such things?"

"Perhaps. But I find myself intolerant of them. Their open-mindedness alone is not enough to bind me to them."

"What about your sister's husband? I have noticed you at ease in his companionship."

Rachel blushed at the perceptiveness of the poetess. She regretted engaging in a discussion of emotions with an artist.

"Shadrach is a fine man, but I cannot think of such a thing."

"Perhaps you would be wise to reconsider," Eliza said. "I can think of no finer man to seal yourself to, especially considering your high standards. You have already lived in that family and it could be no strange adjustment."

"The life of a plural wife. I'm not sure. . . ."

"You might find its rewards outnumber its deficiencies," Eliza said cryptically. "Rather than subordinating your life, you might elevate it to a new level of fulfillment."

Eliza's gaze was finally lifted from her as she turned to recognize a messenger who had noisily bounded up the stairs. He walked immediately to Eliza.

"The prophet has surrendered himself to the Illinois militia," the messenger whispered. "They have taken him to Carthage."

Immediately, Eliza's hand went to her throat and Rachel had to steady her, as she swayed, her white skin unusually pale. All thought of the previous conversation passed and she hurried from the lodge.

Shadrach stood in the shadow of the nearly completed temple as he watched a score of riders galloping up the hill. When he saw them leading a horse with an empty saddle he knew his services were needed.

"They've taken the Prophet!" Hosea Stout shouted as the rest of the workmen stopped finishing their chores. "We ride to Carthage."

Without a word Shadrach swung up into his saddle and galloped off with the riders. In the wake of the destruction of the press of the *Expositor*, confusion had reigned in Nauvoo. Warrants had been issued for the arrest of Joseph Smith on the trumped-up charged of treason. The prophet had fled the city, then changed his mind and returned to Nauvoo. Refusing to call out the Nauvoo legion to defend himself, the Prophet turned himself over to the Illinois militia. Hopeful that his political connections with the governor and the legislature would save him from the fury of the mob, Smith allowed himself to be taken to Carthage to stand trial.

Less confident in the justice of the Pukes were the Sons of Dan. A number of them had gathered as the prophet was taken away. They rode in a small group, following the Carthage Grays, the local militiamen who had taken the prophet. They would infiltrate Carthage and scout it out in case the legion was needed.

The village of Carthage lay to the southeast of Nauvoo, some twenty miles distant. A hard ride by the men of the Sons of Dan brought them to the vicinity of the town as the sun was straight overhead. They reined up their lathered horses by the bank of a creek and held a council of war. Some of the men were in favor of riding boldly into the town, but others feared this would endanger the life of the prophet and suggested that they enter singly and regroup inside the town. Shadrach and Thomas Morse split off from the group and circled the village to enter on the eastern road figuring that the Pukes would be suspicious of riders coming from the west.

They wiped the frothy sweat from their horses and trotted toward the village, looking in no particular hurry. At a bend in the dirt road, a roadblock of a farmer's wagon had been set up. A group of the Carthage Grays was lounging under an elm tree, but they leaped to their feet and grabbed their stacked muskets when they saw Shadrach's approach.

"Hold there!" a seargent wearing a wide-brimmed hat topped with a plume called out. "Where are you from and where are you bound?"

Shadrach's English accent would have given him away in an instant. The only Englishman in Illinois were Saints. Thomas Morse trotted his horse to the fore and did the talking for them.

"We're from Macomb," Morse lied, "We heard they catched old Joe Smith his self and we came to take a peep at him."

"From Macomb, eh?" the seargent said, looking suspiciously at Shadrach.

"That's right! Some fellow said old Joe has cloven feet and horns poking out of his head and we came to rub 'em for good luck," the Danite said quickly.

This brought guffaws from the Carthage Grays who lowered their muskets and leaned casually on them.

"Well if you want a look at him you better step lively," one of them called. "They're going to scoot him off to Missouri right quick, where he'll get a fair and impartial trial and then be hung for it."

"That is, if he doesn't end up as catfish bait on the way across the Mississippi," another taunted.

The two Danites spurred their horses and galloped through the roadblock to the hoots of the soldiers on duty. Shadrach and his partner slowed as they reached the outskirts of the village.

Carthage was, after Nauvoo, the largest township in Hancock County. It had been long eclipsed in the shadow of the city of the Saints and the people of Carthage bore a keen grudge against the Mormons. The village was a typical collection of frontier cabins gathered around a cross-roads. It did boast of a small hotel, a crude two-story frame building which crowned the village like a dry spot in a pigsty.

The capture of Joseph Smith had created the biggest event

the people of the area had ever seen. The town was overflowing by men wearing the gray uniforms of the local militia. Mormon haters had gathered from the nearby parts of Illinois. Shadrach and his partner rode through the crowds, watching the numbers with dismay.

"This place is packed to the gills with Pukes," Shadrach whispered. "We should have brought the Legion with us."

"One sight of the Legion and the prophet's life is not worth a plugged nickel," Morse replied.

Although it was early in the afternoon, a good portion of the crowd was already dead drunk and they stood on the wooden porch of the hotel shouting threats at the Mormon Prophet. Shadrach rode to the back of the hotel, noticing others of the Sons of Dan who had tied their horses up and were reconnoitering the town.

Shadrach hitched his horse and loosened his saddle girth. Walking casually around the front of the hotel, he followed the mob to the Carthage jail where the prophet was being held.

The jail was a two-story log building and appeared far more livable than most of the homes in the town. In fact, the jail could probably have passed for a home for Shadrach could see no bars on the upper floor windows where he assumed the prophet was being held.

The Mobocrats were gathered around the jail, cursing Joseph Smith's name. The Carthage Grays, their muskets slung over their shoulders, were grouped around the front door of the jail. As if on holiday, they smoked their pipes and joked with the crowd.

Shadrach pulled his felt hat down over his face and pushed his way into the crowd. With his large size he bullied his way to the front of the mob. Looking up, he thought he saw the silhouette of Smith pass before the second-floor window.

"What do you boys think you're doing?" one of the mobbers taunted the captain in charge of the Grays. "Protecting us from Joe Smith or him from us?"

The Grays were a volunteer militia made up of farmers from the countryside. Although they enjoyed swaggering around with their rifles and uniforms, Shadrach knew they would be no match for the Legion. He worried that they wouldn't have the heart to protect the Prophet from the mob, either.

"Why, you boys wouldn't mean Peepstone Joe any harm,

would you now?'' the Captain said, winking broadly at the crowd. ''We just don't want him to convert any of you!''

''Let us have him and we'll convert him at the end of a rope!''

''That's right! Don't let him slither away like he's done before! Let's finish that serpent here and now!''

The afternoon was wearing on and so was the patience of the crowd. Shadrach knew the Nauvoo Legion was the only hope for the Prophet's life. Some had to ride to Nauvoo to tell the citizens the seriousness of the situation.

He turned to push his way back out of the crowd when suddenly he was confronted by the pock-marked face he recognized so well! He was looking into the face of his enemy from Missouri. The night of the burning tar and Haun's Mill flashed through his mind.

He ducked, hoping the man had not seen him. Perhaps his new beard would prove an effective disguise. Using his bulk, he elbowed his way through the whiskey smells and sweat of the crowd.

''You there! Big fellow,'' a voice thundered. ''Let's have a look at your face!''

What his beard had hidden, his face had given away. Shadrach kept moving, pretending he didn't hear.

''Stop that man! We have a Mormon spy in our midst!''

Shadrach was tempted to turn and attack his accuser. Perhaps he could get him before the mob tore him apart. But the spark of a fight might set off the tinder-dry mob, so the Englishman broke into run. Half a dozen Pukes launched themselves after him.

Like ripples in a stream, the disturbance widened and soon stones were bouncing off the walls of the jail as the mob ignited in a spontaneous burst of hatred. The Carthage Grays quickly slipped from around the building and disappeared into the crowd. Shadrach fell to the ground like a toppled tree and the Pukes tore at his head with a vengeance.

Three shots rang out and the Pukes attacking Shadrach paused, alert. Six more shots shattered the afternoon and the mob around the jail surged forward.

''It's a trick! The Mormons are busting him out of jail!'' the pock-marked man roared. ''Rally around me, boys!''

The Missourians detached themselves from Shadrach and sped off toward the jail. More shots were fired as the mob roared.

Shadrach stood up, his head ringing. Had the Sons of Dan attempted a foolhardy rescue of their leader? It would be suicide to try. No one was paying any attention to him and he staggered to the perimeter of the crowd.

The jail was a madhouse of confusion as the mob swirled around shouting a thousand different thoughts and orders. Shadrach stared up at the second-floor window of the jail and winced as a volley of shots echoed from inside the room. He saw a man with his hands held on his face in that room stagger to the window and collapse as the crowd cheered.

The Englishman weakened as he saw Joseph Smith rise inside and emerge from the open window to the ledge, as if trying to escape. There was no place to escape to, and when Smith saw the mob standing below him he paused on that ledge. The mob fell strangely silent and for an instant Smith looked as if he was about to make a speech. Shadrach hoped the prophet could inspire the mob the way he had inspired so many Saints.

Before Smith got a chance to speak, however, a musket fired and Smith toppled from the ledge to the street below. Shadrach felt the shot as if it had found his own heart and he staggered backwards, his eyes closed. The mob was snarling like an animal as it closed around the body of the prophet but Shadrach no longer had the strength to look. He walked down the main street of the town insensible to anything around him.

He felt hands gripping his shoulders. He had no will or strength to fight anymore and he calmly turned to face his attackers. Instead of Pukes, he found John D. Lee and the other Danites standing in front of him.

"Let's get out of this hell," Lee said grimly. "We can do nothing more here."

The murder of the Prophet meant that the hopes for the city of Nauvoo were buried in the same grave as Joseph Smith. The news of the assassination stunned the town. Few could believe it happened. Fewer knew what could be done about it.

Some called for armed retribution, others for forgiveness. Most of the Twelve Apostles were out of town, campaigning for Smith's presidential election, so there was no clear leadership speaking for the city. The population of the largest city in Illinois could only watch helplessly as the man who had preached a message of a heaven on earth was buried, the victim of the petty hatreds of Babylon.

Nauvoo was quickly split into factions as the Saints looked for a new leader for the church. The struggle for leadership revealed many of the pent-up conflicts in the community. Many of the Saints had been unhappy about the rumors of polygamy and other new revelations. These people desired a conciliation with the Gentiles and an easing of the tensions. These groups favored the leadership of a stalwart named Sidney Rigdon, a tepid leader who had quarreled with Smith about the direction of the church.

Other Saints realized that the Gentiles would never leave them in peace as long as they clung to their ways. They viewed with alarm the attack of apostates who were swarming back to Nauvoo in order to take advantage of the leaderless Saints.

Shadrach was troubled by these events and gathered his wife and child and sister-in-law around the dining table to discuss what course they were to take.

"Sidney Rigdon is not a happy choice for me," Shadrach announced. "He is weak and colorless. We need a strong leader for the dark times ahead."

"I cannot see how Nauvoo is going to survive," Sarah admitted. "Perhaps we should make peace with the Pukes. The Prophet was such a burr under their saddles that perhaps they will go easier now that he is removed."

"Just the opposite, sister. With the prophet murdered they will be relentless now," Rachel said sharply. "The destruction of all the Saints is their desire and the toppling of the keystone was the first step in razing the arch."

"I agree with Rachel," Shadrach said. "You cannot make peace with mad dogs."

"It is the consequence with trying to mingle with Babylon," Rachel said, the old hatreds blazing in her eyes. "We thought we could do business with the Pukes and remain clean. We have been tainted by their proximity and have fallen back into their ways. We should have followed the first revelations and built our Zion rather than trying to merchandise with Gentiles."

"It's a pity the Apostles are scattered to the four winds," Sarah said, acquiescing to the politics of her family. "By the time they return, old Sidney Rigdon will have sold Nauvoo to the state of Illinois."

*   *   *

A stocky, blunt-jawed man stood on the foredeck of the steamer as it nosed in for a landing at the Nauvoo docks. He stood stiffly in his black suit, his eyes blazing with an intensity that could have guided the boat through a fog. The deckhands sent the coil of rope looping through the air to the men on the dock and when the paddle-wheeled boat was tied up, they lowered the gangplank.

Shadrach had met Brigham Young many times at that dock, but he had never seen the Apostle be the first one to leave the boat. Young hurried off the gangplank, handed Shadrach his carpetbag filled with his books and climbed into the carriage.

Shadrach took the reins of the carriage and clucked the team into motion. Brigham Young's friends gathered around him and in serious tones told him of the events in the turbulent city.

The Prophet had been murdered in the latter part of July and it had taken several weeks for the leadership of the church to assemble. Sidney Rigdon had called for a hurried meeting to vote upon the new leadership. Had a meeting not been cancelled Brigham Young would have missed the meeting and lost his chance to lead the Saints.

The next day, a hard breeze snapped the coattails of the Saints who assembled in a field on the outskirts of Nauvoo to hear the leaders of the church debate the succession of Joseph Smith. The men wore their Sunday meeting clothes, the women their best, but this was no happy gathering. The church had come together to choose a new leader.

Shadrach, Sarah and Rachel stood on the edges of the crowd. Ham was not with them, since children were not welcome at this serious gathering. Everyone shuffled impatiently as a number of long-winded speakers carried on in the August heat. The crowd was awaiting the contest of oratory between Rigdon and Young.

Rigdon's turn to speak came first. He was a string bean of a man, advanced in years. Dressed in a fine new suit, he seemed appropriate for burial, Shadrach thought. His pale bald head twitched nervously and his feeble voice and hesitant manner made him less than a dynamic leader.

Perhaps to compensate for his mediocre oratory, Rigdon chose to speak from the rear of the crowd instead of from the front. This theatrical ploy caused the Saints to have to crane their necks around to see the man who stood on the top of a wagon box.

This novel approach gained a few moments of attention for Rigdon, but unfortunately the wind which blew from the front of the crowd carried his voice away so that only a few in the rear of the crowd could make out what he was saying.

"My spine is cracking," Shadrach whispered uncomfortably as he strained to watch the oration. "How much longer do you think he will be?"

"Quiet, husband!" Sarah hissed. "I can scarce make out his words as is, without your interference."

"Unless Brigham Young speaks from the branches of yonder tree, I will never get the kinks out of my neck," Shadrach said, pleased that the audience was as restless as he was.

Young was up next, wisely remaining at the traditional place at the head of the audience. If Rigdon was a spindly man, Young was the opposite. A dynamic block of a man, he had a physical presence and a steady gaze that riveted the audience before him.

Still, he had been away from the town and many people had lost touch with him. Shadrach was concerned, lest the restlessness of the crowd carry over into his speech. The Englishman buried his face in his hands, afraid to watch the speech.

Suddenly, the voice of Joseph Smith rang out over the crowd! The chills went billowing like waves across Shadrach's skin at the haunting sound of the voice of the prophet. Was he still alive? Was the murder in Carthage a strange hoax that Brigham Young had contrived to remove the prophet from further danger? Was a miracle happening?

Shadrach raised his head and searched for Joseph Smith. The prophet was nowhere to be seen. Instead, his voice seemed to be coming out of Brigham Young. Shadrach could not believe his eyes and looked around to see if he was the only person who heard the voice. The rapt attention and amazed expressions of all the people in the audience showed that they, too, heard the same miracle.

Sarah's hand slipped into his own and Shadrach relaxed to listen to the speech. He felt a sudden confidence about the future. The Saints had a new leader.

Chapter Ten

Ham Tompkins stood on the temple hill. It was a bright sunny day and the sun toasted the freckles which covered his face. The six-year-old boy was not concerned with the sun, however. He watched intently as a large army of horsemen rode through the city of Nauvoo carrying swords and burning torches. Even this did not overly concern the boy until he saw the riders pursuing his mother and father. Shadrach and Sarah were running up the hill trying to reach him, but they were cut down by the riders.

Ham turned to run, but he seemed to be glued to the spot, his legs made out of molasses. As much as he tried to move, he couldn't escape the charging horsemen. He turned in horror as a man with a pock-marked face leaned from his saddle and grabbed the struggling boy by his curly black hair.

The screams of their son awakened Shadrach and Sarah and they ran up the stairs to the sleeping loft. Rachel was already comforting the boy whose undiminished tears showed his terror. The family gathered around him, pressing him to them.

"It was only a dream," Sarah said gently, "Only a dream."

"It wasn't a dream!" Ham insisted through his tears. "The Pukes are coming to kill us all!"

The adults looked at each other. Was this what all the children of Nauvoo were dreaming?

"The Pukes aren't going to kill us. I won't let them," Shadrach assured him. "You've been listening to the talk of children."

"I've heard it from the elders," the boy repeated. "They say the Pukes are ready to wipe us out."

"If you ever hear any adults talking that way, I want you

to tell them to come to see me," Shadrach said angrily. "I'll straighten them out quickly!"

Shadrach knew if the children of the city had nightmares, it was for good cause. He was having the same dreams.

By the fall of 1845, a little over a year after the death of Joseph Smith, the situation in Nauvoo had deteriorated to the point of collapse. The Gentiles had taken advantage of the wounded city to try to deal the death blow to the Saints. All of Illinois and the surrounding states had rallied against the church. Nightriders raided the surrounding Mormon farms with impunity, burning the crops and driving out the tenants. Rumors circulated about armies of Pukes ready to raid the city and massacre its inhabitants.

The legislature of Illinois revoked the charter of Nauvoo, rendering it nonexistent as a city. The call was given for the Nauvoo Legion to surrender its weapons so the Mormons could not rebel against the state and against the federal government. In Washington, the administration of President Polk did nothing to respond to the pleas of the beleaguered Saints. Polk had just won the election, no thanks to the candidacy of the Mormon prophet and he was not about to lift a finger to alienate Missouri. Polk had other more pressing problems. He had promised the voters he would expand the boundaries of the United States to the Pacific ocean. He had no time to waste with a embattled religious sect.

Unopposed in their drive to oust the Saints from Illinois, the Gentiles played their final hand. The leaders of the church were visited and given an ultimatum by the leaders of Illinois. Leave the state by the spring of 1846. Or face a war of annihilation. Nauvoo was doomed.

It was not hard to find an argument that it was possible for the Saints to stay in Illinois any longer. The Tompkins family, the entire population of the city, would be forced to flee the state. The problem was, where would they flee to?

Shadrach knew any of the nearby states were out of the question. If the Pukes had been able to destroy Nauvoo, they would be able to destroy anyplace the Saints settled. The people must find a sanctuary so far removed from the rest of the country that they would be left in peace.

Unfortunately, little was known about what lay west of the Missouri border. The only real explorers of the frontier were the fur trappers and mountain men, but Shadrach knew they were such crazed liars that no one could believe what they described. No maps existed of the area for the trappers jealously guarded their knowledge of the geography to protect their hunting grounds.

All that was known of the West was that families crossed a wide prairie in covered wagons, a prairie blanketed with Indians for one thousand miles west of the Mississippi. If one survived the Indian attacks and the trials of the trail, the Rocky Mountains stood to challenge the boldest surviving traveler. And then Shadrach had heard, if one survived the Rockies, a horrible desert more fearsome than could be imagined lay between the traveler and the promised land of California.

California! Now there was a prospect for the homeless Saints. The fertile valleys of the coastal state were rumored to be for the taking. Only a few Spaniards clung to the shores of the Pacific and they would be no trouble.

Mexico was another prospect. The Mexican's animosity for the United States was shared by the Saints. Perhaps if an alliance could be made, the Saints could find refuge there.

Whatever the destination, Shadrach decided, the first step was leaving Nauvoo for a westward trek. The details could be arranged later.

"Have you heard about Amassa Packer?" Sarah whispered to Rachel, out of earshot of her son. "He's decided to go back to Pennsylvania. Amelia is sick with grief."

"He's leaving the church?"

Sarah nodded. "He says he's had enough. He said Amelia's health couldn't stand another move. Too many people are leaving the fold. I'm worried about these faint hearts."

"Let them go. It will separate the wheat from the chaff," Rachel retorted. "Only the strongest seeds will germinate in the wilderness."

"I wish I had your faith," Sarah admitted. "I fear the prospect of being driven from our homes to dwell in the wilderness again. I had become fond of the convenience of the city."

"Once we build a celestial city this collection of huts will pale in comparison. The spiritual conveniences will outshine any material ones we leave behind." Where once Sarah had been the spiritual cornerstone of the Tompkins, the strength seemed to have passed to Rachel.

"If only I knew the prospect was attainable. My private worry is that we are being driven from our homes to die."

"I see the harassment of the Pukes as a blessing," Rachel said confidently. "The original revelation instructed us to go into the wilderness and build a Zion. When we fled here, we backslid into the ways of Babylon. The death of the Prophet and the attacks of the Gentiles are pointing us in the direction we should have gone a long time ago."

"But we know not where we're bound."

"Then neither do our enemies. I will follow our wagon tracks with a broom to erase the trail so no Puke can follow. And I hope we penetrate so far into the wilderness that we are swallowed up by the land and soon forgotten by the sons of Babylon. This is a test of faith that I welcome."

"Sister, I admire your strength," Sarah said. "You seem unswerving in your sense of purpose."

"It is not easily come by. I hourly have the same doubts as you," Rachel admitted as her eyes darted around the interior of the Tompkins home, the former confidence dissolved. "I worry about what is to become of me. What possibility of companionship can I have in the wilderness? What is there before me but spinsterhood?"

"Nonsense. Your eligibility will increase with every turn of the wheel westward. And the attractiveness of your beaux will magnify the farther you travel from Babylon."

"But what man will have me, even in the remote reaches? It is common knowledge that I was deflowered by the Missourians. And that I shared a bed with an apostate."

"None will care."

"Oh, but they do. I have seen it in their eyes, sister. They turn away when they address me as if the contagion of sin will cross from my graze."

"You are imagining it."

"You know yourself I am not."

Sarah looked levelly at her sister and took her hand.

"Have you ever thought about living according to the Principle?"

"As a plural wife? Yes, I have thought about it," Rachel said defiantly. "Since the Gentiles have no further use for us, I have no compunction against their customs. I view the Principle as an important way of demonstrating our loyalty to the faith."

Sarah studied her sister's reaction.

"Of course, I have the same problem finding a husband who would take me as a second wife as I do with finding one who would take me as the first. Perhaps more so. I would have to gain the permission of his first wife to marry him, and I doubt whether that permission would be forthcoming."

"What if you could find a woman who would be willing and a man you could desire?"

"Then I would do so, gladly."

Rachel looked closely at her sister for the first time in the conversation. Sarah had the serious look on her face, but the aura of controlled excitement reminded Rachel of the way she would look when she played a rare practical joke as a child.

"What are you saying to me, sister?" Rachel asked carefully.

"You have lived with my family, with my husband as long as I. We have no secrets from you nor you from us. As long as we are to leave this imperfect world behind, it is my deepest desire to share my husband with you, not only on this earth, but for all eternity."

Rachel, never at a loss for words, was speechless. Seeing her surprise, Sarah smiled easily and continued.

"That course we are about to embark upon is going to be filled with many hazards. What more perfect way to insure our security than to be sealed to one another with the most permanent of vows. Even if the worst were to happen to one of us, we would be assured that our togetherness would continue throughout eternity."

Not waiting for Rachel to reply, Sarah embraced her.

"This is a more joyous display of affection than I ever hoped to see," Rachel said. "I don't know what my answer would be, but I will be forever grateful for the invitation."

"Only your agreement will make me truly happy," Sarah said, "for it will mean we will be together forever!"

"And Shadrach? What is his view on this matter?"

"I have not proffered the proposition to him," Sarah confided. "But he has so long held you in high esteem that I have no doubt about his answer."

In spite of the fact that the Saints knew they would be abandoning the city of Nauvoo in less than a year's time, the construction of the temple went on as planned. The temple had been the unifying symbol of the city and while construction continued then hope would always be visible. If the progress on the temple languished, then both the Gentiles and the Saints would know the church was doomed.

By the summer of 1845, the building was nearly complete. The craftsmen were putting the finishing coats of white paint on the pine woodwork of the assembly halls and polishing the hardwood banisters which led to the towers. The steeple had been topped off and the workmen were removing the last of the scaffolding. Roofers worked in the hot sun to put the zinc and lead covering on. The expensive metals would surely last for hundreds of years, a testament to the vision of the builders. Even if not one Saint remained in the city, any traveler along the Mississippi could marvel at the industry of these artisans.

The fact that a disorganized and penniless people could be driven from Missouri and then build the greatest structure on the frontier gave the people hope for their future in the wilderness. If they could build a temple in six years, they could easily build Zion in one lifetime.

Inside the temple, the idea that a lifetime was a flick of an eye was being pondered as Shadrach, Rachel and Sarah kneeled before their bishop. They were alone inside a small sealing room where the vows of marriage were said. Kneeling on small oaken stools in the bare room their heads bowed, their hands folded, they listened as the bishop performed the ceremony. Shadrach knelt on one side of Rachel, Sarah on the other.

It had not been difficult to persuade Shadrach to take Rachel as his second wife. After a natural surprise, the Englishman had admitted that the idea had crossed his own mind before. He had not suggested it, unsure of his wife's reaction. Her enthusiasm hastened his own decision and he readily agreed.

For a man to take a plural wife, permission first had to be granted from the leaders of the church. A man's financial status had to be such that he could afford to keep two women as comfortably as one. Shadrach's financial condition was none too stable, but once in the wilderness a strong back would be worth more than banknotes and Shadrach would then be a rich man. The other condition for approval of the marriage was the first wife's consent, so nothing barred the decision.

When the leaders of the church sanctioned this marriage, the news was greeted with joy among Shadrach's friends. Many of the more prominent Saints had already taken plural wives and they were happy he had decided to join them. It created a strong bond between the families and added to the adventure lying before them. The Saints were encouraged to follow the Principle for it created a spirit of solidarity that would be sorely needed in the years to come. Although not one Saint in ten took a plural wife, many of the leaders practiced the custom.

When their vows were exchanged, the Tompkins family left the temple. A dinner was being hosted to celebrate their commitment and they took a carriage to the house of Thomas Morse. A small crowd had gathered inside and the long dinner table had been set with the best china.

The feeling of their new relationship was still as new to the Tompkins as a fresh suit of clothes and they were nervous as they greeted their guests. Their nervousness was increased when they realized that the women significantly outnumbered the men at the gathering. Rachel was afraid to count, but it was obvious that they had joined a new strata of society.

The dinner party wore on, with the men gravely discussing the future of their westward journey at one end of the sitting room. The women circulated at the other and soon Rachel and Sarah were engaged in discussions with some of the other wives. It relieved them to learn that all the women had felt the same degree of discomfiture about their new status after they had been married. The women seemed much more affected by this new arrangement than the men, and the more they talked, the more at ease the women became.

It was late when the wedding party finally dissolved. Shadrach was grateful to see so many of the Nauvoo police on the street as they rode home. Since the dissolution of the city a new breed of criminals had moved into the town, hoping for easy spoils.

A wave of self-consciousness came over the three when they entered the small house. Shadrach lit the oil lamp on the dining table and coughed. Sarah hung her cloak on a peg by the door and kissed both of them.

"I shall retire for the evening, now," she said breezily. "I shall spend the evening in the loft with my son. I trust you will carry on without me."

Both Shadrach and Rachel looked like they would have stopped her, but Sarah bounded up the stairs and was gone. Rachel sat on the bench by the table with her hands folded in her lap. Shadrach fiddled with the oil lamp trying to coax more light from the carbonized wick. Both cast nervous glances at the rope bed in the corner of the cabin.

"I would not expect us to consummate this deed too quickly," Rachel said hesitantly. "Perhaps a platonic relationship could continue for a year or more until we were more disposed to it."

Shadrach frowned. "We have a pact and should observe the proper functions. I have secretly dreamed about having you in a carnal manner for so long that I cannot believe that I shall now have you."

Rachel let out a small laugh. "You also? I had thought I was the one suppressing desire."

"From the first time I beheld you, I have been convetous of you," Shadrach said. "Naturally my fidelity to Sarah prevented any indiscretions . . ."

"Naturally."

"But I have always harbored a longing for you. I was attracted to you before Sarah. That is why I view this opportunity as a godsend for me."

"And for myself. Living under one roof with a man one admires is too great a temptation to continue indefinitely."

"There! Even an old wick burns well if you fiddle with it enough," Shadrach said proudly as the oil lamp adjusted to a steady glow.

Vexed by his attention to the lamp, Rachel leaned across the table and blew out the flame. Shadrach caught her hand and pulled her around to him. The darkness and his desire had suddenly changed her idea about consummating their wedding. Their lips met and their passion was enflamed, hotter than the glowing wick of the lamp.

In the blackness of the room, the years of pent-up desire became unhinged. Shadrach crushed the woman in his arms until he was afraid he would hurt her, but she pulled him tighter still. He lifted her off the floor, as she wrapped her arms around his neck, pushing herself into him.

He carried her without a misstep through the open door of the bedroom and gently laid her on the comforter. By the time he had slipped out of his starched white shirt and new britches, she was ready for him, hungry with desire for a man she had always loved. The idea of a year's celibacy would have made more sense the next morning, for they made love enough times to last them into the wilderness.

* * *

During the fall of 1845, Nauvoo prepared for the evacuation of the Saints. The characteristic organization of the Church, rehearsed on the flight from Missouri, kept chaos from breaking out. The people of the city were organized into companies of twenties, fifties and hundreds with designated leaders who divided the responsibilities for the trek.

Lists were published indicating the provisions each family was to bring for the journey. Foodstuff, clothing, firearms and farm implements were included and the list was detailed down to the last needle and spool of thread. In kitchens and in the graineries, women jerked the beef and sacked the grain. The provisions stored from the fall harvest would have to last them not only through the winter but until they could plant and harvest new crops in the wilderness.

The men worked building the wagons which would carry them an unknown amount of miles over unknown territory. All the timber floated down the Mississippi for the building of homes was turned into wagon boxes and oxen yokes. The forges of the blacksmiths glowed into the night as sweating apprentices bent the cherry-red iron hoops around the wooden wagon wheels. Soon the streets of the city began filling up with strongly constructed wagons which were fitted with staves which held the canvas tops above the wagon beds like the whalebones held a woman's hooped skirts.

Even the children were put to work, crisscrossing the town to fetch needed parts from the wheelwright's shop. Girls sat at their mother's sides sewing the canvas tops for their new homes.

The Saints left nothing to chance. They gathered large inventories of farm implements for the journey. Weaving looms were dismantled and stored in wagons. School books and slates were provisioned for unborn scholars. An organ was packed for a future assembly hall. A gunsmith's shop was loaded on a wagon.

The Saints had reason to hurry. The threat of an armed attack hung over them like the sword of Damocles. The Gentiles had defeated them. Now the Pukes wanted to eradicate the Saints.

Shadrach wearily loaded his few remaining possessions in wooden crates. Was this all he had to show for seven years of work? He looked up as Rachel and Sarah swept into the cabin carrying something behind their backs. Rare smiles were on their faces.

"We have brought you a present to keep you safe on your trip," Sarah announced.

Hope flickered in Shadrach's eyes. "A new Browning rifle?"

"No, something more powerful," Sarah said, holding up a suit of long underwear. Shadrach stared at it, disappointed.

"Underwear?"

"The new holy undergarment," Rachel announced.

Shadrach studied the garment with a new interest. It looked like an ordinary suit of long underwear except for a cut on the right knee, an angle cut in the right breast and a compass cut in the left breast. The garment had no collar and had no buttons and was secured by strings. The arms and the legs were long.

"The three strings on the one side represent the Holy Trinity," Rachel explained. "The others represent a man and his celestial wives."

"The compass with its arms pointing towards heaven reminds you of your spiritual bounds," Sarah said. "Remember your marriage vows and let the priesthood be your guide."

"The three square knots represent fairness," Rachel pointed out. "The slit in the knee reminds you to kneel easily before God. Jesus is Lord."

"Where this garment wherever you go and you will be protected," Sarah said. "Wear it on our journey west and you will arrive safely."

Shadrach took the garment gently in his hands. "I will always treasure this garment and this moment," he said. "With our faith, nothing can befall us."

"When the grass grows and the water runs." Springtime, 1846, was their deadline to leave Nauvoo. The Saints had no intention of waiting that long. The Gentile cavalry could pursue them in the spring, but not in the snow.

On February 6, 1846, the captain of Shadrach's company gave them orders to prepare to leave. As he loaded his wagon in front of his home, Shadrach saw a Gentile profiteer approaching him. The real estate speculators were crawling over Nauvoo, buying homes at prices that would embarrass a thief.

"A cabin as crude as this won't bring much on the open

market,'' the speculator said, pulling his cape around his shoulders. "I'll offer you twenty dollars cash for it.''

"Twenty dollars?'' Shadrach shouted in rage. "There's twenty dollars in nails in that cabin!''

A few flakes of snow were beginning to fall and the speculator dusted them from the crown of his beaver hat. He let the silence carry the sounds of other wagons being packed.

"Take a look around you, Mr. Tompkins. There must be five hundred homes for sale, most better than yours. Why, a brick home can be bought for one hundred dollars these days! The problem is, there's no one willing to buy homes in this city with the threat of insurrection hanging over the town. I'm taking a foolish gamble myself even offering this much for your home.''

Shadrach reflected. The man was right and all knew it. Homes were being traded for a barrel of flour, or boarded up and abandoned outright. No Gentile was going to move into the town until the Saints left, and no Saint was going to remain until they did. The place would be deserted by summertime.

"How much will you offer us for the maple sideboard and the highboy,'' Shadrach asked. "They're heirlooms of my wife's family brought all the way from Boston.''

The speculator grinned in the direction of the two women who sat inside the wagon box listening to the transaction.

"The twenty-dollar offer includes the furnishings. My wife would be more interested in them than I am in the house.''

A combined outburst of rage erupted from the wagon. Shadrach ran to the sidebox and pulled out a cannister of whale oil.

"I'll be damned if I'll take twenty dollars for my home,'' he shouted. "I'll burn it to the ground myself rather than see some Puke steal it from me.''

"Shadrach, don't!'' Sarah shouted from inside the wagon.

Before she had scrambled out of the wagon, her enraged husband had run back into the house and sloshed the oil around the main room.

"Ham! Fetch me a lucifer or some flint and steel,'' he bellowed.

As the speculator watched with detached interest, Sarah seized the arms of her husband and shook them as best she could.

"You know what the instructions are about the departure.

We'll leave no burned-out buildings behind. This entire city will remain as a monument to our persecution."

Shadrach glanced in the direction of the wagon. Rachel, heavily pregnant with his child stood on the wagon box staring at the scene. He remembered how bitterly she had bemoaned the leaving of the heavy furniture. There had not been room in the wagon or strength in the oxen to carry it, but leaving it behind was like leaving the last memory of the old life.

"Leave them the furniture and may they be consumed by the flames for their greed," Rachel said. "I hope their memory of how they came by it bars their happiness."

For one who could be as unforgiving as Rachel to acquiesce to the speculator was the last word. Shadrach held out his hand as the man plunked several gold pieces into his hand. He averted his eyes from the gold and climbed into the waiting wagon.

"I feel like Judas, selling that place for twenty dollars," he complained as he flicked the oxen with his horsehair whip.

"That twenty dollars will buy us enough bacon and bran to make it through the wintertime," Sarah pointed out. "You can't eat a maple highboy when you get hungry."

"That jackal will never get his money out of the cabin," Rachel said. "This city is cursed from now until eternity and it will never flourish as it once did."

At the waterfront of the city, scores of wagons had backed up on the dock as they were laboriously loaded on barges for the trip across the Mississippi. The freeze of January had covered the river with a sheet of ice. Rather than risk the wagons by driving them across the ice, men with axes had chopped a channel for the barges to follow. They poled out into the river and let the current carry them to the Iowa shores.

The trip to the other side was more laborious than had been expected as the ice had to be continually cleared. Despite the careful organization, the evacuation process became confused as unruly oxen broke loose from their yokes and wagon frames cracked as they were loaded into barges. Tempers flared and the ferrymen cursed everyone from the families they were carrying, to the Pukes who had caused it all.

For three nights the Tompkins family slept in their wagon while the freezing wind pushed snow through the blankets they used to block off the wagon tarp.

The cold had numbed their minds as well as their fingers and on the third day on the docks, the news swept the docks that a party of Gentile cavalry had invaded the eastern part of town. Frantic men whipped their teams forward, trying to break into the front ranks of the line. Shadrach's wagon, now sitting on the docks preparing to be loaded, was bumped by the next wagon and the wheel slipped over the edge of the quay.

Women were screaming, children crying and oxen bellowing as men cursed and shouted threats in order to back up the line. Shadrach summoned a party of men who brought iron bars to lever the wagon back on the track. The exertion warmed Shadrach's temper to the boiling point. He rushed back along the line of wagons cajoling and threatening the impatient Saints. What the fear of the Pukes had done, fear of Shadrach undid. The present danger of the hulking Englishman's fist in their faces calmed even the most hysterical teamster.

Shadrach breathed a sigh of silent relief once he was safely on the barge in the middle of the Mississippi. The flat-bottomed boats with the shallow sides were crowded with four wagons and their passengers. The bargemen strained at the long oars, sweeping them back and forth to propel the barges. Two men with steel-tipped poles broke the ice in front of them and in their wake, a second barge carried the oxen.

Every Saint on board the barge stood by the rail, looking back at the abandoned city. Nauvoo stood, like a memory, growing colder and more lonely as they passed farther away.

"Take a good look, boy, and remember this sight well," Rachel said as she placed her sister's son on Shadrach's shoulders. "Never forget the Gentiles have forced you out of your home and into the wilderness."

"Don't stir the boy's mind up. He'll have a clear enough memory," Sarah chided her. "Let him have a moment's peace."

The only sound was the water rushing past the oar sweep. A light snow had begun to fall. The clouds had scudded in and had begun covering the city. Only the temple stood uncovered, bathed in a last sliver of weak winter sun which slipped through the clouds.

As the light was extinguished by a cloud passing over the temple, the snow flew into Shadrach's eyes and they teared up. He pulled his wives to him by the shoulders and made sure his son was firmly seated on his neck. He was afraid to turn to watch the approach of the Iowa shore.

Of all the Saints on the barge, only Rachel was willing to break the silence.

"Vengeance," she said softly, almost as a prayer, "shall be mine."

THE DIASPORA
1846

Chapter Eleven

Soaked in her own sweat, Rachel lay in labor under the crude tent fabricated from the canvas top of the Tompkin's wagon. Around her, half a dozen of the women in her company were gathered. Three of them were assisting with her labor while the other three held their aprons above her head, shielding her from the freezing rain pouring through the seams of the tent.

After leaving Nauvoo, the Saints had traveled some twenty miles inside the borders of Iowa and made camp. Far enough away from Illinois to discourage the Gentile militias from following them, they planned to wait out the winter in canvas tents and push on in the spring.

Unfortunately, the canvas tents did little to protect them from the freezing cold and the blizzards that ripped out of the north skies. Several Saints had already died from the exposure, and many more were ill.

In the flickering light of a lantern, which was held over her abdomen, Rachel looked at the anxious faces of the women who were ministering to her.

"My apologies, sisters, for bringing you out on such a night," she whispered. "I should have had the common courtesy to hold my delivery back in my old house rather than on this plain. It would have been more healthy for both the child and yourselves."

Aldea Higgins, the midwife of the company, continued massaging Rachel's bare stomach without stopping.

"Nonsense. The child will welcome a nice brisk swallow of cold air when he comes into this world," she said. "It's much better for the constitution than the stale air of the city."

Rachel chuckled, relaxing momentarily. She was fortunate to have Aldea in attendance. The spry old woman had delivered hundreds of babies in her time and few women in Nauvoo had felt comfortable unless she presided at their labor. At first sight she looked intimidating in her black dress and matching scowl. Her remarks were always curt and impatient, but her soft gentle hands and her record of successful deliveries were convincing recommendations for a skill learned at the side of her grandmother.

Now the spasms were tearing at Rachel's belly again and she gasped, her eyes wide in amazement at her own endurance. She sucked the chilled air in, saving her cries for the moments of more excruciating pain she knew were bound to come.

"Perhaps we should have a physician or a bishop in attendance," Sarah said anxiously, "she seems in considerable distress."

Aldea looked at her as if her own reputation had been slandered.

"She's not feeling anything the rest of us haven't felt," the midwife snapped. "I'll thank you to keep the bishop and his oils and the doctor and his little pills away from my work."

The woman placed her thin, bony fingers on Rachel's stomach confirming what she already knew. The child inside her was upside down in the womb. She could feel the broad buttocks of the child at the bottom of the woman's stomach and the narrower head at the top. This would be a difficult birth, especially in these conditions, but the midwife showed no outward concern. These ladies around her were panicked enough without any more bad news.

As the child moved its way lower in her stomach, the gasps of air turned into painful whines for Rachel as the rain pelted her face.

"Yep, your time has come, sister," Aldea said, reading her mind. "It's on the move now."

"It's going to be born dead, I can tell. I haven't felt its heart beat for some time," Rachel gasped. "It will be the final blow against me after the bad luck we have suffered."

"Keep quiet, sister," Aldea said. "I deliver only live babies. He may be scrawny but he'll be a kicker."

The midwife lifted back the folds of Rachel's robe and carefully washed her thighs and lower belly for the last time. Her own granddaughter, a girl of thirteen, moved closer with the implements her grandmother was going to need during the delivery. The young girl had watched this process enough times to be matter-of-fact about it.

In the passion of birth, Rachel could no longer hold back her cries of pain. She gave herself over to it, first moaning in a low, unhuman voice and then crying out in an all-too-human scream.

"Go ahead and shout it to the rooftops, sister," Aldea chuckled, grinning for the first time. "I want every man in this entire camp to hear what you're going through. Maybe we'll have a little more respect in the babymaking."

The women formed a tighter circle around Rachel and Sarah held her sister's hands over her head, both in comfort and to restrain her. The woman with the lantern held it near her navel and the golden light hovered close to her birth.

Aldea's granddaughter lost her aplomb for the first time when she saw the feet of the child emerge first from the mother's body. A breach birth was the most difficult and dangerous she had experienced and she glanced at her grandmother to see if the old woman shared her concern.

If Aldea had any fears, she was now showing them as she elevated the rump of the woman in order to ease the child's emergence. The position of the child as it emerged caused more than the normal amount of pain and Rachel tried to free her hands to push on her belly.

"Keep her hands off her stomach!" Aldea ordered. "We don't want to rush this birth."

Sarah restrained her sister although she began to have doubts whether the midwife knew what she was doing.

"He's tearing me apart!" Rachel shouted, fighting against the restraint. "Pull him out. Pull him out before he kills me!"

Like the captain of a ship in the midst of a storm, Aldea steadfastly kept to her own course, ignoring the pleading of Rachel. "We're letting the child come at its own pace," she announced to the concerned women. "Trying to help it along would harm both the mother and the babe."

The legs and hips of the pink baby were now protruding from its mother's body and the rest of its body was following with ponderous slowness. All Aldea could do was to support the fragile body in her gentle hands waiting for the rest of it to emerge.

With a shriek that drowned out Rachel's cries, the storm tore off the top of the tent, sending the canvas flapping wildly and extinguishing the lantern.

"For pity's sake, woman. Get that flame lit!" Aldea ordered in the darkness as the women scrambled to retrieve the canvas. All of them were soaking wet and whimpering by the time they had lashed the flap back on the tent and a sulphur match had been struck to reignite the lantern.

The wick glowed with a coal and then like the rising of the sun illuminated the interior of the tent in an amber light. In front of them Aldea was on her knees, holding the fully emerged baby in her hands, proudly like a magician who has just performed an impossible act of illusion.

"Ladies. We have company," she announced as the wrinkled child choked into a falsetto wail.

The baby was handed to Aldea's granddaughter who cradled it in her arms.

"Not that way!" the grandmother barked. "Hold it up by her feet so the phlegm can drain from her lungs."

The girl gingerly held the baby by its legs, the slick umbilical cord dangling from its navel. Sarah cradled the head of her sister in her lap, dabbing the tears out of her eyes. Rachel was still whimpering, barely conscious that the birth was over.

"Should I cut the cord?" the granddaughter asked, picking up a pair of scissors.

"It appears to be a mite blue," Aldea said with the casualness of a carpenter who has just raised the walls of a cabin and is not concerned about the rafters. "Best leave the cord attached and lay the baby down. Never cut while the cord is blue."

"What's wrong? Is something amiss with my child?" Rachel asked.

The granddaughter laid the baby, cord and all, on Rachel's stomach. Aldea wiped her hands on her wet dress and pulled a shawl around her own shoulders.

"Your baby's just fine. She's going to be a tough little nut, born on a night like this."

By the coming of spring, a large part of the population of the empty city of Nauvoo had established themselves in camps along the western banks of the Mississippi. They had not moved far from the city, but far enough to demonstrate to the Gentiles that they would live up to their promise to migrate west from the city in the springtime.

The shock of a winter outdoors hit many of the Saints hard. The emigrants fresh from the cities of England and the East Coast of the United States were unprepared for the elements and suffered miserably. Others, like the Tompkins family, who had lived on the frontier, were better able to adjust.

With a new baby to feed, Shadrach hunted nearly every day. The snow-covered land of Iowa was barren during the winter, but he was able to bring down enough rabbits to keep his family fed through the hardest times. Hunger stalked all the camps, but through it all the Saints remained cheerful. At one camp, a flock of game birds flew mysteriously into the middle of the camp during a blizzard and the pioneers slew them with clubs. It was interpreted as a gift from God, manna from heaven, and a good omen for the future.

The latter part of the winter was spent preparing the wagons and their passengers for the trip west. The winter had taught the Saints a great deal about life on the frontier and many of the wagons were empty of excess baggage when the spring hardened the ground enough to move.

The leaders of the church had no clear idea about exactly where their destination was, but one thing was sure. It lay to the west and the sooner they were underway, the sooner they would keep their people from thinking twice about the move. When the thawed ground dried out enough, the wagons were organized and rolled west along the banks of the Des Moines River.

The advance party of the Saints was composed of the most able members of the companies. Their mission was to speed ahead of the rest and plant crops that could be harvested by the others who followed later that year.

All along the trail the Saints would plant fields of barley and corn so that the land could replenish what they could not afford to buy in the stores. The impoverished Saints also hired themselves out at the farms of the settlers who were already farming the Iowa prairie. Shadrach's strong back made hard currency for the church's treasury, splitting rails and chopping firewood for the communities they passed along the way.

Throughout the spring and into the summer the wagons rolled across the landscape of the Iowa territory. The gently rolling hills were awash in waist-high grasses which wavered under the blue skies. Groves of willow trees grew along the banks of the streams crisscrossing the land, and oaks dotted the horizon lines.

The euphoria of springtime and the distance from Nauvoo

buoyed the spirits of the Saints and many began looking
longingly at the fertile land.

"Why, there's plenty of land for everyone out here,"
Sarah said. "What's the need of traveling to the Rocky
Mountains when we're in the middle of paradise now?"

"Because wherever the Saints find a paradise, the Pukes
are right behind like fleas on a dog," Shadrach said. "The
farther the distance we put between us and them, the longer it
will take them to bite. But damn my eyes, every mile we travel
takes us farther into this blasted wilderness," the Englishman
grumbled. "I hope Brigham knows where he's going!"

Perhaps sensitive to the grumblings of his followers, Brigham Young called a halt to their trek in July. There, far in the
interior of Iowa, with no Rocky Mountains in sight, they
would make camp for the winter.

As soon as their wagons stopped rolling, the Saints began
preparations for the siege of snow and ice which would soon
come. The tough sod of the prairie was broken with iron
plows and a hurried planting was made. Hopefully the crop
would grow and be made ready for harvest by the time the
frost came.

Other teams of woodcutters traveled into the river bottom
to cut wood for the constructions of houses. Shadrach exca-
vated a dugout home in the side of a small hill. Slashing into
the earth with a pickaxe in a style reminiscent of his mining
days, he carved out an earthern room a dozen feet square.
When he had tamped down the floor and constructed wooden
rafters and front wall, he packed the earth around the top and
sides making a damp but liveable home for his family. Throughout the construction of the house, Ham worked at his father's
side. At first, Shadrach was pleased to have the seven-year-
old boy working, but he soon realized the boy's help would
be a vital necessity on the frontier.

It was from inside this dugout one morning that Shadrach
heard a disturbance outside in the settlement. Pulling back the
canvas wagon cover forming his front doorway, he was surprised to see a trio of U.S. Army officers riding into the
camp. They were covered with dust from the trail and were
pursued by the dogs of the settlement who were trained to
bark at Gentiles.

A sinking feeling hit Shadrach in the pit of his stomach and
he took the rifle Jonathan Browning had made for him and

walked out into the camp to see what the reason for the visit was.

Others in the camp had the same curiosity and most of the men carried rifles as a token of their trust in the United States Government. The officers were taken immediately to the tent which served as the headquarters for Brigham Young. The settlers gathered around the tent, hoping to find out what was afoot but energetic captains shooed them back to work.

The Saints were a people who prized rumors and gossip and made an art out of them. The next few days were spent speculating on what the Army officers wanted. The U.S. Army had jurisdiction on the frontier. Had they come to turn the Saints around? Would they be sent back to face the persecutions of the Mobocrats? Perhaps they suspected the travelers of fleeing to Mexico to aid the enemy? One friend of Shadrach's suspected they had come to arrest Brigham Young. Another suggested they had organized the Indians on the frontier to massacre them.

Shadrach minded his own business, trusting that the president of the church would make the best of the situation for the Saints, but he was concerned when he was summoned by William Macomb, one of the counselors around Young. Once in the presence of the man, Shadrach could no longer restrain his curiosity.

"Tell me what these officers want?" Shadrach pressed. "If they have threatened us, every man is ready to fight them!"

"You may get to fight," the counselor said, "but it will be on the side of the Gentiles rather than against them!"

"What?"

"These messengers from Babylon had brought us an invitation from President Polk. He has invited us to fight on the side of the United States in their war against Mexico."

"So! The war has broken out just as the Prophet predicted!" Shadrach said with satisfaction. "By the time we reach Zion, the war will have toppled Babylon."

"Perhaps," Sampson said. "But in the meantime, Brigham has contracted with them to provide 500 men for their army."

Shadrach was dumbfounded. He stared at the counselor as if waiting for a denial.

"It's true," Sampson confirmed. "The Pukes have few men at arms on the frontier. They need us to send a force to Mexico as soon as possible. We are in the middle of the wilderness already and can be the first to arrive."

"This is outrageous! We are here in the middle of the wilderness because the Pukes have driven us from our homes. How can Brigham have the gall to sell us back to the Gentiles?"

"The Gentiles have agreed to pay fifty thousand dollars in advance for the men, money we need to bring our brethren from the East. They have agreed to provide rifles for them and we need the arms. Finally, here is our chance to place five hundred men in the heart of the Mexican territory to prepare the way for the rest of us, and the Gentiles are going to pay for it."

Shadrach pondered this reasoning but remained suspicious.

"I still think Brigham should be horsewhipped."

"I agree with him, Shadrach. President Young does not want to antagonize the Gentiles while our people are defenseless in camps. If we provide soldiers for President Polk, it would be unpatriotic of the Pukes to attack us. Furthermore, we would be under the protection of President Polk. It pours oil on the troubled waters until we can get our people to safety."

"Why did you need to see me, then?"

"The President has requested you to join the men in the company. We are sending some boys on this mission and the President thinks it a good idea to send some steady men to keep an eye on them. He does not trust the Gentiles and wants you to make sure none of these bucks leave the fold."

"But I have wives and children to care for. I do not wish to leave them alone in the middle of this wilderness with winter coming on."

"Your wives and children will be cared for as if they were our own, Brother Shadrach. We will look after all the families of the men who travel on this expedition."

Shadrach scratched his chin. It was hard to refuse a direct request of the church president.

"We need a stalwart like you to keep these young men true to the cause," the counselor pressed. "As soon as they see Mexico and the ladies of Spain, they may begin to forget the mission we are undertaking. You must be there to see they return to us."

"Very well. I shall go with them though my heart is not in it," Shadrach relented. "I feel that Brigham has just made a pact with the Devil."

Before he left for Mexico, Shadrach had business to attend to.

His son Ham was seven years old. It was time for him to be circumcised. Shadrach consulted his wives and then told Ham.

"No, Pap, no!" the boy cried in mortal fear. "I'm not supposed to be worked on until I'm eight years old!"

"I may be fighting in Mexico when you're eight years old and I want to be there when you become a true man."

"I'll wait for you. I'll become a man when you get back!"

Ham's pleadings fell on deaf ears. Shadrach took his son by his hand and led him to the bishop. The Bishop had no idea that the large boy was only seven years old and he prepared to perform the ceremony frothwith.

The rite of circumcision was a custom borrowed from the Hebrews. Instead of being performed when the child was born, it was performed when the child had grown. The health of Mormon babies was fragile enough without having to worry about the slipping of an amateur surgeon's knife.

"Now hold still, boy!" Bishop Macomb said as he held the razor sharp blade near Ham's young penis. "If you squirm too much, I might cut your manhood off!"

Ham looked at the near-sighted old man, trying to see in the darkness of the tent through his thick eyeglasses. If his father's hand weren't holding him, Ham would have escaped. Ham howled as the man cut the tender cover from his foreskin.

"See! It's as easy as peeling a potato," the Bishop said, holding up the small scrap of skin. "You take this home to your mother and make her a proud present."

Ham walked home with his hand inside his britches, holding the bandage over his ravaged penis. He was glad the ordeal was over with. Now when the older boys unlimbered themselves to urinate on the prairie, he could take his place by their side.

A bugle blew and the Englishman backed out of the earthen dugout that would be his family's home until next spring. In the assembly area south of the settlement, the men for the Mormon battalion had assembled and were loading into wagons for the trip into Kansas.

The five hundred recruits were chosen by the captains so as not to deplete the ranks of able-bodied men who would be needed for the trip. Most of the volunteers were green boys and older men whose work would not be missed. They had left their firearms for they would receive new ones from the

Army. They wore the same threadbare clothes they had come across the prairie in, because for the Saints needed their uniform allowance to bring more settlers from the east.

Even the horses that drew the carts were on their last legs and Shadrach prayed they would make it all the way to Fort Leavenworth, an outpost in the middle of the wilderness.

President Young had made a speech to the men, but had finished by the time Shadrach climbed into the back of the wagon. A bugle blew and the wagons craked off toward the West. The assembled Saints followed the wagons on foot, shouting encouragement to the men. The men of the Mormon Battalion responded by shouting three cheers for Brigham Young and the rest of the pioneers. Shadrach stood in the wagon, watching his small family following in the dust of the trail.

"Keep strong, watch your steps and follow the orders of your bishop!" he shouted at them. "I'll see you on the far side of the Rocky Mountains!"

Chapter Twelve

Ham Tompkin's skinny fingers were so numb with cold they could hardly come together to pick the gray speck of a louse off his baby sister. The child was crying, crying out against the cold, crying out against the hunger, and crying out in the agony inflicted by the lice and fleas.

They had first noticed the vermin soon after the first winter storms had confined them in their quarters. Many of the families had taken their animals into their homes to keep them from being lost in the blizzards. The animals brought the parasites with them and when the animals were put outside the vermin stayed in the warmth. They had quickly adapted to their human hosts and not a Saint in Winter Quarters was not continually scratching through his underwear, night and day.

The bugs came in many shapes, from the tiny fleas which sprang away when one tried to pick them off, to the tanacious lice that burrowed like black scabs in the hair and body of their victims. At first the Saints tried a number of remedies. They rubbed rare lemons into their hair. They boiled apple vinegar and scrubbed their bodies. They would baste each other with a painful dose of lye soap. No matter what remedy was applied, the pestilence always returned and as the winter became too bitterly cold for the curative baths, the pioneers resigned themselves to scratching.

A more insidious menace was visited upon the small community camped in the middle of the frozen wastes. Not long after the fleas began to bite, the first families became stricken with a virulent fever. At first it was thought the fever was a result of the confinement in the stuffy huts, or perhaps a recurrence of the fever of Nauvoo. As more Saints sickened, it was discovered that a plague of typhus had descended on the camp.

Nothing was more dreaded on the frontier than the outbreak of the typhus. The disease spread throughout the camp so rapidly that no one was spared. Within a few weeks, not a household in the encampment existed that did not have some members stricken and the rest fearful.

Ham had watched the disease creep into the family's dugout. First it struck his mother and his aunt. The first signs were always the same. A few sniffles. A headache, a general weakness. Then the fever began, slowly like a pot beginning to boil over a low fire. The two women were soon lying under their blankets on the floor, delerious with the heat of their own bodies. Soon a rash broke out on them and it looked like they had been beaten with a stick.

As the women sank into deleriums, the duty of tending them and the baby fell on Ham's eight-year-old shoulders. He became terrified that something would happen to his family and afraid of letting his father down. The words of trust spoken at Shadrach's departure echoed in his ears and he had nightmares of the women dying during his protection.

Ham threw himself into the care of his family. He would sponge off the women and the baby several times a day. He would boil a thin broth from a piece of suet and spoon every drop into the women's mouths. On even the coldest days he would make the trip to the communal woodpile where he would be issued a few thin twigs to keep the fires going.

The settlement of winter quarters consisted of a collection of dugout dwellings, log huts and lean-tos constructed during the summer months. The Saints had built a stockade out of logs around the settlement in case the Indians attacked the isolated pioneers. As the winter storms drifted snow higher than a man's head, the threat of freezing posed more of a problem than Indians and the stockade was slowly cannabalized for firewood. The granaries which had been filled with the fall harvest dispensed a ration of meal to the settlers, but much of the grain had to be saved for the westward trek next spring.

"Lord, I feel like I am being consumed by the fires of hell," Rachel said. "How is my child?"

"Rebbecca is healthy," Ham assured her. "This plague seems to strike the older ones."

Ham did not mention that the elderly saints had been devastated by the typhus. Hundreds had died and were unable to be buried in the frozen soil.

"Thank God the children are spared," Sarah said. "Thank

God Shadrach has been spared this contagion. I only pray he fares as lucky when the bullets fly around him.''

"I curse those liars who claimed they would care for us," Rachel complained. "I fear they have forgotten about their promise to Shadrach and have left us to perish in this place."

"They have not forgotten about us," Ham assured her, "but they are burdened with sicknesses of their own."

A young man covered with snow stuck his head through the canvas door of the dugout and breathed a steamy breath. "Are there any dead in here in need of disposal?" he asked, unwrapping a scarf from over his nose.

"No, but there soon will be if we don't get some relief," Rachel cried. "Please send the bishop with his oils so that he may pray for us."

"Bishop Macomb? He passed on some three days ago. His wife too. We're waiting for a thaw to bury him."

The Saints were delivered from the typhus into the hands of an even more dreaded killer. Cholera broke out among the weakened people and this time, no ages were safe. A death from cholera involved the victim having diarhea endlessly until the life had drained from their bowels. The gaunt, pinched faces of the victims showed they were being starved from the inside.

In the Tompkins dugout, the children bore the brunt of the attack. Strained from his own ministerings, Ham fell desperately ill. He lay under a blanket on the floor of the dugout, constantly soiling the floor. His mother tried to feed him broth with a thickener of grain, but this passed directly out of the boy.

Rebecca, too, was sick. She constantly cried, adding her wail to the continual moan of mourning which rose over winter quarters like the smoke from the chimneys. The baby became as pinched as a prune and her skin hung loosely on her protruding bones as she stained her swaddling clothes.

"My baby is soiling herself to death!" Rachel lamented, as Aldea Higgins paid a call on the family.

"I know, child, we all are," Higgins said patiently.

"Why are we being punished so? Isn't it enough that we've lost our homes and famlies? Why do the children have to suffer?"

"I can't answer that and I'm not going to try," Aldea said. "Just give your child this salt ever few hours and pray real hard."

"We've been praying harder than anyone I know for eight years and we just seem to be getting worse off. When will be the end of it?"

Aldea turned to leave. "I'm sure a glorious existence awaits us in heaven," she said, "because we sure have spent our time on earth in Hell!"

Thanks to the salt chips provided by the old midwife, the Tompkins children survived. Six hundred other Saints perished that winter and were buried in a graveyard bigger than any other on the frontier.

While the Saints suffered on the prairie the temple at Nauvoo was sold to a religious order. It never saw a chance to be put to use, for a mysterious fire gutted the building. A few years later it was torn down as the people of the neighborhood sought to erase all trace of the Saints.

The springtime which came in 1847 was almost a resurrection for the people of winter quarters. They emerged from their huts like surviving animals. Their faces were white and branded by the desperation of their ordeal. Their bodies were stooped and weakened by the diseases.

Like wilted flowers rising to the sun, the springtime breathed life back into them. To keep the spirits up, the leaders of the church prepared to move the people west as soon as possible. Another winter on the prairie would kill them all.

As the spring grasses pushed up through the winter snows, rheumy oxen licked the stems down to the ground. As soon as the bullocks were strong enough to pull a plow, a crop was put in for the other Saints who would pass into winter quarters in the fall. The remaining grains milled and divided up among the pioneers. The long journey began.

A small party of pioneers including Brigham Young set out in the fastest wagons to blaze the trail. Less than one hundred and fifty people accompanied Young.

This group would scout the trail and choose the spot where Zion was to be built. The others would follow as soon as possible.

Ham Tompkins hitched Castor and Pollux, the family's oxen in the way he had seen his father do many times before. A twin yoke of bent oak frames slipped around the blunt shoulders of the oxen linking them together. A wagon tongue was lashed onto the yoke providing a flexible but firm propulsion for the sturdy wagon.

Sarah and Rachel packed the jerked beef in the barrel of

flour they carried. The flour would preserve the meat and protect it from the heat. They loaded their few belongings and made ready to say goodbye and good riddance to the black hole in which they had spent a horrible winter.

They were assigned to a company of wagons led by Captain Hanson Pettigrew, a dashing young man who had been a riverman before he had stopped off at Nauvoo and found religion. The company consisted of forty wagons, a large enough group for protection, small enough so as not to overgraze the trail.

Pettigrew assembled them all and made a speech outlining his rules. There would be no profanity or hot language on the trail. There would be no discharging of firearms for any reasons. There would be no straggling and all would help the slowest along. There would be no men riding away from their wagons at any time.

A bugle blew and the Saints mounted their wagons. A collective sigh of relief was heard as the party rolled out of winter quarters to the cheers of the weaker ones who remained behind to rest before the journey.

The Pettigrew company headed west, following the ruts left by the pioneer party. The trail followed the north bank of the Platte River which led directly west through the uncharted territory. They passed out onto monotonous rolling plains of dried grasses where trees grew scarcer and the sun burned hotter. They rolled ten, maybe twelve miles a day through dust so thick that all the Saints had to wear mufflers over their noses. The rocking of the wagons and the creaking of the greaseless wheels hypnotized them as they strained to see some break in the horizon.

Sarah and Rachel sat in the back of their wagon, embroidering cloth they had stretched on pine frames. Abel Moreland, an elderly man whose wife had died in winter quarters, drove their team for them. His own son was driving the wagon in front of them and Captain Pettigrew had assigned the old man to the Tompkins women. Ham sat beside the man, alternately holding the reins and flicking the backs of the oxen with a long whip.

"I would much prefer the route on the south side of the Platte," Rachel said, holding a napkin over her face to cover the dust. "I hear the trail is smoother, the grass is greener and there are fewer reports of Indians."

"True, but there are many more Missourians on the south

side of the Platte," Sarah observed. "I want to cross our paths with no Pukes. This journey is painful enough."

"Do you smell fire?" Rachel said, sniffing the air nervously. "Do you suppose the Indians have set fire to the buffalo grass again?"

"If they have, we're near enough water to save ourselves," Sarah said. "What ails you this afternoon? You seem as jumpy as a cat in the cowshed."

"Do you think Captain Pettigrew a handsome man? The other ladies find him so, but I have not decided."

"Oh, I suppose he's comely enough," Sarah said, idly. "I hadn't looked that closely."

"I believe his eyes are too far apart to be classically handsome."

"You have no place looking with that attention to detail," Sarah chided her as she continued her embroidery. "As the wife of a man on a mission for the church, it is unseemly to find interest in such a subject."

Never easily tolerating criticism, Rachel flared, pulling the scarf from around her face. "How dare you make something base out of my observations? When I need a high and mighty judgment from someone I'll ask the bishop. I don't need a supercilious attitude from someone who was carefully looking over Brother Watkins the other day."

Now it was Sarah's turn to flare and she placed her embroidery back in her plunder chest. "Please lower your voice lest the whole train hears our petty bickering."

"I'll grant you that your criticism of me was petty, but my defense was noble. . . ."

"I see no nobility in your attention to another man and I care not about what your true intentions were. We must respect the harmony of the company and remember how quickly conclusions are reached by the people."

"These are a people who have tolerated plural marriage. I hardly feel they will hold my observations of the masculine race against me."

"It is not a woman's place to be promiscuous, either with her emotions or her observations."

"It is my place to do as I please," Rachel huffed, crawling to her child to end the argument. "I have suffered enough to atone for my indiscretions for a lifetime!"

* * *

A bugle call controlled the movements of the settlers. It sounded at dawn to raise them from their blankets. It sounded when the teams were hitched to the wagons and the company began the day's journey. It sounded to signal the period rest stops and finally for the evening retirement.

In the late afternoon, Pettigrew would signal the company to circle. The men would draw the wagons into a protective ring, locking the wheels of consecutive vehicles into each other so nothing could dislodge them. The teams of oxen would be watered and put to pasture under a guard which was always vigilant for Indians. The women, exhausted from the jarring ride, would immediately begin the dinner fires. On the first leg of the journey, firewood was plentiful, but as they cross the plains, trees became scarce. The ground was littered with the dried cakes of buffalo dung. When ignited it would burn cheerfully enough to cook a meal of corn cakes.

"I refuse to touch the excrement of those animals," Rachel announced icily when the first suggestion of the fuel was made. "I refuse to stand anywhere near the smoke of those fires and I absolutely refuse to eat anything cooked on those fires!"

After several meals of cold cakes, however, she changed her tune and was soon collecting the plate-sized chips in the folds of her apron. those who had cooked on peat fires in Europe said the flaky chips burned almost as nicely.

The diet for the traveling Saints was a monotonous one. The beef and bacon they brought from winter quarters was consumed quickly lest it spoil. They were soon left with flour, bran and barley, and they made soups, breads and cakes in any imaginable combination. Fish were regularly caught in the nearby Platte River, but never in enough quantities for any satisfaction. The hunters who rode out every day would return with a few birds, but it was bufflo that provided the real treat.

They had first seen the spoor of the beasts when they crossed the trails the animals followed to drinking water. Sometimes the prints of untold thousands could be counted on the trail. At other times they could see the clouds of dust raised by the migrating herds far off over the horizon.

Whenever the hunters could bring in the carcass of one of the shaggy beasts it was a time for rejoicing. The animals were so huge they had to be quartered by an axe before they could be loaded on a packhorse. A roaring fire would be built and the animal roasted on a spit, its haunches carved by the chefs and handed out on the ends of butcher knives to be gobbled down by the meat-hungry Saints.

Every night on the trail was filled with something to take the weary minds from their hardships. No matter how tired they were, the women would always organize a quilting party where they constructed blankets of imaginative design from the scraps of fabric they saved from their baskets. The children were pitted against each other in spelling bees.

Officially, the leaders of the Church frowned on music and dancing as a frivolous waste of energy. Practically, they encouraged music and dancing as the best way of keeping up the people's spirits. The Pettigrew company had a small orchestra made up of a fiddler, several trumpets and a concertina player. Every night as soon as the cool set in, the band would gather near the central bonfire and begin to play. Their repertoire ranged from the hymns favored by the Saints to the liveliest music they had heard on the steamers on the Mississippi.

Most of the camp would turn out to see the dancers and to whisper as the ordinarily dignified patriarchs of the company hitched up their gallowses and capered around the dance ground.

As the strains of a popular Steven Foster song drifted into their darkened wagon, Rachel looked at her sister, hoping to make peace.

"Let's go to the dance, tonight," she offered.

"I don't think it's seemly for married women to be seen at those dances," Sarah sniffed.

"Don't be such a prig! Of course its all right for married women to be seen at the dances. *Everyone* is seen at the dances."

"But the children. . . ."

"The children are fine. Ham can tend Rebbecca for the few minutes we will be gone."

Ordinarily, Sarah would not have consented. She was just as anxious to make up with her sister and reluctantly agreed to join the onlookers.

"Perhaps the tempo will lift my spirits," Sarah said as they approached the fire. "I have been feeling poorly lately. This separation from my husband is wearing heavily upon me."

The two sisters stood at the edge of the crowd, watching the dancers. As the shadows of the couples hopping in front of the fire flickered across their faces, Sarah broke into a smile.

"Look at Brother Perkins hobbling around like a ruptured gander," she whispered, poking Rachel in the ribs with her elbow. "I never thought I'd see him without that scowl on his face!"

The fiddler was playing a lively hoedown, the violin tucked into the crook of his arm. He sawed away at the ill-tuned instrument and the dancers followed the pace, sashaying wildly in each other's arms with little thought of technique or style.

"I wish our old dancing teacher back in Boston could see this!" Rachel whispered. "In fact, I'd like any of our old acquaintances to see us now! The skinny Tompkins sisters. Smack dab in the middle of the most ferocious wilderness in America."

The fiddler sawed his way to the end of the tune and the crowd broke into applause. The horn players whetted their whistles on a jug of apple cider and the fiddler stepped into the light of the fire.

"Choose your partners for the Mormon Quadrille!" he announced.

The crowd snickered. The Mormon Quadrille was a dance originated in Illinois to mock the Saints. It involved one man leading two women throughout the tune. The dance was great fun and the Saints had good-naturedly adopted it as one of their favorites.

"May I request the honor of this dance, ladies?" a deep voice said behind them.

Sarah turned, startled. Captain Hanson Pettigrew stood behind them, his broad hat in his hand. He was an attractive man at a distance, but up close he radiated a special appeal. He had black hair swept back away from his widow's peak and twinkling gray eyes. A half smile always played on his face as if every action he took had a secret motive behind it. He had grown his muttonchop sideburns in imitation of Brigham Young, and indeed, there were many who could not tell the two men apart.

"I'm sorry, Captain Pettigrew. I am not a dancer," Sarah said firmly.

"Good! Neither am I," the man said dragging both ladies by the wrist into the firelight. "I can't embarrass you if you can't embarrass me."

Before Sarah could resist she found herself in the middle of the firelight where her refusal would have caused a rift in the camp. Biting her tongue and glaring at her sister, who seemed quite happy with the matter, Sarah squared off for the dance.

The dancers formed three parallel lines with the women on the outside and the men in the middle. After bowing to their partners, the men linked arms with the ladies and the skipped up and down the row. Each trio switched partners and repeated the process until they had worked around to their original group. The band bleated out the lively rythym and the onlookers clapped in time, hooting and shouting encouragement to the dancers.

Sarah danced awkwardly, blushing with embarrassment and whispering her apologies to her friends in the audience. But Rachel danced enthusiastically, especially when she was on the arm of Captain Pettigrew. Her smile was broader and her step livelier than anyone could remember.

"Would you kindly slow this conveyance down?" Rachel demanded as she held her child. "I fear the rocking is causing her vertigo to increase."

"We have already fallen a far piece behind the rest of the wagons," Abel Moreland complained. "Much slower and we loose sight of them altogether."

"Then we loose sight of them for a few hours," Rachel said veneomously. "My child is sick and a wagon company sticks out like a sore thumb on the open prairie."

True enough, her child had long since stopped crying. Like a tree whose trunk is twisted in planting, the child had never developed after her birth in winter quarters. Her mother regretted beginning the trip before the child had a chance to age in the sun, and now the effects of the arduous journey were beginning to tell.

Rebbecca had not put on a single ounce of weight during the trip and worse, she had lost her appetite in the recent days. Her tiny body had remained wrinkled, her head hairless. In the last few days she had developed horrible black discolorations on her skin and her glands had swollen. She was so frightful looking her mother would break into tears at the sight of her.

Rachel could not determine what was wrong with the child. The leaders of the company feared the baby had the plague and had permitted the Tompkins wagon to follow the train at a farther distance. The company doctor had no cure, nor had Aldea Higgins.

Convinced the motion of the wagon was contributing to the child's demise, Rachel was nearly frantic. Stopping was out of the question, for the Saints were racing the winter. She realized that if worse came to worse, one baby would not tip the scale against the lives of three hundred pioneers.

"What are you looking so cold at?" Rachel demanded of her sister who sat in the wagon box with her. "You have been that way for days. Is something troubling you?"

"You seem to be spending much of your time in the company of Captain Pettigrew."

Rachel was disturbed at her sister's bluntness. Before the journey she never would have been so forward.

"The captain is a staunch friend and a confidant. I have leaned on his strength to aid me through Rebbecca's illness. I am indebted to him for his time and his talk."

"Where does this leaning take place?"

"No farther than the perimeter of the camp, if you are concerned for my safety. The captain is most gracious to escort me."

"You do not think it unseemly to be observed with such a man. The marriage to our absent husband dictates a certain decorum."

Rachel knew what her sister was trying to do but she kept her temper, refusing to be goaded into an angry reaction.

"For goodness sakes. We are on the frontier now. . . ."

"The more reason to observe a circumspect conduct."

"I have broken no rules of conduct and refuse to have my character impugned!"

"I am not impugning anyone," Sarah said. "I just ask you to think of your duty to your child."

"My child?"

"Perhaps her illness is a sign that you should observe more propriety in your public life."

This remark stung Rachel to the quick, as if she had been whipped in the face. A wellspring of antagonism toward her sister boiled up inside her, but she refused to strike back.

From the front of the wagon, Ham called, "I hear horses coming! I wonder if the company is sending help to us."

"Those horses sound unshod!" Abel said with a hint of alarm in his voice.

The family looked toward the crest of the rolling hill they

were approaching. Their worst fears materialized as six Indians galloped over the crest on painted ponies.

"Lamanites!" Rachel said. "Let's make a run for it!"

"Too late," Abel said. "We must not force their hand with panic. Keep still and perhaps we will be spared."

The Indians did not seem in a hurry to reach them for they galloped easily, talking amongst themselves. They cut back behind the wagon and slowed, trotting like friendly dogs behind a butcher cart.

The women turned and stared at the Indians, trying not to show their fear. The Indians were staring back at them. All were naked, save for buckskin breechcloths which modestly covered their private parts. The older men wore leather leggings that hooked with loops to their belts. The men's bronzed legs dangled idly at the sides of their ponies. They sat in horsehide saddles with high pommels. The hair of the younger men hung in long braids and they appeared wholesome with their lean bodies and countable ribs. The older men had less appealing looks, for their hair hung in stringy strands secured with feathered brochettes. Their sagging breasts and stomachs gave them the appearances of women, but they carried muskets across their pommels studded with the brass nails of combat.

As the wide-eyed women watched, the Indians talked in clipped, husky bursts of speech. They seemed to be deciding what to do.

To prove himself, one of the Indians leaped from his pony and began to run behind the wagon, trying to peer inside.

"Perhaps if we give the Lamanite a present they will go away?" Sarah said.

"We have little enough for ourselves, much less for them," Rachel snapped.

"For pity sakes, can't you see our peril?" Sarah said.

She took her embroidered napkin off the frame and gingerly held it out the back of the wagon. It was snatched out of her hand by the running brave, who yelped and turned, holding his prize up to the rest. Immediately all the younger men jumped from their ponies. Two of them joined the first while one ran to the front of the wagon and tried to bring the wagon to a stop.

"You've done it now!" Abel cried to Sarah. "These Lamanites might be our lost brothers but I will not have them touching our team!"

The teamster gestured to the Indian to back away from the oxen. Castor and Pollux could smell the Indian and the bellowed nervously and tugged at their yokes. With a flick of his whip, Abel stung the Indian on the shoulder.

The yelp of their friend galvanized the rest of the Indians. The older men clicked back the locks on their rifles and the playful appearance disappeared from their faces. One young man reached into the back of the wagon and started pulling out everything he could get his hands on. Bolts of cloth, iron potware, looking glasses and foodstuffs were spilled on the ground behind them.

"Lord have mercy on our souls for I am afraid we face a massacre," Ham said, his reedy voice quivering.

"Merciful God. I commit us to your care," Sarah said, whispering a frightened prayer.

"Is the horse pistol handy?" Rachel whispered. "I want to use it on my child to spare her the suffering."

She held the sickly Rebbecca up, and as she did the wrappings fell off her body. The bloated black markings of the child's sickness were plainly outlined on her naked body.

"*Waggggh!*" screamed the Indian who had climbed in the back of the wagon.

He recoiled off the wagon as if he had been shot, falling in the dust. The others took one look at the child and horror filled their faces. With a shout, they dropped the blankets they had picked up as if they were poisoned and raced away. The young braves on foot ran to catch their horses which had galloped off in the general stampede.

Still ghostly pale with fear, Sarah mumbled her thanks for their Salvation. Rachel wrapped the coverings around her child.

"Ham! Fetch the possibles we have left behind us and be quick about it," Rachel said. "Then I believe we should catch up with the wagons."

Chapter Thirteen

The shout rang out, startling the men of the Mormon Battalion.

"No! I won't take those devil's pills! Get them away from me."

Shadrach looked at Thomas Morse who rode beside him in the column. "It sounds like Doctor Death is at it again," the Englishman said. "We'd better go rescue Perkins."

They spurred their horses and rode to the wagon which served as the sick bay for the caravan of volunteer soldiers. Riding behind it they could see Private Samuel Perkins, a fellow Saint, arguing with a elderly man in a soiled surgeons smock. The surgeon, Dr. Sanderson, had been nicknamed "Doctor Death" by the men for his habit of dispensing medicines to the sick that made them worse off than they had been before.

"Excuse me, sir?" Shadrach said, flipping a salute. "Is there something I can help with?"

"I've warned you men before," the doctor roared. "If you refuse to take the medicine, I'll turn you out of the sick bay. A dose of arsenic from an iron spoon is prescribed!"

Perkins, the wiry young patient blanched at this prognosis. Like many of the older men, he was suffering from malaria picked up crossing the swollen rivers of the Texas frontier. He had run a fever for days before his friends had convinced him to turn himself over to the mercies of the doctor.

"We Latter Day Saints believe that a prayer and a laying on of hands can work a cure as well as powders," Shadrach explained. "Perhaps you should save your medicines in case of an epidemic."

"I have plenty of arsenic, enough for a plague. And this young heathen is going to take some of it if he wants to ride in this wagon."

"I think I'm feeling a mite better," Perkins said weakly, pulling his shirt on and climbing out of the back of the wagon.

Shadrach frowned as he watched the boy pull himself up on his mount. The doctor was purposefully antagonizing the Saints by forcing medicines against their naturalistic beliefs. The doctor showed the same hostility the rest of the Gentile officers showed. The regular army staff seemed insulted to have to command a group of Mormons and they made no effort to hide their contempt. Although they were only a handful commanding five hundred Saints, the officers stayed separate from the men. An unofficial leadership was formed within the volunteers, with men like Shadrach passing on orders given to them by the Gentiles.

The Mormon Battalion had been mustered and outfitted at the frontier outpost of Fort Leavenworth, Kansas. They had been issued spavined, sway-backed horses, mouldering biscuits and beef, and obsolete muskets. They had been ordered to march to the Mexican border a thousand miles away.

The men marched on a trail used once before when the Spanish conquistadors had stumbled after the fabled city of gold. Day after day they marched across grasslands which extended to endless horizons. Shadrach thought that America had seemed large before, but the prairie would have swallowed up the countryside he had seen.

"I'd like to know where we are headed?" Thomas Morse complained out loud. "We have been marching for months and we still have not seen a single Mexican . . . or an American for that matter. Where is General Scott's army supposed to be?"

"I heard that we will not meet with either Scott or the Mexicans," a man said. "The army does not trust us not to ally ourselves with the Mexicans and desert this Pukish Army."

"Not a bad idea," Morse said. "We would probably get a better deal from General Santy Anny than from President Polk!"

"I have it that we are being marched across the continent to attack the Mexican settlements in California from the east where they would not expect it," Shadrach said.

"I don't believe it!" Morse said. "I think we are to be marched across the Mexican desert as a ruse. The Mexicans will think we are the main force and massacre us while Scott slips into Mexico through the back door. They can kill two birds with one stone. Get rid of the Mexicans and Mormons, too!"

Private Perkins piped up. "I say we don't fall into their trap. Let's skiddaddle for the Rocky Mountains with these horses and guns and meet up with Brigham!"

This sentiment was well received by the men within earshot and Sharach knew there would be a mutiny if he didn't move quickly.

"Brothers, don't forget the instructions given us by President Young," he said. "We are bound by our oath to the army and will stay under their orders until we are discharged."

"Whose side are you on?" Morse asked accusingly. "The Pukes or the president?"

"President Young's. That's why I'm going to stay with this command through hell or high water until we've discharged our obligation."

He stood up at his full height and looked challengingly at his friends. They grudgingly acknowledged his leadership and nothing more was said about the mutiny.

Polly Halloran had been watching the tall Saint with the English accent ever since they had left Fort Leavenworth for the dusty march to Mexico. Polly was one of the four laundresses who had traveled with the party.

The trip had been unbearable for most of the women who rocked uncomfortably in the filthy wagons, but Polly was glad to be rid of Kansas. This trek was her free ticket to California where she would make her fortune.

Shadrach had noticed the red-headed laundress with the round face and green eyes. She had a quick laugh and a quicker wit. The others called her Polly.

All the laundresses were prostitutes. They had plied their trade in Fort Leavenworth and had jumped aboard the Mormon Battalion hoping to profit from the Mexican war. The troopers going into battle would pay everything for a woman's love the night before.

The women got the shock of their lives when they met the men of the Mormon Battalion. They were penniless. Their advance pay had been collected by the church. Put together, all of the men couldn't afford one woman.

The women delighted in teasing the Mormons. Only the officers could afford them and they reminded the pauper soldiers of this daily.

Polly leaned out of her wagon and grinned at Shadrach one night as they made camp. "Is it true you Mormons have horns on your head and cloven feet?" she teased.

"Why don't you ride with me and take a look," Shadrach teased back.

"Not a chance! That wide-brimmed hat of yours could hide a deer's antlers and your feet smell so bad that it'd be the death of me to pull off your boots!"

"You shouldn't believe all the rumors you hear about us Saints," Shadrach chided. "We're just people like anyone else."

"Are you Christians or heathens?" she asked with genuine curiousity.

"Christians. Of course."

"Then I don't want anything to do with you," she said coquettishly. "I had enough of priests and their blather in Ireland."

"Ireland? How did you come to end up in the middle of this hellhole?"

"The same way you did, you damn Englishman. Bad luck!"

"I chose to come here," Shadrach insisted. "I've seen good luck and bad. Meeting you has been my good luck."

"I had the bad luck to marry a man from the Wicklow Hills in Ireland. He brought me over to New York City where he got the notion he could get rich as a sutler selling goods to the American Army."

"A husband? Where is he now?"

"A mule kicked him in the chest in Fort Leavenworth and he died the same day."

"I'm sorry to hear that. But how did you end up—?"

"As a whore? Do you know what life is like for a widow at an army camp? You have to beg for your bread. I'd rather lift my skirts and have some bread on the table than be a starving lady."

"What's your future hold for you?"

"California is the new land. The China trade is going to stop there and I'll latch on to a sea Captain. Women are a scarce commodity out there and I should get my price."

"That seems like a hard row to hoe."

"Hah! Look who's talking! When your band of scarecrows showed up at Fort Leavenworth you were starving!"

Shadrach proudly slapped his muscular stomach. "The body recovers quickly if the soul is healthy."

Polly had warmed up to him and was looking apprecia-

tively at his body. Shadrach sat in the wagon, trying to hide
his desire for the first woman he had been close to in months.

"So tell me, Mr. Shadrach Tompkins," she said, mocking
his seriousness. "How many wives do you have?"

"Fifty or sixty, at least. I've lost count."

"What a liar! I've never met a man who could truly satisfy
one woman, much less fifty or sixty."

"I told you that we Saints are special. Besides. With all
those wives, I've had much practice."

This outrageous lie captivated Polly. She laughed, trying to
figure a way of making this Englishman reveal the truth and
to beg for her company the way some of the other men had.

"Do your wives get jealous when you spend the night with
the others."

"Never," Shadrach said confidently. "For I visit each of
them each night."

"Liar!" Polly said, straddling his legs and slapping him
playfully on the chest. "You're telling me you visit all sixty
once a night?"

"Not really. Sometimes I visit each twice a night."

This was too much for Polly and she began unhooking the
tunic Shadrach wore.

"Here. What are you doing?" he asked.

"I'm going to find out how truthful you are. If you have
been spending all these nights engaged in sensual pursuits,
I'll be able to judge this for myself."

"I have no money to pay you with," Shadrach warned.

"If you are truthful, there's no charge," Polly said. "But
you had better be good for sixty times in one night!"

The verbal sparring between Shadrach and Polly continued
as the battalion crossed the Texas plains. Both looked forward
to their evenings when they walked inside the picket lines of
the camp debating among other things, theology.

Shadrach was a good believer but a poor debater and he
suffered at the barbs of the cynical but clever Polly. He
welcomed the encounters, however, and doggedly kept proselytizing her. He had never been much of an evangelist but he
sharpened his skills by parrying her doubts. Polly retained her
lively skeptisim but found the lumbering Englishman's belief
refreshing in a world full of doubters.

Belief will always wear away doubt if it gets a long enough
chance, like water cutting through stone. The stone appears
harder, but it cannot renew itself the way water can and faith

renews itself while doubt cannot. Before a month had passed, Polly was objecting to Shadrach's preaching more for the joy of tweaking his nose than for the pleasure of aetheism.

More than just a philosophical bond had grown between the man and woman as they passed their days in conversation. Both felt a joy in each other's company. Shadrach was uplifted by the red-haired woman's devilish sense of humor and her plucky spirit. Many of the other women he had known had all been so serious that her gay adventurism fascinated him. He felt a tinge of remorse when he thought of the hardships his other wives must be enduring, but he could not restrain his enjoyment of Polly.

She reciprocated his friendship. There was a boyish innocence about this great mountain of a man she had not seen in the other men in her life. The other's always had some secret scheme in mind, even using faith as a tool to get what they wanted. But this one seemed to want nothing in return for his companionship and this made her relaxed and mellow in his company.

The battalion crossed into Mexican territory without incident, and marched without firing a shot into Santa Fe, the capitol of the northern territories. It was a bedraggled column which staggered past the adobe buildings of the town. The men had been without food for several weeks and subsisted on prairie hay and water. The Mormons were in rags and tatters. Their clothing was threadbare when they left Fort Leavenworth months before, but now it almost fell away from their gaunt bodies. Winter had come early to the New Mexican mountains and the last part of the journey had seen their thin boots slogging through the early snows. The mules and horses were in worse shape, their ribs easily countable through their bare skins. It was not an army that could have offered much of a fight.

Luckily, the residents of Santa Fe were in no mood to battle the Americans. Fearing that a huge army was about to follow the bedraggled Mormon Battalion, they welcomed the starving soldiers like heroes, feeding them and clothing them.

Shadrach walked through the streets of the strange town. It was built of mud, and yet the churches and buildings rose many stories from the streets, whitewashed or painted in terra cotta colors, the exposed rafters sticking from the front of them like Indian dwellings. All the houses were surrounded by high walls but within the walls, each home was a paradise with fruit trees and gardens watered by tinkling fountains. A great church dominated the town and while the Temple at Nauvoo was greater in size, the inside of the cathedral was as richly carved as hundreds of Indian slaves could make it.

The men of the Mormon Battalion swaggered around the town. They stared at the exotic Spanish women in their veils and long dresses, their hair richly arranged around the long combs they wore on their heads. Any thoughts of romance were quenched by the grim dueñas in the black dresses, the older women who chaperoned the women around like vengeful dogs. Strange too, were the Indians, dressed in their white blouses and baggy pants. Their sculpted bronze faces stared impassively at the Spanish and Americans alike, revealing little of what they felt as they did the manual labor of the town or sold their produce in the market. The Catholic friars, their bald heads wearing the trimmed tonsures, stared defiantly at the Saints while they whispered rumors of their strange beliefs to frighten their parishioners.

After many hungry months the Saints ate as much as they could of the fatally spicy food the local people supplied them with. The food consisted of beef and beans flavored with the red onions and the scarlet chiles that hung in every kitchen.

"I do believe these people are secretly trying to poison us," Thomas Morse complained to Shadrach. "I think I felt better when I was starving then I do eating this food."

"My bowels have not stopped moving since I first tasted these spices," Shadrach confided. "Living on this fare would be like having cholera all one's life."

At Santa Fe, the beleagured troops refitted for the push to California. Colonel Allen, the army commander had died and was replaced by Colonel Phillip St. George Cook who was less liked by the Saints. A mutiny was narrowly averted by the arrival of Shadrach's friend, John D. Lee. He had been sent across country in a wagon to collect the paychecks of the Mormon Battalion and return them to the Saints in Winter Quarters to pay for their cross-country trip. Lee counseled the men to remain faithful to the army and to return to the Saints only after they were dismissed.

The health of many of the soldiers had become so poor that Colonel Cooke ordered a hospital train to take many of the men to a fort at Pueblo in Colorado for them to recover. He also ordered that the laundresses accompany this train to spare them the danger of the trip to California.

Polly Halloran was furious when she was informed that instead of going to California with the men, she would winter in Colorado with the sick.

"I'll be damned if I'm going to cross halfway across this desert only to turn back now!" she railed at Shadrach.

"Perhaps it's better this way," he said, trying to comfort her. "Marching and fighting are two different things. I couldn't stand the thought of you speared by a Mexican lancer."

"Better that than freezing to death in Colorado. I've dealt with men's lances before."

"I've grown fond of you during our time together," Shadrach said formally, taking the woman by the shoulders.

"And I of you," she said, softening. "Even if you are an Englishman."

"I have a suspicion that a number of our men in this hospital train will be joining up with the first party of Saints who will push across the prairie. If you join them on their journey across the Rocky Mountains, I promise to meet you on the other side. If it is still your intent to go to California, I will personally escort you there myself."

"Now what other intention would I have?" Polly asked him suspiciously.

Shadrach could never hide his intentions or veil his thoughts very well so he usually ended up blurting out his plans.

"I was hoping you might consent to be my wife. It would bring the greatest pleasure to me to be sealed to you to eternity."

Polly stared at him with mortal horror. "What? And have my soul burn in hell for the sin of polygamy? I should say not!"

"Quite the contrary. All the universe shall be yours to reign over when you join me in the heaven of the purest salvation."

"I don't intend to resume our theological debate, Shadrach Tompkins. Let me just say that while ordinarily the prospect of marriage to you would not be overtly offensive, I don't intend to share any man I marry with any other women. Under any conditions. Gentile or Saint."

"I think you might find it a pleasant experience," Shadrach said. "Plural marriage has many advantages. The burden of the wifely chores is shared by several women. The women can experience the sisterhood that comes of the bond and be unified rather than apart. It has greater advantages for the women than it does for the man.''

"I may be old-fashioned, but sleeping in a cold bed while you are off with another of your wives does not impress me as advantageous. I will hold out until I find a man who is prepared to divide his time with no one but me.''

"Farewell, then. And Godspeed,'' Shadrach said, kissing her on the forehead and backing off. "Just remember that sharing a great man with a few other women is so much better than having a lesser man all to yourself.''

His backwards steps were speeded up as Polly stooped to pick up a few loose stones and unleashed them angrily on her fleeing target.

The sun-baked desert in southern New Mexico had reduced the men of the Mormon Battalion to a legion of shuffling ghosts. The landscape was an unrelenting series of mountains and flatlands, barren of anything but the most hearty cactus and sagebrush. The intense light burnished their eyes until they were swollen shut. There was no earth in this region, only sand which found its way into their clothing, their weapons and what little food they had left. There was no water and the brackish supplies they had brought in casks were evaporating faster than it was being drunk.

The mules and horses were not allowed water, and they dropped in their traces. The cattle were dragging their tongues and the men butchered them where they fell.

Shadrach's head felt like a loaf of bread as the noon sun heated up the yeast between his ears. His brain felt like it was rising until ready to explode. He gave a silent prayer of thanks that they did not have to fight any Mexicans in this weather.

Suddenly the scouts came galloping up a dry wash as if General Santa Anna himself was directly behind them.

"Form your skirmishing lines!" Shadrach shouted, afraid they had fallen into a trap.

The bugler sounded the rallying cry and the dazed men dismounted and loaded their rifles. The scouts thundered past without stopping, but instead of the Mexican Army, they were followed by a herd of range bulls.

"Is this the enemy you are terrified of?'' Thomas Morse

shouted as he stood in the middle of the dry wash. "A regiment of Spanish cattle has routed our scouts! Should we surrender to them?"

Before anyone could answer, a mottled bull pawed the earth in front of Morse. Bellowing a challenge it charged, tossing him on its horns and landing him in the middle of a cactus field. The men laughed at his plight, then broke and ran as a score of other bulls charged through the column. The animals had gone beserk when they saw these strangers trespassing and they vented their fury on the Saints. A tan bullock rammed into the hospital wagon repeatedly until the men inside cried out in panic. Other bulls chased the fleeing infantry into the sagebrush as the men ran for their lives. Shadrach was thrown from his horse as a copper-colored bull gored his mount. The Englishman covered his head with his hands as he was nearly trampled by the rampaging beasts.

The rest of the column ran up to assist them after hearing the confusion. They fired on the animals until the bulls had fled into the desert leaving a scattered company in their wake.

Although the bulls which had been killed that afternoon were roasted on spits for a feast that night, there was little joy in the camp. The Saints had fought in their first battle and had been severely mauled by a herd of oxen.

The battalion crossed the rest of the great Mojave desert and made their way into the ranchos of Southern California with hardship but without incident. They found the native residents unwilling to fight. Before they reached the Pacific Ocean the news came that the war had ended and California was now an American territory.

The Mormon Battalion was stationed at several small forts such as the Pueblo de Los Angeles in order to keep an eye on the local ranchers. In the spring of 1847, after nearly one year of service, the Mormon Battalion was dissolved and the Saints left the Army with little thanks for the fourteen-hundred-mile march they had made between Fort Leavenworth and the Pacific.

Two groups of Saints rode out from Lower California bearing their paychecks and the bitter taste of serving with the blue-jacketed Pukes. One group under Thomas Morse rode east along the Old Spanish Trail hoping to meet with the pioneers crossing the Rockies. Another group under Shadrach rode north, heading for the Great Bay at Yerba Buena they called San Francisco.

Shadrach had never seen countryside like the California coast as he rode north past the old capitol of Monterey. The steep mountains plunged sharply into the curving coastline sheltering the ranchos and orchards and trapping the cool Pacific Ocean breezes. The weather was constantly changing as they rode north. They camped on hillsides covered in a thick fog and awoke in a misting rain.

The air was peppery with the smell of pine which grew in rain forests on the slopes. Orchards of orange and almond trees were grown without much effort by the farmers and vineyards and cattle pastures were everywhere. The more Shadrach saw, the more he realized that California was the place the Saints should settle. The Mexicans were so few they could easily be supplanted by several thousand Saints. They could build a Zion on the shores of the Pacific that would stand off any army. The land awaiting them reminded Shadrach of his native England. It would be an Elysium in America.

Shadrach had ridden north on the specific orders of President Brigham Young. He was instructed to meet a boatload of Saints who had sailed from New York City on the ship, *The Brooklyn*. The ship had left in February of 1846, rounded the horn of South America, made a stop in the Sandwich Islands and had left them off at the San Francisco Bay. The affluent New York Saints brought farm implements, a printing press, and most importantly, a shipment of muskets.

The leader of the Brooklyn Saints was an enterprising little man named Sam Brannan who had edited the church's newspaper in New York. Brigham Young mistrusted the ambitious Brannan and he had dispatched Shadrach to keep an eye on him.

The remnants of the Mormon Battalion rode onto the desertlike peninsula which choked off the San Francisco bay like a fist against its windpipe. The community lay at the northern end of this peninsula. A few hotels housed seamen who left their ships on the wharves where they loaded the produce from the surrounding farms. The large party of Saints was not hard to find. They had camped in canvas tents on the edge of town. Sam Brannan, as the official representative of the church, had reserved a room in the best hotel for himself and he greeted Shadrach with an expensive meal in honor of their reunion.

The contrast between Shadrach and his host was great.

Brannan was a dark-haired elf of a man who strutted as if he were the equal of the giant beside him. He wore nattily cut clothing, a silk vest, a tailored waistcoat and tiny polished boots, a far cry from Shadrach's worn broadcloth. Unlike the trusting Englishman, the New Yorker had darting eyes and a volatile manner, always watching his company to make sure he was in control of them.

In this spirit he finished his meal and led Shadrach from the hotel. They climbed the steep hill behind the boarding house until they had a fine view of the sunset. A freshet of a breeze snapped at his tie as Brannan proudly surveyed the land in their view.

"I feel like the prophesy is coming true! We have found our Zion," he said, sweeping his hand across the landscape. "Here we can plant crops and be ready for the gathering of the people."

"But President Young said that Zion was going to be on the west slope of the Rocky Mountains," Shadrach said dubiously.

"Is not the Pacific on the west slope of the Rockies, give a thousand miles or so?" Brannan said, winking.

Shadrach shrugged. There was no denying that this was a delightful land. A thick fog was rolling in and the setting sun was tinting it the color of a twenty dollar gold piece that had been thrown in the fire.

"There! Is that not the land of the Golden Fleece of the Argonauts?" Brannan said, putting his arm around Shadrach. "This is the richest of all lands. A boy with a slingshot could guard that channel against any fleet in the world. This is the land of plenty, but we must act now!"

"I have my reservations about whether the president is going to consider California," Shadrach said.

"I am going to talk him into it," Brannan bragged. "And you are going to help me!"

Riding the swiftest horses Yerba Buena could supply, Shadrach rode with Brannan and another man east to meet the advancing Saints. They rode through the Sacramento River Valley where the black soil cried out for them to till it. They rode over the forbidding Sierrra Nevadas where the melting snows revealed the bones of the Donner party who had been cannabalized the year before by their starving companions.

They picked their way across the pumice and shifting sands

of the wasteland the Spanish called Nevada. This desert was nothing but bare rock, far worse than Shadrach had seen in the Mexican territory. They faced flat sheets of black rock one hundred miles across, rimmed by shimmering mountains. Traveling by the bright light of the stars, the three men rested in the scant shade during the daytime. They surely would have died in the one-hundred-degree heat of the desert.

For three months they traveled, desperate to reach the main party of Saints before they put down roots. After crossing an immense desert in the middle of June, their horses began surging forward, a sure sign they had smelled water. Crossing over a rise, Shadrach gasped as he beheld a huge body of water stretching to the horizon like an ocean.

"This is the Great Salt Lake I have heard about," Brannan said, wiping the sweat from his face. "We're not far from the Rockies now."

They could not restrain their horses as they rushed to the shores of this great lake whose blue waters reflected the snow capped peaks of the mountains in the distance. But at the water's edge, the horses backed away. Shadrach stooped in the sand and sipped a mouthful.

"*Ptttu!* It pickles my tongue!" he cried out. "It tastes of alkali and all manner of salts."

Hoping to cool off, the men waded into the brine of the lake.

"Careful, brothers, for I can't swim," Shadrach cautioned, but before he could stop himself he fell into a deep hole in the lake.

"Help me or I am finished!" he gasped, but the others were too far away to reach him in time.

Just as he said his last wishes and prepared to sink into the briny depths, never to see his family again, he bobbed to the surface like a cork. He wasn't swimming, he was floating. He floundered in the water until Brannan pulled him to the shallow depths.

"What manner of place is this?" Shadrach mused outloud. "Water which you can't drink and in which you can't drown. I will be happy to quit this place forever."

Several days of hard traveling brought them to a river ford on a pleateau east of the great lake of salt. A small wagon train was camped there and through his spyglass, Shadrach was thrilled to recognize Brigham Young by his black clothes and his distinctive beard.

Shadrach had never been welcomed the way he and Brannan were welcomed by the Saints in the pioneer party. The wagoneers who had crossed the plains from winter quarters without a map were overjoyed to see the Saints from the West assuring them that they were on the correct route. Even before they had eaten a meal, Brannan had shown the president a copy of the newspaper he had printed in California and was promoting the land as the perfect location for the new Zion.

Young listened impassively to Brannan's stories and then shook his head.

"You have performed a noble service to the church, transporting our people to California, but now you must bring them East to meet us. Zion will never be built in the Mexican territory."

Brannan stared at the stern leader as if his words had not been heard.

"California is a paradise without an owner. It can be ours for the taking! We can give up this barren desert and live in a land of milk and honey."

"Where the milk runs and the honey flows, the dogs and flies will not be far behind," Young said. "If California is the paradise you claim it to be, the Pukes will overrun it as surely as they have followed us before. Our Zion will not be built in paradise. We will create it ourselves."

Shadrach had been standing by, hoping for a chance to speak. He had never contradicted the president, but felt impelled to speak.

"Pray don't act in haste," Shadrach cautioned Young. "Brother Brannan has not told you the best part. Some say there is gold in California. So much gold that you can pick it out of the stream beds with your bare hands."

He sat back, watching the president, expecting Brigham to leap at the opportunity. Instead, Young's face darkened and a frown creased his brow like thunderclouds gathering.

"If the metal of Moloch is found in California, then it will surely draw enough Gentiles to sink the land into the ocean. Our people will have nothing to do with the place. We will follow our original plan. I counsel you brothers, say nothing to the brethren about California. I want no confusion sown in our ranks."

Brannan rose to his feet, his face reddened with anger. The

scowl on the face of President Young showed it would be no use arguing. The dapper New Yorker stormed from the leader's tent.

"Keep your distance from Brother Brannan lest you be tainted by his ambitions," Young warned Shadrach. "His eyes are fired by greed and they will be burnt out of their sockets by it."

The Pioneer party of one hundred and fifty men led by Brigham Young moved relentlessly west during July of 1847 following the path Shadrach had blazed from the valley of the Great Salt Lake. It was vital that they choose a place soon and put the crops in the ground if they were going to survive the winter. To quell any dissension, Sam Brannan was sent on a mission to Texas by the president and Shadrach guided the band.

They crossed the plains through the country named Wyoming by the mountain men who trapped for furs in the region. A trader named Bridger who had a small fort near the Green River sold them some mealy flour and gave them directions to cross the Wasatch mountains which blocked their way to the West. Bridger laughed when asked about the prospects of life in the valley of the Salt Lake.

"Hell's bells, the ground is so hard, the water so scarce, the winter so long, the summer so hot, the wind so strong and the snows so deep that the grasshoppers have to carry rations to get acrost it!" Bridger laughed, watching the faces of the Saints fall. "If you try to settle there, watch out. The land is so poor I'll give you one thousand dollars for every bushel of corn ye can grow there!"

"We may take you up on that wager," Brigham said, trying not to let the Saints' spirits fall.

"From what I hear, the Missourians may be following ye fellas out this way," Bridger gloated. "Perhaps you should pass on into Mexico to get the odds on your side."

"If I can have ten years of peace to build our strength, I'll ask no odds of any man," Brigham said looking directly at Bridger with such a passion that the veteran mountain man kept his further advice to himself and returned to sipping on the flagon of corn whiskey.

The trail that Shadrach blazed proved true. It led through a narrow canyon where walls of bright red sandstone were marked in stratifications like a gigantic layer cake. The pass was so tight that the sandstone echoed the sound of the creak of the wagon wheels until it sounded like a giant army was passing by. When the company bugler sounded his trumpet, it echoed all the way down the canyon like the trumpet of the angel Moroni signaling the end of the world. The Saints named the place Echo Canyon.

Echo Canyon dropped into a long, wide valley where the company paused to graze their stock before the final descent through the mountains. A party of advance scouts went on ahead but Shadrach remained with the main party.

A group of men from Pueblo, Colorado, had joined the party of pioneers near Laramie, Wyoming, and Shadrach rode back to find them. He was overjoyed to see the scarlet hair of Polly Halloran among them, riding in one of the first wagons.

"So! You couldn't wait to see me again?" Shadrach called out, delighted to see she remembered him.

"I'd be delighted to see the devil himself after spending the winter in Colorado," Polly answered. "And I will take you up on your offer to take me to California."

"I'd be happy to. The snows are beginning to set in, though. We'll have to wait until next year to set out."

"The snows? What are you talking about, man? This is July, the only time of the year when they don't have snow in the mountains!"

"The Sierras are different! Take it from me. I've been there. Only for two weeks at the first of June are the passes open. You wouldn't want to get stuck like the Donner party, would you?"

"If you're lying to me and I'm forced to spend another winter in this wilderness, I'll cannibalize you out of sheer meanness," Polly promised.

Shadrach's attention was caught by the approach of a rider galloping up the wagon line from the valley below.

"I hope it's not bad news," Shadrach said. "President Young has been confined to his wagon suffering from Mountain Fever. I fear for his health."

As the rider approached, he began whooping to get the attention of the wagons.

"We have found our Zion!" the rider shouted. "Even before he saw the valley of the Great Salt Lake, President Young had a vision. He announced to us all with the words, 'This is the right place! We have found our home.' "

"Please, brother, tell me. Perhaps he meant a camping place?" Shadrach said.

"No! *We have found our home!*"

Shadrach's face fell and although he hid his disappointment from the rest of the company, Polly could sense his feelings.

"The valley of the Salt Lake is the most barren place I have visited," he confided in her. "I fear we have made a great mistake."

ZION FOUND

1847

Chapter Fourteen

The chilled winds of autumn were beginning to lash the canvas tops of the wagons as the members of the Pettigrew company paused in the middle of the trail for a brief ceremony. Wearing the black dresses of mourning which had seen so much use in their young lives, Sarah and Rachel Tompkins stood beside a small grave that had been dug in the middle of the wagon ruts. Sarah clung to Rachel, supporting herself on her sister's sun-tanned hands as the stiff wind blew the tears from her eyes.

Bishop McCollough spoke the service as a man laid the tiny body of Rebecca Tompkins into the rock-lined grave. The fragile baby was dressed in the white baptismal gown its mother had made for the annointing that never took place. The child had finally succumbed from the rigors of the trip. Like several others of the immigrants who had passed on during the journey, she would be buried with a solemn but hasty ceremony.

When the service was spoken and prayers said, the grave was lined with rocks and gently covered with earth. Then the entire company passed over the grave to obliterate the signs so no coyote or passing Indian could find the body.

As dark clouds gathered overhead, Sarah and Rachel stood by the grave as the wagons passed over it.

"What a horrible place to be interred, poor little thing," Rachel said, letting a bit of her grief show through for the first time. "The thought of the child who had been frozen and starved for her short life buried on this prairie chills me to the bone."

"She is warmer than all of us now, waiting in heaven," Sarah comforted her. "The time we spend on earth is but a moment and then we will join her for all eternity. When you see her next she will be a beautiful young woman dressed in the most beautiful gown. You have a lifetime to look forward to that reunion."

"I hope you are correct. I have been worried that her life was cursed by our acceptance of the Principle."

"Don't even think of such a thing!" Sarah said firmly. "If a curse was placed on her it was the cold and the privation forced on us by our exodus. The Principle has been our one comfort through this ordeal. When we are reunited with our loving husband, these troubled days will be forgotten in your new children."

"I don't know if I want to bring children into a world as full of persecution as this," Rachel said bitterly. "Better to remain barren and spare them the suffering."

"I'll hear no more nonsense from you. It is our bound duty and pleasure to bear as many children as we can. The road to salvation is gained through motherhood and we must fill the heavens with Saints or eternity will be a lonely time."

The first cold splashes of rain fell on their faces causing them to hurry after the wagon train. Sarah watched her sister. Rachel would rarely show her feelings but Sarah knew she had not been convinced by their talk.

"The only way to true joyfulness is to bear as many children as you can," Sarah said. "A woman will live through the lives of her children."

"And she will die through the deaths of them."

After spending the cruel winter of 1847 at a camp on an island in the Platte River, the Pettigrew company descended into the Salt Lake Valley in the spring of 1848. They passed through the towering walls of Wasatch Mountain granite down a steep pass named Immigrant Canyon.

They were the third company to pass into the valley and they received a warm welcome. Brigham Young and a party of Saints rode out to greet the newcomers and a brass band played as they rolled out of the mountains to a field where a picnic lunch had been set up.

The news of his family's arrival had brought Shadrach Tompkins out with the president's party. He had ridden up to the Tompkin's wagon and scooped the two women in his arms while his son jumped on his neck. It had been nearly two years since the family had seen each other. Shadrach was distraught when he heard of the death of his infant daughter, and the women worried over the weight he had lost during the lean winter. Ham Tompkins had grown several inches since his father had seen him last and it was agreed that Ham would grow, even during a famine.

The immigrant's first sight of Zion did not inspire confidence. The valley Brigham Young had chosen to build the new Jerusalem was as barren as anything they had seen on the trail. Even in the springtime, the grass was brown and coarse, the soil hard-packed.

From the site of their new home they could see thirty miles to the west, and not a tree stood in sight. The land was flat and parched and blocked by the Oquirrh Mountains to the West. The bottomland was filled with the Great Salt Lake, an ocean in which no fish swam and which would water no farmland.

As Shadrach drove their team into the valley, he sensed the reservations of his wives from their silence.

"I know it looks barren right now, but Brigham has promised it will bring forth fruit in very little time," he said.

"My God! We left our homes to travel across a wilderness for this?" Rachel asked. "Out of the millions of acres we have crossed, why on earth did he have to choose this forsaken place?"

"There is a blessing in its sterility," Sarah observed. "If the lizards and snakes don't even want this land, no Gentiles are ever going to try to take it away from us. If we can gain a toehold here, we will live our lives unmolested."

The Saints had named their first community Salt Lake City but to term it a "city" required a great imagination. The pioneers had spent their first winter living in their covered wagons and had only begun to build houses in the spring of 1848.

By the time the Tompkins family arrived in the city, a cluster of adobe huts had sprung up. The wood felled in the nearby canyons was saved for other purposes. The valley had plenty of mud and it served to build the adobe walls the men of the Mormon Battalion had seen in the Southwest.

The industrious Saints had begun work on the city the very day they arrived in the valley. Fields had been laid out and a plot of land was chosen on which to construct the temple which would replace the one they had left behind at Nauvoo.

Joseph Smith once had a vision beholding the plan of the celestial city and it was according to this plan that Salt Lake City was laid out. The virgin land was divided up into square plats and then subdivided into smaller lots. Wide avenues crisscrossed these grids forming a geometrically perfect city plan. Each house constructed on the lots would be surrounded by trees and gardens. The broad avenues would be lined with shade trees. The grids would be divided into wards administered by the church so all could take part. It would be a replica of what awaited them in heaven.

It was hard to recognize the plan in the early days. The surveys had set out the plats, but the streets were little more than stakes in the earth. Instead of elegant houses, the adobe dwellings squatted in the middle of the town surrounded by a small wall for protection. These "dobies" were easy to construct. They stayed cool in the hot summers and warm in the winter.

Shadrach pulled the team up in front of a crudely constructed hut which had a wisp of smoke circling from the adobe chimney.

"This is home," he announced to the hesitant family. "It's not much, but it will be someday."

"It suits me just fine, husband," Sarah announced. "I'm looking forward to some privacy with you. If we are to populate this barren valley we have much work. After two years alone I am anxious to begin. Would you care to be alone with myself or my sister?"

Shadrach tried to speak, but he was unable to mouth his words.

Rachel jumped down from the wagon and took his hand. "If you two are going to stand on politeness, then I will take the initiative," she laughed and pulled him inside the house.

Inside the low-ceilinged hut, the one room was filled with smoke. Polly Halloran stood nervously by a small fireplace in the corner. She was wearing an apron and held a ladle with which she was stirring a pot. A mended set of crockery was set on the wagon box table as if they expected guests. Rachel Tompkins froze when she saw Polly. The Irish woman nodded and curtsied awkwardly to her.

"Who is she?" Rachel demanded icily.

"Well. . . ."

"Sister, you better come in here," Rachel called bringing Sarah and Ham into the house. "Ham. You had best leave."

The boy reluctantly ran out of what promised to be an interesting exchange as the four adults stared at each other.

"Sarah, Rachel, this is Polly," Shadrach stumbled. "Polly Halloran."

"Polly Halloran Tompkins!" she finished for him. "Pleased to meet you both."

Sarah and Rachel stared gap-jawed at Shadrach.

"You see, Polly and I were sealed to each other last winter," Shadrach said. "We had the blessing of the president."

Sarah looked surprised and speechless but Rachel was less restrained. "How dare you?" she demanded. "Did you think your absence from us entitled you to promote your licentiousness?"

"I would have asked your permission for this marriage had I been able to," Shadrach explained lamely, "but we were here in the midst of the wilderness. . . ."

"Celebrating your bacchanals while we froze in the snows of Nebraska? I have a good mind to scratch your eyes out for your troubles!"

"Now, sister, let us accept this development in good faith," Sarah said pouring oil on the troubled waters of their homecoming. "I am sure our husband acted with good intentions and that our new sister is a fine woman."

Her sister's acceptance of the status quo took some of the wind out of Rachel's anger. She was isolated in the group as the intolerant one and she lost the edge of the argument.

"If the marriage was sanctioned by President Young, then far be it from me to stand in the way of his divinely inspired approval," Sarah said. "I think the acceptance of this new relationship can serve as a fine test of our faith."

With this, she crossed the room and hugged Polly kissing her on both cheeks. She turned and stared at Rachel who was caught trying to decide whether to follow her own jealousy if it meant going against the church. Not wanting to be guilty of the sin of pride, Rachel likewise crossed the room and embraced her new partner in plural marriage.

"That's fine!" Shadrach said, clapping his hands together. "Now? Which one of you want to share the privacy of my blanket with me first?"

Sarah looked dolefully at her sister. "I think some of the urgency has gone from my desire. I think I would rather have a hot meal instead."

With the desperation of a people who have known starvation, the Saints began the job of building up their city. Food for the coming winter was the greatest worry, so a summer of labor was put into the farming of the land. The hard-baked soil broke the iron plows they had used in Illinois, so specially forged plows were hitched behind the same oxen which had pulled their wagons west.

Behind the plows, Rachel and Sarah walked with their aprons filled with the precious seed grains. Ham walked before them, jamming a pointed stick into the earth and they placed a seed in each hole. Everyone worked in the fields at planting time and Brigham Young traveled among them preaching and keeping their spirits high.

Since there was little natural water flowing near the fields in the valley, the Saints had to build irrigation ditches to bring the melting snows of the mountains to the crops. Since they had come from lands where the rain fell naturally and watered the fields, the idea of irrigation was hard for the Saints to comprehend.

Shadrach was in charge of a company of men who were digging an irrigation channel down from Cottonwood Creek to the fields on the northern end of town. The work was going slowly because the men longed to privately own land and farm it themselves rather than work on community projects.

"If you ask me, digging a ditch to bring water to the land is nonsense," Thomas Morse grumbled as they worked. "It will work fine as long as the snow is melting on the mountaintops, but what of the later summer?"

"In this land the snow stays on the mountaintops all year round," Shadrach assured him.

Morse's complaints brought the other men's troubles to a head. They put down their hoes and pickaxes to complain about the hard work of the project. In days before, Shadrach might have been helpless against their arguments, but a winter of living with the quick wits of Polly had trained him in the fine art of debating.

"The irrigation of this land is a divinely inspired plan," he argued. "Remember how the Israelites, after traveling forty years in the desert came upon the barren land of Palestine. They settled on the shores of the Dead Sea, a great salt lake with no water running from it. There, they built canals to bring water from the mountains and made the valley green. Just as the Jordon River flowed into the Dead Sea, so does the water from City Creek flow into the Salt Lake. Like the Israelites, we shall make our land rise from the desert!"

Slowly, the Kingdom of the Saints began to rise from their labor. In 1849, the state of Deseret, named for the industrious honeybees of the Book of Mormon, was created. Deseret was an independent territory ruled by the authority of the church and answerable to no one. It extended from the Wasatch Mountains east of Salt Lake City, west to the deserts of California and the Sierra Nevada Mountains, and south to the border of Mexico. These were the enormous boundaries of the Kingdom of God. Filling them, a handful of poverty-striken and starving people equipped with few tools and only a vague notion of where they were.

Deseret needed two things badly. People and food. The people came regularly enough as a continual stream of wagon trains brought the Saints from the settlements in Iowa and Nebraska into the Promised Land. The fall of Nauvoo and the move west had not stopped the flow of immigration from Europe and the eastern States. An organized system of immigration had been established with professional transit agents sheperding the newcomers from St. Louis into the Salt Lake Valley.

Everyone was put to work growing food. The Order of Enoch, the communal ownership of property and its consecration to the church, was revitalized. The fields and lands around them were owned jointly by the Saints and worked cooperatively by them. The harvest was put in church-owned granaries and divided among the people on the order of need.

The Saints also began setting up the industries which would be needed to build Zion. Sawmills and flour mills were constructed. Shops to spin wool into thread and to weave cloth were set up in the adobe homes. Blacksmith shops materialized out of the backs of wagons and wheelwrights and carpenters began work in their backyards. Gunsmiths and doctors worked in their bedrooms.

While the work of building Zion continued, the work of building lives began. The Tompkins family was living under one roof and the friction caused by Shadrach's new wife threatened to split the family apart. He quickly constructed a new addition to the adobe house to separate the wives.

Rachel was unrelenting to her silent disapproval of Polly. She never spoke to the woman, never acknowledged her existence. Sarah was less harsh in her treatment of the new-comer. She would speak and work with Polly, but did so discreetly so as not to start a flareup with her sister.

Shadrach tolerated the tension in the house with a mounting degree of impatience. He felt it was his divine duty to take as many wives as he wished and resented the hostility Rachel was showing. Although most Saints had only one wife, the most promiment had many. His friend John D. Lee boasted of having thirteen wives and an exalted place in heaven because of it. Shadrach had seen as much duty for the church as most men and he felt he deserved the respect that plural marriage would give him.

One afternoon he was called to meet with President Young at the residence Brigham was building in the center of town. Shadrach walked through the dusty lots of the town, past the temple site where surveyers were laying out the marks for the assembly hall that would be built bfore the temple.

Shadrach spotted Brigham Young up in the rafters of the house. Brigham had been a carpenter by trade before he joined the Church and he still swung a hammer with the best of them. Young climbed down from the rafters when he saw Shadrach and wiped the sweat from his brow.

"How do you fare, Brother Tompkins? I understand that your wives are not getting along very tidily these days."

"I think they will do better once they get used to each other," Shadrach answered, embarrassed that the other workmen were eavesdropping on the conversation.

"Time is the great equalizer. I'm sure if you leave them to their own devices, they will patch up their quarrels," the president said. "I would like to send you on a mission for the church. Perhaps that would give them an opportunity."

The idea of getting out of the tiny home seemed appealing to Shadrach. He was tired of listening to the complaints of his wives. Perhaps a mission would relax him and he readily agreed.

"We are a handful living in a land whose borders we do not know," Young said. "We need to send scouts to all the corners of our land to report upon what they find. I want you to lead a party."

"I would be honored, Brigham."

"I want you to make maps and take notes. Find every field where crops can be raised. Find every stream and river, every stand of timber. Look for coal, iron ore, lead and tin. Chart every natural fortification, every possible settlement site. We must get our people to the four corners of the land as soon as possible to keep the Gentiles out."

Shadrach nodded in agreement. Brigham Young took his trusted aide by the shoulders and led him aside.

"In particular, cultivate the friendship of the Lamanites you may find in the wilderness. Give them gifts and promise them our friendship. They may be a great ally if it comes to a fight with the Pukes," Young said. "And keep on the lookout for the ruins of the fortresses of the Nephites which may be found in this remote land. If you find such a site, tell no one but me."

Brigham Young shook Shadrach's hand and returned to his work. The Englishman turned to walk back to his home. His wives were not going to be pleased with this news. . . .

"Over my dead body you'll go on a mission to the wilderness," Rachel said fiercely when he informed them of his plans. "We were separated from you for a time and now they want to drag you off again?"

"I have already told the president that I would do it. I cannot change my mind now."

"Then I will tell him for you," Rachel said, wrapping her bonnet around her hair. "I will tell him to send one of these lazy idlers of which there are so many nowadays."

"He cannot trust them as he trusts me."

"A little less of that kind of trust would make you more visible to us."

"Stay, sister," Sarah said. "If he is called to the wilderness then we should not try to stop him. We must all do our part if we want to set firm roots in this land."

Polly was afraid to interject her own feelings in the tinderbox situation, but her sense of approval fell on Shadrach's side. Realizing the consensus was running against her, Rachel tore off her bonnet and fled behind the blanket partition to her own bedroom.

"Do not worry about my going away," Shadrach assured them. "I will return before the snow falls."

Chapter Fifteen

"Is that a castle or an ancient fortress on that cliffside?" Shadrach said, squinting at the profile of a ruined building on the edge of a cliff. "By the Great Jehovah! I think we have found the ruins of the lost city of the Nephites!"

The light was fading fast in the canyon in which Shadrach and his partner, Thomas Morse, were riding. They had been traveling up the ochre sandstone valley for several days in the inescapable heat. The sun set quickly over the tops of the western cliffs, bringing the relief of the shade and coloring the eastern crags a glowing hue of reddish gold that Croesus himself had never seen. The canyon twisted endlessly like the undulations of a great stone snake and every bend in it brought a view, similar to the one they had just seen. Progress was slow over the painfully hot rocks. Shadrach began to believe that they would never come to the end of their exploration of this land.

The fading light had illuminated one high crag of the cliffside and it shone like the jeweled roof of an ancient temple. Was he looking at the great temple of the Nephites? If so, the journey had been worth it.

Thomas Morse shaded his eyes with his hands and squinted at the shapes. "You are imagining things, Brother Tompkins. That is a rocky crag, like all the rest we have seen."

"No, can't you see? Those are parapets on the side with notches for the archers. There is a main gate of the city, above it the domed roof of the temple coated with gold plate!"

"Your eyes have been blinded by too much sun in this place."

Shadrach stared at the rock, determined to climb to its top and bring back a chunk of gold to Brigham Young. His hopes were dashed, however, when the light shifted and dulled, revealing ordinary rock on the side of the cliff. He stared at his partner and scratched his own beard which had grown thick during the time they were on the trail. Perhaps he had been in the wilderness too long?

For six months, Shadrach had traveled through southern Deseret, charting the land. His party had passed along the rim of the Great Salt Lake and had ridden south, keeping the Wasatch Mountains in sight. They had ridden hundreds of miles as the great valley they were in stretched out beyond their belief. The farther south they traveled, the more dry the land became until it could scarcely hold the sagebrush growing on the plain.

They traveled for weeks noting the red-stained mountains that indicated a deposit of iron ore, the black striations that told them that coal could be found within the cliffs.

They mapped the rivers flowing from the mountains. Only along their banks could farmers plant crops. Pine forests, hidden in valleys in the interior of the desert were duly noted for later use as timber.

At the southern boundary of the Santa Clara River, the land turned into a plateau of broken canyonland resembling the frontiers of hell. The cinder-covered flanks of ancient volcanoes rose above the land. The countryside beyond them looked like the cracked bare skin of an old man.

"That's the desert the Spanish called the Mojave," Morse said. "Twenty-one days ride to the nearest water. Only the Indians cross that desert with ponies stolen from California and half of those don't make it."

None of the scouting party had any desire to die in the desert so they made the Santa Clara their farthest exploration. The men split into small groups in order to efficiently divide the territory among them. Shadrach and Thomas Morse elected to travel east, pushing into the canyon lands.

Shadrach had seen a great deal of America in his short time but nothing matched the sights he beheld as they journeyed into lands so ancient that the gods were not even born when they were made. The clop of their horses hooves was the only noise that dared to disturb the sleeping rock they traveled over. No birds or rustle of wind competed with them. The weathered sandstone towered above them, lined with eons of torment. From the distance it appeared that no life clung to the stones, but as they passed their horses always found grasses growing on the canyon floors watered by pools of rain which had collected from the previous season.

The size of the land was so vast, the silence so overpowering that Shadrach felt as though he was trespassing in a forbidden preserve of the creator. He and Morse ceased making maps and checking for minerals. No one would ever believe the things they saw. It was inconceivable that anyone would pass that way again.

Winter was coming to the high country. They could tell it. Not by the temperature which stayed uniformly hot, but by the angle of the sun and the shortness of the days. The two men decided to return to civilization and were heading north out of the canyons, hoping to find a trail by dead reckoning.

They moved cautiously through an ocean of pines stretching out on the pleateau they were crossing. They had seen many moccasin tracks in the area and were sure that a major group of Lamanites was somewhere about. Shadrach was convinced of his skill as a woodsman and sure they could avoid them.

Rounding a bend in the trail, Shadrach felt a sinking feeling in his stomach. Directly in front of them was an Indian village consisting of a dozen buffalo hide tents supported by pine poles. Several score of Indians were about their business in the village and seemed as startled to see the whites ride into their midst as Shadrach was to be there.

"Lamanites!" Shadrach hissed to Morse. "Let's run for it!"

"No! They've seen us! My nag will never outrace one of those ponies! We must stay calm and pretend like we are here on business."

"Lord help us, I don't know whether I can stay calm."

The two men grinned widely as they rode into the center of the camp. The only reaction from the startled village came from the dogs which snapped at the hooves of their horses. A murmur went up from the Indians and they closed in around the strangers.

The Indians were members of the Ute Tribe that inhabited the mountains of Deseret. They were more akin to the Plains tribesmen Shadrach had seen in Kansas than they were to the nomadic Shoshones who peopled the Mojave desert.

Many of the young boys who chased after the camp dogs were naked, their copper skin smudged with the dirt of their ascent to manhood. A group of little girls gathered in the corner of the village, their black hair hanging stringily over their shoulders, their femaleness hidden by triangles of rabbit skin. In a group, they launched a shower of rocks and stones at the two white men.

The adults of the village, the men wearing breechclouts and beaded moccasins, the women wearing sacklike buckskin dresses followed the riders to a central point of the village. There was some discussion between them in a guttural language and Shadrach guessed that whoever was standing guard would have to explain how the two white men had been able to sneak up on them.

At the biggest lodge in the group, the entrance flap was thrown back and a silver-haired man emerged, pulling on a pair of elkskin leggings. Shadrach averted his eyes at the sight of a naked young squaw behind the man who closed the lodge flap. The powerfully built man had a prominent, flat nose and a lofty manner which reminded Shadrach of Brigham Young's. He was no doubt the chief of this tribe.

"Greetings. We come in peace bringing you the best wishes of Brigham Young, president and prophet of the Church of Jesus Christ The Latter Day Saints."

The chief stared at Shadrach and looked about his people.

"Bienvenidos, amigos!" the man said in an equally loud voice. *"Comme-etes allez-vous?"*

Shadrach smiled at this broken mixture of French and Spanish. Although he spoke neither language, it was obvious the chief had some contact with white men. He swung down off his horse and removed a brass compass from his saddle.

"This gift will seal our everlasting friendship between our peoples," Shadrach said, handing the man the compass.

The chief put the gift to his ear, shook it and threw it down. He stared instead at the horse pistol Shadrach had thrust in his belt. Brashly, the Englishman pulled the pistol from his belt and handed it to the Indian.

"You know the president has strict orders against supplying the Lamanites with firearms," Morse reprimanded him.

"I gave him the weapon. I won't give him the powder and ball."

The chief cautiously cocked the weapon and the crowd shrank back as he searched for a suitable target. He pointed it at a nearby dog and squeezed the trigger. The gun exploded in fire sending a ball between the legs of the dog which leapt for the cover of the pine trees. The chief turned to Shadrach with a grin on his face and pointed to the lodge.

"*Buenos amigos. Buenos amigos,*" he said. "*Allons enfants.*"

By nightfall that evening, Shadrach and Morse were sitting around a smokey fire inside the lodge of the chief sampling fingersful of a greasy gray meat and fermented corn mush. The chief sat in the middle of the lodge surrounded by half a dozen of the elders of the tribe, each wrapped in a buffalo robe painted with the dyes of roots. The old men stared suspiciously at the whites, while the chief assumed an aloof attitude, as if he had nothing to fear from the Mormons.

The parley was conducted in fragments using the universal sign language, the finger talk of the Indians, the Spanish Shadrach knew and the French picked up by Thomas Morse on the border of his native Vermont.

They were assisted by a thin Shoshone slave named Kaleesh, a girl the chief had captured on a raid into California. Kaleesh had the look of a frightened rabbit and was thin and drawn from life as of a slave in the Indian camp. She spoke enough Spanish to be able to communicate with the Saints.

From the Canadian trappers who had taken the beaver from the Rocky Mountains, the chief had learned a guttural dialect.

"*Comme s'appelez vous?*" Morse asked him.

"*Je m'appellez Walkara,*" the chief said proudly announcing his name. "*Como se llama sus gentes?*"

"He wants to know the name of your tribe," Kaleesh translated.

"We are the Latter Day Saints," Shadrach answered. "We are three thousand strong and growing in numbers with each passing day."

"Santees?" Walkara mused as the information was translated.

The elders of the tribe were visibly disturbed over the vast numbers of people pouring into their hunting grounds. Their faces darkened and their voices lowered as they instinctively fingered the knives all had thrust in their belts.

"Our Chief Brigham Young desires to live in peace with the Utes," Shadrach said hastily. "There is plenty of water and grass for all of us and we will show our appreciation to our brothers by gifts of horses and cattle."

This offer didn't mollify the Utes at all. Apparently they had received the same offer from others passing their way.

"We are grateful to see you because we believe your tribe to be the descendents of the Lamanites who were descended from travelers from across the sea. Because some of them fell into evil ways, they were punished by a darkening of their skins. In the coming days, a great upheaval will be visited on the earth and your people will be their heirs to all that is bountiful. Until that day comes, we wish to live in harmony with you as brothers and equals."

This was laboriously translated to the Utes and they seemed much more interested in this talk. They had never heard a white man state such a novel relationship before.

"We wish to live amongst our new-found brothers, to teach you to farm and raise stock and to present you with gifts of cloth and many other things."

"Muskets? Can you give us many muskets?" Walkara asked cautiously.

"Yes, certainly. Other whites will come this way who do not feel the brotherly love for you that we do. They will want to kill you and drive us from this land. With the muskets you can ally yourselves against them."

This news caused a ripple of excitement as it was translated.

"In the meantime we will preach to you about the restored priesthood," Shadrach continued, pressing his advantage. There are many things to learn about the Kingdoms of Heaven, the principles of eternal progression, the plurality of marriage. . . ."

"Wagh!" said Walkara, slapping the ashes off the knees of his leggings. *"Les Santees son tres bons!"*

"He says the Saints are very good and welcome here," Kaleesh said. "He has no use for the Catholic priests but with the Santees he is much more comfortable."

Thomas Morse was dispatched back to Salt Lake City to return with gifts for the tribe, but Shadrach remained behind to learn the language of the Utes and to ingratiate himself with them. He would not be able to keep his promise to his family to return before the winter set in, but it was a unique opportunity to observe the Lamanites in their natural state.

The group he had settled with was a small part of the tribe. Apparently Walkara was a most powerful man amongst the Utes. He occupied the most abundant hunting grounds and fished in the fullest rivers. He was the recipient of gifts and tribute from the other tribes and had the most slaves in his camp.

Walkara was the foremost in a large family of many brothers, all of whom seemed covetous of his chiefship. He had at least five wives that Shadrach could count and a number of concubines. Kaleesh, his translator, was one of them. His other wives were contemptuous of the young girl and beat her frequently around the face, perhaps hoping to spoil her beauty.

The Utes prized strength in their leaders and Walkara was the strongest. He strutted about the camp, ready to menace anyone who didn't yield him the proper respect. His main fame was his reputation as a horse thief. He bragged to Shadrach of his many expeditions to Mexico and California. He would always return with hundreds of captured ponies.

Bragging was the chief's pasttime and the presence of an white guest in his camp added to Walkara's prestige. Whenever neighboring tribes would send representatives, Walkara would always throw a feast and Shadrach would be the main attraction. As the carved stone calumet was passed around the fire and the Indians puffed on the smoking herbs, Walkara would brag about his friendship with the great Santee chief, Brigham Young, and the gifts he soon would be receiving.

During the summer and fall, the Utes lived on the cool mountain slopes covered with twisted pines and hemlocks, in valleys deep with grasses and bright yellow flowers. The turning of the aspen trees into shimmering golden signals of winter sent the Utes into the lower elevations of their range. The lodges were folded and loaded into travois, which were dragged behind the spotted ponies as the tribe moved in a talkative caravan to their winter home.

They settled on the banks of a shallow stream in a sunlit canyon. A variegated sandstone butte rose above them and from its heights Shadrach could see a vast maze of canyons which stretched out to the horizon.

The winter went slowly, with Shadrach spending the evenings around the fire telling the stories of the founding of the church and its beliefs. Walkara and several braves made a horse-thieving expedition into New Mexico, but came back empty-handed.

The failure of the hunt and the idleness of the camp put Walkara in a black mood. He began beating Kaleesh more often and then started on his wives. Shadrach, too, was growing restless and he determined to liven up the winter with some further exploration.

"My chief is most anxious to find the cities of the ancient ones who were gone long before your people can remember," Shadrach said one night. "Do you know of the existence of any of these ruined cities?"

"Of course. I know many," Walkara grunted. "What would your chief pay for a sight of these?"

"Fifty horses," Shadrach offered.

"For a hundred horses I will show you a place only I know about," Walkara said. "The stone houses of the ancients. I will take you there. I have been in this camp too long."

For several days they traveled into the interior of Walkara's domain. Their trail wound through canyon after canyon, forded river after river. They crossed forested plateaus and led their horses over breathtaking stone bridges which would have arched over the Nauvoo Temple with room to spare. Had Walkara fallen to his death from one of these natural spans, Shadrach might have well jumped after him, for he would never find his way back through this maze of stone.

Walkara had brought only his youngest wife and Kaleesh with them. They traveled quickly eating only the parched corn and the jerked elk meat they carried in buckskin parfleches, the wallets of the Utes.

They had traveled far when their way was blocked by a huge dome of red rock which extended a thousand feet above them. Shadrach could see no way around it, but Walkara led them onto it. For half a day they climbed a hairline trail which curved around the mountainside. The Englishman leaned in his saddle towards the edge of the mountain, not watching as his horse kicked rocks over the edge of the trail, the stones disappearing soundlessly to the valley below.

By nightfall they crested the ridge and Shadrach found himself in a delightsome place. Instead of being barren, the crest of the dome was pleasantly forested with spicy smelling pine which grew undisturbed on the back of the mountain. Several springs fed a small lake where the fish jumped to feed on the evening flies. The game seemed plentiful and were such strangers to men that Walkara was able to shoot a doe that approached within twenty paces of their horses.

"I shall call this place Eden," Shadrach said as they roasted the haunches of the doe that evening. "I have rarely seen such a comforting place."

"Only you and I have seen it," Walkara said. "My grandfather showed it to me. He would not show it even to his own son."

Shadrach slept fitfully that night, on the eve of a great discovery. He was tormented by the sound of Walkara making love to his young wife not ten paces from his own bed.

The next morning Walkara led the Englishman to the back edge of the dome. The cliff on this side was even steeper than the one they had come up so they left their horses on the top and made their way down on foot, clinging to the rock walls with their fingers.

Beneath an outcropping of rock, hidden to all but the most careful climbers was a ledge of rock. Walkara pointed proudly to the ledge. Hidden in the shadows at the rear of the ledge was a small tower made of stone. Shadrach's heart almost stopped despite his exertion.

The lost city of the Lamanites!

A group of huts built of flat gray stones were hidden behind the tower and Shadrach climbed to them. Climbing through a hole in the top of the tower, Shadrach lit a small candle and peered around. Instead of the engraved tablets he had hoped for, or intricate carvings on the walls, the stone chamber yielded nothing except for a few scraps of woven matting.

"I've found it! The Great Temple of the Lamanites!" Shadrach roared in the hollow chamber. "This is living proof that the ancient tribes of Israel did come to this continent!"

He looked up through the square entry hole. Walkara was staring down at him with a sad look on his face. "These Lamanites could not have been a smart people if they lived in a dark place like this," he said. "I prefer it up above where the sun is bright."

The remainder of their time on the mountain was spent lounging in the sun and strolling in the forests. The dome was the one place in the west winter seemed to have missed. The days were warm and balmy, the nights pleasant. For the first time that Shadrach could remember his time was his own. There was no task to perform, no mission to accomplish. He could spend his hours breathing the fresh air and watching the sun cross the sky.

One afternoon he walked through a meadow with Kaleesh who was teaching him the names of the wild plants growing on the plateau. They were startled to hear the sound of laughter coming from a nearby stream. Stalking through the woods they saw Walkara and his wife frolicking naked in the brook. Shadrach felt Kaleesh's eyes upon him.

"Why have you never wanted a woman during your stay with the Utes?" she asked him bluntly. "Do you not know you are the butt of jokes from the women?"

"I have wanted a woman, it's true, but I have been reluctant to advance upon the women of the tribe for fear of causing offense."

"You cause the offense of ignoring them. They think you are too good for them."

"That was not my intention."

"And what about me? Would you like to lie with me?"

Shadrach blushed at the woman's forwardness. Not even Polly would have broached the subject so broadly. "I do not know what claims Walkara might have upon you?" he said, glancing in the direction of the stream."

"I am his property, scarcely of concern to him," she said. "Any of his tribe can have their way with me. The boys use me when they like. I am given to guests of his. Why do you think I was brought along on this journey?"

Shadrach cleared his throat and looked around. There was nothing more to be said and they both understood it. Kaleesh walked into a stand of aspens which closed around them like a shroud. In the sun-dappled grass she pulled her grease-stained buckskin dress over her head and smoothed it out, pressing down the grasses around her. She straightened out her long black hair and knelt on the buckskin, her brown skin glistening in the sunlight.

Kneeling in front of her, Shadrach held her bare shoulders in his hands. Her skin was warm from the sun falling upon her and smoother than any he had touched since he left his wives' beds. Looking at her body he noted she was still lean but she felt firm and robust in his hands. She boldly snatched his broadcloth shirt from his pants and unhinged the buckler of his belt.

"I wonder if Lamanites kiss?" he said out loud as he pulled her toward him. He placed his lips awkwardly on hers and she nipped back at him as a horse might nip his leg. Her musky scent was intoxicating and more powerful than any perfume he had ever smelled. It stirred the deepest primitive instincts in him. His mind was clouded by a fog of desire that isolated him with this woman in the sunny meadow.

He was out of his shirt and trousers in an instant and she lay back on her dress to receive him. They made love in the sunlight as freely as the world around them. Shadrach was afraid the small woman would not be able to stand his weight but she had apparently had rougher lovers than he and she thumped him vigorously. Her muscular little body clung to his, urging him on.

When Shadrach had finished with her, he looked up to see Walkara and his woman standing above them, smiling widely.

"You see, Santee," he said. "This is a special place."

Shadrach could sense something was wrong in the camp before they had reached the shores of the stream. Living in the wilderness had sharpened his appreciation of the spirit world.

Evil emanations hung above the tribe like a thundercloud.

When Shadrach rode into camp the scowls of the Utes made him think they had lost a battle. The people were in a terrible mood and he feared a war with the Saints had broken out. Kaleesh came running to him and pulled him from his horse.

"The chief's youngest son is dead," she informed him. "You must stay in your lodge until this is over."

"I must go to Walkara and express my condolences as one brother to another.

"No, the Utes turn into animals around death. They will kill the first stranger who comes into ther midst as a way to appease the gods. Do not remind them that you are not far removed from a stranger."

For three days and nights Shadrach hid within the buffalo hide tent that served as his home, shivering without a telltale fire, eating the cold meal cakes and meat that Kaleesh managed to bring him. Outside the Utes wailed in a nonstop dirge of mourning, crying out in awful shouts as they wound their way through the camp. The few glimpses he got of Walkara found the chief to be disheveled and overwrought.

On the third day of the mourning, a horrible cry went through the camp. A small band of captured Indians wearing the woven reed clothing of the Shoshone were brought into camp. Walkara was summoned from his lodge bearing a war club. Before Shadrach's eyes, the Ute chief struck down a young woman who had been the first in camp. In his rage, Walkara dashed the brains from a second captive and then a third as the others dropped to their knees as if expecting this kind of fate at his hands.

Shadrach was sickened by what he had seen and resolved to leave the village if he could to preserve his own brain pan. The killings of the slaves seemed to ease the grief of the Utes, for their was little lamenting after their bodies were dragged away.

On the fourth day, Walkara visited the lodge of Shadrach and slumped wearily in a skin seat hung from the side of the lodge.

"It is passed. It is over," he said briefly. "My son has been buried."

"I grieve with you for your son and I am reminded of my own whom I wish to see," Shadrach said carefully. "I will soon be taking my leave of you."

"The Santees and the Utes both cleave to their families and that is good," Walkara said. "Do not forget that your president owes me one hundred ponies."

"I will not forget and I offer you twenty-five more for the slave Kaleesh."

"If I still owned her, I would give her to you. But she belongs to my youngest son now."

"But he is dead."

"She has been buried with him to serve him on the other side."

This news shook the Englishman but he showed no emotion.

"Do not forget my muskets, either," Walkara said in farewell.

Shadrach tied his horses to a laurel bush well off the trail well away from the village. Doubling back, he swung wide along the base of the cliff so as not to be seen by the Utes.

The grave of the chief's son was on a high crest of a mountain, a difficult climb from the stream. The snows of winter still clung to the trail. It was unlikely that any of the superstitious people would be visiting the mountain.

A pile of huge boulders marked the burial pit. The stones were placed to keep the wolves from attacking the body, for the Utes felt a mutilated body would remain so in the afterlife. Shadrach stood above the grave and said a prayer over the soul of Kaleesh. He swore that he would undergo baptism for her to save her soul to join him in eternity.

"Is that you, Santee?" a familiar voice called from inside the rockpile.

"The great Jehovah, is that you, Kaleesh? How be it that you are still alive."

"I am buried alive to preserve my body for serving his corpse," she replied. "They want me whole in the afterlife. Do you have some water? I am thirsty."

Shadrach sat on the rocks and peered into the darkness. He could barely make out the flicker of her dark eyes inside the sepulchre. He poured a trickle of water down the hole and heard her greedily licking the water from the rocks.

"How are you feeling?"

"I am hungry," she answered, "and this boy's body is beginning to stink."

"Hold on. I shall prise these rocks from over you."

"Do not disturb them, Santee. If they catch you it will mean your death as well as mine."

"I have seen enough barbarity," Shadrach said. "I can stand no more."

One by one, he lifted the stones it had taken many men to place until the skinny girl was ready to wriggle free. When she had scrambled out, she stood lookout while he carefully replaced the stones until no sign of disturbance was visible.

"Come. I will send you back to your people," he told her.

"My people are dead. I will be your slave."

Chapter Sixteen

Polly Halloran Tompkins blew the steam off her spoonful of watery barley soup she held in her red fist. The spoon was loaded to the brim with the thin broth and as she moved it to her mouth several drops splattered on the table. The broth was not nutritious, but it was filling. To cool it Polly drew the liquid into her mouth with a slurp.

The noise was magnified by the dead silence of the rest of the table. Polly took another spoonful and slurped again. Looking up she saw Rachel sitting rigidly on the other side of the table staring scornfully at her. Sarah averted her eyes while Ham watched the developing argument.

"What are you staring daggers at, sister?" Polly asked.

"Would you mind not spilling your soup all over the table while it is in transit?" Rachel said tightly. "And when you place it inside your gaping jaws would you do so quietly?"

The anger flashed in Polly's eyes. She had suffered under the disapproval of Rachel long enough. "Whenever I need a lesson in etiquette, I shall ask for it from someone who has a hint of it herself."

"And what do you mean by that?"

"It seems to me that manners is a way of living that makes it easier to get along with your housemates and to make things smooth in society. For the six months you've been out in this hard country you've done your best to make life intolerable for everyone around you."

"I resent that! I've worked as hard as anyone out here."

"And you keep on working when decent folks are trying to eat. I may not have been brought up in a manor, but I know that everyone's digestion is put off when someone at the table is harping all the time."

"I do not harp! And I have been exceedingly tolerant of the coarse manners some of us have shown. This is the first time I have spoken up."

"You've spoken up with your eyes, sister. You're a regular chorus with your eyes!"

"I'm not going to sit idly by while my house . . ."

"Your house? My hands shaped these walls themselves!"

"While we were stranded in the plains."

"Don't go giving me your hard luck story again," Polly said pushing back from the table. "Everyone in this valley has a hard luck story, else they wouldn't be here. And most everyone has the common courtesy to keep it to themselves."

Rachel clenched her fists into tight balls and rose from the table. The tears exploded from her face and she ran under the gray wool blanket which separated her sleeping area from the rest of the house. The adobe home was one large rectangular room filled with the possessions the Tompkins family had managed to salvage on their journey. The rafters of the home hung with drying onions and peppers and small sacks of grain safely out of the reach of the mice.

Sarah gave Polly a sympathetic nod and then disappeared behind the blanket to comfort her sister. "I can't stand it anymore, being cooped up with that shanty-Irish charwoman," Rachel cried.

"Listen, Miss Highborn. You're under the same roof I am so don't put on any airs," Polly shouted back.

"I won't let her ruin what little civility we have left," Rachel sobbed. "I hate her. Hate her!"

"Hold your tongue, sister. That's far enough," Sarah said with a menacing ring in her voice. "If there is a fault in the house it is your own sin of pride. Do you think that table is your own? Or this house? Or our husband, for that matter? All these things you have consecrated when you left the material world behind."

"I don't have the strength to take the burden anymore. Our lives have been sliding downhill for a decade and I can't see bottom yet!"

"Then this is the time when you must hold the tightest," Sarah said, emerging from behind the partition.

A better rapport existed between Sarah and Polly. The first wife of Shadrach hugged the third in a sisterly embrace.

"You have to pardon my sister. The years have been hard on all of us. Her fuse has been cut too short recently."

"The fault is my own," Polly said. "I should learn forbearance for it will be a skill that will come in handy in these lean times. I sometimes wonder if I am making a poor Saint for my selfishness. The spirit of cooperation and consecration comes hard when I have spent my life trying to attract a few worldly possessions rather than give them away.''

"Don't be troubled by human nature, sister," Sarah comforted her. "In this bleak land, we will not be often tempted by worldly things."

The temptation of luxurious goods was the last worry of the Saints as they struggled to build their capital city. The grand designs they envisioned were replaced by the necessity of raising food and providing shelter for the thousands of immigrants entering the new land.

The unyielding soil of the valley was not kind to the crops the Saints planted. Many seedlings were drowned in the flood of irrigation water provided by the inexperienced farmers. Next, the hot sun of the summer scorched the life from the young shoots leaving them brown and listless.

In the late summertime, a giant swarm of locust loomed up through the northern passes and descended on the valley. The first warning of their appearance was the sound many likened to the crackling of a prairie fire or the rustling of a stiff wind through the dried leaves of a northern forest. The first of the dull brown grasshoppers fell on the fields like the first warning drops of a rainstorm and then a general deluge of the vermin followed. Like a wispy brown cloud, the swarm hovered over the young city as the field workers turned out to pick the bugs from the nearly ripened grain.

Women wearing shawls over their heads to keep the loathsome creatures out of their hair picked the voracious beasts from the stalks of grain and crushed them underfoot. Overcoming their reluctance to touch the fragile insects, their rage at seeing the harvest consumed before their eyes drove them into a frenzy. They soon were smashing the heads of the locust between their fingertips, squeezing the brown juice from the papery bodies.

But the pestilence kept coming. The entire community had to be mobilized. Hundreds of Saints poured into the fields armed with brooms and shovels. The crops on the edge of the fields were burned in the hopes of stopping the advance, but the locust leaped over the flames and moved on to the next field. The appetites of the insects were so great that they were able to strip a field as if a battalion of cavalry had trampled it under foot. The food supply for the coming weather was threatened.

If the black cloud of locust was the agent of the devil then the capricious God who had watched over the progress of the Saints dispatched a white cloud to the rescue of the crops.

A seagull, a great white quarrelsome bird, landed in the most ravaged field and speared a grasshopper with its sharp beak. Its brothers and sisters followed, spinning wildly in midair to catch the flying locusts, or swallowing them whole on the ground. The air was soon crowded with flocks of the white and dirty brown gulls devouring the vermin in the same way the grasshoppers had attacked the fields.

And then they were gone. They had arisen magically from the shores of the Great Salt Lake, had eaten their fill and then departed. Unfortunately for the Saints, the birds left before they had eaten all of the grasshoppers, but they had eaten enough to save the harvest.

Rachel Tompkins stood in the field at the end of the week-long siege. Her face was tanned by the clouds of dust that had risen from the beating of the fields and when she took her bonnet off, the dark demarcation of the soot from the fires contrasted with the pale skin of her forehead. She watched the retreating gulls and twisted her foot on the body of the last of the locusts.

"God continues to slap us in the face and then give us a pat on the head," she said, savoring the irony of their situation. "I hope in my lifetime he makes up his mind about us. I would like to know where he stands before I go off to bask in that opinion for eternity."

A different and more dangerous plague of locust descended on the valley of the Saints after 1849. Brigham Young had chosen a remote valley in the middle of nowhere to build his Zion hoping this barren land would be bypassed by civilization. The discovery of gold in California in 1849 brought a wildfire of immigration by Easterners anxious to grab the yellow metal. The 49'ers chose two ways of traveling to San Francisco. The first was by boat around South America. The other path cut straight through Salt Lake City.

The Saints had barely put down their roots in the valley before the California-bound travelers began passing through.

At first they came in small groups of half a dozen men who were mounted on fast horses racing toward the gold. Later they came in wagons bringing their families and livestock.

The Saints reacted fearfully to the newcomers. The wagon trains would recruit their stock in the valley, eating up the precious forage. The leaders of the church watched the growing numbers of settlers and worried that if California filled up, the eyes of the Gentiles would turn to Deseret.

"I distrust these Pukes who rest their stock here before pushing on to the Sierras," Rachel said at the Tompkins table one evening. "I believe they are spying out our land and will return with the army to drive us from our homes."

"I understand Sam Brannan has made a fortune from the gold fields and refuses to give any of it to the church," Sarah said. "Some of the brethren from the Mormon Battalion were among the first to discover Gold on the Sacramento River. They have been corrupted by the fever like that damned apostate Sam Brannan, may he burn in Hell! Thank God, Brigham was wise enough to keep us here in Deseret away from the temptation of California. Nothing good will ever come of that country by the Pacific. It is filled with greed."

"I have been offered a position by some of the brethren who are opening a store to service the travelers to California. My experience with the quartermasters in Fort Leavenworth will prove valuable," Polly informed the diners. "I can be of service both to the Church and to this family."

A chilly silence greeted this news as Rachel turned to her.

"Cooperation with the Pukes smacks of treason to me."

"If we provide the Pukes with fresh stores we can turn a handsome profit and move them on more quickly at the same time," Polly said, defending herself. "The church needs the hard currency to bring immigrants from the East and we might as well take their money before they spend it in California."

"Over my dead body will you sell anything to the Pukes," Rachel said, flaring. "The honor of our husband and the memory of our family precludes it!"

"Our husband isn't around to have a say in the matter and you both have more family growing in your bellies who are going to have to eat this winter. Do you think we have grown enough food to make it on our own? We are going to need money—and the Pukes are going to give it to us!"

*   *   *

The famine was visited on the Saints with the same severity as the locusts. It arrived more slowly but it lingered longer. The harvest had been lean. The freshly cultivated earth was too poor to yield much, and what grew had been consumed by the locust. The barley, the wheat and corn had been stored in the bishop's warehouses for the common use of all the Saints, but there were too many immigrants and too little grain.

The bishops alloted a ration to the families in their wards but as the gray winter wore on, the ration was cut in half and then cut again. The snows cut off the mountain passes to the east and to the west isolating the Saints in the bleak valley.

The Tompkins family planted a crop of turnips, chard and cabbages which they hoped would grow throughout the winter, but a prolonged freeze in January killed off the plants. When the family's supply of cornmeal ran out, Sarah appealed to the bishop for relief, but the man was besieged by pleas from every family in the ward and had to refuse further rations.

Sarah and Rachel had recently borne children, their family biologies separating their deliveries by less than a month. Now they stood by the Dutch oven of the adobe fireplace boiling a buffalo robe in order to scrape the hair from it. When the hide was cleaned it was boiled until it became soft enough to chew, and then it was eaten by all the family.

Ham Tompkins was ill with rickets, which weakened the joints of the children in the community. Skin diseases broke out with alarming frequency and the population became listless from the meager diet.

"They promised our husband we would be taken care of in his absence," Rachel complained as they huddled around the oven one night. "Yet where is our supply of firewood? The other families in the ward have a gracious plenty and yet we are lacking. Where is the fairness of this?"

"The snow has been too high for the woodchoppers to make much progress," Sarah pointed out. "We will get our cords when the sledges can move again."

Sarah was boiling the hides, which had covered the roof of their home, in order to soak them into a glue they could eat. The wet smell of the hides made the room smell like a slaughterhouse but the scent only whetted the appetites of the family.

"The head of my baby is soft," Rachel said with alarm. "I can feel by thumb indent its skull when I press on it!"

"The skulls of all children are soft," Sarah said quickly, knowing how prone to panic her sister was. "But pray you, don't press too hard or you'll leave a permanent indentation."

The door opened and Polly entered, pushed by a swirl of snow which followed her from the black night. She shook the snow off her ragged cloak and warmed herself by the fire as puddles formed under her thin boots.

"Whew! You should've given that buffalo a bath before you biled him," Polly said cheerfully.

Her sense of humor elicited no reaction from the two hungry women.

"We had some good fortune today, darlings," Polly continued.

"I saw a man I once knew in Fort Leavenworth and he gave me some flour."

"Was he one of your customers, there?" Rachel asked bitingly.

"He's a winter Mormon, now," Polly said, ignoring the jab. "He's staying in the valley professing the faith, but in the spring I expect he'll move on to the gold fields."

The women hesitated about whether to use the flour.

"Let's make Lumpy Dick!" Ham pleaded, not shy about his hunger.

This solved the question and the women cleared the stove to make the dumplinglike meal of water and flour called Lumpy Dick. To enhance the meal, Polly pulled two freshly skinned carcasses out of her cloak.

"Meat!" Sarah said. "What are they? Rabbits?"

"Rats," Polly said. "Bishop Warner has been trapping them in the grainery. He has not forgotten our need."

The drive of their hunger was so great that the rats were quickly filleted and fried up in the flour. It would be the first fresh meat they had in two months. Reaching one last time into her cloak, Polly produced a blue bottle capped by a cork.

"Colic medicine for your babies," she announced. "They are crying for all the wrong reasons."

Sarah rushed to her and embraced her.

"Apologizing is not a trait that comes easily for me," Rachel said, extending her hand. "But I have said some mean and contemptible things to you and I'd like to set them right."

Polly pumped the hand of the stern woman.

"You're a hard woman to unthaw, Rachel," she said. "Come talk to me by the fire while the cakes fry up so we'll make sure you don't freeze again."

The spring had brought torrents of water rushing from the mountains flooding the irrigation ditches and spilling over the muddy fields when a party with several horsemen in it stopped before the Tompkins house. The horses were fetlock-deep in the mire and the leader of the party had to leap from his mount onto the front doorstoop of the house to avoid soiling his recently newbought clothes.

His heavy pounding brought Polly to the door where she stared suspiciously at the bearded stranger in the white linen shirt and the black homespun jacket purchased at the Mercantile Association.

Shadrach was hard to disguise even in a beard and new clothes but even so, he startled the rest of his family when he picked Polly up and carried her into the house like a highwayman kidnapping a victim. Pandemonium broke out as three wives and a son embraced their husband and father while showing him their new arrivals. Shadrach reverently examined his new babies and felt the ribs of his family.

"That was the last time I will leave you," he vowed. "I am now determined to tend my own garden and let the rest of the world pass me by."

"We will be pleased to have you, husband," Rachel said, speaking for the ladies. "You have been sorely missed."

"I have a surprise for all of you that will bring much credit to this house," Shadrach said, stepping back out through the door.

He returned pushing a woman before him. The members of his family stared at the bronze-skinned woman who stood awkwardly in the doorway, terrified of going inside.

"This is Kaleesh who we have given the Christian name of Mariah," Shadrach announced. "I want you to take her to the bosom of our family like one of our own."

"Welcome, Mariah," Sarah said, mustering up as much enthusiasm as she could. "Please come in."

The Indian girl stepped over the threshold and onto the packed clay floor of the strange dwelling. She was highly uncomfortable in her scratchy black dress that rustled noisily like the leaves of a sycamore tree each time she moved. The strange underclothes they wore under these dresses constricted her body. The covers these whites wore over their hair both restricted her vision and her hearing at the same time. Her horror of meeting these whites increased as she saw them staring at the muddy moccasins she wore under her skirts. Had she broken some taboo the whites kept?

"The ladies at Spanish Fork were kind enough to contribute some civilized clothes for her to wear," Shadrach explained. "But they had no shoes to spare."

"Is Mariah going to be a student in our community learning the ways of our church before she goes back to her people?" Rachel asked solicitously.

"We are her people now."

"Oh, is she a ward of the church?"

"She is my wife," Shadrach said easily. "I have just made my report to President Young and then was sealed to Mariah with his blessing this afternoon."

"You have taken her as your wife? How could you do such a thing?" Rachel asked. "Are you going to mingle our blood with hers?"

"I have been living with her as man and wife in the wildnerness. President Young was pleased with my decision. He believes it will bind us into a closer alliance with the Lamanites."

"And what of your alliance with us?" Polly asked, taking Rachel's side. "How do you expect us to receive the news of this new dalliance?"

"With good faith," Shadrach said, noticing that Mariah was observing the opposition and anger of his wives. "For you have but to accept this with good grace."

"I should say not! Ham, leave us to a private counsel," Rachel said as she waited for the boy to leave the room. "Husband. I shall not share a bed with you if you will sleep with that Lamanite wench!"

"Nor will I," Polly added. "The good Lord knows where she has been before your attention."

"For shame on you both. Is this a greeting for our husband and our new sister?" Sarah said, moving to the side of Mariah. "It is our bound duty to welcome them both joyously."

She was about to embrace the Indian when she was repelled, even in her zeal, by the smell of the maiden. She delicately sniffed her own husband who had been without the benefit of civilization for almost a year.

"That is, we will welcome both of you into our home after a good scrubbing down with lye soap."

Chapter Seventeen

Ham Tompkins fidgeted nervously in his seat on a bench in the family's kitchen. His aunt Rachel was conducting a lesson for the children who lived in their neighborhood. Outside the spring rains were pouring down and Ham could only think of joining his friends in fishing the streams swollen by the melt-off.

At thirteen he felt too old for school. What did a priest of the church need to be squinting at a copy of McGuffey's Reader for? Besides, he knew the reader by heart, it being one of the few primers to make the trip from the east. He idly opened a page and looked at the first sentence:

> *Beautiful hands are those that do,*

He closed his eyes and finished it from memory;

> *Deeds that are noble, good and true,*
> *Beautiful feet are those that go,*
> *Swiftly to lighten another's woe.*

The education of the children of the Saints was first carried on by women like Rachel who conducted the classes in their homes. Schoolbooks and primers had not been a survival item when their trek was made and the few that existed were ragged from use. Many of the books printed in Babylon seemed unfit for the children of Zion and religious tracts were substituted in their place. Rachel would gather the young around her, some of whom could not remember Nauvoo, and tell and retell the story of how the persecutions of the Saints began. This she believed to be a fundamental part of the children's education.

"What do you call her?" the young girl asked Ham as they walked from the home after the lessons had ended. "Do you call her your mother?"

Hezibah Clayton had been dogging Ham ever since the lessons began. She lived with her family in a nearby house and believed that just because their fathers were both English, she and Ham should be close friends. The pudgy girl with the complexion which stayed red the year round was making life unbearable for him. The rest of the children his age laughed at her broad accents and he did not want to become their target by associating with her.

"What do I call whom?" he asked testily.

"Sister Rachel. Our teacher."

"Her? She's my aunt."

"But she's your father's wife, too."

"And my mother's sister."

"What do you call Sister Polly?"

"She's my aunt, too."

"But she's not your mother's blood kin."

"She's my aunt all the same," Ham said impatiently trying to outpace the girl. "And what I call her is none of your business."

"My father says you Plurals are a disgrace to the church."

"Who cares what your father said? We'll settle that score in heaven. The followers of the Principal have the first crack."

"I can have just as good a place in heaven as you plurals have," Hezibah said angrily, "and there are no two ways about it. My father said so."

"Your father? If he wasn't so poor he'd have as many wives as he could!"

"My father is not poor. He keeps my mother in better clothes than your mothers have! He could have as many wives as he wanted. My mother said she'd leave him if he ever thought of marrying again."

Ham felt he had gotten the best part of the argument and he used this point to shrug and walk away leaving the girl behind.

The families where plural marriage was practiced made up not one household out of ten, but the numbers of church leaders following the Principle was out of proportion to these numbers. If there was disapproval among the brethren for the practice of plural marriage it wasn't voiced loudly. In the valley the practice was equated with true belief.

"My father says that the children of plural marriages are bastards!" Hezibah yelled in frustration. "Do you know what that means?"

* * *

By 1852, the celestial city was beginning to take shape. The adobe wall which had been built to protect the settlement now had wide avenues like Temple and Main Streets running out of it, north and south. Numerical streets like First and Second Streets ran east and west, forming the planned grid pattern.

When the Saints celebrated their fifth year in the valley, their lot was beginning to improve. Salt Lake City was beginning to grow. Adobe and pine buildings were springing up away from the center part of town. Brigham Young had constructed a home called the Beehive House not far from the temple site and conducted his business there. A grist mill and an armory was established nearby. Not far away the houses of his close associates had been constructed and the trees which lined the broad, dusty streets were beginning to grow.

Not far away, a group of tents had sprung up around the Mercantile where the Saints were able to buy clothing and utensils brought in from St. Louis.

Some brought chickens or garden vegetables to barter for their goods. Credit was extended to those without anything to barter.

Oxen plowed the fields surrounding the town and hauled the pine logs still smelling of resin down from the canyons. A sawmill had been constructed and the first wood frame houses had been built for Saints wealthy enough to buy this luxury.

Immigration was the chief concern of the Saints and during the season when the snows did not block the mountains, wagon train after wagon train crossed the Wasatch Mountains to deposit a fresh cargo of pilgrims in the promised land. A good many of these new Saints were from Europe, not only English but Scandinavian, Swiss, French and Danish families who heeded the words of the missionaries and had been transported to the strange land.

These people were welcomed in the new land by the established Saints who were now able to help them settle with more ease than the first companies. Salt Lake City had such a burgeoning population that many of the newcomers were shunted straight through to settlements like Ogden to the north and Fort Utah on the Provo River. There they would get a real taste of pioneering.

On the weekends all the city worshipped and then turned out to see the drills of the Nauvoo Legion. The defense of their homes was no longer debated in this wild land. Every able-bodied man and boy was expected to perform military duty. On the plains outside the city, the cavalry and infantry wheeled and paraded, ready to meet the enemy from within or without. Although there was not enough powder and shot for the militia to take target practice, the drilling went on as planned.

In order to manufacture the powder and shot needed to repel an army of Pukes, President Young ordered his scouts to find the necessary lead, charcoal and sulphur to manufacture their ordinance. A supply of lead was found, but it had such a high silver content it was useless.

A Swiss chemist arrived in Utah and promised to make a passable saltpeter out of hog's urea. He was later discovered to be working on a distillery and was asked to leave the territory.

For the Tompkins family, the early fifties was a period of consolidation. Weary from his missions, Shadrach turned his energies to providing for his family.

His first order of business was to build a new addition to his house from sun-dried adobes. He made sure each wife had her own private room and threw a room for himself in for good measure. Privacy was becoming a rare item in his household.

The business of the household was carried on in an orderly fashion. The family rose shortly after dawn and enjoyed the morning breakfast together. In accordance with the Words of Wisdom set down by the Prophet Joseph Smith, no coffee or tea was served in the house. The family avoided serving hot foods as much as possible and their breads were always served cold. The family avoided eating meat dishes, for beef and pork were rare in the valley. Chickens scratching in the back of the house had their necks twisted and provided the main course for the family's meals.

The hardships had toughened Shadrach and his family. A new air of formality took over the house. At the dinner table Shadrach presided at the head of the pine table while the wives sat on the sides. A smaller table was reserved for the children who generally ate before their parents.

Shadrach had begun a business hauling freight between Salt Lake City and the southern settlements. He was in partnership with several old friends from the Sons of Dan and had borrowed his share of the capital for the venture from Brigham Young.

Polly worked a full day at the Mercantile keeping the inventories and managing the bookwork, often arriving home after the sun had set. Rachel divided her time between a wool spinning venture she had organized in their home and her duties as a schoolteacher. Sarah worked at the Relief Society tending the needs of the Saints who had fallen on hard times, and at the Church tithing office where she helped with the job of administering the state of Deseret.

After a day's work for Deseret, the family turned its attention to the home. Shadrach had the constant job of building luxuries for the Tompkins home like the two-holer outhouse which stood twenty paces behind the house.

The women divided the chores of the house between themselves. At first, they rotated the jobs of cooking and cleaning but certain skills gravitated to those who did them well. After sampling Polly's cooking, an uninspired cuisine of boiled meat and vegetables, the kitchen became the domain of the two sisters. Polly was clever with her hands and attended to the chores of mending the family's clothing and utensils. Mariah, as the junior wife, was given the cleaning duties which included scouring out the cast iron cookware with sand, and sweeping out the grit which constantly blew off the plains into the loose seals of the windows and doors. Of all the women, Mariah worked the hardest. Her previous employment as a slave for the Utes comforted the family's conscience regarding their use of her.

Dinnertime, after the grace was said and coarse food had been ladled onto the tin plates, was a time of gossip about the progress of Deseret. The talks aways centered around the influential members of the community.

"I heard that Brigham is sorely vexed at Brother Markham," Polly volunteered. "That lowers his stock in this city."

"It must be because he falls asleep so easily in the Tabernacle," Sarah said, referring to the small assembly hall where services and meetings were held.

"He falls asleep because his wives are always fighting at home," Rachel pointed out.

"None of those are the reasons for Brigham's displeasure," Shadrach confided. "Brother Markham has not been turning over an honest 10 percent of his income to the tithing office.''

"Now all of you stop this idle gossip," Sarah said. "I'll check at the tithing office tomorrow and find out the truth.''

A full range of topics occupied the family as they tossed some pine logs into the fireplace after the meal. Most important were the rumors of what the Pukes were up to in Washington and Missouri. Had they forgotten the Mormons? Or were they plotting to seek them out and destroy them? The situation of the immigrants pouring into the valley troubled the Tompkins. Food was a problem. There was little work for the people to do. Worse, many of the new immigrants could speak no English. Rachel feared that so many foreigners would ruin the perfectness of Salt Lake City.

When the fire burned low, the delicate choice of a night's partner for Shadrach was decided. An informal consensus based on desire often dictated his choice. Shadrach divided his nights among his wives in order to prevent jealousy and disharmony. An unofficial order of rotation allowed him to spend one night a week with each of them with three days by himself in order to recruit his strength. If a whispered invitation was given to him on his free nights, he could satisfy the wishes of any wife for whom the one night a week was not enough.

The carnal appetites of the family were considerably reduced in proportion to the amount of work they had done during the day. When the business of hauling freight to the south had involved so much work that Shadrach went to sleep in front of the fire, not much in the way of sex was expected of him that night. But other nights the thin walls of the house could not hide the playfulness of a partnership in high spirits.

The most randy of the bunch was always Polly who used her once-a-week by filling the night with bouts of lovemaking. None of the children in the house could have much doubt about what transpired between a man and a woman when the raucous laughter of the Irishwoman rang through at midnight.

More restrained in her exercise was Sarah who gave up her nights with her husband more often. Her desire was for the warmth of his body on the cold nights and for the comfort of his company. Her belief that lust was a flaw in the human spirit restrained her, but in her bed Shadrach found the most peace.

Rachel fluctuated in her passions according to her moods.

On some nights she was melancholy and showed no desire for him, but when her spirits were up she was a tigress on the horsehair ticking and would flay his bones until he cried out for relief.

Mariah had not adjusted well to the new civilization she found herself in. Like a wild animal brought into captivity she was confused and frightened by what she had seen. She tried to hide her anxiety. Her dreams at night made her cry out and Shadrach could not enjoy the pleasure they had felt together when they were in the mountains.

Shadrach's freighting business failed in 1856. The fragile peace between the Saints and the Indians of the southern areas had broken down and the colonization of lower Deseret slowed. The poor management of Shadrach's partners was the final blow and the Englishman found himself with a growing family and without employment.

With a heavy heart he journeyed to the office of Brigham Young to inform him that he was unable to repay his loan for the freighting company. The president was no longer able to spend his hours working at his carpentry. A host of petitioners and visitors filled the waiting room of the Beehive House while a dozen clerks worked at desks lining the room attending to the business of state.

Shadrach had the privilege of being led to a private meeting with the president. Brigham's hair was beginning to gray and the fuzzy mutton chop sideburns had grown into a full beard. The president had put on a little weight since the days of the immigration, but he still stood powerful and energetic as he shook Shadrach's hand in a firm grip.

To the Englishman's surprise, Young waved aside the news of his inability to pay the debt.

"We have much more important business at hand, Brother Tompkins. I have a mission I want you to undertake."

Shadrach gulped. He had resolutely sworn never to assume another mission, having no wish to leave his family again. But he could hardly refuse the man who had waived his debt aside.

"We have set up a revolving account to provide money to bring destitute Saints to Deseret. We call it the Perpetual Immigration Fund," the president continued. "We provide the money to bring a Saint to our city and when he earns his keep out here he pays the money back in order to bring more Saints."

Shadrach nodded. He knew how the fund worked.

"The problem is, the price of a wagon and a team has been driven through the roof by all the Pukes desperate to clamor to California. In order to save money, we have devised a novel way to bring our people to Zion . . . at a bargain price."

"How is that?"

"On foot."

Shadrach stared in disbelief. "A journey of one thousand miles on foot? What about their possessions?"

"We have begun the construction of hand carts, similar to those the porters use in railway stations," Young confided. "We intend to have them pull their belongings out here. Our experiments have shown they can make the trip as fast as a team of oxen."

The president was looking proudly at him.

"And what is it you wish of me?" Shadrach asked hesitantly.

"You are going to do *what*?" Rachel asked in amazement.

"I am going to lead a company of immigrants to Zion on foot," Shadrach said, repeating his announcement to his family.

"Can I go with you, Father?" Ham piped up.

"No and neither can he," Rachel snapped. "What have you done to offend the president that he should always be punishing you with these missions?"

"I view these missions as an honor and not as a punishment. The president has called me his 'strong right arm.' "

"It is certain that you are not his brain, for if you were Deseret would be in grave danger," Rachel said caustically.

"I will be gone for but half a season," Shadrach said. "No more than that, I promise."

"Let him go while his back is still strong. We can manage here," Sarah said. "There could be few missions available in the future."

"Then it is settled," Shadrach said.

One boon I beg of you, husband," Rachel asked. "Please refrain from marrying anyone on this trip!"

Chapter Eighteen

Eighteen years had passed since Shadrach had last seen Keokuk, Iowa. The tiny settlement had grown into a major jumping off place for the western frontier. A row of livery stables and drygoods stores had grown around the main street selling provisions to the settlers who traveled up the Mississippi by steamer. Coming from the isolation and privations of Deseret, Shadrach felt uncomfortable with the bustle and the sophisticated air of Keokuk. The traders and rivermen stared at his homespun clothing and Shadrach realized how many years he had spent in the wilderness.

Brother Moab Wheelock, the son of the man who had welcomed the Englishman to Missouri in 1838, greeted him as he rode in to Keokuk carrying the latest news from the valley. All the Saints were anxious to hear of the progress of Zion and Shadrach filled in the man as much as he could as they rode to the embarkation camp operated by the church on the outskirts of the town.

"I fear ominous forces are gathering against us," Moab confided as they rode. "Two Mormon-baiters are running for the presidency using us as their whipping boys. Buchanan hates us and John Fremont is even worse. The dogs of war are being sicced on us by the Missourians and other enemies in the government."

"On what grounds? Surely we can no longer be a threat to them?"

"They are determined to pursue us to the ends of the earth. They even put a plank in Buchanan's campaign. You have heard of the twin relics of barbarism, have you not?"

"The twin relics of barbarism?"

"Slavery and polygamy. The two institutions Buchanan has campaigned against. They are trying to take the public's attention off the fight between the North and the South over slavery by starting a fight with us."

"Polygamy and slavery?" Shadrach mused. "I can understand the opposition to slavery for no human would ever voluntarily choose to live under such a system, but why single out polygamy? Who does plural marriage hurt? Surely there are worse evils in the world?"

"But none as vulnerable as the Saints. They can pick upon us with impunity. If they attack slavery they offend the southern states. But if they attack us they rally everyone behind them."

The cold fear of a repetition of the episodes in Missouri and Illinois crossed Shadrach's mind. Were the forces of evil conspiring to drive them from their homes one last time?

"This is why we want to get these people to Deseret as soon as we possibly can," Moab said. "If the Pukes attack us, they will first cut off our supply lines."

"Let them come and try!" Shadrach said belligerently. "They will find the helpless Saints have grown claws in the last ten years. We have no place left to run. It is their turn to do the running!"

His brave words began to sound hollow as Shadrach rode into the staging area for the trip to Zion. The camp was in a small grassy knoll surrounded by willow trees. Covering the hill were immigrants living in tents, their bundles of possessions scattered around the site. A babble of foreign tongues greeted his ear.

"Danes. Swiss. Italians. Swedes. People from all over the world," Moab said proudly. "Our missionaries are gathering the tribe wherever they find them."

"I wish they would gather some who spoke English," Shadrach grumbled. "Following directions is hard enough when you speak the tongue."

At the edge of the camp, carpenters and wheelwrights were constructing the carts which would carry the immigrants to the West. Each cart was made from several woods. Stout oak hearts formed the axles and wheel spokes for strength. Lighter hickory formed the bodies of the carts for ease in pulling. The entire contraption weighed one hundred pounds and resembled the carts which hauled the coal about the towns where Shadrach had grown up.

"Each cart costs less than thirty-five dollars," Moab said. "Compare that with over one hundred dollars for a wagon, plus the expense of a team. The man on foot needs only his shoe leather and some barley to keep going. Livestock needs to be grazed and fed and tended to.''

"Oxen are used to pulling their weight. Are people?"

"We have way stations every hundred miles or so to keep them moving. Our routes are charted and well-planned. We know the water, the weather, the times and the fords. Everything has been provided for.''

"I have a bad feeling in the pit of my stomach about this," Shadrach commented. "Every time I see a Saint get confident, I know something is bound to go wrong.''

Shadrach looked over the one hundred expectant travelers facing him on that bright July morning. Their cheerful smiles and happy chatter were the opposite of his own feelings. The difficulties in manufacturing their carts had delayed the start of the journey to midsummer. They would have to hurry to beat the winter snows.

"Brothers and Sisters, I'm not one for speechifying," Shadrach shouted to the assembled company, "but we are embarking on the most glorious journey of your lives. With nothing but our faith to guide us, we will pass out of Babylon and enter into the kingdom of heaven to assist in its building. The road ahead is long and difficult, but with a little shoe leather and a lot of sweat we can cross into the promised land. We are being given a rare opportunity to show our devotion to the Lord by the sweat of our brow. God bless you and let us meet on the banks of the Jordon!''

He paused, waiting for the applause and the amens which he expected to follow. Nothing happened. The crowd stared blankly at him.

"What is the matter? Is something wrong?"

"Those are noble words, brother," a woman said. "But I don't think anyone understood you. They don't speak English so good.''

Shadrach stared at the woman. Even her speech was thickly clogged with an accent he couldn't identify. She stood looking at him. Her jaw was jutted out, her white skin clear. Under a straw bonnet her blonde hair was severely pulled back as her blue eyes sparkled with an intensity as bright as the July sky.

"If you speak their language, ma'am, would you please put it in their words.''

The woman turned to face the crowd and spoke a burst of guttural words with the same intensity Shadrach had spoken.

When she finished the crowd broke out in a polite cheer and clapped their hands together. They then siezed the long handles of the pushcarts and heaved until they began to roll westward on the wagon road.

Each cart was loaded with the household goods and worldly possessions of the immigrants. Bundles of clothing and kitchen implements were tied under tarps while clocks, zithers and the personal items of lifetimes were lashed on the sides. Some of the children of the party were too small to walk and were placed in the shade of blankets on top of the carts. Twenty carts made up the Tompkins company, each one pushed and pulled by four or five of the immigrants. The men dug their heels into the soil and pulled on the long cart handles while another strained his shoulder against the back of the cart. The women stood by the four-foot-tall wheels turning the spokes with their hands.

Slowly, miraculously, the creaking carts rolled along the rough road. Step by step they made their painful way toward the western horizon. The burly Shadrach made his way up and down the line of travelers, pulling a stubborn cart here, giving a word of encouragement there. He stopped when he came to the blonde woman who had translated for him earlier.

"My thanks to you for talking to these thick-headed people," he said offhandedly.

"You would be thick too if you were in the Alsace pulling a cart while someone yelled at you."

"The Alsace? Is that where these people are from?"

"Alsace. France. Denmark. Switzerland."

"And you can speak to all of them?"

The woman shrugged. I speak French. Italian. German and . . . some Danish," she said. "Enough to get a few thoughts across to them. That's all they need. They can do the rest."

Shadrach looked at her incredulously. "Where did you learn to speak all those languages? Did your husband teach you?"

"Is it so strange that a woman should know language?" she said, offended. "I did not need a man to teach me, either. I learned them at the university in Geneva."

"The university? You went to a university?"

"Does that surprise you? I am a medical doctor. What do you think about that?"

"A midwife?"

"A real doctor!"

"That's impossible."

"It's not—and I am."

Shadrach looked suspiciously around him as if a great joke was being played. "Your husband?"

"I have no husband nor any need to prove myself to you."

A brilliant idea overcame Shadrach as if he had cracked the case. "If you are a doctor and have no husband, why are you traveling on foot to Zion?"

"I came to the point at which I had no more hope for the human race," the woman said. "The world made me want to cry when I considered it. I heard of the city of heaven being built on the shores of the Salt Lake and when I heard the missionaries I decided that it was for me. I hope the ones in charge in Zion are more clever than you are."

"And when you meet them, I hope you are more polite than you are to me," Shadrach said, striding off.

After several weeks on the trail, Shadrach's fears for the worst began coming true. The pale Europeans were unused to both the intense heat of the American plains and the heavy labor of dragging the carts before them. They had endured the bloody blisters which soaked their thin shoes with blood and the muscle wrenching energy required to haul the carts over the wagon ruts. They ran short on water, drinking several quarts a day to replace the sweat. Their thin rations of meal and bacon couldn't replace the weight they lost on the trail. The Saints kept their spirits though, singing the hymns about their mission and making up ditties they sang behind Shadrach's back, which poked fun at their lumbering captain.

As the pilgrims collapsed around their campfires at night, scarcely strong enough to eat dinner before they curled under their blankets, Shadrach marveled at their bravery. Every mile of the journey was counted in faltering footsteps and broken knuckles and sunburn, yet they kept going. In spite of his anxieties the Englishman appreciated the power which drove them to Zion. It replenished his faith to remember how desperately he had wanted to arrive.

The carts were a different matter.

The cheapness of the carts, the very reason for using them, was their downfall. The Saints had saved money by not wrapping the wooden wheel rims with the iron belts they used on the wagon wheels. After hard miles, the strong oak rims could no longer stand the strain and broke under the constant pounding. The green wood with which the carts had been constructed dried out in the summer heat. The joints loosened, the wood split, and the carts began to fall apart.

As the carts began to disintergrate, so did the morale of the Saints. At first, a few began complaining about the design of the carts. Next they began complaining about the choice of the route. Shadrach feared that if things became worse, he might be forced to turn back. If they were caught in the snows of the mountains he would have more than a mutiny on his hands.

Shadrach redoubled his efforts to keep his company together. He enforced a tight discipline, rousing the pilgrims at dawn and keeping them going until sundown. At the waystations where they stopped to repair their carts, he browbeat the station masters until they had given up precious materials to keep the carts together.

Theresa Gluck, the Swiss woman doctor, served as the translator of Shadrach's demands, passing them on to the rest. She made her antagonism to him very clear and relations between the two were chilly. She resented his authoritarian manner and his brusque command of the company. He was irritated by her insistence on being treated as an equal by him.

She went out of her way to infuriate him. She was not young, perhaps thirty years old, but with her blonde hair and tight skin she looked much younger. She always insisted on carrying a man's burden and she shouldered the carts as well as any of the rest. In spite of her sex she was a natural leader, perhaps because she symbolized a feminine alternative to Shadrach's command. The pioneers looked up to her and she egged them on. She had assumed a role as the ghost captain of the company as Shadrach watched his authority erode.

"Why are you always shouting at us?" Theresa demanded one afternoon as Shadrach berated a group of pilgrims who had lagged behind to put bacon grease on their cart's creaking axle.

"Because if I don't shout, none of these blockheads will pay attention!"

The party of pioneers gathered around the two to watch the confrontation. Shadrach could tell they all sided with her.

"Perhaps you should try lowering your voice," she admonished him. "I thought we were all brothers and sisters here and harmony was our rule of order."

"Brotherly love begins in Salt Lake City. Out here our rule of order is to pass through before the snow flies."

"What is the point in acting harshly? We are all in God's hands now."

"I have found the less you give God to worry about, the happier both you and God are going to be," Shadrach said. It was not easy to defend oneself against a self-righteous person.

"Perhaps you should try being a little more gentle."

The pioneers nodded their agreement. This was a dangerous challenge to his authority. She was telling him how to lead.

"Madam, you do not know these western plains as I do. My temper cannot match the severity of the winter in these parts. My sole purpose in sternness is to keep this company moving until the danger is passed. When that is over I will kiss every man, woman, and child in the company. Until then, you will obey my wishes."

Shadrach's voice had risen to a rolling roar. There would be no appeal from this tryant and Theresa swirled her pleated skirts around her as she stalked out of the circle. The rest of the company balefully followed her, glowering at the ogre who led them.

"I know now how President Brigham Young feels when he is criticized by the brothers and sisters for being too harsh with us," Shadrach said. "To undertake a great mission a few sore spots must be rubbed in the journey."

"Do not compare yourself with one so great," Theresa yelled at him, finally losing her temper. "And don't think you can abuse us so, and then make excuses for it!"

"As Sampson slew the Philistines, so am I embattled," the Englishman roared. "By the jawbone of an ass!"

The stern directions of their captain and the rigors of the trip hardened the pilgrims. As they crossed through Nebraska their pace quickened. Much of their load was consumed or left on the trail. The carts were cannabilized to make fewer but more sturdy conveyances.

Lean and brown, the men, women and children had transformed into self-sufficient frontier people in a shorter time than those who jolted in wagons. The efficient Europeans adapted quickly to the rigors of the journey. Unlike wagon parties where death usually accompanied them, the pushcart pioneers were hale and hearty as if the exercise of walking one thousand miles had kept the disease from their bodies. There were fewer complaints and more expectant talk of Zion as they progressed. Shadrach was pleased with his flock but was reluctant to show it. It was too early to relax his image as a taskmaster.

The Saints rested a few days at Fort Laramie while the mountaineers stared at this strange company who had the gall to cross on foot. Then they pushed west sometimes traveling across Wyoming at the rate of fifteen miles a day.

Their speed was not enough. Three weeks after they had left Laramie, the sky clouded over and the first flakes of snow fell upon Shadrach's tousled hair. The tiny flake sent a chill through his body like no icy wind before it. He looked up. The sky was filled with tumbling swirling flakes.

Winter had come to the high country.

They pushed on and so did the snow. The next morning they awoke and found six inches of white powder covering their blanket tops. They shook it off and pressed onward. Before nightfall, the ordeal of pushing the carts through the three-foot drifts had become impossible. Shadrach led them into the shelter of a shallow gorge.

"We will make camp here and wait for better weather," he announced. "This freak winter storm is a passing thing. A thaw will bring us through in a few days."

The camp was made but the thaw never materialized. Instead, the snow flew heavier, obliterating all signs of their path.

The pioneers wrapped themselves in blankets and huddled around the fires they built in the center of the gorge. They blew on their frostbitten fingertips and watched the sky for providence to send them clear weather.

The early arrival of winter was grimly noted in Salt Lake City. The scouts were sent out for a break in the weather, but none came. The woodchoppers were driven down from the mountains by the blizzard and stock in the highlands froze to death.

The organizers of the immigration noted the absence of the Tompkins company. A hasty meeting was called at the Beehive House. Noting the few provisions the carts were able to carry, Brigham Young ordered a rescue mission to be organized.

The Tompkins family watched with concern as the fastest teams of oxen and horses were gathered. Sarah and Polly helped in the collection of the winter clothing and food which would be carried to the travelers. Rachel managed to requisition a few bottles of brandy from some of the brethren who indulged in the forbidden pleasure.

So many Saints volunteered for the rescue mission that only a select few were chosen. They buttoned up their wool blanket capotes around their necks and whipped their teams into the mountains.

The days and nights kneeling in prayer had brought the Saints in the company no deliverance. The snow was falling with ominous regularity. The last of the cornmeal had been divided out to the families so the children could eat. The bitter winds swept down into the ravine at night cutting through the thin canvas tents and covering those who were able to sleep with as much snow as outside.

One fire after another flickered out as the starving pioneers no longer had the strength to fetch firewood. More of the pilgrims stayed in their tents during the daytime as walking about consumed too much energy.

Shadrach alone stumbled through the deep snow to the ridgeline to gather the stunted pine limbs so the fires could burn. Several times he had almost perished when the blizzard had become so fierce that its whiteness had disoriented him. Everything turned white around him and he could see no features of the land. He felt as though he was tumbling in the air and he lost the feeling of what was up or down. Only by dropping his firewood could he tell which way was down.

The only other active Saint in the camp was Theresa Gluck who ministered to those who had fallen sick from the cold and hunger. Disease went hand in hand with the privation and almost everyone showed signs of some malady. Although she was quickly out of the medicines to treat them, Theresa's gentle words and soft hands were enough to comfort them.

As the conditions became worse in the camp, the relationship between her and her captain improved. They progressed from a few rough and grudging words to whispered consultations about their deteriorating situation. Soon, they were sharing Shadrach's ragged tent. Their partnership was not a passionate one for even had they wished it to be it was too cold for any carnal behavior. Rather, it was a bone of mutual support, for if the man and woman had nothing else in common, their shared determination to survive and to pull the others with them dissolved their rivalry.

Six weeks after they had first made camp in the ravine, the first Saint died. Shadrach was huddled in his tent, wrapped in a wool blanket. Theresa walked to the doorway, her feet bound up in rags and clothing which had been pressed into

service as shoes. She crawled into the tent and kneeled on the
pine boughs which formed the floor.

"Madame Clerot passed away last night," Theresa whispered.

"Oh my God! Are we beginning to die?" Shadrach asked.

"It was a blessing for the old woman," Theresa said. "In
her last words she told me that she was looking at the holy
city of Zion. She died happily."

These words of consolation could not stem the tears which
were flowing down Shadrach's cheeks, freezing before they
reached his chin.

"My leadership of this party was a curse to the woman. I
should have ordered us to winter in Laramie. It was my pride
that drove us to this end."

"Don't blame yourself for nature's ways," Theresa said
with her loving Swiss sternness. "You did the correct thing.
Winter was early."

"No, you don't understand. It was a matter of pride for me
to lead this company in before the wintertime to show the
president his trust in me was justified. I forced us at a
reckless pace."

Theresa slid beside him and crawled under his blanket. She
took his numb hands in her own warm fingers and rubbed
them as if to chase not only the cold but the pessimistic
thoughts from his body.

"I know that no one in the company has anything but
admiration for you," she promised him. "I was your enemy
at first. Yes, it's true, but I've realized you are a good man.
Not a diplomat, perhaps, perhaps not a great leader even, but
a good man and the people will follow you. I will follow
you."

"Follow me where? Not only am I not a great leader, I'm
not a very good scout."

"Shhhh, the people will hear you and they have enough
doubts themselves," Theresa said, putting her fingers over
his lips. "I had a dream of seeing Salt Lake City last night. I
know we will come through."

Warmed by the heat of the woman beside him, Shadrach
drifted into a light sleep. The light scent of her under the
blanket comforted him and for a brief time he forgot about the
cold. He rested his head against her breast and she supported
him drifting into a sleep herself.

They awoke with a start as the sound of gunfire echoed

through the ravine. They looked at each other to find out if they had shared a mutual dream. The shots reported again and Shadrach searched through his possibles for a pistol.

"Indians! They've waited until we are the weakest to begin their attack!" he said. "At least death will be swift and merciful!"

He found his pistol, but it was uncharged. He cursed and crawled out of his tent hoping to locate a loaded rifle among the company. The other pioneers were already on their feet, but instead of screaming in terror they appeared to be cheering.

Shadrach turned. On the ridge above them he could see the familiar long hair of O.P. Rockwell and several other scouts. They were firing their rifles in the air both to alert the stranded pilgrims and to signal the rest of their train.

"What's the matter, Brother Tompkins?" they shouted when they spotted him, "Did you lose your way?"

WAR
1857

Chapter Nineteen

The crowd of assembled Saints packed into the tabernacle leaned forward on their benches as Brother Hays unleashed a speech so full of hellfire and brimstone that Shadrach was afraid the adobe assembly hall was going to burn to the ground.

"There is a great apostasy loose in the church today," the high priest roared. "Barely ten years in the wilderness and already we have begun to backslide. Now, as we face a united enemy from outside, we must deal with an inner rot. We must purify the church. We must cleanse Deseret . . . with blood if need be. If there is a sin against the church, it can be atoned in blood!"

A revival was sweeping through the church. As the pressures from the outside built, the inner fires were stoked to revitalize the people's spirit. From one end of the territory to the other, Saints reconsecrated themselves to their faith. Shadrach had disciplined himself by cutting out the pinches of snuff he had begun using and attending more Sunday services than he had in the past.

More troubling to him was the fear the Saints had of apostasy. Apostasy, the falling away from the faith, was one of the most serious offenses. Apostates were traitors and worse. They threatened the very existence of Deseret. Now the threat was made against anyone who would turn traitor to his people. Blood would be shed if anyone imperiled the security of Zion.

Shadrach was uneasy about the newfound zeal of some of the brothers and sisters. He believed in belief and rock steady commitment. But too much belief in the minds of a few hotheads could be as dangerous as backsliding.

The headline of the *New York Herald* fluttered in the breeze as Shadrach held it in his trembling hands. No matter which way he turned it, it was impossible for him to read. A small crowd had gathered near the tabernacle. A workman on the temple had brought a copy of an eastern paper left off by a passing wagon train of Gentiles bound for California.

"Here, you read it, the talent escapes me," Shadrach said to his son, Ham, as he handed him the newspaper.

The gangling boy took the faded paper and held it up. In the last year he had begun to grow like a freshly watered sprout and now he was nearly as tall as his father. A few more years in the fields would fill his body out, but even now he stood above the workmen who jostled to hear his reedy voice.

"Turkey is in our midst! Modern Muhammadism across the Rocky Mountains. The Mormon pasha Brigham Young keeps a harem of helpless women chained to a life of celestial slavery in his desert kingdom," the boy read carefully.

This inflammatory headline caused the workmen to try to shout the truth all the way to New York, but Shadrach quieted them so his son could continue.

> How long are we to permit this barbarity to go on inside our own borders?" the editorial trumpeted. "Innocent maidens lured to Utah. Blushing brides snatched from younger men and married to aging bishops. This last vestige of paganism must be eradicated. The Christian citizens of our country call for the president to act! Already an army stands prepared waiting for his orders to march on the polygamist capital. Why stand we here idle?

"Lies!" one of the stonemasons shouted.

"Read on. What does it say about this army preparing to march against us?" another urged.

"I can't read father. The backpages are missing," Ham said, thumbing the well-worn newsprint.

"What is the date on the paper?" Shadrach asked.

"May 10, 1857."

"Then that news is already three months old," a workman shouted. "They could be marching on us at this moment!"

"Let's not get worked up, brothers," Shadrach said, trying to calm the crowd. "The papers have been lambasting us for years without visible effect. This is a ploy to sell papers."

"They've been trying to murder us for years, and they've done pretty well at it!" someone yelled. "Just think how many papers they would sell if they had a war with the Mormons?''

"We're not going quietly like the sheep to the slaughter this time!" a worker yelled, brandishing his adze. "If they mean to have truck with us, we will give back better than we receive!"

The workmen moved off in a crowd to look for more support leaving Shadrach and his son behind. The Englishman watched them go. The rumors of war had kindled similar feelings across the state of Deseret. The citizens were fearful of the gathering storm and they took out their worries in braggadocio. The Saints claimed they were ready for war, but he was afraid they had been isolated too long and had forgotten the vastness of the country on the other side of the Rockies. There were more factories in St. Louis alone than in all of Deseret. And the Nauvoo Legion, however organized and determined, could not hold off the United States Army.

"I fear an adze won't stop a cannonball," Shadrach remarked.

"You think there will be war?"

"When both parties seem so eager to fight, a war always follows."

"If there is a war," Ham said, with a waver in his throat; "I intend to fight at your side."

Shadrach looked at his eighteen-year-old son. He seemed like a willow wisp, scarcely past from a child. He recognized the look in his son's eyes, the burning desire of belief that has not recognized pain.

"If there is a war, you will fight in it."

The boy was startled, as if he had expected his father to object. "I can?" he asked, his timing thrown off. He was ready to rebut his father's refusal and now he ran after him.

"You will have to fight," Shadrach said impassively. "Just don't tell your mother until we're ready to leave."

Mariah Tompkins died in the spring of 1857 just as the sego lilies she had taught her husband to identify were beginning to bloom in the mountain valleys. She succumbed to an attack of the ague, a minor illness seasonally affecting the community. The whites who caught it suffered through sniffles and a phlegm-blocked chest, but the Indians were unprepared for the disease's onslaught and died in fevered agony.

Her body was prepared for burial in her favorite Sunday dress and carried to the cemetery on the outskirts of Salt Lake

City which was beginning to fill with Saints who left for their eternal reward from Zion.

Shadrach himself presided at the service and spoke over her grave. "She was a delicate creature who had survived war and deprivation under the Shoshones, rape and slavery under the Utes, and found salvation with the Saints," he said sadly. "I will miss her laugh and I look forward to our reunion in heaven but I praise God she passes on under our care rather than on some pine-covered mountain in a heathen grave."

The loss of Mariah was felt by all the Tompkins family. She left a young child less than a year old who had been nursed by Sarah at the same time as a child of her own. The Ute chief Walkara had died in 1855 without receiving his horses from Brigham Young, and in his honor the child was named Walker.

The pain of the loss was cushioned by the size of the Tompkins family. The grief was shared, not just by a man and his wife, but by a man and his three wives. The death was explained not to just two or three children but to eight children in the growing clan. When the Tompkins prayed for the soul of Mariah, it was with twelve voices. When the family went to the Endowment House to perform their temple work, it was the entire family which underwent baptism for the dead members of Mariah's tribe so they could join her in heaven.

The loss of Mariah was partially offset by the addition of Theresa Gluck, who had been invited to stay with the Tompkins family. At first, Shadrach's wives had suspected that his relationship with the attractive Swiss woman might have been more than just survival, but as they came to know her they grew to trust and like her. Theresa, who had abandoned her friends and family in Europe, was grateful for the hospitality of the large family who clothed and fed her.

Theresa was suspicious of the practice of plural marriage and made her feelings known to the women of the house.

"I don't know how you can share one man?" she would confide in Rachel, who seemed the most independent.

"If the man is important enough, there is plenty to go around," Rachel answered, tolerant of her suspicions.

"But aren't you giving up your own claim on his life to live in his shadow?"

"We Saints are patient folk," Sarah would explain. "We

will live out our time on this earth preparing for eternity. We have plenty of time to make our claims on life.''

''What about your children? Do they not get confused over this situation.''

Polly smiled. ''When I was carrying my last child I felt too ill to take care of my first borne. Having two other mothers in the house kept the child cared for during my absence. On the frontier we do not have the luxury of staying at home all the time. While some of us are in the fields, there is always a woman in the house to care for the children.''

''There is always someone to share the load with,'' Sarah added. ''If one of us is sick, or tired, or ill at sorts, the others are able to step into our shoes and take the responsibility.''

''What of the criticism of the outside world?'' Theresa asked.

''The criticism of the outside world stopped bothering me a long time ago,'' Sarah said. ''It's the contentment of my inside world I cherish.''

''The outside world is full of adulterers and philanderers anyway,'' Rachel pointed out. ''It is better to have this done at home than on the sly in some filthy brothel.''

Theresa shook her head with good-humored disapproval.

''I'm afraid I'm too modern to live under such an arrangement,'' she admitted, ''. . . or too old-fashioned.''

Every messenger from the east brought more news of threats against the state of Deseret. Mormonism had become the whipping boy for a United States divided over the issue of slavery and states rights. As if to avoid the bitter feud that raged between the North and South, the country diverted its attention to the struggling desert kingdom.

As the threats grew more menacing, the church stepped up its immigration plans to gather as many Saints before the immigration was cut off. They called in the settlers who were colonizing the remote reaches of Deseret. All people and resources had to be saved for the coming fight.

Shadrach had barely the time to step back into his life before President Young summoned him to the Beehive House where preparations for war were being made. Shadrach was admitted to the office of the church president who seemed to be taking their desperate situation calmly.

''Well, Brother Tompkins, Babylon appears to be falling,'' Young said good-naturedly. ''Within a year I expect the

North and South to be at each other's throats like dogs and eventually the South will win. But before they set on each other they seem likely to have a go at us!''

"It wouldn't come as any surprise, Brigham. We know it and we are ready for them.''

"The longer a confrontation can be delayed, the more likely they will be fighting each other than us,'' Young said. "It is imperative that we not give them any provocation to attack us in the next year or two. The slightest spark can set off the powder keg.''

"The brothers are sparky enough,'' Shadrach observed. "Many are spoiling for a fight and think we should strike first.''

"That is why I have called you here,'' the president said gravely. "I want you to ride South to the fiesty wards in Dixie. Keep the brethren down there on a tight rein. Don't dampen their fighting spirits, but don't let them catch fire. There are wagon trains of Pukes passing through that country. I don't want anything to happen to them. If the devil himself is riding in the wagon box of those trains, I want him to pass through unmolested.''

"I will do as you say but the brethren in Dixie are a rough breed. They might let the devil pass through but they'll bite off his tail to make him remember the trip.''

Dixie, as the southern part of Deseret was known, covered a vast area. Shadrach had helped explore the region but each time he traveled the trail south he was amazed at the size of their land. Despite the vastness, the wagon trains passing on to California followed a single trail which led through the important settlements. In Spanish Fork, Lehi, Nephi and Parowan, Shadrach found the settlers worked into a fever pitch by the rumors of war and the offenses of the passing wagon trains.

"Half the Pukes in those wagons are from Missouri,'' an elder in Parowan told Shadrach as they shared an evening meal together. "They brag about how they wiped us out in '38 and they swear they're going to do it again.''

"The Fancher party that just went through claimed they was going to give the U.S. Army a map of our settlements when they got to California so they could use it against us,'' the man's wife claimed.

"They must have been putting a practical joke on you,'' Shadrach said, trying to lighten the mood.

"Practical joke, my eye!" the woman said. "We've seen 'em making maps of our springs and fields. They're spies! Every other man was in the Missouri militia."

"They've been poisoning wells along their route," the elder claimed. "In Cedar City they left some poisoned meat for the Indians. When they ate the meat they died and now they blame all white men for this. The Pukes are trying to turn the Indians against us, then leave us to contend with the consequences."

"They are poisoning our minds as well," his wife said. "They had named their oxen in the lead wagon 'Brigham' and 'Joseph.' They would whip them around the settlement every day. Our children were very upset by this and would have the most terrible nightmares."

"The boys around Cedar City are worked up and aim to set things straight," the elder pointed out. "John D. Lee and his boys are going to set an example for anyone who thinks they can flaunt our ways in front of us. You know Brother Lee, don't you?"

"I have known John since we fought together in Missouri," Shadrach said. "He means what he says."

"And he says he means to 'use up' some of those Pukes to let the world know we aren't going to lie in the dust while someone beats us with a stick."

Shadrach whipped his horse into a sweaty froth as he rode south in pursuit of John D. Lee and his men. In every community he passed he heard the same tales of the Gentile threat. He heard of the cattle which trampled the Saint's crops and of the shots fired at the children who played along the route of the wagon train. He heard stories of the waterholes polluted by running livestock through, of the Gentiles antagonizing the Indian populations. He recognized the Puke's arrogance and felt the same anger and resentment against them he had felt in Missouri.

Still, orders had been given that they would pass quietly from Deseret and there would be no breaking this commandment. He and the other Saints he would tell the order to would not violate the wishes of the president.

At Cedar City, a small stockade and a handful of houses that formed the southernmost terminus of Deseret, the Fancher wagon train took a westerly route into the mountains. South of Cedar City the land descended into the Mojave Desert and the Gentiles were intent on pasturing their stock before they began the trip through it.

The trail led him up into the pine valley, a delightful series of small mountains covered with fresh-scented pine trees. It was early September and while the lower deserts were still deadly hot, the valley was tolerably cool. The end of the summer was bringing a breeze down from the north and it blew the sun baked smell of pine resins to clean up his dust clogged lungs.

There were few settlers in the valley. Fear of the local Indians had kept out all but the most fearless. Those Saints told him an ominous story. The Fancher party, over one hundred men, women and children, passed that way not more than two weeks before. A few days ago, John D. Lee and an equal number of men who had been associated with the Danites had passed, hot on their trail. Signs of Indians had been seen in the valley as if a war party was gathering. This gathering of forces alarmed Shadrach and he spurred his mount. He must reach Lee before these mortal enemies met.

He was watering his horse near a creek when he heard a rider approaching on the trail. Cautiously concealing himself in a thicket near the trail he waited for the rider to cut the creek. Presently a young man on a sweating horse galloped up and stopped so his thirsty horse could drink. As he did so, Shadrach stepped out of the thicket.

The man drew a Patterson revolver he had in his belt, but he startled his horse so badly he was thrown into the creek. Shadrach picked up the revolver and helped the startled boy to his feet.

"You're Ebeneezer Pringle's boy aren't you?" Shadrach said handing back the gun. "You seem pretty jumpy today."

"You frightened the beejeesus out of me, that's why!"

"Have you seen John Lee and his party?"

"I just come from him! I'm riding to Cedar City to round up some more men."

"More men? Is there trouble?"

"All hell has broken loose at Mountain Meadows. We are currently skirmishing with a well fortified band of Pukes."

"Skirmishing? Has it come to this? We must put a stop to this nonsense before the damage is done."

"It is too late now. We had been using Indians friendly to our cause to pin them down. Yesterday we caught four Pukes trying to escape from their camp. We killed three, but the fourth returned to his camp to tell his story. If we break off the attack now, they will escape to California to sing their songs."

Shadrach grabbed the boy by the jacket collar and pushed to to his horse. "What is done can be undone," Shadrach said. "You lead me to Mountain Meadows as fast as you can."

Mountain Meadows was not near any mountains, nor was it much of a meadow either. It was more of a shallow ravine running down a sandy bottom north of where the volcano cones grew. A series of low hillocks ringed the draw. The foraging was lean that year with only the sparse sagebrush growing with any success around a water hole. The land was composed of a maroon sand the color of blood.

Shadrach felt a chill when his guide led him to a knoll overlooking the meadow. Below them, a wagon train had been pulled into a tight circle and he could see the defenders crouched in a rifle pit at the center of the ring. Facing them, Shadrach could see the warriors of several tribes of the local Indians occupying a harassing position. Behind them on the high ground Shadrach could make out white men wearing the plain cloth clothing of the Mormon settlers.

These settlers seemed cheered to see Shadrach when he rode down, believing he was the first of the reinforcements the boy had been sent to collect. Their cheer faded when they found out he was alone.

Shadrach was shocked by the appearance of the Saints. All the men, normally calm in the face of danger, seemed nearly hysterical. They were wild-eyed and confused, as though they were divided about their mission.

The leader of the men, John D. Lee, was in a state of agitation unlike anything Shadrach had ever seen. Lee had been one of the coolest heads among Saints. During the hottest trials in Missouri and Illinois, the bearded man never lost his aplomb. But now he rode about the ranks of the men shouting orders, and Shadrach had to drag him off his horse to get his attention.

"Good Lord, John? What is going on here?" he demanded.

"War! This is war!" Lee answered. "These Gentiles have begun the fight and we aim to finish it! We will not let them ride roughshod over our land and not punish them."

"I bring specific orders from the highest authorities of the church that these wagons are to pass unmolested."

"Let the highest authorities come down here and try to contain these men! They have seen their land trammeled and their lives threatened. They are out of anyone's control."

This remark frightened Shadrach more than anything else.

"You had best bring your men under control, Brother Lee!" he shouted. "Or there will be hell to pay for this and you will be left with the bill!"

"The boys have their dander up now. Joshua Monkton was gutshot by one of the Pukes yesterday. The Indians are in a fouler humor. Two of their braves have been killed outright and their chiefs wounded. They are all for having done with it or going home."

"Then let them go, and send your boys too."

"It would show a bad example to the Indians if we engaged our enemies and then let them off. They might think us cowards."

"Let them think what they want, damn you!"

"I have already arranged for a truce," Lee offered. "I have sent a good talker under a white flag who has convinced Captain Fancher that this is the Indians' business. If they will leave their weapons and depart the valley on foot, the Indians will spare their lives."

This was the first good news Shadrach had heard in many days and a look of relief crossed his face as he slapped his old comrade on the shoulders.

"Thank God, John. Let us take advantage of this parley to bury the hatchet and see these Pukes safely from our country. Perhaps we can take the credit for saving them and come out of this pigpen smelling like a rose."

Resting wearily on the knoll overlooking the Meadow, Shadrach had a fine view of the truce. Below him, the Fancher party was being led out of the valley under the escort of armed Saints. The wagons of the Pukes led the way, driven by Mormon teamsters carrying the children of the Gentiles. Behind the wagons, the women marched in single file, protectively flanked by heavily armed Saints who would guard them from Indian attacks. Bringing up the rear, the Gentile men walked two abreast, also guarded by the mounted riflemen.

The peacefulness of the scene reassured Shadrach that he had done his job. He could relax his sleepless body in the bright sunshine of the afternoon now. Reason had prevailed and his diplomacy had effected a peaceful end to the volatile situation. God knows what might have happened without him.

The peace was shattered by a rifle shot. Another rang out and then a volley echoed across the low hills. The gray puffs of powder were exploding in the valley and the screams of men and women reached his ears.

Shadrach sprang to his feet. In the valley below him all was confusion. A party of Indians had hidden in a narrow draw near the trail and now had descended on the wagon train. The mounted Saints rode among them, but instead of firing at the Indians, they were firing at the fleeing Gentiles.

Cursing, the Englishman ran down the slope into the valley forgetting his horse. "Stop! For God's sakes, stop!" he yelled as he ran until his breath was too labored to shout.

His supplications were drowned out by the reports of rifle and pistol shots and the cries of the victims. By the time Shadrach had reached the site of the slaughter, his lungs were as near to bursting. All around him on the valley floor the dead lay where they had fallen.

Dozens of dead lay on the ground. Many of the Gentiles in the party had been cut down by the first fusillade of the Indians. The others had been cut down trying to flee to the sides of the narrow valley.

There was still sporadic firing. A Gentile who had hidden amongst the dead jumped up and started sprinting away. The Indians, crazed by the killing, joyously whopped and set after him on foot. Shadrach could hear the man's terrified screams as the Indians closed in on him and shot him to the ground with muskets.

John D. Lee, Shadrach's old friend, had ridden to a small hill to survey the valley. When Shadrach rushed up to him, he found the normally unshakable Lee was trembling.

"In the name of God, stop this killing," Shadrach shouted. "Have we all gone mad?"

"This is war. War!" Lee shouted as if Shadrach was one hundred miles away. "This is a battlefield of that war! They have come to take our land. They have come to start their bloody cycle against us and we are fighting back!"

"Then fight in honorable battle!" Shadrach shouted back. "Not against women and children."

"There were women and children at Haun's Mill," Lee countered. "We shall spare the children. That is more mercy than they showed us!"

There were tears in Lee's eyes. Shadrach realized he was as helpless as himself to stop this. It had all started a decade earlier.

Shadrach looked down. The Indians were scalping the dead.

"For pity sake's, stop the scalping at least," Shadrach argued.

"It's better that way. It will be read as an Indian massacre," Lee said gravely. "I take this day as my personal responsibility. I will stand for it in history."

"I'm afraid we will all suffer the responsibility for this," Shadrach said angrily. "It is a black day."

Turning, Shadrach ran into the midst of the dead where an Indian was stooped over the fallen body of a woman. The back of her dress was soaked in blood. The Indian pulled the top of her hair back and drew a long steel knife from his belt.

The woman groaned.

Before the Indian could draw the sharp knife through the flesh of her forehead to take the scalp, he felt the barrel of Shadrach's pistol placed against the back of his neck.

"You take that woman's scalp with your knife and I take yours with powder and ball," Shadrach said menacingly.

The Indian didn't move. Instead, he yelped, and his friends surrounded Shadrach. The clicks of muskets being primed resounded in the valley.

Shadrach pressed the barrel deeper into the Indian's neck. He could feel the inner trembling of the man's shoulder muscles. The Indian relaxed his shoulders and slipped the knife back into his belt.

Shadrach kept the hammer of his pistol back as the Indians backed away from him, cursing and threatening him. He had broken the bloodlust and all around him the valley quieted.

He stooped and gently picked up the woman. Her eyes were glazed, her breath shallow. Flecks of foamy blood were on the corners of her lips.

"My babies," she whispered.

Shadrach felt a chill pass over him as the woman shuddered and her breath stopped. He held her for a time, unsure of whether she was alive, for her eyes remained open, staring at him. He pressed his thumbs over them to close them and gently set her on the earth.

Several children walked among the dead. They made no sound. In the strange events of the day, no one seemed to be concerned about disturbing them. Determined that they should not see any more of the carnage, Shadrach picked two of them up in his strong arms and carried them toward a wagon that was still hitched. Only then did the children begin to cry.

"Harm a hair on these children's heads and answer to me for it," Shadrach shouted angrily.

Several other of the men retrieved more of the motherless children and put them in the wagon. Now some of the men had tears in their eyes.

John D. Lee stood alone as the men began the job of giving the dead a proper burial.

"We shall swear an oath. If any man breathes a word of what has happened today, he will join the dead," he said quietly. "No one shall hear of this place—ever!"

Then there was silence. A wind had snapped up from the south and it buffeted the men still in the valley.

Chapter Twenty

The Tompkins home was more cheerfully dressed up than it had ever been. New curtains hung on the windows, prizes of Polly's connections and Theresa's abilities as a seamstress. New furniture filled the low-ceilinged adobe, the bequest of a departed Putnam aunt. The furniture was fine-quality cherry dining tables and walnut dressers. A sum of money had also been left in the will, but it had been spent sending the furniture to Deseret. A box of Wedgwood china arrived in hundreds of shattered pieces and the children saw Sarah in tears for the first time any of them could remember.

In spite of this new decoration, Shadrach's homecoming was a somber one for their husband seemed unusually quiet and uncharacteristically depressed.

"What ails you husband and be forthright about it?" Sarah demanded. "You have scarcely touched the first beef on this table in two months. Out with it and no more dissembling!"

Knowing that he would not be able to keep a secret from these canny interrogators, Shadrach sent the children to their rooms with Theresa. Then he told them of what he had seen.

A shocked silence greeted this account. None of his wives spoke. After a few moments Rachel was the first to comment.

"Vengeance is mine, sayeth the Lord. And it was," she said. "Now the dead in Missouri can rest in peace."

"As a mother yourself, how can you say that?" Sarah demanded. "Two horrible wrongs don't equal a right. It was a dastardly act."

"It was my fault. I failed in my mission to stop them," Shadrach said, despairing. "The task should have been entrusted to one more persuasive than myself."

"Don't shoulder the blame for them," Polly said. "The deed was underway before you arrived. It was none of your doing. You tried to stop it."

"What does Brigham say?"

"He was heartsick when I made my report. "It is a black day for our cause. He is convinced the war dogs will be unleashed on us and I fear he is right."

"As if the Pukes needed any excuse to make war on us," Rachel snorted. "If a company of Saints is murdered, the country cheers. If a company of Pukes is used up, you brave men run and cry!"

"I can't believe my ears?" Sarah said. "Are we the same people who came to build the kingdom of heaven? Have we fallen so low that we are coolly apologizing for murder?"

"Not murder. Atonement of blood," Rachel argued. "The Pukes sewed their seeds of hatred and this is their harvest. Now the world will be warned that none can trespass against us."

"Hold your tongue!" Sarah ordered. "Never assume you have the right to take another's life, even if they be in the wrong. You will call down unmerciful judgment against yourself and your house. We should be on our knees praying for forgiveness!"

Not long after Shadrach returned, news came that an army of United States soldiers had been on the march since midsummer. The war was about to be joined.

The eastern newspapers and politicians had whipped the American public into such a frenzy of hatred against the Mormons that President Buchanan had no choice but to send an army against them. The reasons for sending an expedition were vague. The state of Deseret appeared to be in open rebellion against the United States. Its secession from the Union would set a bad precedent for the slave-holding states. The rumors of polygamy outraged the ministers of all religions who used them to denounce the Mormons from their pulpits.

Looking for a thin excuse for an invasion, Buchanan removed Brigham Young as the official governor of the territory and replaced him with an Indian agent named Alfred Cummings. When Brigham refused to step down, Buchanan ordered an army of 2,500 men under a Colonel Johnson to accompany Cummings.

In July of 1857, the army marched westward. They brought with them eight thousand tons of supplies in hundreds of covered wagons. Six million dollars was spent to outfit the expedition and the eastern newspapers sarcastically called the march "the contractor's war."

Alfred Cummings was an obese man who spoke with the drawl of his native Georgia. A thin moustache covered his puffy cheeks. The finest silk waistcoat and top hat covered his corpulent body as he bounced out of Fort Leavenworth in his wagon. Cummings was unhappy with the assignment. He would have preferred the lights and parties of Washington to shepherding a bunch of bearded rebels with barely enough money to pay a small bribe. His wagon was loaded with Cuban cigars, French champagne, salted hams and pickles, all gifts from his political allies. He would make the best of this wilderness.

The approach of the American army was reported by the last wagon trains passing ahead of the columns. The oxen of Johnson's command were making slow progress, but they would be in Salt Lake City by late fall.

A general alarm was called throughout the territory. The Nauvoo Legion was mobilized to fight the foe. The harvest was rushed to get the wheat in the granaries before the troops arrived.

A restrained mood of fear spread throughout Salt Lake City as riders, galloped in bringing fresh reports to the Beehive House. In the Tompkins home, Shadrach took down the rusted saber which hung by the fireplace and keened it to a sharp edge on his whetstone. Sarah watched his preparations for war with a heavier heart than the other wives. She was not as convinced of its righteousness. But when she saw her oldest boy Ham oiling the musket his father had given him several years before, Sarah's silent disapproval ended.

"And just what do you think you are doing, Mister?" she demanded, trying to seize the gun from his hands.

"I am going to stand beside my brothers," Ham answered trying to gently pull the musket from her grip.

"Indeed, you are not. If your father is a participant in this madness, he will not sacrifice you as well."

"I am almost twenty now, an elder in the church and a crack shot. To stand idly by the greatest fight of our history would be an act of shameful cowardice."

"Don't talk to me of cowardice!" Sarah fairly shouted at him. "We have spread enough bravery across this continent to stand for many years."

Ham had never seen his mother so angry and he nodded to Shadrach who busied himself on the whetstone, trying to avoid this talk. "Father has given me permission and I have volunteered to fight with my friends."

"Oh, he has, has he?" Sarah said, turning her rage toward her husband. "And why was I not privy to this decision? Have you gathered so many women about you that you no longer remember the mother of your offspring?"

"Bite your tongue, woman," Shadrach said stoically. "The boy has a duty to perform."

"What about your duty to me? Have you forgotten the times when we used to plan our lives together? Have you grown so cold to me that my deepest desires no longer count."

"Your desire is the continuation of our lives in this place, is it not? We are protecting no less than that. The boy is fighting for all our children."

"Then bring him back alive or don't come back yourself."

The smoke curled lazily up from the farmer's log barn as the riders circled it throwing more torches through the doorway. When the flames finally burst through the roof, the riders hooted their cheers and galloped off to burn what remained of the stubble in the fields.

Shadrach was in charge of the company of horsemen who were burning the Mormon farms on the eastern frontiers of Deseret. He turned to the local bishop who, with the help of the farmers themselves was directing the burning.

"We want every blade of grass and every seed of grain carried off or burnt down," Shadrach said. "When those Pukes oxen come this way we don't want them to even smell any food nor do we want a single roof to shelter the army."

"Brigham has all the grain we raised this year; the people have all moved to Salt Lake and the buildings are burned," the bishop said. "The only thing left to do is to dig up the mountains and take them with us."

"Do you really believe we can whip the entire United States Army?" the bishop's wife asked anxiously.

"We can't whip all of them, that's for sure," Shadrach said. "The president wants us to hold them off as long as we can. He wants us to avoid taking life wherever possible and to harass the enemy. If we can keep them on the eastern side of the mountains long enough, maybe there will be trouble back east and they'll go fight each other."

The Saints prepared to meet the advancing American army

with the same sacrifice they had shown in building their kingdom. All the farmlands so laboriously scraped from the earth were razed, the buildings burned, the fields plowed under, the orchards chopped down, the wells filled in.

Along the steep walls of Echo Canyon, the main entry into the Salt Lake Valley, a series of forts were built to withstand a siege.

The men of the Nauvoo Legion remained at their work, ready to be called up at a moment's notice. A corps of observation was formed, a group of seventy-five experienced and disciplined men, including Shadrach and Ham Tompkins. This corps was charged with scouting the advance of the army and delaying them as much as possible.

Brigham Young had been given his ten years to build his strength in the valley. Now he must face the odds.

Shadrach shivered in the biting cold of the mountain pass as the snow fell relentlessly around him. It was Christmas Eve, but instead of celebrating with his family, he was waiting in ambush with his son at his side. Both men had wool mufflers wrapped around their heads, holding their broad felt hats over their ears. Shadrach loosened his scarf so he could listen for the sound of a horse's hooves approaching.

The horseman returning to the camp of the American soldiers was carrying a bundle of firewood across his saddle. The collar of his blue campaign coat was turned up against the storm and he hunched over to escape the wind. So bundled up was he that Shadrach was able to spur his horse and ride up next to the man before the officer realized what had happened.

"Good evening, sir. You are my prisoner," Shadrach said good-naturedly, trying not to startle the man.

"Damn your eyes, sir. I am not."

"I have a colt revolver in my pocket. If you show any defiance I will shoot you from your mount and leave you to die in the snow."

"What do you intend to do with me, then?"

"I intend to induce you and your comrades to leave our mountains."

"That will not take much doing. We are sick of these mountains and their climate."

Seeing the man was subdued, Ham Tompkins signaled for

the half dozen other Saints in their party to mount their horses and follow his father into the enemy camp.

The snowstorm and the Christmas rum that the army troops were drinking had caused the pickets to leave their posts and Shadrach and his men were able to ride unopposed into the wagon ring. A dozen supply wagons bringing material to Johnson's army had camped for the duration of the storm, not suspecting a Mormon attack. They had built a roaring fire in the middle of the ring and were eating dinner. Their weapons were stacked in the center of the ring and by the time they looked up it was down the barrels of the Saint's muskets.

The snow-covered cloaks looked like ghostly apparitions lending a fiercer appearance to the bearded men.

"Don't anyone make a terrible mistake," Shadrach calmly bluffed. "This camp is surrounded by one hundred armed men of the Nauvoo Legion!

"Do as he says," the woodcutter said nervously. "The place is crawling with Danites."

The soldiers and the teamsters crowded closer to the fire to avoid any appearance of resistance. While Shadrach trained his revolvers on them, Ham and the other men drove the oxen and horses away from the ring and began setting the wagons on fire.

"Not the wagons! How are we to make our way back?" the officer protested. "Do you mean to leave us here?"

"Fort Bridger is twenty-five miles to the west. If you walk fast you will make it there tomorrow."

"In this storm? You can't be serious?"

"Our women and children have walked through worse than this many times," Shadrach laughed. "This may give you a new appreciation for the people you are fighting."

By the light of a dozen burning wagons, the soldiers shuffled off into the west. Ham and his men drove the oxen and cattle of the soldiers before them and carried as much of the food as they could make off with.

Shadrach rode up beside his son and uncorked a bottle of the rum he had been able to salvage. He pulled a swig from it and passed the snow-covered bottle to Ham.

"Here. This will take some of the nip out of the night."

Ham gagged as he took a poke from the bottle and passed it back as the night settled in around them.

"Merry Christmas, father."

*   *   *

The daring raids of the Saints were able to stop the advance of the American troops during the winter of 1857–58. Small bands of guerrilla raiders burned the supply wagons and drove off the livestock of the Pukes. They captured tons of supplies and kept the enemy on the eastern side of the Wasatch Mountains. Johnson's army was forced to spend the winter in the sub-zero temperatures of Fort Bridger.

Several years earlier, the Saints had burnt the greedy Gentile trader out of his fort, but he had returned with the Federal troops and was ready to take revenge on Brigham Young and his people.

The Saints were granted a respite by the snows which sealed off the mountain passes for the winter. The population of the valley rejoiced and thanked God for their deliverance from the Gentiles. But Shadrach knew that when the thaws came, there would be little stopping the American army. For every wagon they burned, ten more came in its place. During the first stage of the war, only one American soldier had died, killed in a fall from his horse. In the coming year, things would be different.

Spring came but the army waited. Pressure was mounting back east for a quick end to the war. The expenses of maintaining the corrupt army in the field were astronomical and Buchanan was under pressure to bring it to a finish. The delay the Mormons had caused him proved a great embarrassment. If they succeeded in defeating his army, he would be ruined.

From Salt Lake City emissaries from the office of the church president made secret trips to the headquarters of the army in Wyoming. During these meetings the leaders of the opposing sides discussed ways of bringing the conflict to a halt. The talks were troubled at first. The Americans had convened a frontier grand jury composed of army teamsters who had indicted Brigham Young on charges of high treason. The leaders of the Saints distrusted the Pukes and demanded that they leave their territory. As pressure from Washington mounted; the army relaxed many of its demands.

Shadrach was given the mission of accompanying the church leaders to the army camp. When some of the more hot-headed of the Nauvoo Legion discovered he had been guiding the peace missions, they visited his house late one night. Shadrach had been sleeping when he heard the dull whistle used in the old days by the Sons of Dan. Still wearing his nightshirt he opened the front door and stepped out into the moonlight. In the front yard, half a dozen shadowy men stood. Shadrach immediately recognized their leader, Thomas Morse.

"Good evening, brothers," Shadrach said. "What brings you out so late?"

"A traitor in our midst," Morse said.

"An apostate? Who?"

"Have you been party to these negotiations with the Pukes?" Morse demanded.

"I have acted as bodyguard and guide to the deputies of the president."

"Do you know it is their intention to offer surrender terms to the Gentiles?"

"They have not informed me of their talks, but I heartily doubt whether surrender is one of them."

"We have it on account that the president is set on compromising with the Pukes to avoid bloodshed."

"If it avoids the shedding of innocent lives, then I am for it. I have seen enough of killing," Shadrach said firmly.

"You have lost your nerve, Brother Tompkins. Every time we have compromised with the Gentiles, they have used it to destroy us. Joseph made that mistake and now Brigham has fallen into the same trap and is leading us into annihilation. We aim to stop him before he does."

"Watch your words, Brother Morse."

"And watch your actions, Brother Tompkins. Remember your Danite oath to defend the faith against the Gentile. If you side with those who are trying to sell us out, a bowie knife across the throat will be your reward."

"Gentlemen, don't you have wives and families who need your company more then we do in the middle of the night?" a voice said behind them. Rachel Tompkins stood with a candle in her hand in the doorway of the house. "In this time of peril we have better ways to spend our time than by making threats to each other in the moonlight," she said sternly. "Brother Morse, your wife is about to have a child. Don't you think it better to be on hand for that?"

Morse glared at Shadrach and walked away. Shadrach backed into the house, the cocked pistol still held behind his back."

The signal man stood on the highest cliff of Echo Canyon and wigwagged a torch signaling the advance of the American forces. Below him, the red sandstone canyon dropped one thousand feet straight down the vertical walls to a narrow defile. This was the only passage through to the Salt Lake Valley. Like the Athenians at Thermopylae, a handful of men could hold the pass against an army.

In the narrowest part of the canyon, the Saints had built a series of fortresses out of the stone and earth that blended in with the red rock. The canyon at some points was less than two hundred yards wide and a rifleman in these barricades could not miss the enemy.

At night the stark walls were silhouetted against the night sky.

Shadrach was mounted on Bellerophon, his favorite horse, and was surrounded by his company of men.

The firefly signal of the torch waggled on the mountain top and Shadrach turned to address his troops. "They're on their way!" he said. "Look sharp and follow me."

A few minutes later the carriage bearing Alfred Cummings, the would-be governor of Utah, came rattling down the canyon. Cummings had been invited, alone, by Brigham Young to Deseret. He was to be driven in a carriage through Echo Canyon at night to attend a meeting the next day.

"Light the fires!" Shadrach ordered.

His men ran along the canyon walls lighting piles of timber which had been set up to simulate the watchfires of the barricade's defenders. Twenty fires flickered, tended by two men.

Cumming's open carriage drove into view and Shadrach would see the fat man still wearing his top hat and a formal coat. Cummings seemed highly nervous about riding alone into enemy territory and Shadrach planned to make him more nervous. His guard of horsemen stood on the side of the trail as the carriage passed and saluted the Gentile with their rifles.

As soon as the carriage had passed, Shadrach and his men spurred their horses. Looping around the edge of the canyon, they bypassed the carriage and arrived at the next barricade as the men there were setting more watchfires. They lined the top of the barricade as Cumming's carriage passed and saluted him again.

Once more, the phantom army rushed to get ahead of the carriage to the next barricade, half a mile down the canyon. In this manner they were able to create the impression that the canyon was guarded by a force of a thousand men when barely one hundred were present.

When Cummings met to negotiate with Brigham Young the next day, he would be dealing with a man who commanded a powerful force . . . of nonexistent soldiers.

The Mormon war ended without further bloodshed. The Gentiles were so anxious not to have to fight the belligerant Saints that they offered Brigham Young amnesty in exchange for a peaceful solution. The church president reluctantly agreed to allow the federal troops into his sacred valley if they promised not to camp within Salt Lake City. They were to march directly through and camp many miles away, south of the lake.

The Saints did not trust the Federal troops.

Brigham Young had promised Cummings that if a single incident occurred he would burn Salt Lake City to the ground and take his people into the mountains where they would fight to the end.

Once more the Tompkins family was loaded into their wagon. The family was packing all their worldly goods and joining the evacuation of the Saints from Salt Lake City. By the time the Federal troops marched in, the city would be a ghost town.

Castor and Pollux, offspring of the oxen which had brought the family to Deseret stood patiently by as the household goods were loaded. The family had grown so great that not one, but four wagons was needed to move them, and they still could not bring all their furniture.

"I can't believe that in our impoverished condition for the last ten years we have collected so much paraphernalia," Sarah complained. "Where does it all come from?"

"The Pukes would do us a favor if they broke their treaty so we would burn some of this," Polly joked. "It would protect us from the sin of possessions."

"I hate to leave Aunt Priscilla's good cherry furniture behind," Rachel said sadly. "Is there no way to bring it with us?"

"The wagons are loaded to the gills, woman," Shadrach said impatiently. "If we are forced to burn our homes and flee into the mountains, there will be no use for dining tables."

"The time to think about that was when you had the Pukes

on the other side of the mountain," Rachel said, bitterly. "Letting them into the valley was like letting the fox into the chicken coop. They can do anything they want now. If you had been true to your faith you would have stopped them."

"Brigham will get everything he wants, you watch," Shadrach assured her. "The fox is in the chicken coop but the chickens are high enough in the rafters for the fox to starve."

A group of the Nauvoo Legionnaires drew up in front of the Tompkins house with a load of straw. The wives of Shadrach helped carry the straw into their house. Despite the trouble it had taken them to build the adobe and wood home, they piled the straw knee-deep on the floors until a match would have consumed the place in minutes.

They stood in the hay-filled living room, reluctant to leave.

"As much as I love this place, as hard as it has been to build it," Rachel said. "I would throw the first torch into the house myself rather than have one Puke defile it."

"I will hold the torch for this house myself," Shadrach promised, "and if a Puke looks hard at it he will see ashes."

Under the strict orders of the church, the entire population of Salt Lake City fled north to Ogden while the Federal army passed through. The stone cutters working on the temple left their tools lying where they labored. The millers left the grain their were grinding in the stones. The mercantile clerks locked the doors of the store. The school mistresses left the textbooks. As the 26th of June, 1858, dawned, not even the barking of the dogs could be heard in the town.

The Federal troops who had camped in Immigration Canyon the night before were presented with an eerie spectacle. Below them at the foot of the mountains an empty city stood. The adobe houses and white clapboard homes were freshly painted, the fences covered with new whitewash. The stores lining the streets were fully stocked and the markets full of the first products of the spring gardens. But only the rustling of the young trees lining the city streets greeted the army of Colonel Johnson as they marched in smart formation into the eastern end of town.

The city was not totally deserted.

Mounted on their fastest horses, the men of the Nauvoo Legion waited on the sidestreets. Each man carried a blazing torch. At the first sign of the federal troops trying to occupy the city, they were to throw their torches into the straw-filled buildings until none was left standing. As the column of troops moved west through the town, the shadows on horse-back moved with them, staying a discreet distance away.

The federal troops had brought a brass band with them and the sweating musicians played their entire repertoire over and over again as they marched through the town. Whenever they stopped, the sound of marching feet was the only thing disturbing the silence of the city.

The officers of the troop cantered nervously on their horses looking for signs of a Mormon ambush. They didn't like the idea of marching through the capital either, but Alfred Cummings had ordered it as a symbolic display of their victory over the Saints. Cummings himself rode fearlessly in an open carriage, although his eyes scanned the windows of the houses for a sign of O.P. Rockwell, the Mormon sharpshooter.

The troops maintained their discipline as they marched through the town, but the teamsters who followed were a different breed. They were not under the military law and the long winter had whetted their appetites for a little fun. As their wagons followed the army into the town, a teamster jumped from the back of a moving wagon. Running up to a dry goods store on Main Street, he smashed the store window.

The sound of breaking glass pricked up Shadrach's ears and he guided Bellophoron toward the sound. An army officer had also heard the sound and he spurred his own horse toward the looter.

"Get back in your wagon!" the officer ordered.

"Hell, captain. I need some new buttons and nobody's going to miss them. The damn Mormons we've been hearing so much about have run away," the man sneered.

The officer drew his service revolver and cocked the hammer.

"Get back in your wagon or I'll blow the rest of your buttons off your pants," he said.

Shadrach watched the cloud of dust hover over the western part of Salt Lake, tinting the afternoon sun a hazy brown. The dust was all that was left of Johnson's army. The Pukes had kept their promise and marched out of Salt Lake without disturbing it.

Both sides had preserved their honor and their lives.

The rest of the mounted horsemen converged in the empty main streets of the town, their pine torches still burning.

Halfway down the street, Ham Tompkins spotted his father

and galloped up to him, whooping and swinging his torch around his head like a sword.

"We have been delivered!" Ham shouted. "It was a tricky game but I believe Brigham has dealt us the best hand!"

Shadrach nodded with the restraint that comes of age.

"Would you really have thrown a torch in our home if they had wandered off the street?" Ham asked.

Shadrach looked at his son and smiled. Then he blew the fire off his torch and left it smouldering in his hand.

Chapter Twenty-One

The Endowment House was a two-story adobe building standing on the northwest corner of Temple Block. Carrying a bundle of special clothing, Theresa entered the house early on a chilly winter's morning. Ahead of her was an experience she had awaited for years.

The reception room in the Endowment House contained a clerk's desk and wooden benches occupied by other Saints clutching the same parcels as she. A clerk seated at the desk recorded her name and the "recommend" of her bishop who had advised her she was ready for one of the church's most cherished rites.

Theresa was led to a small dressing room where a kindly woman helped her disrobe. She was then led to a long tub where she was bathed. After the bath, Theresa stood trembling as she was dried off.

"You're shaking so, sister," the woman observed. "Are you suffering from the cold."

"No, I am trembling with excitement." Theresa replied.

Another woman entered the room and anointed Theresa with a sanctified oil. Starting at her brow the woman dabbed the oil on different parts of her body blessing each as she touched her.

"For your head, that you may have knowledge of the truth of God," the woman recited tenderly. "For your eyes, that you might see the glories of the kingdom. For your mouth that you might speak the truth. For your arms that they might be strong in the defense of the gospel. For your bosom, that you might nourish children whom you will raise with your husband."

Theresa involuntarily flinched when the oil was rubbed on the most private part of her body.

"That you should raise up goodly seed," the woman said

without hesitating, "that they might be pillars of strength for the upbuilding and strengthening of God's kingdom on earth."

The woman kneeled and anointed Theresa's feet with oil.

"That you might be swift in the paths of righteousness."

After this anointment, the woman whispered the celestial name of Theresa in her ear. She would be called "Shimona" when the Millenium came.

Slipping into her holy undergarment, Theresa joined a group of similarly clad men and women who were also receiving their Endowments.

The Endowment was a magical time for Theresa. It created a feeling of being present at the beginning of Creation, and then swept her through the development of mankind and into Heaven.

Theresa overheard a conversation taking place between Elohim and Jehovah concerning the creation of the earth. Several of the brethren acted out the parts of the deities as they created the Garden of Eden and populated it with Adam and Eve.

The men and women were led into the Garden of Eden Room, which had been beautifully decorated by a frontier artist in the imagined lushness of the fabled garden. The birds and beasts of paradise were painted on the walls. The blue ceiling sparkled with gold stars and a giant sun and moon. An apple tree was painted by the doorway and an altar stood at one side of the room.

As Jehovah spoke to the assembled Adams and Eves, a man wearing an apron representing the Devil entered the room. He threatened the group with temptation, trying to lead them out of the ways of the church.

The rest of the day passed as a dream to Theresa. The assembled group was shown the grip of the Aaronic priesthood and donned the special robes, caps and moccasins they would wear for the rest of the ceremony. The robes consisted of straight pieces of cloth in the front and the back worn loose at the shoulders and gathered around the waist. The women's hats were muslin coverings held on by strings. The men's were like those Theresa remembered the pastry cooks wearing in Switzerland, white and rounded slightly.

The properly clad group was led into the World Room, also painted with imaginative scenes of present life on earth. Three men representing Peter, James and John presided in this room and instructed the group in the tenets of the faith.

They were shown the grip of the Melchizedek priesthood, a higher order of worthiness than the Aaronic.

Next, they were led up a flight of stairs to the Instruction Room where they sat on wooden benches. In the middle of the room, a delicate piece of fabric called the Vail was suspended as a recreation of a similar fabric in Solomon's Temple. The Vail contained the same enigmatic marks as their undergarments.

During the afternoon, the group was instructed in the revelations about the Resurrection and the life in Heaven. Theresa was floating on the new knowledge, not learning it consciously but letting it cover her with its glory. They learned of the three states of heaven. The telestial kingdom would be occupied by all who are saved and would be least in its glory. The terrestial kingdom would be a higher place surpassed only by the celestial kingdom where all who entered would be exalted in their glory.

Theresa was still heady with what she had witnessed as she walked out from the Endowment House into the dark chill of the Salt Lake evening. A few flakes of snow were falling but the warmth inside of her made her wonder how she could ever be cold.

Sarah and Rachel were waiting in the darkness to escort her home. "How was it?" Rachel asked, rushing to her.

Theresa could only smile at her. She opened her mouth to speak, but no words came. Tears of happiness poured from her eyes reflecting the glow of the lanterns burning in the square. Sarah and Rachel understood. They wrapped their arms around their sister and escorted her from the Temple Square.

Theresa's spiritual life had progressed but her medical career was bogged down in the mire of prejudice against women doctors.

The Saints were traditionally suspicious of doctors of every stripe, preferring the practice of prayer as the first curative of disease. If that failed, then a laying on of hands and an anointment with oil was in order, with the presiding members of the congregation around them. If that failed, there was always an old woman with the knowledge of herbs and wild roots who would prepare a comfery for the afflicted. At last resort there were a number of doctors of differing persuasions that one could see.

Not a woman doctor.

The midwives of the community looked with jealousy at this foreign woman with her high-bred education and her black bag. Her modern notions about birth and disease frightened them and they spread the distrust about her methods across the back fences of the city. The local doctors were even more vicious in their desire to stop the competition of this newcomer. They appealed to the church authorities to bar her from her practice and when that failed they sent off to Geneva to verify her license to practice. When this was confirmed they mounted a secret campaign to keep her from the medical clinics of the city.

"I am moved to tears at the intransigence of these people," Theresa complained at the dinner table. "If I was doing their laundry I would be welcomed into their homes but when I arrive to heal their bodies I am scorned."

The women of the Tompkins family might have felt the jealousy other women felt for the educated Theresa, but since she had lived in their home they felt a comradeship and sympathy for her. Her struggle became their struggle and they tried to keep her spirits up.

"What does the community have against a woman contributing to the cause?" Theresa asked. "Surely it is not the teachings of the church which hold it so? Brigham Young himself has encouraged women to work as long as they do not neglect their families."

Shadrach was mopping up the gravy from his plate when he felt all eyes at the table staring at him. "What do you want me to say?" he asked as he stuffed the biscuit in his mouth. "This is not Geneva or London; this is Salt Lake City. New ideas are not going to take hold as quickly out here. If you are patient, you will get your reward."

"She wants patients, not patience," Sarah reprimanded him. "How can you sit there and let her be shunned by a community in need of doctors. Surely there must be something you can do to help?"

"Perhaps I should go over to brother Jonathan Moses and threaten to break his leg if he doesn't let Theresa look at it."

"This is no time for jokes!" Rachel snapped.

"An unmarried woman is viewed with suspicion," Shadrach observed. "Both morally and spiritually. It is difficult for a woman doctor to gain confidence, but twice as hard for an unmarried woman doctor."

"Perhaps in some of the outlying regions of the south?" Polly asked. "Perhaps in Dixie they could be more appreciative of her talents? When a place has no doctor, perhaps they could turn a blind eye to her sex?"

"That's right. You know the countryside and you know all the people," Sarah said. "You could make inquiries of the folk in Dixie and find her a position."

"It's a hard life in the South," Shadrach said. "It might be too much for her."

"I would go anywhere to practice," Theresa said, "Even to the desert itself."

"Very well, then. I will make the necessary inquiries."

The invasion of the federal troops into the valley of the Great Salt Lake changed the life of the Saints very little. It was like the loss of virginity. No longer would their valley remain purely their own preserve, but the effects of the defilement were not altogether harmful.

The United States Army stayed only two years before it was called back to meet the threat of the Civil War which was beginning in the southern states. While they were in the territory, the Mormon farmers made large profit from the army by selling them forage for their livestock and food for the men.

When the army marched east to fight a new war, Brigham Young proudly occupied the rostrum in the tabernacle to proclaim victory for the Saints."

"The apocalypse of Babylon which was long prophesized is now coming true!" he claimed. "The Pukes are at each other's throats and before the North and South have done with each other the corrupt empire of the West will have fallen. God has spread his protection over us. Even with a hostile army in our midst he has calmed them and delivered us from them. We are now free to build our haven as the rest of the world falls into ruin around us."

The war which raged in the East turned the attention of the Gentiles from Zion's shores, but the Saints were not left in peace for very long. A detachment of California Volunteers marched into the valley in 1862 under the command of a brash young officer named Colonel Patrick Connor.

These soldiers were not content to set up their camp outside the Mormon capital but instead requisitioned the high ground at the foot of the Wasatch Mountains. There, they built a fort named after the old enemy of the Saints, Stephen Douglas, within sight of the dome of the Tabernacle.

To add insult to injury, the soldiers positioned a battery of cannon at the front of the fort and pointed it at the headquarters of Brigham Young. They bragged that if any threat was made to them they would 'knock Salt Lake City flatter than a corn cake.'

The soldiers came as a warning to the Saints about taking advantage of the Union's troubles with the South. They also served to encourage the growing number of Gentiles who were trickling into the valley to establish a challenge to the Saint's dominance of the valley.

The Saints watched this transformation of the valley with great suspicion. They generally felt that perhaps Brigham had not made such a fine bargain after all. The Gentiles showed no promise of growing sick of the valley and leaving. Worse, many of them appeared very happy there. The soldiers of Fort Douglas had very little to do, so they spent their hours prospecting for ore in the mountains around the city. Since the Saints had been forbidden by Brigham Young to prospect for precious metals, the soldiers had the run of the mountains.

The families who gathered on the temple grounds for afternoon strolls after service on Sundays watched the growing presence of the Gentiles with concern. Shadrach often took walks there with his ever-increasing family—three wives, house guest, and eleven children in tow. He greeted his friends and colleagues in the community and commiserated with them on the pernicious influence in their midst. Thomas Morse, with whom he had patched his friendship since their falling out during the war, often brought his large family to the grounds.

"Have you seen the way those soldiers look at our women?" Morse complained. "They have publicly stated that if plural marriages flourish in Deseret, they will take as many women as they please."

"I have seen them staring at us in a lewd manner," Rachel said. "If they lay so much as a glove on me I will scratch their eyes out!"

"The Gentiles have opened a saloon and a whorehouse on South Main Street and the soldiers are flocking to it," Morse complained. "I remember when I could walk the streets of Salt Lake and hear no profanity. No longer!"

"A group of soldiers broke the head of Brother Akins the

other night," Shadrach observed. "I'm afraid when the brother recovers he is going to get a pistol and avenge himself and then all Hell will break loose."

"We should burn Fort Douglas to the ground while we have the chance," Rachel suggested. "Now that the Union is losing the war to the South, they will never retaliate against us."

"It is too late for that," Sarah said. "Gentiles are flooding this valley. A Puke named Auerbach has opened a dry goods store not far from the Mercantile. He is going to undercut our prices."

"Then we will undercut his!" Polly said. "The Mercantile will drive him out of business. We will also take down the names of any Saint who shops at his store and they will be disfellowshipped."

A group of blue-jacketed soldiers strolled by and tipped their hats to the Tompkins and Morses. All of the Saints turned their backs on them, pretending they had seen nothing.

Shadrach shook his head.

"This valley is changing all right," he said. "I hope we do not change with it."

During the early part of the 1860s, a transcontinental railroad was constructed that would link up the Pacific Coast with the eastern United States. The line would run through the northern part of Deseret just above the Great Salt Lake and its existence was the source of great debate among the Saints. A railroad near the valley could bring Gentiles pouring into Salt Lake Valley, or an army at any time of the year. It could tempt the younger, more restless Saints to move to the more lively haunts of San Francisco.

Brigham Young considered the railroad and realized that if it could bring Gentiles into the valley, it could also bring Saints who would be spared the arduous overland journey. It could also ship Mormon merchandise out of the valley and bring manufactured goods in, an advantage that would speed the building of Zion.

The leaders of the church reluctantly agreed to not oppose the railroad. One of the conditions was that the contracting work for the Utah section be awarded to the Saints.

Shadrach Tompkins, with his background in mining and his faithful service to the cause, was made a contractor on the Union Pacific. He was in charge of overseeing the construction of a tunnel through the Wasatch Mountains, a tunnel dug by a large gang of Chinamen with materials supplied by his fellow Saints.

The work brought Shadrach a measure of financial security he had not seen before, a reward from Brigham Young for the missions he had undertaken at great cost to his family. With the income from the work, Shadrach was able to build a second house in Salt Lake City, a large frame house built from Utah pine high on the hill above City Creek. The more distinguished of the pioneer families were all building homes on the hill where the view of the growing city of the Saints was unsurpassed.

By agreement, Sarah and Rachel Tompkins would share the new house while Polly and her children remained at home in the original adobe house on Main Street. This new arrangement took a great burden off the growing family and the extra room seemed to be a great luxury.

Sarah and Rachel had each borne Shadrach three children, ranging in ages from four to eight. Polly was the busy mother of five children who more than overran the adobe house.

Shadrach divided his time between the two households, spending his weekends and two days on the hill, the three other days at his Main Street residence. His principal joy in his life was the sound of his children running to be scooped up in his arms when he came back from Ogden where he oversaw the railroad work. The children would show him the new toys the old men of the city had made for them, the corn dolls and carved wooden animals that were jealously handed down from child to child. The new prosperity of the family had not extended to the clothes the children wore. They were the same threadbare hand-me-downs the family had kept for years.

Extravagant dress was frowned upon in the frugal city.

The clothing of the children did present one crucial problem for Shadrach. It made their identification more difficult. A little girl wearing a small calico frock trimmed with lace would skip by and he would remember her as Susanna, the daughter of Rachel. But Susanna had outgrown the dress the year before and now it had been passed to Erin, the youngest daughter of Polly.

Before Shadrach entered one of his houses he would always recite the names of the children to be found within. Walker Tompkins was the easiest to remember. He had the pleasingly tanned skin, the sculpted features and dark black hair of his Indian mother. Since Mariah's death he had been raised as one of Rachel's own children. Rachel's three other surviving children had the same sharp personalities as their mother. John and Nathan Tompkins, ages ten and eight, were named after John and Nathan Putnam, murdered at Haun's Mill. Her daughter, Eliza, was named after her grandmother.

Sarah's children showed the more even disposition of their mother. Zina, twelve, was a caretaker who shepherded the other children including her brothers Orson, eleven, and Lehi, whose speech was impaired by a hairlip until a surgeon operated on him at age nine.

Polly's children were the wildest of the family, perhaps because of their run of the adobe house. Finnegan Tompkins, a gangly troublemaker at eight, led his brothers Brian Boru and Wolf Tone in a ceaseless tormenting of their sister, Erin.

Once he had committed to memory the names and habits of his children, Shadrach was a kind but stern father to them all.

Shadrach loved to sit in the middle of a circle of his children and quiz them about the Book of Mormon.

"Who knows who the Gladianton Robbers were?" he asked.

"I know! I know!" an angelic little blonde girl shouted, raisng a pudgy hand in the air.

"Very well, Zina, tell me," he said.

"I'm not Zina, I'm Laura," the child replied.

"Laura? Laura?" Shadrach said. He was ashamed to admit he didn't remember who her mother was. "Aren't you Rachel's youngest?"

"No, Brother Tompkins. I'm Brother Morse's little girl."

The rest of the children tittered but Shadrach tried to continue as if he hadn't made a mistake. "Very well, Laura. Who were the Gladianton Robbers?"

For years, the legal disputes of the Saints were handled by the bishops or special church juries. When a citizen of Deseret had a problem, he went to the church, not to the government.

The U.S. Government was trying to change that.

When the army marched in, they brought something more threatening than guns. They brought the Federal judges. The Saints felt these men were political hacks who were intent on destroying the church. The Federal judges hunted for cases to try. They were eager to bring Deseret to its knees.

The massacre at Mountain Meadows was their biggest target. Rumors of the massacre had spread east and relatives of the missing pioneers were clamoring for an investigation. The federal authorities, eager for a case with which to discredit Brigham Young, siezed upon this as a crime to investigate. A grand jury was impaneled to look into the matter and various men were sought for questioning.

John D. Lee's name was prominently mentioned in connection with the incident and Lee fled into the rugged canyonlands of the southern mountains to avoid questioning. The others who came forward claimed little knowledge of the crime, and others kept to themselves.

Shadrach Tompkins name had been linked to the incident as a witness and the growing investigation made him nervous about the intentions of the authorities. Although he had no complicity in the matter, he would be reluctant to give testimony against his friends.

In a discussion with some church officials, the mention of an overseas mission caught Shadrach's ear. Perhaps an absence from Utah would be convenient at this delicate time?

Shadrach called his wives together for a formal dinner for Pioneer Day on July 24, 1865. They sat in the two-story house whose bay-windowed dining room looked out over the twinkling lights of Salt Lake City. The three women wore the best dresses yet available at the Mercantile, while Shadrach was uncomfortably dressed in a new black suit.

The four spent a quiet evening of reminiscence about the struggles they had seen in the past eighteen years to protect the church and to build the city.

After dinner, Shadrach sipped from a glass of mineral water and cleared his throat.

"I have reached a decision about undertaking a mission for the church," he said. "I have chosen to journey to help reorganize the affairs of our ward in the Sandwich Islands. I leave for San Francisco immediately."

The women were surprised by this announcement.

"The Sandwich Islands? Where on God's earth is that?"

"Three thousand leagues west of San Francisco. The islands called Hawaii. The church's mission had encountered some setbacks there."

"Are the heathens in those parts dangerous?"

"The whites are more dangerous than the heathens."

"How long will you be gone?"

"Until the federal authorities forget about me," Shadrach said, supressing a twinkle in his eye.

"What about your affairs here?" Rachel demanded. "What about the railroad?"

"Ham has been at my side for the entire labor," Shadrach said. "He knows my business as well as any and can step into my shoes. You will, I trust, give him the benefit of your wisdom if he needs it."

"Then that settles it," Polly said.

"There is one more piece of business before you leave," Sarah brought up. "Theresa is coming back from Washington County to practice medicine here in Salt Lake."

"That's good news, indeed," Shadrach said.

"We feel that it is important that she be married right away to gain the proper standing in the community."

"I agree," Shadrach said. "Pity's that she couldn't find anyone to her liking in Washington County."

"She is very particular," Sarah continued. "She has already chosen a man of her liking in Salt Lake and has confided his name to us."

Shadrach looked crestfallen. Whoever the man was, he was already jealous. The thought of Theresa in another man's arms was too much for him to bear. He tried to conceal his disappointment in this news.

"Oh? Who is the gentleman? Do I know him?"

The women hid their smiles as they looked at each other across the table. Shadrach breathed an inward sigh of relief. He nodded gravely, trying to hide his inner excitement. The idea of increasing his celestial glory and his earthly pleasure with the addition of the comely Swiss woman made his years of yearning for her and his abstinence worthwhile. The virtue of chastity had rewarded him.

THE ISLANDS OF THE SEA

SEA

1865

Chapter Twenty-Two

The Pacific typhoon had whipped the ocean into a snarling enemy as the barkentine, *The Wave Hound*, plowed west toward Hawaii. Their mortal peril was clear to the passengers of the sleek sailing ship as they were thrown about their cabins by the pitching of the storm.

Shadrach could stand no more of the stomach-floating gyrations of his bunk. He had to be in the fresh air where perhaps the wider view would ease his seasickness. He pulled himself up as boot-deep water poured down the companionway.

When he poked his head through the hatch cover and looked around, he was terrified by what he saw. It was midday, yet the sky was as dark as evening. The clouds poured rain on the ship like buckets of water being thrown on a screaming cat. The ship rose lazily and then began to fall with a sickening velocity. Shadrach watched in horror for the ship was not falling. Instead, the seas were rising above it until they stood taller than the cliffs of Southern Utah.

The water broke like an avalanche and fell on the ship with such a force that Shadrach was sure it would be driven under. It survived, but he was knocked to the bottom of the companionway. Checking to see if his legs were broken he scrambled up the steep steps and lurched out on deck.

A series of lifelines had been strung across the deck for the sailors to cling to. Shadrach followed them to the stern of the ship, gripping them tightly to keep from being washed overboard.

He was not the only member of his party of Saints who had been unable to stand the buffeting below decks. Lorenzo Snow, Joseph F. Smith, and several others shivered in the deluge. Hanging on to the pin racks of the mizzenmast they looked like Ulysses about to pass the temptation of the sirens.

They were a powerful group: leaders of the church sent on an urgent and delicate mission. Smith was the nephew of the murdered prophet. Snow was an apostle and one of the most influential men in Deseret. Yet huddled together, soaked to the skin, their beards dripping with rain and ocean spray, they looked like a collection of wet rats on a raft, hoping to stay afloat until a landfall could be reached.

"I do believe the storm is abating," Shadrach shouted over the roar of the wind.

As if to dampen his optimism, a giant wave broke over the bow of the ship and crashed down on them. Shadrach was swept over the rail into the boiling ocean. His powerful hands never loosened from the lifeline he was holding and with the next surge of the ship, he was pulled back on board the ship by the other Saints.

"I am going to ask the captain how much longer the storm is going to hold," he announced when firmly back on deck.

The captain of the ship was a bitter looking little man who stood in a black oilskin at the helm of the ship. He gripped the brass binnacle of the *Wave Hound* as if it was his salvation and he cursed impiously as each wave smashed down over himself and the helmsman who gripped the wheel.

When the captain saw Shadrach approaching he took off his sou'wester and rubbed his hand across his bald head.

"God damn it! Every time I carry a load of missionaries with me I run into heavy weather," the captain shouted. "If God sees fit to test the faith of you people, why can't he do it on someone elses ship?"

"Perhaps we are good luck!" Shadrach shouted back. "The storm might be worse if we weren't along."

"I doubt that. The mercury in my barometer has just about disappeared. This storm is just beginning to pour on."

"How much longer can it last?"

"If I was smart enough to be able to predict the longevity of storms, I would've been smart enough not to have entered a career on the sea!"

The captain and the helmsman grinned as they watched Shadrach's face fall at the prospect of the continuing storm.

"Captain, is there anything my brethren and I can do?"

"Yes. Go below and make yourselves scarce. Some of the crew say that having Mormons on board is bad luck. They want to chuck the lot of you into the drink."

"Don't worry, captain," Shadrach assured him. "We will all offer our prayers for our deliverance. I prophesy that we will make it through intact."

Now it was time for the captain's face to fall.

"No! Don't do that! Every time a group of damn missionaries get us into a storm, the first thing they do is fall to their knees and pray for deliverance. This caterwauling always makes the storm ten times worse!"

As the gangplank was lowered onto the dock at Honolulu, Shadrach was the first to stagger, wobbly legged onto dry land. He stood on the granitelike permanence of the dock taking in the beauty of the tiny port.

The first thing he noticed was the delightful perfumed air of the island. It smelled like a dream of one hundred ladies wafted by the balmy air of the mountains towering over the harbor. The sky was a tranquil blue, not unlike the blue of his Deseret skies, but it reflected upon a glowing green carpet of vegetation that extended in every direction. Hawaii was as lush and verdant as Deseret was barren and rocky. Even on the busy wharf the warehouses and chandlers were dripping with red and yellow flowers of such brilliant color that he had to feel them to see if they were real. The weather here seemed to mimic springtime.

This observation was borne out as a speedy little packet boat carried them south of Maui. The dolphins leaped by their bow and the frigate birds soared above their mast as they passed the chartreuse hillsides of Molokai. Shadrach had been burned a permanent tan by the blazing sun of Deseret, but he still felt the rays of the Hawaiian sun. When the brethren were not watching him, he loosened the tie of his shirt to relieve his sweating.

When they reached the whaling port of Lahaina on Maui Shadrach could only contrast the village with the places he had known in Deseret. All around him the profanities of the sailors were woven through the mast tops and grog shops lining the crowded harbor. Before the sun was over the tops of the houses the carousing whalers were staggering through the streets clutching the breasts of the willing native girls with such immodesty that Shadrach was forced to turn away.

Drunkenness abounded in this depraved section of the island paradise. The church delegation scarcely left their lodgings for the abuse the sailors gave them. Only in the company of the powerful Englishman would the church leaders venture around the blasphemous seafarers.

Gratefully the delegation set sail for Lanai, across the channel, and the final leg of their journey.

*   *   *

The church had always been evangelical. From its earliest days in the 1830s missionaries had spread the word, not only through the United States and Europe but throughout the rest of the world. Seafaring Saints carried the news of the restored church to the Pacific Islands in the 1840s. A flourishing Mormon community was established in Hawaii despite opposition from the New England Congregationalists. During the exodus from Nauvoo and the war with the United States, the support for the Hawaiian mission fell by the wayside and the community dwindled in numbers.

In the early 1860s an itinerant snake oil salesman and platform speaker named Walter Murray Gibson arrived in Salt Lake City. He quickly professed a miraculous conversion to Mormonism and began to attract a following for his speeches. Soon he was speaking at the tabernacle and outdrawing the leaders of the church.

Brigham Young sensed he had another Dr. John Bennett in his flock. A two-year mission in New York was abandoned by Gibson in six months and the slippery huckster was back in Salt Lake speechifying again. The charlatan had a beautiful daughter named Talulah who had been turning heads wherever she went. Many of the most prominent men of Deseret had cast their eyes on Talulah, including President Young, and the thought of his precious daughter in a plural marriage so terrified Gibson that he proposed a mission to the Pacific Islands to reestablish the church.

He had been successful in gathering the Hawaiian Saints to the island of Lanai where they cultivated a six thousand acre farm in the crater of an extinct volcano. Using the free labor of his converts, Gibson profited enough so he no longer needed the church. He set himself up as the monarch of his own island.

Brigham Young received an anguished letter from a faithful Saint complaining that Gibson had sold the priesthood and offices of the church to the highest bidders and was holding the congregation as slaves who worked his fields. Young furiously ordered a delegation to set sail immediately for Hawaii to depose this false prophet.

At the landing at Lanai, a lighter was tied up at the dock while a herd of cattle was loaded. The cattle were strapped into a harness and the crane swung the bellowing beasts out onto the deck of the sailboat.

Shadrach's own arrival was more dignified as the Saints stepped off the boat. A line of carriages was waiting for them at the dock. A group of white-shirted, smiling native drivers sat in the carriages waiting to take them to the steep mountain.

"Gentlemen! Welcome to Zion in the Pacific."

The words were spoken by Talulah Gibson who looked even more beautiful than the few times Shadrach had seen her in Salt Lake. The young woman wore a white lace dress which revealed her constricted waist and hinted at her ample breasts. Although the dress rose to a high collar, it was cut from a thin material and when she stood against the light, her body was revealed through the sheer material. She wore a wide-brimmed straw hat that hid her mahogony-colored hair and she carried a parasol that protected her alabaster pale skin from the sun.

The men of the delegation were flustered by the broad smile and outstretched hand of their hostess. "I'm sorry my father was not able to greet you personally," the hostess said, "but church business keeps him so busy that I have volunteered to take you on a tour of what he has created here before we meet with him."

The men dutifully climbed into the carriages and the drivers cracked their whips. The narrow road spiraled around the precipitous slopes of the extinct volcano. The road was cut into a pumice-covered cliff. If a horse were to bolt, their carriage would plunge straight down into the breakers crashing on the rocks below. The dizzying climb took them three thousand feet above the beach until they could no longer see the white combers breaking on the shore.

As they crested the top of the volcano's crater, Shadrach caught his breath. The interior of the cone had been turned into a garden. The shallow valley had been created by the filling of the cone. Sheltered by the lips of the crater and fed by a crystalline stream which poured from the sides of the lips, the place was ten thousand acres of unsurpassed fertility.

"If the garden of Eden had been as bountiful as this, Eve and Adam would never have bitten the apple," Talulah called to the men as they rode. "This was a barren plain when my father first set eyes on it, but his faith and the work of our brethren have turned this into a heaven on earth. Think what we could do with the proper support from Deseret?"

The fields inside the crater were growing all manner of crops. The brown-skinned natives who tended the fields bowed and waved with unabashed affection as Talulah rode by. She acted as though she was the queen of the island, Shadrach noted. And the squat islanders in their long white shirts and full dresses were working like serfs in the mid-day sun.

Along the road that led through the valley, poles had been placed at intervals. On the poles, crucified with nails, pages of the Book of Mormon were visible.

"What is the meaning of that?" Lorenzo Snow asked angrily.

"You have to understand. You are in Hawaii now. The Kanakas do not act the same way folk in America do," Talulah explained breezily. "In the old days they worshipped images of their Gods which they placed on poles. Now they understand the significance of the book more easily if we ape their customs."

The carriages drove on until they came to a shrine which had been set up by the side of the road. Talulah disembarked from her carriage and led them proudly into the hut made of palm fronds. Inside, a large polished boulder stood higher than a man. The delegation stared at the center of the rock. A lone copy of the Book of Mormon rested in the interior of the boulder, displayed like an ornament.

"There it is, a jewel set in our crown," Talulah exulted. "This is father's proudest accomplishment. For centuries this boulder has been worshipped as sacred by the natives of this island. Father put a Book of Mormon in the middle of it. The superstitious darlings spread the rumor that if any man touched it, he would die. That taboo has worked wonders for their belief. A chicken flew in here one morning and keeled over. We made a lot of converts after that. I am the only one who is able to come in here."

The delegation was astonished beyond words at what they had seen.

"What makes you so dad-gummed special?" an incredulous Saint asked.

"Father has made me a high priestess of the church," Talulah said smiling. "I keep all the shrines on the island."

Shadrach winced as she spoke. Lorenzo Snow almost suffered an apoplectic stroke. There would be some explaining to do.

That evening, few of the delegation were hungry for the roast suckling pig wrapped in taro leaves being carved by

Gibson. A dapper, middle-aged man with a syrupy voice and a calculating eye, Gibson lived in a more regal style than Brigham Young himself. His white-washed wattle home was kept spotless by a small army of smiling native members of the church. The natural cooling properties of the thatched palm roof were enhanced by rotating ceiling fans kept turned by small boys who pedaled iron treadles hooked to pulleys. The spacious cottage was furnished with furniture requisitioned from Yankee Saints and when Gibson entertained, it was on white linen and a sparkling china service.

Gibson spoke with a broad drawl that reminded Shadrach of a Missourian. The white-haired patriarch of the island looked unusually calm for someone who was under suspicion of wrongdoing. He wore a white waistcoat and open neck shirt and lorded over the meal, as if he were king of the island.

The delegation of Saints were visibly agitated by what they had seen. They were used to the way business of the church was done in Deseret where the proper decorum and respect was shown to church officialdom. This popinjay threw all tradition in their faces.

"Eat your dinnahs, Gentlemen!" Gibson drawled. "Eat! Eat!"

"Frankly, sir, I have no appetite for food after what I have seen today," Lorenzo Snow said. "You have made a mockery of the practices of our church on this island and you have led a number of goodly Saints astray."

Gibson hardly blinked an eye at this impeachment. "You have to understand that in the islands, things are done differently. What may appear to you to be mysterious has actual basis in the habits of the natives."

"The ordinances of the church are universal!" Snow replied evenly. "They apply in Deseret, they apply here or in Siam, and they will apply on Jupiter as soon as we can send a mission there."

"The Hawaiians are a childlike race, barely removed from paganism," Gibson purred. "The church suffered when it attempted to bring them too far, too fast. If we tune our strings to their natural and gullible natures, they will follow us in droves. We have already outdistanced the Congregationalists in a very short time."

"What good is leading a people easily if the path you are taking is a false one?"

"I am following the path of the church doctrines."

"You are not, sir!" Snow said, raising his voice as his anger seeped through. "What I have seen this afternoon borders on idolatry! How dare you nail up the pages of the Book of Mormon like pagan images? How can you countenance the chicanery of that shrine? The blasphemy of your daughter in the priesthood?"

Now it was Gibson's turn to raise his voice. "For several years I struggled alone on this island without a word of encouragement from the church. When I asked for money to buy this sacred land at the price of twenty-five cents an acre, I was refused. I was forced to raise the money myself and did so without any help from you."

"We appreciate your industry, Brother Gibson," Hale said, "but that does not excuse you from the charge of breaking the convenants of the church."

"I didn't allow you on this island to lecture me!"

"Allow us, Brother Gibson? Do you know what you are saying?" Hale asked, trembling with rage. "Do you realize we are a mission from the highest level of the church sent here to investigate the gravest charges against you?"

Hale had lost his temper. He was no match for the wily orator and Gibson knew it. Gibson smiled comfortably and looked at his daughter.

"On my island, only I bring the charges," he said.

"Your island? This land is consecrated to the church and to God!"

"You are mistaken, Mr. Hale," Talulah said. "For the sake of convenience, the deed to this property was made out in my father's name, not the church's. He is the sole owner and can dispose of it any way he wishes."

"This is monstrous!"

"And if you have any doubts about it, please test it in court," Gibson said, smiling. "I have the goodwill of the king of the islands on my side as well as the friendship of the major planters. The church does not have a pot to pee in."

"We will bring this case before the people of the congregation," Hale said, trembling with anger. "When they find out what a charlatan you are they will throw you bodily off the island."

Gibson pressed his hands together and touched his lips with his fingertips to conceal his smug smile of victory. "The good Saints on this island think of me as a god, as their father. I had prophesied that a group of evil men were coming to harm their father and they believed me. I doubt whether you will receive one vote against me in a test of confidence."

Hale stood up and threw his napkin on the table. The other Saints stood and prepared to follow him. "I now have a prophesy to make," Hale said. "Before this decade is out, you will be roasting in the eternal flames of hell for your treachery to God and to the church!"

The next day the congregation of Hawaiian Saints was called together in a muggy assembly building. From the beginning, Gibson controlled his flock like a shepherd, leading them in spirited hymns and then addressing them in fiery Hawaiian. He was as effective an orator in Polynesian as he was in English and when he had finished the Saints voted against the Utah delegation almost unanimously.

Only one Hawaiian sided with the Saints. He was an old chief named Ha'oke who had sent the original letter of complaint to Brigham Young. When the voting was over, Ha'oke volunteered to take the Utah delegation back to port on Maui.

It was a dispirited party which rowed the narrow dugout canoe across the strait that separated Lanai from Maui. Hale and the rest of the delegation felt that they had failed the president. They had lost the congregation, the land and the victory to the scheming Gibson.

Ha'oke was cheerful in spite of the circumstances. He smiled as he dug his broad paddle into the swells of the Pacific. "Don't worry, now everything be fine," he said in his sing-song English. "People tired. When they see we leave they soon follow. Nobody like Kipona anyhow."

"Then why did they so overwhelmingly vote for him?" Hale asked.

"They not agree with him, but not friendly to fight with him," Ha'oke said easily. "Before long they come follow us."

Shadrach sat hunched over in the canoe gripping the gunwales with his fingers. He was convinced that if he sat upright his weight would tip the canoe over and they would all be eaten by the sharks. These islanders could swim like fishes but if he fell into water over his head he would drown.

Ha'oke's daughter sat in front of him paddling as easily as her father and brothers. Her name was Wamoa and Shadrach's only consolation on the dangerous trip was watching her supple bronzed skin and muscles ripple as she followed her father's rhythmical singing to pace her strokes. Wamoa felt Shadrach watching her and turned to flash a smile at his nervousness.

To relax him, she would sweep an oarful of water on him, drenching his new suit. This prank relaxed all the members of the crew, save Shadrach, and the tension of the trip was broken as they all laughed at his discomfort. Wamoa kept drenching him until he could take no more and scooped a gallon of sea water up in his top hat. He poured it over her, soaking her new white dress. The rest of the long trip to Lahaina went more pleasantly. Shadrach was pleased to note that wetting down her dress clearly outlined the contours of her body as the material became transparent when it stuck to her brown skin.

The defeated Saints went first to Honolulu where they planned what to do next. A quick vote disfellowshipped the traitor, Walter Murray Gibson, cutting him off from the covenants of the church and banishing him to the buffetings of Satan.

It was decided not to try to sue Gibson for the return of church property. The Saints had never fared well in Gentile courts and news of the schism would only embarrass the church. Instead, they looked for a new place to build a Polynesian Zion and to regather the Hawaiian Saints. Ha'oke suggested a deserted stretch of island on the eastern shore of Oahu. Here, land was plentiful. The farmlands were protected from the storms coming from the west by a chain of mountains. The same mountains would protect them from the prying eyes of the Gentiles and would shelter a community of the faithful until they had time to build their strength.

A packet boat was engaged and the Deseret Saints spent their last money buying building supplies and food to last them until they had become self-sufficient.

About forty Hawaiian Saints had been collected at Honolulu, the remnants of the congregation that had existed before Gibson settled at Lanai. Led by Ha'oke, the Saints told stories about how they would rebuild the faith and sang hymns in the enchanting harmonies of the island. To Shadrach, the singing sounded like choirs of celestial angels and he was moved to join the rhythmical clapping that accompanied each song.

On the afternoon of the tenth day of the voyage, the packet boat rounded a hook of land that created a shallow harbor in the windward coast. The ship dropped anchor and the Saints crowded the hot deck to admire the view of their new home.

Wamoa hugged Shadrach as she leaned over the rail. "There is Laie," she said, pointing to a deserted beach. "Is it not as beautiful as we have foretold?"

Shadrach had to admit it was. The strip of sand rimming the cove was as white as the rims of his fingernails. The green jungle marched up to the edge of the beach and they were saluted by the raucous calls of hundreds of wild birds. Even at anchor they could smell the scent of the orchids growing in the forest. A heavy mist hung over the peaks of the mountains in the background.

As they watched, a brilliant prismatic crescent of a rainbow arched over the bay and anchored itself on the beach. The assembled Saints broke out in a burst of spontaneous applause.

"That is a good sign," Wamoa said, thrilled at the sight. "That means the Gods are pouring their blessing onto our choice of a home."

"Not the gods, Wamoa," Shadrach cautioned. "God!"

A herd of pigs had broken loose from their pens and came racing out of the burning forest, screaming like Lamanites. Shadrach cursed and made a grab for one piglet but it was too fast for him. In anger he threw his torch after the squealing shoat.

"Run, damn you, run! Run into the forest and get burned alive. At least I'll have some roast pork for my troubles!"

He had run out of patience. The lackadaisical Hawaiians had let the pigs escape again. It would take days to bring those hogs out of the forest and they would have leaned out by running so far. Shadrach had begun burning the jungle to clear some farmland that morning. He had been assisted by four of the Hawaiian men, but by noon he was all alone. The Kanakas showed great enthusiasm for every project they began, but the enthusiasm faded as the sun rose in the sky. He was beginning to think that perhaps Gibson was right. Forced slavery might be the only way these happy people would work.

"At this rate it's going to take one thousand years to build a Zion in these Islands," Shadrach said, slumping to the ground in the ashes of the forest. "The Millenium could be scheduled for tommorow, but these people would still go fishing."

Shadrach's impatience was the source of great amusement for the Hawaiians. Ha'oke had tried to reassure Shadrach that there was plenty of time to build up the community. More and more Saints arrived every month. Gibson's charm was wearing thin on Lanai and his flock was deserting. A village of grass huts had been constructed around the inlet at Laie. Ha'oke tried to convince the sunburned haole that they were succeeding in their mission and that he should relax and have some fun. But relaxation had been an unknown ideal to Shadrach before he had come to the islands. He had worked constantly to build a new life, in Missouri, Illinois and in Deseret. He had seen how constant labor was rewarded wherever they settled. Relaxation of this work was almost a sin.

Now, in this paradise, Shadrach took personal responsibility for all the labor. While the congregation was swimming, gossiping or singing, he was in the fields. He would burn away the jungle, plant yams and watch the jungle grow back again and consume the fields. Even if he did get a harvest from the garden, the land was covered with only a thin layer of topsoil and the heavy rains would wash the good earth away leaving only the lava base. The soil, he concluded, was like the people. Beautiful but not fond of work.

Shadrach got up out of the ashes. This day, a certain laziness had finally overtaken Shadrach. He longed to go for a swim to clean the ashes and grime from himself. Perhaps it would not be a great sin to lie in the sun that afternoon and rest from the labor of single-handedly building the community? Perhaps these Hawaiians had a point?

Although Shadrach had adopted the habit of relaxation, he had not succumbed to the other habits of the islanders. He was shocked at the promiscuous ways of the natives, both in the neighboring communities and in some instances, in the Saints themselves. The younger people seemed more inclined to the pleasures of the flesh than their more restrained parents. At any time of the day, the children could be found swimming within the reef, as naked as the day they were borne.

Shadrach had been forced to whistle as he walked through the forests surrounding the community. Several times he had chanced on the young people in positions of carnal ecstacy that would have made Nero blush. He had been particularly disappointed to find Wamoa engaged with young men, not just on one occasion, but several times.

He had complained about these practices to Ha'oke, but the old chief had just dismissed these observations with a shy smile and a wave of his weathered hand. "These people are young," the wrinkled man said, as if that were all the explanation necessary.

Ha'oke himself was no model of deportment. He had taken a number of wives and on Saturday nights when the music made the shift from the staid church hymns back to the wilder drumbeats of the ancient music, the wiry old fellow would always select the youngest and prettiest girl he could, and drag her out in the firelight. He would dance in a pelvis wiggling contortion that would have had him arrested on the streets of Salt Lake City.

"Kahuna! Kahuna!"

A voice calling him in his Hawaiian name summoned him from his thoughts. Looking up, Shadrach saw Wamoa running toward him on the jungle path. He looked discreetly in back of her to see if she was with anyone. She always called him "Kahuna," the Hawaiian word for *priest*.

"Look at you! Have you fallen into a volcano?" she said, laughing as she brushed the ashes from his clothing.

"I was going to the beach to clean up," he said, embarrassed.

"I will come with you."

They walked on together in silence, with Shadrach leading the way with his giant strides, Wamoa following with quick steps as she held her white skirt above the dirt path of the jungle. They left the jungle at the edge of the beach. The inlet was filled with the children of the village splashing in the surf, while the elders of the village sat in the shade watching them.

"I cannot join this display," Shadrach said, frowning. "You stay here. I will bathe farther down the beach."

Shadrach walked north along the beach, stepping quickly inland when the dying surf lapped around the soles of his boots. A stiff offshore breeze was blowing, ruffling his hair and soothing his jangled nerves. He continued to walk north before he turned around. He knew Wamoa was following him but he was afraid to admit it, afraid he would angrily order her back.

Sure enough, when he turned around, she was standing behind him, grinning the cheshire cat grin of hers. Shadrach looked back down the beach. He had walked so far that the rest of the community were barely visible specks on the shimmering horizon.

"Come with me," Wamoa invited. "I know where some of the most beautiful shells on the island are."

Before he could stop her, she lifted her muslin dress and pulled it over her head. She wore nothing under her dress and she stood teasingly before him for a few moments before she ran into the surf. As she came to the line of breakers she dove under them and beckoned the embarrassed Englishman to join her.

Shadrach said a silent prayer begging for guidance. He could not get the image of the woman's body from his mind, the firmness of her breasts, the whiteness of her inviting smile, the graceful lines of her body. He reasoned that this was a sign. Hopping on one foot, he pulled off his boots and pants, tore off his soiled shirt and waded into the water after her.

The surf was waist-high when he crashed through the waves. Wamoa back-paddled in front of him, laughing as he charged after her. The sand was soft under his feet, the water delightful as he made powerful strides after her.

Her laughter was infectious and soon he was laughing as he reached out his arms to take her hand.

Suddenly, the earth fell away beneath his feet. He flailed helplessly in the water, unable to stand, unable to swim.

"Help me! I cannot swim," he shouted as he desperately tried to turn around and get back to the shelf he had been walking on.

It was no use. The more he struggled, the further out he was carried. He was swallowing gallons of seawater now and he sank under the surface, rose, gasped, and sank underneath once more.

He felt a soft but firm pair of hands slide up his waist and spin him around. He tried to grab hold of Wamoa's shoulders, anything to keep from sinking again. She kept him on his back and put her arm around his chest. She swam back toward the shallow water with Shadrach flopping as helplessly in her arms as a great fish. The assuredness of her strokes calmed him and he relaxed, trusting himself to her care.

They were both breathing heavily when Shadrach felt Wamoa touch the sandy floor of the ocean. Gingerly, he felt for the bottom, still in her arms. As his feet stood firmly on the ocean bottom, he clung to her. Their chests were rising and falling together and neither wanted to separate. Shadrach wrapped her in his arms. The beads of water were glistening on her lips, her eyes were wide, staring expectantly into his. As the surf burst around them, angry that it was cheated of his life, Shadrach bent down and pressed his lips on hers. Their bodies intertwined and they were carried by the gentle tide onto the beach. The floating petals of the flower Wamoa wore in her hair stuck to their bodies like kisses.

A log drum pounded out a Polynesian salute as Ha'oke pronounced the wedding vows to seal his daughter and the giant haole. Both bride and groom were grinning broadly in the light of the torches which flickered in the night breeze. The assembled congregation had turned out to wish the couple well. The smell of fish frying in the cocoanut leaves permeated the air and as soon as the ceremony was over, they adjourned to the feast. Shadrach wore a garland of bright flowers over his suit; Wamoa wore a linen dress brought all the way from Honolulu for the occasion. Both beamed with happiness, the dark island girl and the tanned Englishman experiencing the intoxication of the night.

Ha'oke was the happiest of all it seemed. He circulated amongst the guests bragging about his new son-in-law who was an important haole.

He would continually pop back to their place at the feast, feeding both of them lovingly the pork and fish bits that everyone was consuming by the fingerful. He would squeeze between the bride and groom, hugging them, and then move on again.

"I knew you could not resist our ways. No haole ever does—for long," Ha'oke confided. "The island ways are too powerful. The old gods don't give up so easily."

"I disagree. It was Wamoa who gave up the island ways to trod in a more righteous path," Shadrach insisted. "We must sanctify the carnal spirit and end the odious habit of free love amongst this nearly perfect people."

Ha'oke grinned at his son-in-law. "You can't lie any better than you can swim," he said. "I was hiding in the forest while you took your walk. You have no secrets from me."

THE BOLD DAYS

1869

Chapter Twenty-Three

"Women's suffrage is not just the right to vote," Theresa Tompkins said to the group of ladies, assembled in the basement of the Salt Lake Theater. "Women's suffrage is the right to an equality that has been denied for ten thousand years."

The ladies politely applauded these sentiments as they might clap for a speaker at the Female Relief Society. They were seated on caned chairs in a room used for rehearsals for the traveling players who performed in the large hall upstairs. A woman sat at a melodean, ready to play the hymns and songs that linked the women's rights movement to the spiritual revivals sweeping the country at the time.

In the wake of the Civil War, women saw that the same tactics the abolitionists had used to gain freedom for the slaves in the South might be used to gain women the right to vote. Spontaneously in churches and meeting halls across the nation, a new breed of woman began organizing her sisters around the rallying cry of "one woman, one vote."

A small group of women traveled around the country giving speeches to the ladies who flocked to hear them. Susan B. Anthony, a portly woman with the disposition of a schoolteacher facing a room of rebellious students, was the most well-known. Although the women's rights movement was not a large one in Salt Lake City, Theresa Tompkins and several other women had taken up a collection to bring the noted suffragette out to Deseret to address the local population.

The fiery lady had suffered through the long coach ride from Denver, and her arrival in Salt Lake caused a stir, with reporters from the *Deseret News* vying with the Gentile reporter from the Salt Lake City *Herald* for printable quotes from the first lady of feminism.

They got their quotes, and the meeting that evening drew a packed audience. Theresa was pleased to see women from every strata of Mormon society, from the wives of church officials to women who had only recently been gathered to Deseret. Attendance at the meeting was frowned on by the male leaders who distrusted any tampering with the social fabric of the close-knit society. In addition to the male reporters and curiosity seekers, a number of church observers were present to report on what was said.

The small but powerful Susan B. Anthony rose to her feet and adjusted her wire rim spectacles, glaring out at her audience. "They say that the hand that rocks the cradle rules the world," she observed acidly. "If that is true, then why can't we even elect a dog catcher by any other means than whispering in our husband's ears?"

She paused for a few beats to let this logic sink in. Then she launched into a spirited speech which flayed the ruling class of men up and down for their thousands of years of ill treatment against women. Who suffered the most during wars? Who worked for the poorest wages, either in the spinning mills of the North, or over the washtubs of the Midwest? Who were prey for every quackery of medicine, or ignored by the panjandrums of the medical colleges? Who were denied decent jobs, then forced to beg or be sold into white slavery when they had no one to support them?

Anthony's stirring catolog of the crimes against the female race moved every listener in the room. At the end of it there was one simple solution proposed to these injustices. Universal women's suffrage.

Theresa beamed as she sat on the dais behind the charismatic woman. Theresa winked at the other Tompkins women sitting in the front row. Everyone in the room seemed moved by the speech; even Rachel seemed stirred by the message.

"Miss Anthony! What do you feel about the practice of polygamy here in Utah?"

Theresa glared at the Gentile reporter from the *Herald*. A murmur went through the crowd. Quite a few plural wives were in attendance. Susan Anthony coughed delicately, looked at Theresa, then resumed her defiant glare.

"I would be less than honest if I did not speak my mind. With all due respect to my sisters in this territory, I find polygamy to be the harshest oppressor of women for it assumes that a number of women should be satisfied with one man, but the reciprocal of this arrangement is not true."

This statement caused a commotion to break out in the hall.

Part of the crowd applauded enthusiastically while the other part gave catcalls that disrupted the proceedings.

"Equality is all I am asking for. Is that too much?" Anthony shouted above the crowd. "I say there's no great wrong for a woman to live in a polygamous situation if her sister has the opportunity to live in polyandry and take as many husbands as she wishes!"

The reporters dashed from the meeting hoping to go to press in the next issue. A man burst into the room and seized one woman by the arm.

"Come along, Elsie," he said. "You've heard enough nonsense for one afternoon!"

The woman resisted and she was aided by several of her woman friends who pulled in opposite directions and poked her tormentor with parasols. Susan B. Anthony was mobbed by a crowd of woman, half partisans of her cause, the other half against her.

Sarah patted Theresa on the back as the Swiss woman pressed her handkerchief against her eyes. The parlor was filled with the sobs, for Theresa cried as vociferously as she spoke.

"There, there, it wasn't that bad," Sarah said, encouragingly. "At least the speech drew a lot more attention than if it had gone peacefully. A thousand speeches are given in Salt Lake City every year and not one of them will draw as much discussion as this one will."

"We looked like buffoons up there," Theresa said bitterly. "I have set women's rights in Deseret back at least ten years."

"Perhaps that's a good thing," Rachel sniffed as she stiffly watched the upset woman. "I personally believe that the divinely revealed place for a woman is in the home with her family rather than in a polling place."

Red-eyed, Theresa looked up from her handkerchief at her husband's wife. "You can't really believe that, can you?"

"That's not all I believe. I think women's suffrage is a plan, if not an outright plot, to undermine the authority of the church in Deseret. If the women were to rise up against the leadership at this crucial stage, the church could suffer irreparable harm."

"Why don't you just come out and say it?" Theresa said

angrily. "You believe that any espousal of women's rights is akin to apostasy, don't you?"

"I'm not saying I do, but there are some who would agree," Rachel said. "Any dissension in our ranks is the devil's work, no matter what the cause. You saw how fragile the peace is after that fight started tonight. Do you want the same thing happening to the church as a whole?"

"We're not questioning the authority of the church; we just want the right to vote," Theresa said. "Even Brigham Young himself has advocated women's place outside the home."

"In supervised church disciplines. But this business of getting involved in politics is dangerous. Let men's lives be troubled with the worries in the world. Our duty is to provide a haven for our husbands and children so they do not get overcome with their troubles. That's much more important a duty than being overcome with fly-by-night politicians."

"Some of our worst enemies are not bigoted men, but our own deluded sisters," Theresa said, biting her tongue. "You have swallowed their dogma, hook, line and sinker. You are the poison from within and will be the hardest to overcome."

"I shall have a word about your attitude with our husband when he returns from his mission," Rachel snapped. "We shall see what he thinks about your actions while he is suffering so terribly in the South Seas."

"You do that, you bitter, vindictive woman," Theresa said, rising. "I hope your insides turn to vinegar before he comes back, for your mind is pickled enough already."

She wrapped her shawl around her. Polly Tompkins had been standing silently as the fight had developed and together they swept past Rachel's glare and left the house.

"You shouldn't be so hard on her," Sarah said when they were alone. "She is doing what she thinks is right. I agree with some of what she says. I do not agree with a radical like Susan Anthony, but I believe the world would be a better place to live if men weren't so high-handed."

Rachel was staring after the departed wives and didn't acknowledge what her sister had said. "Theresa will have to be watched closely," she said. "If she will betray the church, she will betray our husband."

The Civil War in the East ended somewhat disappointingly for the Saints. The Babylon of America had not crumbled, although some large cracks had occurred. The Union had held together and the eyes of the country began to turn West again. Thousands of new immigrants passed through Deseret on their way to California and Oregon, many fleeing from the destruction of the South.

The victory of the North made the troops stationed at Fort Douglas more cocky than they had been before. The soldiers made their anti-Mormon sentiments more widely known, both in their newspaper, *The Vedette,* and in their remarks on street corners. The soldiers now knew that if they faced any threat from the Saints, they could summon help from an army no longer tied down in the South.

The Saints tolerated the fort and its soldiers like a thorn in their side. The church had a policy of 'shunning' the soldiers and any fraternization with the troops was forbidden. Even so, occasional fistfights and skirmishes between hotheads on both sides required diplomatic efforts on behalf of both the church and the army to calm things down.

Even hotter were the skirmishes between the federal judges and marshals and the recalcitrant Saints who refused to recognize their authority. Under the thin disguise of legalities, both sides sniped at each other.

In 1862, the Gentiles had managed to promulgate a regulation that prohibited the practice of polygamy in the territory. The Saints had ignored this ridiculous provocation and had gone about their business. President Brigham Young was, at the time, courting a young woman named Eliza Ann Forbes, an attractive and popular woman in the community. After several false starts, the president took the Young woman to the Endowment House where she was sealed to him.

This was the opportunity the Pukes were waiting for. An order was issued for the arrest of Brigham Young on the charge of participating in a polygamous marriage.

Immediately, over one thousand armed Saints turned out to guard the president in his Beehive House. Angry eyes turned toward Fort Douglas and threats were made to "use up" the Federal troops if they dared lay a hand on the prophet.

Urgent messages were flashed to Washington where President Lincoln was requested to rescind the proclamation against polygamy. Lincoln had been asked how he would treat the Mormons, his old political rivals from Illinois. Lincoln had replied that he would treat the Saints the way a plowman treated a sunken log in a field. "Sometimes you find a log that can't be burned out, dug out, or dragged out," Lincoln explained. "In that case I'd just plow around it."

With the Civil War going badly, Lincoln "plowed around" the Mormon question, leaving the Saints and the Federal judges to fight it out.

To defend their president, the Saints called their own grand jury. Filled with loyal Mormons, the grand jury investigated the charges of polygamy brought against Brigham Young. It surprised no one when the grand jury found there was "no evidence to suggest that Brigham Young had at any time entered into a Polygamous relationship."

In spite of this verdict, it was common knowledge that the president was an appreciator of feminine pulchritude. "The Lion of the Lord" had a number of wives in the Lion House a short walk from the Beehive House. The official counts varied, for many of his wives were platonic "celestial wives." Popular counts put the number of his wives at around fifty.

The Saints would wink at each other when they told of the system Brigham used to keep track of his partner for the night. He would chalk an *X* on the bedroom door of the lucky lady to allow her to prepare herself. If another wife was jealous of this attention, she would erase the original *X* and chalk a replacement on her own bedroom door.

When the Saints weren't skirmishing with the federals, the 1860s were a peaceful time for them. Or as quiet as things could be on the American frontier. The Saints used the lull in their fight for survival to build up Zion.

Most important was the securing of Zion's borders. The original Mormon colonies like Las Vegas and San Bernadino had been abandoned during the war of '57.

In order to spread his umbrella over as wide an area as possible, Brigham Young dispatched missions to stake out Deseret's borders. Pioneer families traveled into Idaho and south to the borders of New Mexico. A string of settlements running on the trade route to California became the Mormon corridor. These settlements were instructed to cultivate the land, build their homes . . . and keep the Gentiles from moving in.

Wherever the Saints settled, their villages conformed to the plan for the Holy City. Even in high mountain valleys, the uniform grid system of plats and wide avenues was marked off. The stockaded villages always had plats set aside for schools and assembly halls. A visitor crossing a high mountain could look down and see a perfectly squared-off village and know he had found Mormons.

Salt Lake City itself was sprawling past its original plan. The city had long since spilled past the adobe wall. Pine houses were being built miles south of Temple Square. Fine brick mansions were being built in the hills flanking City Creek Canyon.

Work had never stopped on the Salt Lake Temple. The foundations had been dug deep in the earth. Huge blocks of Wasatch granite formed the thick walls. The walls were rising past the first floor height and workmen rushed to top off the building before anything could stop them.

A new feature on the Salt Lake skyline was the new Tabernacle, completed in 1867. It was a remarkable arena whose gleaming domed roof could be seen for miles. Inside, a high-arched ceiling was free of any visible supports. A speaker could stand on the podium and be seen by anyone in the hall. A pin dropped on the lectern was audible at the back of the room.

The Tabernacle was always filled with Saints coming to hear Brigham Young or the apostles speaking. Visitors from all over the world agreed there was nothing like it anywhere. To see the Tabernacle was to imagine you were in heaven.

Only a few grumps complained that it looked like an upside-down soup tureen.

A short walk from Temple Square, downtown Salt Lake was beginning to look like a big city. The old Tithing Office was surrounded by buildings several stories high. Main Street was crowded with dry goods stores set up by Gentiles and Jews to attract the trade of the Saints. Despite the disapproval of the church, Saints patronized these stores which gladly gave them credit.

To counter this threat, Brigham Young ordered that the Saints should compete in this trade. The Zion Cooperative Mercantile Institution was formed. The bishops carried the word and the ZCMI did a thriving business. The ZCMI sold everything, from the holy undergarments and gray jeans made in church factories, to goods brought from the East. Angry Gentile merchants lowered prices to attract the pennywise Saints but the ZCMI fought back, driving some Gentiles into bankruptcy and the remainder to living on their savings. For the people of the valley, the price war was a chance to buy the goods they had been unable to afford for so long. To the stockholders of the ZCMI, Brigham Young included, the prices the new enterprise was forced to charge gave them many sleepless nights.

With the Utah spur of the Union Pacific railroad drawing to completion, Ham Tompkins had more of an opportunity to spend his evenings at the family home in Salt Lake. The contracting business started by his father had yielded a small profit at the expense of wearisome days and nights in the mountains near Ogden. The building of the railroad was a perpetual struggle. If Ham was not fighting with his foremen or his workers, he was fighting with the engineers and accountants who worked for the Union Pacific.

So many of the Saints he had hired proved to be such poor workers that he was finally forced to fire most of them and hire Chinese laborers who did twice the work for half the pay. This had not made him a popular man in the community, but Ham preferred being unpopular to being bankrupt.

Now, at home in Salt Lake, his peace was interrupted as frequently as it had been in Ogden.

"When are you going to get married?" his aunt Rachel confronted him one night as he sank into his father's armchair in front of the fireplace. "You are almost thirty years old and still a bachelor. Others your age have taken several wives already."

"Now, Aunt Rachel, I will take a wife when the right one is revealed to me," the soft-spoken man said.

"It's not just a matter of your personal convenience," Rachel pointed out. "You have your soul and your place in the heavens to consider. What if you were to die tomorrow? What if a tunnel should collapse on you or a rail drop on your head? Who would accompany you throughout eternity?"

"I'm sure you would be along directly to remind me of what a mistake I made."

"Don't make fun of me, young man!" Rachel snapped. "I'm not thinking just of your eternal soul. You know how the church leaders frown on unmarried men. You will never advance in the church hierarchy if you do not marry. Look at the respect your father is given."

"I promise I will marry as soon as I can."

"And what of Deseret? With the Gentiles pressing us on all sides its important that we produce as many of our host in order to stave off annihilation, or having them wash over us.''

"I promise, Aunt Rachel. I will go out the front door and marry the first woman I see, if it will make you feel our people won't die out.''

"I know a great many women whose daughters have inquired about you, Ham. Please let me bring a few of these young ladies for dinner so that you make make an acquaintance with them.''

"Please, I will do my own hunting. I am now free of the railroad and I will spend my time building a family.''

Rachel was not easily put off, but to her regret she had run out of things to badger him about.

"Just promise me one thing, Ham. In your haste to marry, don't be too hasty.''

"What? First you beg me to marry, then you tell me to go slow?''

"Be hasty to marry a Saint,'' Rachel said, "but for the love of God, please don't marry a Gentile!''

Wearing the new three-piece wool brown suit his Aunt Polly had selected for him at the ZCMI, Ham hitched up the family's springboard trap to their most gentle mare and trotted across Salt Lake to the 'dobie house occupied by John Clayton. Clayton was surprised to see the Tompkins lad and even more surprised was Clayton's daughter Hezibah, who was the real object of Ham's visit to the household.

Ham further startled her by inviting her for an afternoon drive. The flustered woman accepted as her large family gathered around the visitor. While the young woman left the main room of the house in order to dress for the afternoon, John Clayton and Ham sat on the front porch of the house talking about the latest news of church business.

John Clayton was a loyal and true Saint, but he had not risen far in the affairs of the church. He was employed as an administrator of the irrigation ditches south of the city, a sinecure for his loyal service. This employment required his attendance at the gates which channeled the water into the ditches leading to the fields and his settlement of any disputes leading from that apportion, but otherwise his time was his own.

Ham sat on the hard bench looking out at the heights of Ensign Peak, the tallest point of the Wasatch Range. Clayton talked about Sister So-And-So who fell asleep during the president's talk at the Tabernacle or Brother What's-His-Name who was hiding his earnings from the Church tithing offices. While his host talked, Ham's mind was thinking about the woman he had come to spark.

To Ham, Hezibah Clayton had always symbolized desirable womanhood since he had first known her in school. She had been the first girl whose body the boys had noticed as her blouse and bussle filled out with the contours of her body. At thirty years of age the fullness was as ripe as it always had been and the color in her cheeks was still as fresh. Her curly hair was the color of the desert sands and somehow it complemented her rebellious spirit and wise-cracking mouth.

Hezibah had never been a stirring example of Mormon womanhood. Chief among her sins had been her marriage to a Gentile mining engineer who had barely saved her from the flames of hell when he converted to the faith. The man had proved to be a winter Mormon for he stayed in Deseret only long enough to exhaust his financial resources. He lit out for California, leaving his twenty-five-year-old bride in the lurch. This soured most of the other men in the community on the bubbling woman, but if she missed their attentions she didn't show it. Although there were always a bumper crop of bachelors in Salt Lake City, she showed little interest in remarrying. She had found employment at the Salt Lake Theatre where the idle gossip of the town had linked her name to several itinerant actors who brought second-hand New York productions to Salt Lake on the way to San Francisco. The amusement-starved Saints filled the house.

Hezibah made her proper entrance on the front porch wearing a indigo blue silk dress which had seen use only at opening nights at the theatre. As a horde of young Claytons razzed the couple from the windows of the house, Ham helped the woman into the carriage and they set off for an afternoon at City Creek Canyon.

A narrow road up the steep-walled valley was one of the few forested spots near Salt Lake. The canyon was a favorite place for young couples, a private place where they could be alone, but not too alone to cause gossip.

"You certainly like to surprise a woman," Hezibah observed. "Showing up unannounced wearing your best suit."

"I don't stand much on formalities. I guess I get that from my father," Ham explained. "I apologize and appreciate your good nature."

"Good nature is the handmaiden of a jilted wife in this place. I'll catch no flies with vinegar."

"I expect you have them buzzing around you all the time. In this arid land they can tell honey miles away. After all, this is the land of the honeybee."

"I'm not so interested in flies anymore. I gave up my comb to one of them some years ago and now I keep my fly whisk close and handy."

Ham laughed and stopped the springboard. Tying the reins to a cottonwood tree, he and Hezibah walked up the canyon, staying discreetly apart, close enough to converse privately, not close enough to touch. Where the trail banked steeper up the mountain side, Ham took a seat on a grassy hummock and plucked a piece of grass to put in his mouth.

"Remember when we were in school together?" he asked, chewing thoughtfully on the straw.

"Sure I do. You were always a tow-headed little sap. I was always following you around but you had better things to do."

"I was a fool in those days. Not that it was anything personal mind you. Young boys are always fools. But even in those days I thought you were the prettiest girl in the entire city."

"Maybe I was wrong. Perhaps you weren't such a fool."

"I still think you're the prettiest girl in the city."

Hezibah laughed, partly out of derision, partly out of embarrassment. "I shouldn't laugh. I don't know how much longer I'll be getting those compliments," she said, catching herself. "I'm no spring chicken."

"Hell. Have you ever had a spring chicken? Nothing on their bones. I like a nice summer hen any day of the week."

"Ham, don't think I don't appreciate the attention. But during this conversation you have compared me first with flies and now with chickens. I don't want to get the whole damn zoo thrown at me."

Ham laughed again. "I wish I had had more time to study my Latin or Greek. I could compare you favorably with any goddess who ever walked the earth. None of them could ever hold a candle to your beauty or to your charm."

"Now that's more like it. Keep it up."

"Ever since I was a boy I have worshipped the ground you walked on, and that's no lie. No sir, I always kept my eye on what you were doing. I always dreamed of having you as my own. I was so jealous when you married that Puke, no offense meant. I was so darn happy when he ran off, no offense meant again. I always wanted to work up the gumption to ask you to be my own."

"Well? Why the heck didn't you? I've never thought you were half as bad as I let on."

"I always had too much work to do, lady. First I had to grow up so I knew what I was doing. Then I had my mission work. Then I had to help the family out. Now's the first time of my own I've had all my life."

"What are you going to do with it, then?"

"There is a ceremony being held up near Ogden to drive the final spike into the Union Pacific Railroad. I was wondering if you would go up there with me?"

The smile faded from Hezibah's lips and a look of hurt crept into her eyes. "That's more than a day's journey. I have enough trouble with wagging tongues without bringing an affair like that upon me."

"Tongues won't wag if you go up there as my wife."

Hezibah's pained look turned to one of genuine shock.

"As your wife? You don't waste any time, do you? At least your father would have spread the proposal out over an hour or so!"

"Time's a wasting," Ham said impatiently. "Yes or No?"

"What do you have? Another appointment this afternoon? Did you have another woman waiting in case this one didn't go through?"

"I reserved a room at the Endowment House a week ago. They raise holy hell if you don't show up on time."

"What time did you make it for?"

"Four o'clock," Ham said, looking at his watch. "That gives us half an hour."

Hezibah looked confused, but this confusion drove her to the challenge. "I will do it on one condition."

"Anything."

"I saw how my mother suffered as a plural wife," Hezibah said, firmly. "I have sworn I would never suffer the same way. If I marry you, it will be one man and one woman for eternity. Is that agreeable to you?"

Ham looked at his watch, considering carefully.

"I've always observed that plurals usually have more trouble than they need," he said. "I'd be willing to risk my eternal soul for a little peace on earth. If I don't loose my deposit at the Endowment House, then we have a deal.''

He reached over to kiss her, but she pried his arms off her bodice. ''After the sealing,'' she cautioned him. ''Don't think I haven't seen this trick played before.''

The brass band was playing despite the stiff wind whipping off the salt flats sending the ladies's hats soaring. Two giant steam locomotives were drawn up facing each other as men and boys clamored on the boilers for a better view of the ceremony.

Ham stood beside his new wife, Hezibah, and held his bowler hat in his hand. He wanted his face to be clearly seen in this commemorative photograph. Leland Stanford, the president of the Union Pacific, spit on his hands and joked about the weight of the sledgehammer he was wielding. The photographer ducked under the canopy of his camera and looked at the upside-down composition of the plate that would photograph the joining of the continent.

The assembled crowd consisted of railroad officials, politicians, contractors, laborers, tourists and anyone else who could squeeze into line. Conspicuously absent was Brigham Young, the man who had sworn to shoot any railroad employee who trespassed on his land. Brigham had relented in the face of the inevitability of the railroad and he had helped the Saints make a tidy profit from it. But, he was miffed that the Gentile politicians had planned the railroad to run north of the city rather than passing through Salt Lake. They had planned to starve the city out by bypassing the Mormon capitol and helping establish a Gentile rival city in the North. Brigham Young had responded by raising money to build a Saint-owned spur railroad to connect the city with the Union Pacific.

The Union Pacific was relieved that the Mormon leader was not in attendance on May 10, 1869. The feelings still ran strong in the East about the rebellious Saints. ''Frigem Young'' was the symbol and embodiment of their cooperation with the railroad. They were much happier to have clean-cut young contractors like Ham Tompkins representing the church than the wild, bearded patriarchs.

When the photographer signaled his readiness, Stanford posed with the sledgehammer. The crowd quieted down. Stanford swung the hammer with a weak motion which would have brought laughter from any gandy dancer on the railroad. The carefully prepared golden spike sank into the hole which had been dug for it. The whistles on the locomotives howled with a wild hoot and the crowd cheered and threw their hats in the air. Ham held on to his. It had cost him too much to throw it about. He watched as the employees of the railroad quickly removed the golden spike from the ground and had replaced it with an iron one before the crowd was dispersed.

"That's just like the Gentiles," he whispered to Hezibah. "They make a big show of putting something into our land, and then they take out anything of value they can carry away."

One of the first passengers on the east-bound train from San Francisco was Shadrach Tompkins. The investigations into the Mountain Meadows Massacre had cooled off and he was no longer wanted for questioning. His family had sent word to the Hawaiian Islands summoning him back to Deseret. He had reluctantly left the idyllic existence he had come to know at Laie. He would miss the cool evenings on the beaches, the warm sunny days in the mountains, the soft soulful singing of the islanders. His duty was with his family and he came back to his home.

Wamoa bravely endured the strange sights as the steel volcano wagon carried them farther from the ocean. San Francisco was not too different from Honolulu, but as they traveled over the snow-covered Sierras and crossed the hot sands of the desert, a quiet homesickness overcame her.

Her two children, Aaron and Bethany, saw no such reason to remain quiet. The two tanned children howled as though they were being murdered as the train crossed Nevada and the other passengers in the rail car quickly were moved from amusement to irritation at the spoiled children.

Shadrach was relieved to reach Ogden where his son would be meeting him with a carriage to take them to Salt Lake. He was getting too old to deal with the problems of small children and he longed for his own quiet home and genteel family. He had resolved to build Wamoa a separate home so the two children could be kept at arm's length.

A burst of fatherly pride overcame Shadrach as the train hissed into the brand-new station at Ogden. The tall lad was standing on the platform and Shadrach jumped off the train and gawked.

"Isn't it beautiful?" Shadrach said in awe. "Oakland's station ain't half as pretty as this one."

The sniffles of children alerted Shadrach to his wife and offspring stepping off the train. Ham helped his father carry the carpetbag luggage and strangely scented woven bags of food and clothing off the train. He stared at the delicate, brown-skinned woman in the black silk dress who stood beside his father, who was over fifty years of age. The girl could not have been more than twenty.

"This is Wamoa," Shadrach said briefly. "My new wife."

"And this is Hezibah," Ham said, as the cheerful woman strode up and took her husband's arm. "My new wife."

Chapter Twenty-Four

Fifteen-year-old Walker Tompkins stood boldly on the Main Street sidewalk and lit a match. He inhaled the droopy, hand-rolled cigarette that hung in his mouth. He savored the smoke, letting it roll from his tongue and steam out of his nostril's like a dragon's breath.

He hitched his thumbs in his suspenders and leaned against the wall of Auerbach's drygoods store, the weed dangling menacingly from his lip. He pulled the saucer-shaped hat down over his forehead and whistled brightly at two young women who were entering the store. The two girls, daughters of a well-known and disliked Federal judge, ignored the Mormon half-breed, but Walker's friends who loitered nearby snickered over the frostiness of their prey. The boys were really hoping for some Mormon girls to come along. A cigarette in the lips of a Saint could cause a minor scandal at the school they attended.

Walker sneered back at three old women who scolded the boys for their truancy. He was so busy glaring at the women that he didn't see the hulking shape of Shadrach bearing down on him.

"Cheese it! Here comes your old man!" one of the boys yelled.

Walker turned around in terror. He jettisoned his cigarette, but it was too late. Shadrach had seen the smoke pouring out of his mouth. Walker sprinted across the street, dodging behind a carriage. Shadrach tore off right behind his son. The passers-by on the busy street stopped and stared in amusement at the efforts of the scrawny boy to elude his lumbering father. If Walker had been born the son of a banker or a lawyer, he might have had a chance at escape. But his father was a frontiersman; his life had been hardened and tempered by a life out of doors. As much as the boy darted and twisted

down the street, Shadrach stayed on his tail. In a final burst
of speed, he caught the boy and shook him like a terrier.

"How dare you flaunt the Words of Wisdom?" Shadrach
roared. "Right here in the public street? Have you no shame?"

"Don't, Pap, don't! They made me do it," Walker cried.

"Don't add a lie to your guilt! They weren't pulling on
your cheeks to draw the air in!"

Shadrach cuffed the boy on the head, knocking his hat to
the ground. "I've just come from seeing the President. What
if he knew my son was smoking cigarettes? Would he have
any faith in me?"

"I won't do it again, Pap!"

"Why when I was your age I had already been in the mines
for ten years. Plenty of boys your age born under the Covenant died during the hard times we Saints have seen. You
should be out working for the common good rather than
hanging around with common criminals."

"I don't want to hear about the hard times you had,"
Walker said defiantly. "Those days are gone and now the
Saints are getting as fat as anyone else."

"Don't talk back to me, boy!" Shadrach said, cuffing him
again. "I've seen too many good people die to take that kind
of talk lightly."

Walker could see it was dangerous to antagonize his father
and he kept silent. Shadrach looked at his son and thought of
his mother, dead these fourteen years. He realized how hard it
must have been for a half-breed boy to grow up in the
all-white community, of how his classmates must have ragged
him unmercifully about the color of his skin. It would do no
good to humiliate him more in public.

"We'll settle this later, son," Shadrach said, softening.
"Run along home and cut yourself a piece of stout hemp
rope. When you get your hiding, I will do it in private."

The early 1870s found the Tompkins family in dire financial trouble. Shadrach had been out of the territory for several
years and had lost touch with many of the leaders of the
church. The railroad, which had brought the family prosperity, was completed. The fertility of his wives had caused the
family to grow so large it was bursting from the two houses it
occupied. Ham Tompkins had been forced to move in with
his father-in-law, accepting the hospitality of that ne'er-do-
well family.

The mounting stack of bills that accumulated worried and angered Shadrach. When he would escort his wives to the Salt Lake Theater for a performance, he would sit looking at the fine clothing worn by his friends instead of at the performance.

When he took his wives for weekend drives in the city, he would fume at the houses built by Saints who had entered into profitable businesses and made fortunes.

"How much tithing money has Malichi Jarvis paid this year?" he demanded as he passed a fine hillside home. "When he lived in Nauvoo he could scarcely pull on his own boots and yet now he lives in a mansion!"

The state of his own impoverishment troubled Shadrach so much that he called his family together in his home for a pronouncement.

"The Saints are growing too fat," he said, echoing the words of his son Walker. "All around me I see signs of corruption and decadence. Big houses, fancy clothes. This is not right."

"Since when was it a sin to live in a nice house?" Polly said, contradicting him. "Were we not promised that we would be living in a heavenly place? Why remain in a pigsty?"

"I fear we are giving up our brotherliness in sacrifice to the material world. With some Saints living in mansions and others living in 'dobies, how can we remain one people?"

"We are all equal in the eyes of God," Rachel said. "If we don't wish to be equal in the eyes of fleas, we get a better house."

"Even Brigham Young has taken up some ostentatious ways," Shadrach said, encountering unexpected resistance from his wives. "He has furnished the Beehive House in a manner that would shame a bawdy house!"

"The president entertains important visitors from all over the world," Sarah pointed out. "The Saints will be held in higher esteem for his furnishings. How can the world treat him with respect if we don't treat him with respect?"

"Well, I won't have it in my house. I am cancelling all our credit arrangements until you ladies learn to live in a more spiritual manner. I will not be one of the original founders of this territory who lives on the charity of the church."

"Instead of cutting off your nose, why don't you smell which way the wind is blowing?" Polly asked angrily. "A goodly number of faithful Saints have earned a living. Why can't you?''

"I will not sacrifice my soul for profit-making."

"And no one is asking you to. But don't sacrifice your children's necessities for your own misguided pride. You have done plenty for the church. Now do a few things for us."

"Madam. I will not be lectured in my own house!"

"Husband, it is not my intent to lecture you. Merely to point out that twenty-five lives are dependent on your largess. You must shoulder your responsibilities and earn some money."

Shadrach looked around the room. The eyes of all five of his wives were in agreement with Polly. Even Wamoa, who not long ago had never heard of money, had taken their side. All the older children who sat in the sparsely furnished living room seemed united against him, their homespun clothing echoing his insistence upon thrift.

He couldn't stand and he couldn't run. Shadrach shook his head, helpless against their onslaught. "Allright. I shall go seeking after profit like everyone else in the church seems to be doing," he said. "And if I lose my mortal soul, I hope you will wear your finest clothes when you visit me in hell."

Shadrach's task of making a better living for his family was not an easy one. He could barely read and write. He had spent most of his life on the frontier and had no mechanical skills nor a way with figures. He could not learn a profession at his age. There were not enough businesses in Deseret that could afford to train a man over fifty, no matter how outstanding his church credentials. And the idea of moving from Salt Lake to become a farmer in the fertile valleys of South Deseret was vetoed by his family.

His first impression that everyone else was making a fortune was wrong. A few had made fortunes by luck or skill, but most Saints labored on in the quiet businesses of feeding, sheltering and clothing their people. Prosperity was not a problem in Deseret.

Shadrach went calling on his old friends he had accumulated in his thirty years as a Saint. He met with counselors of the church, sawmill owners, freighters, manufacturers and leather tanners, all of whom offered advice about businesses to get in to.

"Take a look at your past experience and take your clue from that," Thomas Morse advised him. "What you've done in the past will be something you'll be good at now."

Shadrach was sitting in the new offices Morse had opened up in a new brick building on South Temple Street. Morse ran a contracting business and had made enough money to take a beautiful young wife and put her up in a fine house on Orange Street.

"I did plenty of work on the Nauvoo Temple," Shadrach said. "Perhaps I should become a contractor like yourself?"

"Can't teach an old dog new tricks," Morse said dismissing the idea. "This business would eat you alive in one minute. One mistake and you'd be gone!"

"I worked as a freighter, Tom. I know the Corridor like I know the back of my hand."

"You're too old for that. It takes a young man to do that type of thing."

Shadrach had exhausted his list of skills rather quickly and was fishing for something that would spark Morse's imagination.

"In England I spent ten years of my life working in a mine," he said. "I did a bit of tunnel work when they put the Union Pacific through."

"You might have something there!" Morse said, snapping his fingers. "Those Gentile miners have swarmed all over the territory putting holes in the ground. If they strike it rich, they take it all out of the state. It's about time some Saints got into the mineral business so we can keep a little of it for ourselves."

"You know how Brigham feels about mining. He thinks a man who finds gold or silver is going to be harmed more than he profits."

Morse waved his hand to dismiss the objections. "Deseret needs the money to grow, otherwise the Pukes will own us all. If you can make money grubbing metal from the ground, Brigham will give you all the blessings you need."

"I wouldn't know how to start."

"Leave it to me," Morse said. "I know a group of fellas that have started a company that's sinking a shaft in Parley's Park. They need a good man to look after the excavation. I can put you in touch with them and you can get right to work."

"Are they Saints?"

Morse answered with a wink. "Would I be putting you in touch with them if they weren't?"

Chapter Twenty-Five

"I never thought I'd be taking another wagon trek," Sarah said glumly as they rolled across the frozen tundra of Parley's Park. A sprinkling of snowflakes was the only movement livening up the gray and chilly morning.

"I'm getting a little too old for it myself," Rachel said as she pulled the blanket tighter around her. "You may say we've grown too used to the comforts of the city, but after a lifetime of suffering I can live with a little pampering."

"Kiss it goodbye, sister. Our fifty-year-old bones are going to have to get used to hard living," Sarah said, nodding at the mountain ahead. "Abandon all hope, ye who enter here."

She clucked her tongue but the mules continued at their same place. In the back of the wagon, Wamoa tried to smile optimistically, but her eyes betrayed her fear of their new home.

Shadrach had gone broke again. His mining partnership with two other Saints had produced a succession of mineshafts but they had not struck any ore. His two partners had quit the business leaving the headstrong Englishman with a barren mining claim and backlog of unpaid bills. Still believing that the mine would produce, Shadrach had sold his fine home in Salt Lake City to finance the operation of the diggings, which the local Gentile miners had nicknamed the "Mormon Folly."

Shadrach's decision to sell the Salt Lake home met with a storm of protest from its occupants: "I refuse to let you sell this house or touch a single one of my possessions," Rachel had announced. "I will shoot you dead if you try it."

"You have no choice in the matter," her husband informed her. "Either we sell it for a good price, or the sheriff will auction it for a pittance. My signature is on our debts and the creditors will swoop down on this place like locust when I default."

"I rue the day when I urged you to enter the business

trade," Rachel said. "I would sooner try to teach a monkey to play the piano than allow you near the purse strings of this household."

The hillside home was soon sold. The family divided, depending on who was keen on moving to the mountains. Theresa was adamant about staying in Salt Lake, where her medical practice and struggle for women's suffrage required her full attention. Polly was needed to help keep the books at the ZCMI. Most of the young women of the family were determined not to abandon their beaus and friends in the capital city for the bleak life near the mine. These moved into the Tompkin's 'dobie on South Third Street and Shadrach moved the remainder to Parley's Park. Rachel and Sarah went quietly. Better seclusion in the mountains than to face their friends in the Female Relief Society after losing their home.

Parley's Park was a small valley cradled in the granite hands of the Wasatch Mountains, some thirty miles above Salt Lake. It was the last plateau before the steep trail dropped through Immigrant Canyon and had been a favorite pasture for the wagon trains passing down into the valley. The wagon trains had been replaced by the railroads, but the park was still a favorite summer pasture for the herds of cattle kept by local farmers.

In the winter, when the air grew gray and thick, the farmers knew they were breathing in the clouds passing over the mountains peaks and they moved their stock to the lowlands. The snows settled in over the park ten feet deep, leaving only the miners to appreciate the beauty of the winter.

Greed will lead men to the most inhospitable places on earth. The Gentile miners who clung to the back canyon mountainsides were no exception. The sites they chose for their mines would have discouraged anyone else. On sheer granite hillsides, far above where the last few scrub pines could grow, the men sunk their shafts. If their mules died pulling the carts up to the diggins, they pulled them by hand. If their partners died when a spring flood inundated the mineshaft, they dug alone. If their neighbors decided that theirs was a better claim and tried to take it by force, the sheriffs in the valleys below never heard the gunshots echoing through the mountains, or ever found the bodies left to rot in deep ravines.

Many of the miners had been Federal soldiers. General Connor himself had turned to mining after the Civil War. The men were veterans of the Nevada Mother Lode and when that had expired they went looking for the treasures of Utah. Gold was scarce, but silver was plentiful, so plentiful that the Mormons had not been able to use the lead from the mountains to make bullets because it had such a high silver content.

Mining was the one place a Gentile could edge out a Saint in Utah and they made the most of it. In the mountains to the west of Salt Lake, in hell-roaring camps like Bingham, Gentile strongholds sprang up in fierce opposition to the Saints in the lowlands. The mining camps were some of the few places in Deseret where, if a man had the gold, he could find a bad bottle of whiskey and an even worse woman to entertain him through the night. The Gentiles claimed the mining camps as their own and were vigilant lest the Mormons try to take them away from them.

The Mormon Folly was little more than a six-foot-high tunnel dug into the side of a granite mountain face in a dead-end canyon above Park City. Shadrach's former partner had bought the claim from an old Gentile who declared his health was shot. The mine proved to be twice as shot as the miner's health but the men kept digging deeper into the mountain side in spite of that. From the front porch of their tiny cabin in Park City, Rachel and Sarah could keep an eye on the mine. The cabin was a rustic shack, built of split timbers and roofed with a pine shakes that threatened to catch fire each time the small sheep-herder's stove in the kitchen was lit. The women had tried to domesticate the house by decorating it with lace curtains and cable-coiled rugs, but the cabin steadfastly refused to be tamed.

The two women sat in discouragement looking at the sight of the small community that ran in the valley beneath their porch. A score of similar shacks hugged the hillside trying to stay above where the creek flooded every spring. A few larger dormitories housed the bachelor miners who worked the diggings. A number of saloons housed the gambling wheels and the prostitutes who worked the miners who were not too tired to throw their money away after a day's work.

"It looks like the Lord took a hoe and gouged out a rut up this valley and then the fools came in and built houses in it," Sarah lamented. "I reckon they hope this place will sprout like a garden some day."

"The Lord could come back with his hoe and scrape all the

weeds out of this valley and it would be a more fit place to live," Rachel said, her breath frosting in front of her face.

"I haven't heard as much cussing and swearing in twenty years in Salt Lake as I've heard in one afternoon here. Not to mention the drinking and whoremongering. I wasn't sure whether we had succeeded in building the city of God in Salt Lake but after seeing this place I know we did."

"This is the city of the Devil, for sure," Rachel said. "I thank God we didn't bring any of the children up here. The sins of this place are palpable enough to corrupt the Nephites themselves."

"I had thought we had been delivered for good from the torments of our early years but it seems this is not the case," Sarah said. "I believe in my heart we have slid far backwards."

As she spoke, the ladies heard a boom in the mountains over the city. If a gigantic cannon had fired in the heavens it might have made as loud a noise. Their bodies were rocked by the concussion which swept down the valley.

"An avalanche!" Rachel shouted, as she held onto the post of the porch looking fearfully up the mountain behind them.

The avalanche was on the opposite side of the valley. With a *whoosh* it tumbled down the side of the mountain like a frozen waterfall. A plume of white powder rose from the swirling snow as it tumbled downward, sweeping a forest of pines with it as easily as a scythe cuts grain.

Rachel and Sarah watched in mute horror as the avalanche flowed down a narrow chute directly above the Mormon Folly mine. The tiny figures of the miners saw the danger approaching and scrambled toward the mouth of the mine just as the white cloud swept across the face of the mountain. In an instant the shack which served as the offices for the mine vanished in a cloud of snow, trees and timber. The avalanche exploded at the foot of the mountain and vanished as the wind carried away the last whisps of snow, leaving the blue skies of the valley shining as if nothing had happened.

Instantly the two women joined the rest of the people in the town as they slogged up the muddy streets toward the shaft. A barricade of debris blocked their way. A fortress of snow and pine trunks was piled so high that shovels and axes had to be sent for before they could even approach the site where the Mormon Folly once stood.

The men dressed in their high boots and thick canvas overalls worked ceaselessly with no mention of the victims' religion. When a disaster struck, all the miners pitched in without regard to past feuds. Any of them could have been buried in the avalanche and would have had to rely on the work of strangers to save them.

Using axe handles and pine branches the men moved up the mountain probing through the snow beneath their feet. Several times the branches hit something solid in the snow pack but after anxious seconds of digging, no bodies were discovered.

Sarah and Rachel stood shivering in the knee-deep snow while the miners searched for their men. For once they didn't mind the cursing grunts of the men who labored over shovelfuls of sodden snow. Pausing every few minutes, they at last heard voices beneath them. Digging harder, they struck metal against metal.

"Glory be! We found 'em!" the leader of the rescuers shouted. "The buggers all seem to be in one piece."

Sarah and Rachel pushed their way through the rescuers who were clammy with the smell of sweat and wet wool. Looking through a small opening in the snow, they could see the dark opening of the Mormon Folly mineshaft. In the flow of a lantern in the shaft, Shadrach and his crew were huddled. They had been spared the force of the slide by retreating inside the mountain.

"Sarah! Rachel!" Shadrach shouted. "Thank God you're all right."

"We're all right? Thank God you and your men were delivered from the avalanche!"

"Avalanche? Is that what it was? I thought the Pukes were trying to dynamite us out!"

Shadrach thrashed on his bed as Wamoa grumbled and tried to sleep. Her husband was sleeping less and less, waking up in the middle of the night to worry about his failing mine. His two other wives had refused to sleep with him due to his restlessness and only the amiable Polynesian would share his bed.

Everything Shadrach owned had gone down the Mormon Folly hole. He had been forced for the first time in his life to borrow money and even that was threatened by the barren workings. His crew had been without salary for a month and he was worried about how long he could keep them loyal.

As he slipped into a fitful rest, he dreamed that he was alone in the Park City Canyon. All the workings, all the cabins were deserted, the people gone. Shadrach himself was sitting outside his abandoned mine when an old prospector came wandering down the road leading a starving mule. The man was dressed in a suit of black leather so worn and ragged that had he so much as set foot in Salt Lake City he would have been arrested.

"Where have all the people gone?" Shadrach asked.

The old man let out a high-pitched laugh. "Gone. All gone away," he said. "Moved back to the flats where they belonged."

"Did the mountain play out?"

"Hah! The folks played out a long time before the mountain. They gave up looking before they knew where to look."

"What about this mine?" Shadrach said, pointing toward the Mormon Folly. "We never did find the vein."

"You just din't know how to look," the man said, taking an object from his saddlebag. He handed Shadrach what appeared to be a clear crystal rock with a number of facets circling it. He hefted it in his hand for it appeared to be unusually heavy.

"Go ahead! Take a look through it. Don't just stand there like a lummox!" the stranger said impatiently.

Reluctantly, Shadrach bent over and peered through the crystal. As the murky image focused in the rock, he was shocked to see his naked foot and leg through the leather of his boot. He jerked his eye away from the rock. His boot was in sound condition.

"Yep! That's what a peepstone's for, all right," the old man said, excited. "See's what needs to be seen, right through everything. Try 'er again."

Shadrach put the stone next to his eye and held his hand in front of it. He recoiled as he saw the sinews and bones of his hand laid out like a steer on a slaughterhouse floor, but still moving.

"Try it on the mountain," the old man suggested impatiently. "That's where the real fun is!"

Holding the crystal against his eye, Shadrach could see the clear outline of his mineshaft as it descended into the mountain. On all sides of the shaft he could see the minerals they had passed on their way into the interior of the mountain. Great masses of feldspar and quartzite were massed in huge lumps untouched by pickaxe or blasting powder. Streaks of gray lead ran through the mountain while the fissures in the rock led off like the cracks in dry stone.

Shadrach gasped as he saw a vein of silver shooting through the mountain like a lightning bolt of the precious metal three hundred yards long. It was flecked with gold that sparkled like tiny explosions in the granite. From what he could tell, they had missed the vein as they ran parallel to it, not more than a dozen feet away.

"That's the damndest thing I ever saw," Shadrach gasped, turning to the old prospector. The man had disappeared.

"Go back to sleep," Wamoa growled, her patience gone. "You've been dreaming."

When the miners arrived at the Mormon Folly the next morning before dawn, Shadrach was already at the shaft pouring over the maps they had made of their drift. By the time the crew had lit their candle lanterns and attached them to their hard leather helmets, Shadrach was already towing the foreman down the tunnel.

"We have been mining the wrong way," the Englishman explained. "We have been tunneling inwards when we should have been going off to the side. We have missed a vein of gold as wide as our cart tracks."

"That's geologically impossible," the foreman scoffed. "We haven't gone deep enough to hit a vein yet."

"We're taking the drift off to the side."

"Who have you been talking to?" the foreman asked suspiciously.

"I had a revelation last night. I was shown where the vein was by one of the Nephites."

The crew gathered around their leader, looking at him suspiciously. Reluctant to question his sanity, the foreman stalled until Shadrach picked up a chisel and hammer and pounded into the side of the tunnel.

"We drill here!" he ordered. "We have been shown where the gold is and we're going to get it."

The men slowly followed the instructions of their employer. As Shadrach watched with righteous certainty, they hammered their cold steel drills into the mountain side. When they had tapped a deep hole in the granite, they tamped a charge of blasting powder into the hole and lit the fuse. While the miners retreated up the tunnel, the blast would tumble a pile of gray rock onto the rock floor. The muckers with their wheelbarrows would clean up the debris while the engineers built timber supports above the men who widened the hole left by the blast. Repeating this process over and over again would lengthen the tunnel as it pushed into the mountain in search of the sparkling flecks that would signal the vein of gold.

Shadrach stayed below the earth for several days, convinced that his revelation was correct and that it would be a matter of hours before they struck it rich. When he could no longer swing a pick, he returned home, the light of a full moon reflecting off the canyon walls.

His wives were asleep by the time he returned, but Rachel awoke and wrapped herself in a woolen robe. Shadrach sat wearily at the table while she served him a plateful of cold beans.

"What is this I hear about your revelation?" she demanded. "Something about a location of a vein?"

"It's true. An old man came to me in a dream and gave me a wondrous stone which revealed the innermost parts of the mountain."

"Husband, have you been breathing the thin mountain air too long?"

"It's true. I swear it!"

"I'm not questioning its truth. I'm questioning your wisdom. Why did you have to involve Revelation in the business of profit-making?"

"Other brethren before me have been guided in business by revelation."

"Perhaps, but they have not broadcast the source of their inspiration. Now every man woman and child in the valley is talking about the Mormons and their strange ways."

"What of it? We are used to talk."

"What happens when no vein of gold is found? You and the church will be the laughingstock of the entire valley. They will think us a backward people who obey strange men in dreams."

"When the spirit speaks to me, I do not try to hide it."

"The gift of prophesy was not meant to be cast like pearls before piglets. Do not amuse the Pukes by flaunting the divine word."

"And what if my revelation proves correct? Will it not convince the Pukes that we are the righteous ones."

"Eat your beans, Brother Shadrach. You have grown too old to continue thinking in dreams."

The Nephite's prediction became a joke among the people of the valley who daily would gather around the Mormon Folly to taunt Shadrach with questions about his prophesy. Each day without a strike, the joke of the Mormon's dream was told to more skeptics.

To speed up the process, Shadrach took charge of everything. He mucked the rock out, he carried water. Stripping to the skin in the heat, he was the first into the mine in the morning, the last to leave at night.

One afternoon, the men had set a blasting charge into the mine wall and had scurried to safety. They stayed far up the shaft, their fingers in their ears, but the explosion never occurred.

"The damn fuse must have gone out," Moroni Callahan said, as the men looked at each other.

It was common practice to wait for fifteen minutes if a charge did not explode in case a smoldering spark was still burning in the fuse. The inactivity allowed Shadrach to think about the possibility of a cave-in, and to forestall that he strode down the tunnel to reset the errant fuse.

The coming of the Millenium could not be more brighter than the explosion that picked the Englishman off his feet and hurled him back up the mineshaft. His consciousness was snuffed out as easily as the lanterns behind him, but instead of lying in the darkness, he was in a place of great light.

At first Shadrach thought he had broken open the wall of the mountain and discovered the treasure he was promised. Instead, he was pleased to see his brother approaching him surrounded by angels. His brother looked exactly as he had on the day he was killed some forty years before. The only difference in his appearance was that the boy was finally clean of the coal dust which always covered him. In fact, forty years of death had improved his looks for he was healthy and rosy-cheeked. The boy was wearing a solid white garment.

"Is that you, Lemuel?" he asked cautiously. "It's good to see you after all these years."

"That it is, brother," the boy said naturally.

"I'm pleased to see that the Baptism for the Dead took hold in your case," Shadrach said, pleased that his religion had delivered what it had promised. "Are mother and father and the rest of the family equally provided for?"

The boy nodded pleasantly.

"I notice that you are wearing your temple garment and I guess you wonder why I'm not wearing mine," Shadrach said, embarrassed. "The truth is, it's so hot in these mines that I can't wear it. But I think I will have a change of heart after this."

Lemuel nodded patiently and Shadrach raised himself up on his elbows. "Where are we? Is this Heaven?" he asked. "Have I died and gone to my eternal reward?"

"Look to your family and imitate not the Gentile," his brother said. "Why are you in these mountains? Is your greed so great that you forsake everything to pursue it?"

This rebuke took some of the pleasure out of their meeting.

"Is this any way of greeting the brother you have not seen in so many years?" he asked, hurt.

Lemuel smiled and bent to help him up. As he put his hand to his sleeve, Shadrach could feel a chilly breeze on his face and the kiss of snowflakes. He opened his eyes and found himself inside an ore car. Moroni Callahan bent over him and held Shadrach's eye open with a calloused thumb.

"Can you hear me, Brother Tompkins?" he asked. "We thought you had been blown to Kingdom Come."

His eyes refused to focus and his tongue refused to move. Shadrach stared up at the mountainside they had just removed him from. Moroni hefted a large piece of granite and held it in front of his employer's face.

"Take a look at this ore. It's shot through with sulfides."

"Is it gold?" Shadrach asked, forgetting the warning of his dead brother.

"Nope, but if this isn't some of the best silver ore I've ever seen, I'll eat this rock."

"Silver?"

"Yep. Wait 'till the Gentiles hear that your prophesy assayed out! They'll have you and your peepstone walking through every mine in the canyon!"

"Tell my wife Sarah to get up here!" Shadrach ordered.

"We'll do it. We'll send one of the boys and tell her that she's a rich lady!"

"Never mind about that," Shadrach whispered. "Just tell her to bring me my Holy undergarments!"

Chapter Twenty-Six

Lilly Lamont, the "Mormon Thrush," was warbling out the lines of the song, "Forever, My Darling," as the musical presentation *Frontier Romance* played its final engagement at the Salt Lake Theater. No sooner than the last notes had died in her throat, Shadrach Tompkins leapt to his feet to lead the applause of the packed house.

"Bravo! Bravo!" he called and hearing his booming voice, Lilly paused in her bows to pat her lips with her fingertips and blow him a soft kiss.

Shadrach had every reason to know the musical by heart. He had attended every performance of the syrupy melodrama and could have acted as the show's prompter if need be. He was enthralled by Lilly, the blonde-haired, white-skinned pride of Deseret. Lilly was a local girl, born in the valley, who, without musical instruction, had risen in the choir at the Tabernacle until she had been offered the lead in the Theater's first local production.

Lilly had been an instant success and was idolized by the Saints, but none more than Shadrach Tompkins, the prosperous owner of the Mormon Folly. So much high-grade silver ore had been taken from the mine that Shadrach and his family had become one of the more well-to-do families in Deseret. Their long years of poverty had prevented them from becoming ostentatious with their money, but everyone knew that Shadrach could now afford to spend all his evenings at the theatre and his days escorting the lovely Lilly Lamont to the finest stores in Salt Lake.

After the performance Shadrach hurried backstage. The cast of the musical and the stage hands nodded politely to the rugged Englishman whose new San Francisco suit and starched white shirt could not conceal the times he had spent on the frontier. The Salt Lake Theatre was not large enough to give Lilly a private dressing room. The one she shared with the other ladies of the cast was filled with the cut flowers Shadrach had sent there during the last act.

When he politely rapped on the door, she answered it and gave him a firm handshake of thanks. In deference to her privacy the other girls filed out of the room, leaving them alone.

"The flowers are beautiful, Mr. Tompkins! They must have cost you a fortune!"

"The cost was nothing compared to the pleasure you gave me, Miss Lamont. You sang more beautifully tonight than anything I have ever heard."

"How you do flatter me? I don't deserve it."

Shadrach took her hand impulsively and the girl blushed.

"If the angels sing half as sweetly in heaven, all my trials will be worth the trouble."

"Please, Mr. Tompkins. You're making me blush."

Shadrach kept a tighter grip on her hand and pulled the slender girl closer to him. "Call me Shadrach, Lilly. Call me Shadrach forever, as I would have you sealed to me for eternity."

This burst of forthrightness on the Englishman's part made the blush in the singer's cheeks disappear. She turned white and slipped into his arms.

"What? What did you say? No, don't tell me. The memory of it is making me feel faint-headed."

Shadrach supported the girl as easily as he held his walking stick. His powerful arms encircled her slender waist and her helplessness excited him.

"Forgive me for my directness for I am a simple man. I have not learned the arts of romantic seduction, but I know when a woman pleases me and you do so more than any other woman I have ever known. The short time I have spent in your company have been the happiest moments of my life. You must allow that to continue."

By this time, Lilly had partially recovered from her case of the vapors and had taken a seat in front of her mirror where she briefly checked her appearance as she fanned herself with Shadrach's theatre program.

"I am flattered and honored by the attention of such a respected man, but I am hesitant to say 'yes' to your proposal."

"Why? Is it because of my age and that you are only seventeen? I can assure you that I can outrun and outlove any younger man. I have satisfied six wives in my lifetime and sired a score of children which attests to my virility. My experience is worth that of a dozen Casanovas.''

"No one doubts your masculinity, Shadrach," Lilly said, "but I am a young, and I think, worthwhile woman. . . ."

"More than worthwhile, my darling."

"More than worthwhile. I am loath to marry into a plural household. I fear getting lost in the crowd."

"Believe me, there is no danger of that. I would buy you your own house, with servants, if that is your wish. My own wives are growing older and can get along without my company. I'm sure they won't object if I spend my days with you."

"It's not the days I care about—it's the nights."

"Of course. You would have me all to yourself. Excepting of course, the times when I have to discharge my familial duties."

"As much as I admire you, I hesitate to give my consent. I am anxious to continue my career as a singer."

"As you must, as you must! I insist on it," Shadrach said sternly. "All the more reason to marry me. With me as your patron you can devote yourself full-time to your singing."

"What if I want to travel and give concerts in other cities?"

"We will travel together. As far away as San Francisco, if you like."

Showing the first signs of her decision, she jumped into his arms and held him around his shoulders.

"Oh, Shaddie! This sounds so wonderful! Tell me that it is all true and that I'm not fainted under the lights out there on the stage."

"It is all true, my desert flower," Shadrach assured her. "We are going to spend some delightsome times together."

"And you're sure your other wives won't object?"

"My other wives are of an age where they begin to turn from thoughts of the flesh to more spiritual matters. They can only be pleased that I have found such happiness with you!"

"There's no fool like an old fool!" Rachel spat when she heard the news. "Have you gone senile in your dotage? What do you think you are doing, marrying a woman one-third of your age?"

"She and I love each other," Shadrach said hopefully.

He was without hope. Sitting in the middle of the living room of the new house he had built on upper State Street. The house was of genuine brick. The bright interior was made of hardwoods shipped from San Francisco and ornately carved by local craftsmen. The furnishings had come from New York, picked out of a catalog by Rachel and Sarah. He had given his wives everything they wanted. New homes for all of them. Servants if they wanted. New dresses and fabrics—even if they didn't need them. Credit arrangements at the ZCMI.

And what was his thanks? All five of his wives sat on the expensive linen fabric of the exquisite living room suite and stared at him with more hostility than they had ever shown him when they were starving.

"We would much prefer you to travel to San Francisco and visit one of the best bawdy houses to get this out of your system rather than drag our family's name through the mud with your juvenile antics," Polly remonstrated.

"I resent the implication that this is a childish fling!"

"And we resent the way your behavior reflects on us," Theresa said. "All my friends have been remarking upon your cavorting around the city with your child sweetheart. Our children are teased about it at school. I'm surprised you have not frequented the Bowery with the other eighteen-year-olds."

"That is enough! I will not have you and your man-hating friends cast aspersions on Lilly," Shadrach said, fighting back. "If you must besmirch a name, use mine. But kindly leave hers out of this."

He looked at Wamoa, hoping that her Hawaiian morality was still intact enough to sanction his love interest. Wamoa had gained much weight in the nine years she had been in Utah. Her bronzed face was now round and full-cheeked, her body hidden by the hooped dress she wore. As the junior wife in the family, Wamoa had been assigned more kitchen duties than she should have been. Her role as a housekeeper had not made her too happy. Now it appeared she would take out this unhappiness on Shadrach.

"We are not in the islands anymore," she said firmly. "My children have grown up here like any Americans. With their skin so dark they have not had an easy time in school, but they have managed. Now you bring disgrace on both our children and ourselves by your chasing this young girl around. In the islands I was embarrassed when my father would dance with the young girls. Now I feel a similar shame for you."

Shadrach groaned and turned to Sarah. She was his last

hope. If she approved of his match, the other women would listen to her. If she didn't, he would have to go it alone.

"Gentle Sarah, you have always understood me. Say that you understand me now."

"I cannot understand this foolishness, husband, after all we have been through. Cannot you enjoy your increasing years and your new-found wealth in a dignified manner. Why must you act the fool when you have been so wise? The leaders of the church have looked disapprovingly at this public display. Would you ignore them? You have a duty not only to us but to the church."

"My duty to my soul is to look after my Increase. My marriage to Lilly will do that for me."

"Hogwash on your Increase! Don't you realize the Federal authorities have been using polygamy as their cudgel with which to beat us Saints. Now is the time to be discreet about our private relationships and not flaunt them!"

Shadrach had rarely seen his first wife so angry. Sarah had aged well, for she had eaten sensibly and had always worn her bonnet in the blazing Deseret sun. She now wore wire-rimmed glasses which betrayed her age. The flashing anger colored her cheeks and reminded him of the woman he met forty years before.

"You are a patriarch of this community," she reminded him. "Our young children are falling away from the old ways of the church. How are we going to inspire them with you caterwauling around in front of God and everyone?"

"I have had enough of this," Shadrach said, standing to end the meeting. "Brigham Young himself desired the hand of Lilly and if he hadn't fallen so ill, he probably would have gained her. For all my life I have given unstintingly of myself to both you and the church. Now I have found someone who brings me great happiness. I intend to have her for now and eternity and there is nothing that anyone can say to stop me!"

In Deseret, a man's word overruled the words of his wives. Shadrach was sealed to Lilly Lamont in a private service in the Endowment House. He moved her into the new house he had built for her, a two-story sandstone fairy castle in a new residential neighborhood being built on the eastern side of City Creek Canyon.

Salt Lake was growing faster than anyone could compre-hend as the population pushed fifty thousand Saints and Gen-tiles into living cheek to jowl. Prosperous Saints and newly arrived Gentiles were investing money in the territory and there was no longer any question of whether or not Deseret would survive, but who would control it?

The federal government had saturated the city with carpet-bagging administrators and judges who struggled daily with Brigham Young to wrest control of the territory from his fingers. Brigham had firmly planted the Saints in the Utah soil, but his own authority had ebbed as the society took root. The president had sought to perpetuate the existence of the church and he had succeeded. The price he paid for this survival was coexistence with the Gentile. The Pukes were forever at his throat. . . .

In 1875, John D. Lee had been arrested by the federal marshals and charged with the murders of the one hundred and seventeen Gentiles killed at Mountain Meadows. Lee had been on the run for almost twenty years, ever since the massacre took place. Although there had been many others involved in the incident, Lee's name and reputation had made him the prime target.

Lee had fled to the remote interior of Deseret. For years he was rumored to be operating a ferry that carried the rare traveler across the Colorado River, not far from the Grand Canyon. Some twenty years after the murders took place, the Federal marshals tracked Lee down and found him hiding beneath the chicken coop of a wife's home. He was arrested an brought to Salt Lake City for trial.

Shadrach made himself scarce during the trial. He was afraid he would be called to testify against his old friend, or worse, he would be arrested as an accomplice. He and Lilly traveled to San Francisco where a voice teacher was hired to give his young wife the singing lessons she had demanded.

The Federal judges were satisfied to have one Mormon leader in their net and they never prosecuted any others for the murder. Lee's first trial ended in a stalemate, but his second trial convicted him of the murders and sentenced him to death.

Shadrach rushed back to Salt Lake when he heard of the verdict of his old friend. He took a carriage out to the territorial prison, a giant fortress patrolled by blue uniformed warders who walked the crenellated walls like vultures. The Englishman was shocked when he saw his old friend.

Lee, formerly a robust man, had aged terribly in the years

since Shadrach had seen him. His hair on his head had fallen out and his long beard had turned as white as a Nephite's. He was still as stocky as Shadrach remembered him, but the shackles that bound his hands and feet and the striped prison uniform he wore made him look fragile.

As Lee walked into the room he rubbed his hand beneath his ear in the sign of the Danite alarm he had taught Shadrach many years before. He winked at the surprise of the younger man.

"I don't see too many of my former Danite brothers since I've been given quarters in this pokey," Lee said. "Most of them have grown faint hearts with their gray hair."

"John. Is there anything we can do for you?"

"Nary a thing. We lost our chance in '58 when we let those Federal troops into the state. Now they are like a scar on your body. You'll never be quit of them."

"What about Brigham? I will talk to him."

At the mention of the president's name, Lee scowled.

"Brigham? He betrayed me, Shadrach. He threw me to the Pukes like he would throw an angry dog a bone. When they use me up, they will forget about Mountain Meadows. I am the scapegoat and perhaps in his place I would have done the same thing. But I can never forgive him for not standing beside me. Remember when we all stood beside each other?"

"I remember, John."

"Perhaps it couldn't be helped," Lee said wearily. "The world is too small a place for us to get away. The Pukes didn't want to have us stay in their midst. They were even more reluctant to see us leave, damn 'em. Now they're closing in around us again. I'm kind of glad I won't be here to see it."

"Do you have any regrets, John?"

"None. Not for anything we've done for it was done in the cause," Lee said defiantly. The tough old man softened and the tears began to flow down his cheeks.

"They took my wives away from me, Shadrach. That was the thing that hurt the most. They took my wives away from me."

"Who did? The Pukes?"

"Not the Pukes, they couldn't do that. It was Brigham and the church. They disfellowshipped me. Cast me out of the church to suffer the buffetings of Satan. My wives were deprived of their rightful place in heaven. The life I was living was too much for them. They all left me to die alone."

Lee broke down in sobs and Shadrach gripped the old man by the shoulders. "If there is any God in heaven he will watch over you," Shadrach said. "You will be reunited with your loved ones when the time comes."

"Do you know what they are going to do to me?" Lee asked. "They are going to take me back to the Meadows, tie me in a chair and shoot me."

"Then be brave and do credit to us when you die," Shadrach said gravely. "You are giving your life for the peace of all of us; you are taking that weight on your shoulders. I swear that as soon as I hear you are dead, I will be baptized in your name to save your soul from damnation. This I promise you."

This pledge cheered Lee up considerably and he stood to end the visit. "There is one further favor I would ask of you, old Shenpip," he whispered.

"Anything."

"My boys have sworn to get Brigham for what he has done to me. Brigham is terrified because he knows they mean business. I want you to go to my boys and tell them I told you to stop them. I want no more blood spilt."

"I will do that directly."

"Just don't tell Brigham about it. I want him to look over his shoulder wherever he goes."

Lee was executed at Mountain Meadows by a firing squad in 1877. True to Shadrach's request, he died proudly with a pledge to the faith on his lips. The Englishman kept his own promise to his friend by riding to meet with Lee's sons who were plotting to revenge themselves on Brigham Young. The president himself barely outlived Lee and passed away in the same year.

Brigham Young's funeral was the biggest event Salt Lake had seen since Johnson's army had passed through. Saints came from all over the world to pay homage to the man who had single-handedly kept the faith alive and intact through the long years of persecution.

When Young's body was taken from the Temple Square, under the sight of the unfinished temple, thousands of mourners marched in its wake. Shadrach and his entire family marched in the long line, behind a muted band which played the president's favorite hymns.

The tears formed in Shadrach's eyes as he looked around the city on the way to the cemetery. He remembered the first time he had seen the valley of the Salt Lake, barren, lifeless and hopeless. He remembered the Saints, starving, persecuted and disorganized. In thirty years, Brigham had built a city and a kingdom like he had promised. The temple was rising on solid ground. Salt Lake had spread out over the valley, the biggest city between Denver and the Pacific. And the Saints were strong and still free. There would be no uprooting them now.

Thomas Morse was walking in the procession with his wives and family and he guided them over to Shadrach's flock. The two old friends walked side by side, nodding to their acquaintances in the procession.

"I see fewer and fewer old faces. Most of these people are strangers to me," Morse complained. "I remember when we walked in Joseph Smith's procession and I knew every Saint."

"Let's just hope the succession of leadership is smoother after Brigham than it was after Joseph," Shadrach said.

"I hear Brigham's sons are going to try to fill their father's shoes," Morse whispered.

"The church will have none of that. The Twelve Apostles are ready to appoint John Taylor president at an appropriate time. I think everyone will agree that is a good choice."

"I feel much better having the old crowd at the reins than these youngsters," Morse grumbled. "Why, there are men coming up in the church who don't even remember Nauvoo, much less Missouri! I don't believe they have the fighting spirit like we have!"

Shadrach smiled wryly. He thought about his own boys, about Ham, now a responsible man in the church, about Walker and Brian. "We had the fighting spirit to survive and now the need isn't as pressing," Shadrach said. "I think having a little less fighting spirit and a little more loving spirit is going to help us out. We aren't rebels anymore. We should let bygones be bygones."

Morse frowned at this apostasy. "The Pukes won't forget and neither should we. As soon as we drop our guards, they are going to hit us."

*　　*　　*

Wearing nothing but a cotton nightshirt, Shadrach tiptoed down the hallway of the house he had built for Lilly. The carpeted hallway was as dark as the night outside, but Shadrach felt his way to the doorway of his wife's bedroom and rapped lightly on the frame.

"My darling? Can I come in?"

There was a long pause, then an irritated voice spoke. "Go away. I'm trying to get some rest."

Undeterred, Shadrach pushed open the door and tiptoed into the room. The floor squeaked as he felt his way over to the brass bed where Lilly lay, a black eyeshade over her face to screen out the moonlight. Shadrach lifted the quilt on the bed and slipped under the cotton sheets. As he did so, his wife rolled over in the bed, turning away from him.

"Do you not feel well, my angel?" Shadrach said, rubbing her back. She felt so smooth through the silk nightgown she wore that Shadrach began breathing heavily at the thought of making love with her.

"No! I have a pain in my chest and I haven't slept well for days," she complained. "The moonlight is behind it, I am sure. A full moon always causes this problem."

"Perhaps I have an idea of how you can relax, my beauty?" her husband suggested mischievously, caressing her silken rump.

"No! Is that all you ever think about?" she snapped at him. "I am beginning to believe I married a sexual pervert."

"But Lilly. It has been over three months since we last slept together," Shadrach whined. "I don't think it is too much to ask for my matrimonial obligations."

She rolled over and pulled off the black eyeshade, a cross look on her face. She stroked her husband's jaw and looked imploringly at him as if to beg his forgiveness.

"Let me recover my spirits, Shaddie. I have been feeling so melancholy lately. Perhaps later this month I will be more receptive."

"But that's what you said three months ago. . . ."

"Perhaps if you were a little less crude in your demands, I might be more more inclined! You are so . . . so . . . unromantic."

"I want to give you everything you want. A good home, a good life, a good family. . . ."

"Don't bring up children again," she groaned. "I told you

I am not a baby factory like the rest of your wives. I don't intend to become a breeding sow like most of the women of this city. I have my audience to think about. I must preserve my diaphragm and my figure."

"It is your figure I am so fond of," Shadrach said in a last-ditch attempt at seduction. "That is why I am here tonight."

"Please leave," she said in a strained voice. "If you worry me much longer I will never get to sleep tonight. I feel a nervous collapse coming on."

Chastened, Shadrach backed out of the room and shut the door. The first inkling that he might have made a bad match occurred to Shadrach not long after his marriage to Lilly. The vivacious young woman enjoyed spending his money in the stores of Salt Lake and San Francisco. He was excited by her girlish enthusiasm and the pleasure she took in a bolt of bright cloth or the modeling of a new cameo. He was inspired by the beautiful way in which she fixed up her new house until it had a salon that rivaled any in Salt Lake.

"High spirits! That's what I like about the girl. She knows how to have fun in life," Shadrach confided to his friends. "My other wives, bless their hearts, have had a tough life. It has killed their spirit of levity. Lilly may have expensive tastes, but she's worth it."

Lilly lived up to her desire for fine living.

The money from the Mormon Folly kept rolling in and then rolled back out to department stores in New York and Chicago. Shadrach was at first annoyed by the money Lilly continued to spend, then irritated. Finally he confronted her with a demand that she economize.

She ignored him.

In retaliation for his reducing her allowance, Lilly began reducing her contact with him. Their frolics in the large brass bed he had bought her became less frequent. Their afternoon carriage rides around City Creek Canyon became rare. Instead, Lilly surrounded herself with her old friends who were considerably younger than her husband. Not only was Shadrach shut out of her company, but he felt his age was being mocked by his wife and her friends behind his back.

When he took his problems to his friends, their response was more amusement than sympathy. He believed most of them were envious of his new arrangement and were making fun of his predicament.

His wives were even more hostile to his problems. Rachel was openly sarcastic. Theresa was scolding. Polly laughed at him. And Wamoa shrugged her shoulders without listening. Not even Sarah would sit still for his complaints.

"Troubles with your child bride?" she said mockingly.

"Why don't I get any sympathy around here?" Shadrach moaned.

"When you marry a girl young enough to be your grand-daughter, don't come whining to us with your problems. If you lie down with a very young dog, you still rise up with very old fleas!"

In an effort to patch things up with Lilly, Shadrach imported an Italian voice teacher from San Francisco, Enrico Viscardi, who demanded and received a rehearsal studio in the Salt Lake Theater. When the piano in the studio was not up to his expectations, a finer one was rented and moved to the theatre. Viscardi moved into a room in the Fairfax Hotel, a gathering place for the Gentiles of Salt Lake, and proceeded to run up a staggering expense account while complaining about his sacrifices in coming to this desert town.

Lilly was much more pleasant to her husband after he bowed to her demands. Breakfast and dinner was once again a civil practice. The long hours spent practicing her voice lessons left Lilly exhausted, however, and at night she was asleep well before Shadrach could make any conjugal visits.

So pleased was Shadrach with Lilly's improving disposition that he went to great lengths to insure her happiness. He never once complained about the expense when the two weeks of lessons were extended into a month's time.

Shadrach made an effort to become more romantic during this time. One afternoon he was in a particularly good mood and left his Salt Lake office with the intention of dropping by the theater. Purchasing a bunch of flowers from a street corner stand, he whistled happily until he came to the theatre, a building with the fluted Doric columns of the Greek revival style. Nodding to the workers inside the theatre, Shadrach mounted the stairway, pausing on the landing to listen to the sweet voice of his beloved wife singing the scales. His wife's voice was not ringing out in the hall that afternoon. Viscardi must have been explaining the fine points of harmony, Shadrach concluded.

Walking down the hallway, he paused outside the rehearsal

studio door. Lilly hated him to barge in and he had second thoughts about the visit. He listened, hoping to hear a break in the lesson during which time he could easily step in.

Some faint murmurs and silences came from the room. Perhaps they were going over a musical score, in which case they would be offended by his interruption. To save himself a scolding, Shadrach decided to scout out the territory before entering.

The transom above the door was tilted to admit the breeze. Reaching up with his long arms, Shadrach gripped the sill and pulled himself up. He felt proud that a sixty-year-old man could chin himself so easily, for with no difficulty he was able to raise his eyes above the transom sill.

What he saw inside took his confidence away. At first he thought Viscardi was attacking his wife for they were both writhing on the floor. The bald-headed Italian was kissing her passionately on the lips as they lay on the hardwood floor, the music scattered around them. Shadrach paused a moment too long, for he could clearly see Lilly kissing the professor back. With great suppleness she pulled his suspenders down over his arms and unbuttoned the teacher's striped pants. She was lifting her own silk dress above her waist when her cuckolded husband shut his eyes. He dropped back to the floor outside the door way. The flowers fell silently from his weakened fist to the toes of his boots.

What could he do?

He could walk away, pretend he saw nothing and never bring the subject up with his wife. Perhaps this was just a passing infatuation and if he ignored it she would be true to him from then on. Or he could go inside.

Enrico Viscardi, his arms encased in plaster casts, boarded a train for San Francisco. He had thought about instituting a suit against his employer but realized he didn't stand a chance in a Mormon court.

For his part, Shadrach and his young bride were soon sitting before John Taylor, the president and prophet of the church. Taylor had known the Englishman from the days at Nauvoo and he was surprised and dismayed that his old friend was seeking a divorce. The young lady seemed to have no objections. She was receiving her house and a healthy income from her ex-husband and seemed anxious to be free of him.

The church had a realistic attitude toward divorce. Marriage was one of the holiest covenants of the church, but if it became an earthly burden, the bond was better dissolved.

"You realize that once divorced, you will both forego the reunion in heaven and the eternity spent together?" Taylor asked.

"Good," Lilly said petulantly. "The idea of spending an eternity with him turns my stomach."

Shadrach nodded in sad agreement. Taylor granted the divorce, Shadrach wearily shook hands with the president and searched for his hat. It was time for him to go back home.

Chapter Twenty-Seven

"Sisters! Take off your sunbonnets!" Theresa Tompkins shouted, waving a copy of the *Deseret News*. "We have won the right to vote!"

The crowd of women seated in the Young Women's Mutual Improvement Association meeting hall jumped to their feet and embraced each other. The members of the Deseret Women's Suffrage Society had just won a great victory. The territory of Utah had just become the first area of the United States to grant women the right to vote. The year was 1882.

"I know none of you are wearing real sunbonnets tonight," Theresa said, beaming at the crowd. "But are you wearing mental sunbonnets? We women of Deseret have been slaving under the ideals of sacrifice and subjugation that were necessary when we were driven out here. Times have changed. We no longer live in a primitive place. Salt Lake City is taking its place among the major metropolises of this country. We Utah women are showing the way for our sisters in the states. We no longer have to stand in the shade of our more cosmopolitan sisters. We can finally take off our sunbonnets!"

Once again the ladies cheered and Theresa felt her eyes misting up. This was the moment she had awaited for almost twenty years. Through all the struggles and disappointments, through all the hardships and discouragement, she and her friends had kept pressing to give their women an equal say in the affairs of state. And now that they had achieved the victory, she was ashamed to show her tears of joy. Other women in the audience were bawling but as the leader, Theresa felt she should show some reserve.

"Maybe it's because we Mormon women have been through so many other struggles that we aren't afraid to keep on fighting in order to get the right to vote," Theresa continued. "Maybe we had to show our men that they might rule the roost, be we're going to have a say in how that roost is run.

But one thing is sure. We've got it and we aren't turning back now. This group isn't going to disband until we see Deseret become a state."

The desire for Deseret to become a state was not a new one. Brigham Young himself had tried on numerous occasions to get the United States Congress to vote statehood for the territory. The eastern politicians were wary of the Mormons, however. These independent people could not be counted on to follow the traditional political parties and could be thorn in their side. Using the excuse of Mormon rebellion and polygamy, the congress refused Young's request.

As federal officials moved into the state, the Saints became afraid of a land grab by the Gentiles. Each year saw fewer Saints immigrating into the valley and more Pukes. At first only Gentile miners and lumbermen settled in the state, made their money, and then left. But a new breed of settler was coming. The railroad brought Gentile farmers in, ranchers and sheepherders, mostly immigrants who had no knowledge of the Saint's battles with the United States.

If these Gentiles settled, they might be able to swing the tide of the voting population. If the Saints lost the vote, they would lose the territory.

A practical decision had been reached. Since the Saints came from big families with a goodly share of women, why not give the women the right to vote? Many of the Gentiles were bachelors. If women's suffrage passed, it would give the Saints the edge in any election. A loss of manly pride was a small price to pay for a solid Mormon legislature.

"Yes, we are going to keep organized and keep on fighting," Theresa told her assembled sisters. "We are going to fight to see that Deseret is admitted to the Union. We are going to vote in the election that sends the first Senator to Washington. And when that Senator is elected, she is going to be a woman!"

After the meeting, Theresa walked home along the wide streets of the city. The trees planted thirty years before had grown tall and the cottonwoods, alders and scrub oaks diffused the light of the street lamps into shadows on the sidewalks. En route, they encountered one blue-coated policeman who tipped his conical hat to them as they passed. The women's suffrage movement had been a peaceful one in Salt Lake.

Theresa's oldest daughter was walking beside her mother.

Ilsa was tall and straight, with the blonde hair of her Swiss ancestors wreathing her pale, serious face. Ilsa wore a gray wool dress and a matching jacket over her white blouse. A straw-boater hat with a blue ribbon kept her in fashion with the rest of the girls in Salt Lake.

She had been at her mother's side throughout much of the struggle to get the vote. She was eighteen years old now, and Theresa hoped that by the time statehood was granted, perhaps the girl would be running for office.

"Congratulations, Mother. I know plenty of people have been saying that to you, but I want to add my admiration," Ilsa said. "None of them have seen the tears you shed in private. There would have been no victory without your efforts."

Theresa wrapped a strong arm around her daughter and squeezed her until the girl squealed in mock pain. "I could not have done it if it weren't for my family," Theresa said.

"Even father?" Ilsa teased.

"Especially your father. Even though I think he still doesn't understand why we are fighting, he gave me the freedom and the encouragement to do what I wanted. That's what I will always love about him and about the Saints. This religion is always dynamic. It seems to be of one mind, but it is always willing to accommodate its people whenever it is necessary to do so."

"Mother. May I talk frankly with you? About such a matter as changing one's mind?"

"Of course you can."

"I was moved by your speech this evening," Ilsa said, solemnly. "Especially the part about fighting for what you believe in. Even if sometimes it means going against what everyone around you believes in."

Theresa nodded understandingly. "This is very important, perhaps the most important things in the world. Without it we are not individuals in God's eyes."

"What if what you believed in went against God? Or at least what the church stood for."

"It would be a very serious matter. But if you truly believed it you should say it. The church has been known to be wrong before. What is it that you are concerned about?"

"Mother, I'm in love."

Theresa looked relieved even though she tried to remain

serious. "My goodness! That's wonderful news! But why all the talk of belief and fighting?"

"He is a geologist for the Interior Department."

"A Gentile?" Theresa said, sobering quickly.

Ilsa nodded.

"With all the nice Mormon boys in this town, why a Gentile?"

"Because I don't want a nice Mormon boy. I want Morris!"

Theresa paused to hug her daughter, patting her on the back while she herself gazed up at the stars with the look of one who has completed one struggle only to start on a second.

"There, there, my darling," Theresa said. "I'm sure that if you truly love him things will work out fine."

"What about father? He will be furious when he finds out."

"Your father is a stern man, but he's not an ogre. He is true to the faith, but he will not force his way upon others. Let me talk to him. I'm sure he will object but he won't try to stop you."

"I forbid it! I absolutely forbid it!" Shadrach bellowed as he leapt out of his chair. His voice rattled the window panes of the dining room where he was supping with Theresa and her six children.

With this reaction, Ilsa burst into tears and fled from the room leaving Theresa and the five younger ones staring at the red-faced Englishman.

"Of all the apostasties I have heard, this is the one that beats the band," Shadrach grumbled, regaining his composure and sitting down. "After fighting those sons-of-bitches away from my doorstep for forty years, now one tries to sneak in to my own house by marrying one of my daughters!"

Theresa was stricken at this reaction, embarrassed that she had handled the sensitive matter so poorly by bringing it up at the dinner table.

"It is not that great a catastrophe, my dear," she reminded him. "The girl's happiness should be closest to our hearts."

"The girl's immortal soul should be closest to our hearts," her husband thundered back, banging the table with his fist. "If she marries out of the church, she will be cut off and we will lose her for eternity in heaven. Her temporal happiness on earth is of less importance to me. Once we are in heaven, she will thank me for it."

"But she will hate you on earth."

"I have been hated before. I can bear it."

"I think you have selfish motives in your refusal," Theresa said, accusingly. "You want her under your thumb to satisfy your own sense of power. You want her in heaven to soothe your own loneliness."

"Woman, I will not have you impugn my faith before anyone, especially our young children for whom you are setting a poor example."

"And I will not have you ordering me about in my own house!" Theresa flared, knowing that her only defense against his unreasonable rage was to attack.

Shadrach threw down his napkin and took his coat off a peg in the hall. "I will never let my family be broken up by a Puke. I forbid any further discussion of this distasteful subject from henceforth on. I will adjourn, and since you have encouraged our daughter in this matter, I charge you with straightening it out."

If all the Saints were a little jumpy in 1882, it was with good cause. The United States Congress made another frontal assault on the Mormon theocracy which so far had resisted the efforts to tame it. The Edmunds-Tucker Act, passed by congress in that year, outlawed polygamy anywhere in the United States and made its practice a federal crime.

For the first time, federal marshals were empowered to arrest a man on the suspicion of having more than one wife. The territory of Utah, which had been immune from such justice as long as the Deseret legislature sat, was suddenly wide open.

Only a small portion of the Deseret population practiced plural marriage, perhaps 10 percent or less. But those that did formed the cream of Mormon society and included the leaders of the church, the militia, and the business community.

In a second blow to the kingdom of the Saints, the church itself was targeted by the federal authorities. If the church leaders resisted this drive to stamp out polygamy, they would feel the sanctions of the government. The U.S. attorney's office threatened to confiscate church property, which included many of the manufacturing plants in Deseret.

To the Saints assembling on the front porch of the Salt Lake Hotel to talk the matter over, it was very clear what was happening.

"This is it, boys, the final battle," Shadrach announced to his friends. "They sent in Johnson's army and that didn't work. They sent in the federal judges and that didn't work. Now they're sending in the federal deputies, and that just might work. They haven't been able to kill the body of the kingdom, but now they're going after the head."

"When those deps arrive with their arrest warrants, I say we meet 'em with shotguns," Thomas Morse argued.

"Not with two regiments of blue coats in Fort Douglas with shotted cannon pointing down on the city. That's just the excuse the Pukes want to blow us to smithereens!" Elohim Cooper argued.

The men who sat on the benches of the hotel stuck their hands in the pockets of their coats and contemplated their alternatives. "We can't sit still and we don't want to run," Ruben Parsnip, the owner of the brick factory and the husband of three wives said. "What is left to us?"

"Brother John Pratt is conducting some negotiations with the president of Mexico," Morse informed them. "He has the intention of starting a colony of plural families south of the border where the Deps can't touch us."

"Why should we run and abandon everything we have built here?" Shadrach argued. "I'm too damn old to begin my life over again. By my reckoning I've begun it four or five times already."

"We should have been fighting them with guns instead of words all these years. We're all too fat to do it now," Elohim said gravely. "We fell away from the true religion and got ourselves in this pickle."

"Brothers, it's too late to start thinking that now," Ruben pointed out as a squad of U.S. soldiers swaggered by the front of the hotel. "We just have to stick to our guns and hope we can wear them down like we have so many times before."

The church and the citizens of Deseret stood firm against the newest swarm of locust which swept down on the valley. Every train arriving in Salt Lake had a new complement of federal deputies on it. The deps were all humorless men in bowler hats pulled down over their shifty eyes. The men sported handlebar moustaches and shiny stars on the breasts of their store-bought suits. The deps acted like they were entering enemy territory. To show they meant business, they carried the familiar bulges of Colt police pistols in their pockets.

The deps made their presence felt by checking into the Carlysle Hotel and prominently displaying their badges in public places. They were followed around town by the young boys of the city who would sing "The Battle Hymn of the Republic" to warn the population about the approach of the marshals. Then the deps began making their first arrests and the laughing stopped. A state of siege settled in over the city. The first arrests were of the well-known polygamists, the patriarchs whose religious zealotry prevented them from renouncing the way of life they felt divinely inspired. These men were hauled before unsympathetic federal judges, fined, and imprisoned in the Utah penitentiary for up to five years.

The deps widened their search. They swarmed over Salt Lake and broadened their hunt to Ogden and Provo. No member of the community was safe if he lived with more than one woman. Doctors, legislators, bishops, all were fair game. In the daytime, no man would dare visit his wives for fear of drawing the marshals. At night, the back streets and alleys were full of dignified men jumping over picket fences and crawling in windows.

Shadrach had to separate his five wives into five different dwellings to avoid suspicion. Rachel kept the house on the hill while Sarah moved into a smaller cottage near Cottonwood Canyon. Wamoa was given the old 'dobie house and Polly and Theresa each had their frame houses in the flats of the city.

Shadrach divided his time, skulking around to the wives who were scattered about the capital. He would attend to his affairs at his office and have a leisurely meal at the Salt Lake Hotel. In the evening he would briskly walk through the darkened streets until he came to the house where he was scheduled to spend the night. If a light was burning in the front window of the house, it was safe for him to slip into his own backyard.

One evening as he clamored over the fence, a figure rushed from the bushes and bumped into him. Shadrach seized the man by the throat, outraged at this trick and shook him.

"You damn dep! Why can't you leave us alone?" Shadrach snarled. "If you try to keep me from my family tonight, I'll break your neck, I swear it!"

"I'm not a dep!" the man said, choking. "I'm your neighbor Eli Cobb! Take your hands from my throat 'ere your strangle me!''

"Eli? What are you doing here in the dark?"

"The same as you, Shadrach. Trying to sneak into my own house, in my own town, to see my own family."

Shadrach released his neighbor and brushed him off. "Things have come to a pretty pass when respectable men like you and me have to sneak around like thieves in the night."

"This affair is wreaking havoc on my family, that is sure," Eli said.

Shadrach shook his head and continued through his own yard, stumbling through the flower garden his wife had planted in the back. Three quick raps on the back door and a towheaded child admitted him.

"Go keep a watch on the front door and tell pretty Polly I'm home," Shadrach said.

"This isn't Aunt Polly's house the child replied. "This is Theresa's."

As the decade wore on, the relentless federal prosecution of the polygamists began to bear fruit. The Utah penitentiary began filling up with bearded men and the church relief rolls began filling up with women whose husbands were breaking rocks. The businesses of Salt Lake began to suffer as their owners spent more time dodging the law than balancing the books.

The leadership of the church, dependent on stability, began to be taken over by younger men, many of whom had only one wife. These younger men, free from the problems of hiding their households, could concentrate on the affairs of the church. There was much to be cared for.

The Latter Day Saints were nearly flat broke.

The federal judges had fined the church and assessed so many judgments against it for its sanctioning of polygamy that the Saints could hardly pay the bill. When the money finally ran out of the church coffers, the deps began seizing church property and padlocking some of the bishop's warehouses. These actions outraged the citizens of the territory but the federal authorities were not moved. It was a war to the end.

To escape the persecution of the dep's, many "polygs" moved into the wilder and unsettled parts of Deseret. A colony was established in the province of Sonora in Mexico, out of the jurisdiction of the United States.

Closer to home, Deseret's Dixie offered many refuges to the plural families looking for sanctuary. In the Zion canyonlands not far from St. George, a dozen communities of matrimonial outlaws sprang up. Further South, in the unmapped canyonlands that had hidden John D. Lee, tiny agricultural communities sprang up where a man and his wives could live according to the Principle.

In hidden towns like Fredonia, Arizona, named for the "free women" it sheltered, Glen Canyon, Kanab or Paria, the polygs took up residence and lived as they pleased. In that remote land, where a trail might twist five miles to travel what a raven could cover in one mile, few federal marshals would come looking for them. In the northern edge of the Arizona territory, where the Grand Canyon blocked off access from the South, they could live without interference in the Principle.

By 1885, Shadrach Tompkins had gotten a bellyful of the dep's harassment. The church was bankrupt and running on the credit of its members. The leading men of Deseret were scattered or in prison. Bickering had broken out in the community over whether the Principle was worth the price of the harassment.

"My sixty-seven-year-old bones can't take the punishment of crawling over that fence anymore," Shadrach told his wives, all secretly assembled in the Hill House. "I can't stand to see the church torn apart by the Pukes."

The women nodded in agreement. Life for them had been equally difficult. The job of bringing up children called "bastards" by the Gentiles of the city, the nights of sleeping alone, of watching for the marshals night and day, had worn them down.

"I propose moving to Dixie until the harassment of the deps is passed," Shadrach said. "It won't be an easy life. I'm not demanding that any of you join me. I am putting the deeds to your houses into your own names. I have given Ham the control of the Mormon Folly. If anything happens to me, you will all be provided for."

A quick counsel determined that Sarah, Rachel, and Wamoa would accompany Shadrach to Southern Deseret. Polly and

Theresa would stay in Salt Lake to manage the affairs of the family.

Since so many of the family's children had reached the age when they would be working or marrying, the choice of moving with the family would be an individual one.

Being driven out of their native city by a bunch of interlopers was a bitter pill for the family to swallow. Living the life they had chosen in the wilderness was preferable, however, to living under the thumb of the Pukes.

The family businesses were put in the hands of Ham Tompkins and his younger brother Walker. In 1884, Ham was forty-five years old and Walker, twenty-nine. The men and their younger brothers were rising rapidly in the church. Ham was a member of the seventies, busied with guiding the church through the hard times. He was a leader in the Mormon Chamber of Commerce, seeing that church businessmen got a fair share of the business of the territory.

Walker had completed his church missionary work. He had proselytized in Georgia and had nearly been lynched by an angry mob. His father could never say his religious experience had been easy.

The rest of the family's children were grown, by 1884, the youngest being ten years old. The younger ones would accompany the family to Dixie. The married children would remain with their spouses in Salt Lake. The children attending Deseret University would live with Theresa and Polly in the city.

The Hill House was closed up. The furnishings too valuable to take to Dixie were covered with sheets and left to the care of Ham. Four wagons were loaded with the household goods needed for the trip into Southern Deseret. Amidst jokes about their first arrival in Salt Lake, the family set out. The three wives traveled in separate wagons driven by teamsters in the employ of the Mormon Folly. Shadrach followed separately in a buggy, for the roads south were crawling with deps. As his horse led him through the open valleys and the quiet mountains of the South, he began to breathe easier than he had in several years. The deps would never follow him here. . . .

Ilsa Tompkins looked sadly at the crystal clear light of the Deseret dawn breaking over the Wasatch Mountains. She knew she would never find a home with the same purity of air and light, or a purity of the citizens, like she had enjoyed in Salt Lake. But Morris Clement, her geologist and fiancé waited for her in Denver.

The Union Pacific train waited in the shade of the Ogden Station. Steam jetted from the escape valves as the engineer built up the pressure and prepared to get underway.

Theresa Tompkins looked at her daughter and squeezed her hands. She lovingly arranged the bonnet over her golden hair for the tenth time that morning.

"I know what is going through your mind and you musn't worry about your father," Theresa said firmly. "In the long run he will be happy for you when you make yourself happy."

"I can't get over feeling horrible about what I am doing," Ilsa said. "In the best of times I would still feel badly about defying father and running off with a Gentile, but now I feel I am taking advantage of his bad luck. He will hate me for it."

"Don't worry my darling. It's better this way. Everyone has to make unpleasant choices in life," Theresa assured her. "Look at my choice to leave Switzerland and come to America."

The conductor shouted his final boarding call and walked impatiently toward them.

"Was it worth it, Mother?"

"Without hesitation I would do it one hundred times again!"

Ilsa flung herself on her mother, kissed her and stepped onto the train without looking back. The conductor swung up after her and waved his hand. With a lurch, the lines of cars rumbled slowly out of the station leaving Theresa in the soft quiet of the morning.

UNDERGROUND

1885

Chapter Twenty-Eight

A small buggy carrying the silhouettes of two men was kicking up a cloud of red dust as it rattled down the trail leading into Polyg Canyon. The single horse picked its way carefully, hugging the steep walls of the cliff, for one false step would have sent the carriage plunging into the chasm below.

The progress of the carriage was carefully watched by a young man wearing the frayed straw hat and gray jeans of a back-country Mormon. He was sitting on the dizzying edge of the cliff two thousand feet above the buggy. He steadied a brass telescope on his knees and made a positive identification of the two U.S. deputy marshals riding nervously in the buggy.

On the other side of the cliff, a small community of adobe homes sat in the shade of the ridge. A series of orchards and fields lay up the canyon watered by a stream running out of the mountains.

Standing up, the boy picked up a large green flag attached to a pole and began wig-wagging it to get the attention of the people in the village below.

Shadrach Tompkins was kneeling on the floor of his kitchen, his elbows resting on the seat of his chair as he said his prayers. His wives and children were likewise praying when the door burst open and a breathless boy with greasy black hair rushed in.

"Pa, Pa! The deps are coming!"

"Just a minute, boy. I'm conversing with the Lord," Shadrach said. He squeezed his eyes tighter and moved his lips faster so he could stand and listen to the boy.

"The deps are coming up the canyon road. They should be here in about five minutes."

The family burst into action. Lucille Tompkins, thirteen years old, rushed to the side wall and pulled a canvas rucksack from a peg. The rucksack contained his flint and steel, a heavy coat and a blanket. Sarah grabbed the bag from her child's hands and thrust a loaf of still-hot bread into it. Then she handed the rucksack to her husband, received a quick peck of a kiss, and opened the back door for him to bound out.

The adobe house was a two-story dwelling which resembled the other homes in the village. They each had separate entrances for each wife's family so that the husband could visit in privacy. Now the back entrances of these homes were flying open and bearded husbands were sprinting out to avoid arrest by the deps.

With his long legs and healthy lungs, Shadrach led the running men up the narrow canyon. Where the spring poured from the red rock cliff, the men scattered like quail and clamored up in the mountains to wait out the chilly night when the deps would be gone.

Marshals Reilly and Cooper looked nervously around as they descended into the quiet village. They scanned the rocks above the village where an army of riflemen could hide and ambush them at will. No marshal had been killed enforcing the ban on plural marriages, but some nasty incidents had seen the bullets fly, and threats against their lives were common. The two men covered an area of over ten thousand square miles of fierce canyon lands. The men who were their quarry were no strangers to violence.

Reilly clucked his tongue and flipped the reins sending their sorrel mare into a trot that brought them up into the middle of the village. Only chickens and scruffy hound dogs scratched in the dry dust at their feet as the two men stepped out of their buggy carrying the blank warrants they had brought from St. George.

A dozen sets of eyes watched them approach a 'dobie house and pound loudly on the barrel stave door. No one answered. They continued to pound until some movement was heard inside the house and the door cracked open.

In the narrow slot, Rachel Tompkins peered angrily at the men, her frayed silver hair and threadbare clothes testifying to the hardship of the life in Dixie.

"Afternoon, Ma'am. Is your husband to home?" Reilly said, tipping his flat-brimmed, straw-boater hat politely.

"No."

"Might you be expecting him shortly?"

"He went to California. He'll be back in a couple of months."

"Mind if we come in and look around? We have a warrant."

Rachel diffidently let the door swing open. She stood back glaring at the two men who walked into her crude kitchen. Reilly removed his boater, but Cooper left his bowler hat on his head and twiddled his handlebar mustache as he looked around.

"Might you be Mrs. Tompkins?" Reilly said, looking first at Rachel, then at Sarah.

"I'm Mrs. Tompkins. This is my sister, Sarah."

"Her sister!" Cooper snorted. He was fingering some of the personal effects of Shadrach that he had left in his haste. A pair of eyeglasses lay on the table and several pairs of boots that had been cleaned were by the door. A basket of clothing was waiting to be mended and a shotgun was resting against the fireplace.

"Now we know you are lying, Mrs. Tompkins. The back door of this place is covered with a man's tracks," Reilly said pleasantly. "Now why don't you call him back in and have done with it."

"Have you seen enough, you damn scum?" Rachel said icily. "Why can't you leave us in peace?"

"An old lady like you shouldn't be left alone," Cooper said, examining a pair of Shadrach's britches with holes in the knees. "Not while your man is off scallywaggin' with a young gal he probably has stashed in the next valley."

Several of the Tompkins children sidled into the kitchen, resentful of the deps but still curious enough to want to see the enemy.

"Well, lookee here. They don't look too cretin-ified," Cooper said, rubbing twelve-year-old Daniel on the head. "I always heard the children of polygamy were misshapen morons."

"Get out of my house!" Rachel ordered, "before I take that shotgun and cause a spark which will set this whole land against you buzzards!"

The two deps replaced their hats and sauntered out the door. "Tell your man I'm going to get him," Cooper warned happily. "And when we do we're going to throw him in the pen with the rest of the horny old goats!"

*   *   *

The onslaught of the Pukes was beginning to be successful. In 1885 the penalties for polygamy were increased. A man convicted of cohabitation with more than one woman could be fined and imprisoned and his right to vote stripped from him.

To the dismay of Theresa Tompkins and her sisters in the women's suffrage movement, the same bill abolished the right of women to vote in the territory of Deseret.

So many men had been arrested for polygamy that many judges in the South were fining some of the smaller fry the sum of two dollars. The more important Mormons, the leaders of the church and the community, received stiffer sentences. The courts claimed they wanted to make examples of the top men. They effectively crippled the Mormon establishment.

No one was too powerful to escape the deps.

The president and prophet of the church, John Taylor, was hounded throughout Southern Deseret until he was captured and thrown into the penitentiary outside Salt Lake. His incarceration outraged the citizens of Deseret. They were helpless. Taylor languished and died inside the Puke jail. After living a life to free himself of the bonds of Babylon, after fleeing Missouri and Nauvoo and building Salt Lake, after fighting the Gentiles in the snows of Wyoming and in the courts of Salt Lake, he died in a row of cellblocks shared by horse thieves and claim jumpers.

And the Saints could do nothing to revenge his death.

Willard Woodruff was made president of the church to succeed Taylor. He inherited a bankrupt church, an embattled kingdom and a divided people. Many of the Saints were ready to relinquish the Principle in order to secure peace from the Pukes. The survival of polygamy mattered less than the survival of the church. If the federal authorities were only interested in stamping out plural marriage, let them do so and make Utah a state.

In the isolated canyons of Deseret's Dixie, a different view was held. "If we give up the Principle, the next thing the Pukes will outlaw is baptism for the dead. Then they will outlaw the priesthood," Rachel declared. "They won't stop until they have converted us all to Presbyterians."

Shadrach lay on his stomach on a sandstone rock overlooking the small home he had built for Wamoa. The crickets chirped brightly in the thin night air. The moon had not risen yet but the stars gave plentiful light, enough to show that no one else was about.

Satisfied that he was alone in the night, Shadrach tiptoed down from the rock. In another part of the village, a dog barked and Shadrach froze. Silence fell over the community and once again he moved until he stood by the back door. He was puzzled that Wamoa had not left the lantern in the window. He attributed it to the forgetfulness of the Hawaiian personality. He was so anxious to get out of the cold, he had quit caring about their precautions.

"That's far enough, right there! Stand stock-still or take a bullet!"

Shadrach froze in his tracks, afraid he had been mistaken for a horse thief.

"Don't shoot, brother. It's me, Shadrach Tompkins."

A light shone on him from a lantern held by his captors. When they started advancing on him without speaking Shadrach realized that he was not being held by Saint, but by strangers. Ducking out of the light, Shadrach raced around the corner of the house and charged for the cover of the corral.

"Stop! Hold or I shoot!" a voice shouted and bullets whistled over his head.

Shadrach leapt over the corral fence and dashed between the nervous horses inside. On the other side of the corral he sprang over the fence and sank hip deep in the manure pile gathered by the villagers for use as fertilizer. Floundering in the pungent-smelling manure, he tried to pull himself free but was unsuccessful.

Pounding feet rounded the corral and a light was shone upon the Englishman as he struggled out of the manure pile. Looking up, he could see the grinning faces of deputies Reilly and Cooper staring down at him.

"I've been waiting a long time to meet you, Mr. Shadrach Tompkins," Cooper said. "It looks like you got yourself into something you just couldn't shake off."

The black wagon used by the federal marshals to transport prisoners clattered through the streets of Salt Lake as the citizens watched in scorn. Inside, staring through the iron bars of the "black widow," Shadrach watched the familiar tree-lined streets and newly painted houses go by. He was a prisoner in his own city, just convicted by a federal judge of "unlawful cohabitation" and sentenced to a term of six months in the Utah Territorial Penitentiary.

It could have been worse, his lawyer had told him. Some polygs were getting four- to eight-year sentences in the prison. Nonetheless, the sentence broke Shadrach's heart. It proved that in their painfully built Zion, the Saints were no longer the masters of their own fate. The federal judges had the power to separate a man, not only from his wives, but from his religion.

The penitentiary was a forbidding complex the Pukes had built on a hill near the old sugar house. The original "pen" had consisted of a group of adobe barracks ringed by a high adobe wall. Both the wall and the barracks were whitewashed and gleamed until the winter rains splattered them with the local mud. So many polygs had been incarcerated in the building that a new addition to the pen was being constructed with a massive brick wall and a gingerbread administration building.

Shadrach whispered a prayer as the gates of the pen swung open and rifle-wielding guards unlocked the "Black Widow" to let him out.

The inmates of the prison wore the familiar zebra-striped suits of jailbirds. Although each man wore the same suit, each wore a different type of hat. Shadrach could immediately separate the hardened criminals, the horse thieves and murderers, from the polygamous convicts. The Gentile thieves were scar-faced, swaggering scoundrels who, with their weatherbeaten hats, appeared to belong in the pen. The Saints, on the other hand, with their backgrounds as church and community leaders, were decidedly uncomfortable in their prison roles, and kept their stetsons and straw hats as clean as their consciences.

The blue-jacketed wardens shoved the new prisoner into the barrack that would be his home for the next six months. The dimly lit building consisted of a long room lined with wooden bunk beds. A wood stove at the far end of the room.

The prisoners were lounging on their beds waiting for dinner to be served and Shadrach immediately recognized a number of prominent Saints. Church leaders and the president of a woolen mill lounged on their blankets, looking woefully depressed.

"Look what just walked in," a scar-faced man at the end of the building roared when Shadrach walked in. "A nice fresh fish!"

Shadrach glared at him, assuming "fresh fish" referred to him. All the inmates in the barrack were sizing him up.

"Good afternoon, Brother Cannon," Shadrach said to a white-bearded patriarch, sitting on the top of the bed. "I haven't seen you since the last church assembly."

"Good afternoon, Brother Tompkins," Cannon said pleasantly. "I had been informed you were convicted of U.C. Welcome to the Territorial Prison Ward."

Shadrach grinned. *U.C.* was short for "Unlawful Cohabitation," and the creation of a new ward inside the prison amused him.

"Hey, fresh fish!" the scar-faced man called out, angered at Shadrach's ignoring him. "You listen when I speak."

"Where do I find a blanket for my bunk?" Shadrach said, ignoring the loudmouth.

"There are no more bunks," Cannon replied. "And your family has to provide your blanket for you."

Shadrach frowned but before he could object, a rough hand seized him and spun him around. He found himself staring at the scar-faced man who was shorter than Shadrach, but his crossed eyes and short-cropped hair made him look as vicious and tricky as an Indian's dog.

"I'm Mean John Mopt, a murderer and renegade," the man snarled. "I'm been sentenced to die by the firing squad so I fear no man. I run this barrack and those that do as I say get along."

To show his contempt, Shadrach plucked the man's hand from his prison uniform and straightened the wrinkles from it. Seeing this, Mopt grinned and knocked Shadrach's bowler hat from his head. As it rolled across the floor, the prisoners in the barracks sat up on their beds to watch the fun. Shadrach made no attempt to retrieve his hat.

Mopt was a head shorter than he and as wide in the shoulders. But Shadrach had thirty years on the younger man and Mopt had all the meanness. Still, if he let this bully beat him once, every prisoner in the barracks would follow the example.

"That's a fine beard you have there, old-timer," Mopt said, staring at the foot-long whiskers on Shadrach's chin. "Someone bring me a scissors for I intend to shear this old goat of his fleece."

"I spent five years underground growing this beard and

you shan't touch a hair of it," Shadrach warned. "I am a patriarch of the church and my beard is my soul."

"Your soul and you are going to be parted, reverend," Mopt said mockingly. "You'll be much more attractive to those girls in Salt Lake when you are shorn."

The murderer looked around to make sure his friends were watching him. As he did, Shadrach saw his chance and struck the bully a blow that would have lifted an ox's head off its shoulders. Mopt fell to the ground, but jumped up again and leapt at Shadrach. The two men fell to the floor and thrashed around, but Mopt's young strength got the better of the older man and he came out on top, punching Shadrach in the nose. The years underground, tilling the soil of Southern Deseret had hardened Shadrach, and he was able to strike Mopt in the Adam's apple with such force that the scar-faced bully fell choking to the floor.

Like a bouncer in a mining town saloon, Shadrach picked Mopt up by the scruff of his neck and hurled him into the wood stove at the end of the barracks, sending a cloud of smoke and soot into the room. The inmates clamored to put out the fire before the guards noticed and Shadrach stood over the fallen Mopt like a puma stands over a deer.

"I think I will sleep in this gentleman's bunk," he announced. "And I will wrap myself in his blanket until I can obtain one of my own."

The morale of the imprisoned Saints was low when Shadrach entered the pentitentiary. The men had chosen to follow a path of civil disobedience, preferring to go to prison rather than abandon the Principle. They had flaunted the laws of the United States, which they claimed violated their religious freedom.

Once inside the prison and away from the stirring speeches in the Tabernacle, some of their bravado wore off. Most of the men had never seen the inside of a jail cell before, and the caliber of their cellmates shocked them. The pious Saints could not get used to the vulgarity of the criminals' language nor to the coarseness of their thoughts. The stench of unwashed bodies violated their sense of cleanliness.

But Shadrach's arrival lifted their spirits.

Polly Tompkins clasped the bundle of blankets and the basket of jams and bread she had brought her husband as she entered the visiting area of the penitentiary. The Pukes had refused to allow her children to see their father and they waited outside.

At first, Polly didn't recognize her husband when he was shown into the bare, sunlit visiting room. He had lost weight behind bars. The striped prison suit made him look like the pictures of hardened convicts she had seen in the newspapers. At the sight of him, Polly burst into tears and Shadrach had to pat her on the hand until she stopped crying. Even the warder who watched over them was forced to turn away in pity.

"You look ghastly," Polly wept. "I thank God the children cannot see you."

"I am actually enjoying myself," Shadrach said. "I am getting the first rest I have had in a long time."

"How are they feeding you?"

"Three kinds of beans and a piece of hard bread once a day," Shadrach said. "It reminds me of the meals we used to eat during the Starving Time. In fact, it reminds me of the way you cook now."

Polly bit her tongue, bouyed by his sense of humor.

"How are the children taking it?"

"They are proud of their papa. They want a picture of you in your prison outfit. It would remind them of all the times you punished them," Polly said, brightening. "Ham's children are embarrassed about it for the children tease them in school."

Shadrach chuckled. He adored his grandchildren as much as he loved his children.

"We got a letter from Theresa's Ilsa," Polly said cautiously. "She and her husband are living in Washington D.C. They have just had a baby son."

Shadrach cast his eyes downward to hide his disappointment.

"Did they say if they would raise him as a Saint?"

"They didn't say."

"Some of the brethren in here are mighty downcast and miserable," Shadrach said, changing the subject. "They are getting real antsy sitting around doing nothing."

"They should take up their missionary work inside the penitentiary," Polly said firmly. "What better place to preach the gospel than to a bunch of damn sinners who have no place to get away to?"

Shadrach smiled at the idea. "You may have a point.

When we stand on the street corners or pass out tracts at a meeting, the Gentile can get away. In here, we've got 'em cornered.''

In fact, Shadrach and some of the other brothers did begin proselytizing to the criminals while they spent their time behind bars. While the convicts labored under the hot sun in the prison garden, or lounged around the exercise yard, Shadrach would speak to whoever would listen about the restored priesthood of the Church of the Latter Day Saints.

The convicts listened to his preaching with amusement. Most drifted away from him, a few stayed out of interest or boredom. The penitentiary mission was not a great success in getting converts, but it rallied the spirits of the imprisoned Saints and reminded them of the faith that they had sacrificed their freedom for.

The one convict Shadrach was not able to reach was John Mopt, who he had defeated on his first day behind bars. Mopt had not troubled Shadrach since. Like all bullies, he went looking for easier game. But the Englishman had chosen this convicted murderer as his personal challenge: to save his soul before the firing squad claimed his life.

On the Fourth of July, 1888, the prisoners in Shadrach's barrack held a party in the afternoon. The wife of one of the Saints had supplied a keg of cider and several boxes of sugar crullers which the guards had eaten a portion of while checking for hidden contraband. The men sat smoking hand-rolled cigarettes and drinking the cider as several inmates played some popular tunes on a jew's harp and a harmonica.

Shadrach was tapping his feet and as the music quickened, he jumped to his feet and capered out on the floor. The prisoners whistled as he clicked his feet together and danced over to John Mopt.

''My I have the pleasure of requesting your company in a dance?'' Shadrach asked bowing deeply.

''You're asking me to dance?'' Mopt growled.

Shadrach nodded and Mopt looked around to see if a joke was being played on him. The other men were surprised as he.

''I would oblige you, but I am carrying this cannonball on my leg,'' Mopt said.

Shadrach stooped over and picked up the heavy iron ball which was fastened to Mopt's leg with a shackle. Holding it under his arm, he extended his hand to the murderer and pulled him to his feet. The band played a slow waltz as the two men pirouetted around the room. The men applauded and howled as the two men danced, and Mopt broke out in the first smile Shadrach had ever seen. Soon, all the men had chosen partners and were sweeping in grotesque parodies of a waltz.

"That ball must be getting kind of heavy," Mopt said to Shadrach. "Come on, reverend. Let me buy you a drink."

"Mopt, I want to do you the most important favor you've ever gotten in your sorry life," Shadrach said as he and the murderer toiled in the penitentiary's garden.

"The best favor you can grant me is to get me a file, a set of keys and a colt revolver," Mopt said. "And then have a fast horse waiting for me over the wall."

"That would only save your mortal body," Shadrach said. "I can do better than that by saving your immortal soul."

"I was figuring on saving my mortal body and then having the time to work on my immortal soul in Mexico."

"Mopt. If you renounce these misbegotten ways of yours and enter into a covenant with Jesus Christ, there is still hope for you to spend eternity in heaven."

"Reverend, I murdered my wife and her mother and father with an axe, then I robbed their home and spent the proceeds on liquor and whores. If there is a way to get me into heaven after that, then you damn sure could get us both out of this lousy prison."

Undeterred, Shadrach kept proselytizing the murderer. Mopt was the most resistant man he had ever seen, but occasionally he would slap a knot or two on Mopt's head to get him to listen better. As logically as Shadrach explained the church's ways to him, the murderer would find some dodge to avoid being saved. Doggedly Shadrach kept preaching. Mopt would complain less and listen more, although he never admitted belief.

When the day arrived for Mopt's execution, the warden of the prison called Shadrach out of his barracks. "Tompkins, John Mopt has requested that you be his pastoral counsel during his execution. Since in your peculiar religion, everybody seems to be a minister, I guess you're elected."

"I have no stomach for executions. I'd rather not witness this act."

"You are not being called as a witness, you are being ordered to minister to this man!" the warden said testily. "If your religion is as genuine as you claim, you'll heed the call."

The warden was a fire breather who did not like to argue with prisoners. He had threatened many times to shoot recalcitrant prisoners and no inmate had seen fit to test his determination. Shadrach agreed to stand by Mopt at his execution and he followed the warden outside.

At the far end of the prison compound, a cottonwood post had been sunk in the ground in front of a whitewashed adobe wall. A squad of guards carrying Sharps single-shot rifles had drawn up in front of the post. Nearby, John Mopt was being held, his arms and legs bound by shackles.

"Welcome to my goodbye party," he said when he saw Shadrach approach. "I'm glad you could see me off."

"This work displeases me," the Englishman said.

"It displeases me one hundred times worse," Mopt laughed. "Come now and say a prayer for a good Mormon boy gone to hell."

Both men sank to their knees and bowed their heads in prayer. After a minute of silent devotion Shadrach raised his eyes to the heavens.

"Oh Lord, John Mopt, here, is one of the lowest sons of bitches you ever created. He's a murderer and a thief and he admits it freely. Now he's about to be shot for it and nobody deserves it more. But he was once a good Mormon boy, baptised and all that. So if you can see it in your heart to forgive a Jack Mormon like him, then everybody on earth has a chance!"

Shadrach looked proudly at Mopt who struggled to his feet under the weight of the chains. "Thank you, Brother Tompkins. I can face what's comin' much happier now. Tell my ma that I died in the faith and I'm sorry about all the deeds I've done."

"We'll do your temple work for you, son," Shadrach said. "And we'll meet on the better side of Glory."

A guard fitted a floppy black wool hood over Mopt's face and secured it with a string. With a piece of chalk he x-ed a mark over the man's heart and led him to the post. Mopt stood motionless as his wrist and leg irons were attached to hooks on the stake. When he was prepared the two guards hurried off.

"Ready your weapons!" the warden said.

"Shadrach?"

"Yes, John?"

"Aim your weapons!"

"If there's an afterlife where I'm going, I'll send you back a hailstorm as a signal!"

"Fire!"

The muskets thundered and Mopt slammed back against the post, the bullets raising a cloud of dust on his dirty uniform. He slumped to the ground, hanging from the shackles.

The prison doctor examined him and pronounced him dead.

Afterwards, Shadrach stood over the bare grave which had been prepared in the prison cemetary just outside the walls. A group of trustees had set Mopt's body in a pine coffin and had carried it outside the walls under the watchful eyes of the guards in the towers.

His coffin was set down in the grave and a trustee shoveled the clods of dirt down on the pine top. The clods drummed on the wood like a thunder clap. As if to accompany this sound, a gray cloud passed in front of the bright July sun.

Happy to work in the shade, the men kicked the rest of the dirt in while Shadrach tried to preach a final word.

"Here he is Lord, and welcome to him. The only way he got out of prison was to be carried feet first, but at least he's free of his pain now. . . .

Before Shadrach could finish, the first hailstone smashed on the ground next to him. The next piece of ice hit, then a shower of the hailstones showered the ground like a cascade of diamonds. The men couldn't believe it was really hailing at first, but when the stones began stinging them sharply, they dropped their shovels and ran. Shadrach tried to walk with dignity as the stones bounced off the brim of his hat. When a stone two inches across fell at his feet, he raced with the other men until they took shelter under the protection of the prison gate.

Inside the penitentiary, the inmates took note of Mopt's prediction of an afterlife by banging their tin cups on the bars of their windows.

"Damn, old John didn't waste any time letting us know," a toothless trustee said, grinning up at Shadrach. "I just might take up religion again myself."

Shadrach rubbed his face where the stones had left red bruises and welts on his shoulders.

"Next time Brother Mopt sends us a prophesy, I'm going to request a light snowstorm instead."

Chapter Twenty-Nine

In 1890, with its leaders in prison, its assembly halls padlocked, its membership divided, the church was forced to relent on the issue of plural marriage.

President Wilford Woodruff announced that plural marriage was no longer officially sanctioned. From that moment on, the Principle was disowned.

The Woodruff Manifesto sent shock waves through Deseret. The Principle had been one of the tenets of the faith. The defense of plural marriage had been part of the history of the territory. The long struggle with the federal authorities had symbolized the Saints' desire for freedom.

Now the battle was lost. The Saints had conceded the bitterly fought contest.

Many citizens of Deseret breathed a sigh of relief. No longer would they have to fear federal marshals. No longer would Mormons be a joke to the rest of the country. No longer would the church be persecuted. The millstone of polygamy was lifted from their shoulders.

The younger Saints were anxious to put the past behind them. They wanted Utah to become a state. They looked forward to moving into the Twentieth Century, now only a decade away. Salt Lake City could take its place among the important metropolises of America.

On July 4, 1890, the younger Saints gathered on the shores of the Great Salt Lake. A huge amusement park had been built. Its gingerbread spires and Victorian architecture contained tunnels of love, thrill rides and the new nickelodeon machines. The young people cheered as the fireworks shot over the lake, and their cheers were for the United States.

The faraway fireworks were visible through the windows of the Hill House where a different kind of gathering was taking place. This group was not happy about the recent surrender to the federal authorities.

Shadrach Tompkins had assembled his wives around his dining room table. The five women sat stiffly, their silence betraying their unhappiness. Sarah rested her brow in her hand, her tears staining the lace tablecloth.

"It appears that we are not going to be allowed to grow old gracefully and be forgotten," Shadrach said, trying to pick up the spirits of the women. "This Woodruff Manifesto places another burden on our backs."

"We have been betrayed!" Rachel said pointedly. "These younger upstarts in the church have sacrificed us. All they can think of is statehood for Utah and everything else be damned! *Utah!* What a name for a state! To name it after a pack of flea-bitten Indians! The least they could have done was to keep the name 'Deseret.' "

"The younger people have yielded everything. They have taken the vote away from the women. They have taken the women away from the men. And they have taken the man away from the church," Theresa said.

"Saints used to stick together," Polly complained. "Now all I hear is what Saint is getting rich and what Saint is getting poor. What Saint is going to be a Republican and what Saint is going to be a Democrat."

"Salt Lake used to be a beautiful town. Now it reminds me of Lahaina when the whaling ships came in," Wamoa observed. "I see drunks and whores on State Street now. Salt Lake has become another Babylon."

"The new manifesto will force men to leave their wives and children to become bastards," Sarah said. "What are you going to do, husband?"

The women turned to Shadrach.

"When I was sealed to my wives I was sealed for eternity," Shadrach said, drawing the words up from his heart. "I will not abandon them on the whim of any man or institution. My vows will not be changed to suit the politicians."

"Amen, brother," Rachel said.

"I have watched this community change," he continued, "and the changes have not pleased me. Perhaps I am old-fashioned; but I intend to cling to the old ways. I will be always true to the faith."

"But how can we, in these times?" Theresa asked.

"Religion was not meant to be practiced in the city. There

are too many temptations from money and machines," Shadrach said. "I am ready to quit this Babylon and travel to the remote countryside where I can live close to God in the faith we have followed all these years."

"Back to Polyg Canyon?" Sarah asked.

"No. To a better place. A place I was shown by an old Indian many years before. It is so remote it has no name. Once we go there, no one will ever trouble us again. We can live out our lives in simple harmony. I call the place 'Eden.' "

The women looked at one another. There was no discussion.

"Wherever you shall lead, husband," Rachel said quietly, "we shall follow."

On Pioneer Day, July 24, 1890, the whole of Salt Lake City closed down for a celebration. The streets were swept clean and the street lamps hung with bright bunting in anticipation of the huge parade which would wind through the streets.

For the first time in forty-three years, the Saints could expect a peaceful future.

At the Hill House, every living descendant of Shadrach Tompkins gathered for a special family celebration. From his seven wives, Shadrach had produced forty-three children of whom thirty-nine had survived to adulthood. These had produced one hundred and fifty-five grandchildren. The fourth generation of the Tompkins clan were represented by Ham's children.

Nearly two hundred Tompkins gathered at the Hill House that day. They had been arriving in the city for days. Cousins, brothers and sisters who had not seen each other for years opened up their houses and took their family in, forgetting past feuds and sibling jealousies.

At Hill House, the poorer relations of the family had gathered, sleeping on mattresses in every one of the upstairs rooms. The young men slept out on the back lawn. The house was never quiet, children running around screaming at all hours.

Shadrach wandered around, trying to soothe the tempers of his granchildren like a lumbering old giant among a tribe of ill-behaved dwarves.

He wandered into the kitchen where a dozen ladies were tripping and fighting with each other as they prepared the picnic lunch.

"Are all these noisy brats part of my spawn?" he asked Polly, half in pride and half in bewilderment.

"Children are Utah's most important crop," Polly answered, wiping the sweat from her brow. "They are all yours, one way or another."

"Perhaps we should not have surrendered to the Gentiles, then," Shadrach mused. "Given a few years we could have outbred them."

"We're still going to need to breed if we want to outvote the Gentiles," Hezibah said, "and since breeding is the one sin the church encourages us to perform, then I don't think a Gentile politician has a chance."

Polly and Hezibah suddenly fell silent. Shadrach turned to see what had quieted two garrulous women like themselves. In the doorway to the kitchen stood a woman dressed in a fashionably cut dress. The woman was taller than the others in the family. Her blonde hair had not lost its lustre since the angry time he had seen her last.

"Hello, Ilsa. Welcome home," Shadrach said gently.

"Hello, Papa. It's good to be home," the woman said, relieved at his acceptance.

She held out her hand. A young boy wearing a scaled-down sailor's suit came shyly out of the living room and placed his small hand in hers. He looked frightened when he saw the imposing presence of Shadrach.

"This is your grandfather I have told you so much about," Ilsa said. "Go up and give him a kiss, Jonathan."

The boy hung back, and had to be pushed into his grandfather's arms. "I don't want to kiss him," Jonathan screamed. "That big beard is scratchy."

Laughing, Shadrach roared like a bear and shook his long gray beard in the boy's face.

"I guess I've scared you and your son in turn in my lifetime," he said good-naturedly.

"Papa . . . about the time I left. I wanted to say. . . ."

Shadrach shook her comments aside with a wag of his hand. "Those were hard times for all of us. There is no need for explanations. I am simply relieved that you are visiting us."

Ilsa rushed forward and fell into his arms. She buried her face in his beard as he patted her on the back.

"The old beard is still as scratchy as ever, Papa. You haven't changed a bit."

"What about this Gentile you married? I hope you have come to your senses and left him?"

"Not a chance, Papa. He is staying in the Hotel Carlysle. I didn't want him along in case there were any fireworks over here."

"Well go and fetch him before the festivities start," Shadrach roared. "I have everything else in my family. I might as well have a Gentile or two."

That afternoon Ilsa's husband, the geologist from Washington D.C. sat in the middle of two hundred Mormons as they crowded into the back yard of Shadrach Tompkins home. The man sweated quietly in the heat. The midday sun was not diluted by the shady elm trees like a canopy over the green yard.

Shadrach sat at the head of the table, his wives proudly sitting at his side. No federal marshal would have dared disturb the peace of Salt Lake that day. Around him, Shadrach's eldest sons, Ham, Walker, Nehi, Jared, sat in their solemn black suits, their wives wearing dresses of identical color. Seated at a greater distance from the head of the household were the younger members of the family.

A steer had been slaughtered and roasted over coals in the backyard. This horrified the young girls of the family who wanted a more sophisticated meal. They were embarrassed their grandfather was acting like a frontiersman.

Shadrach watched with pleasure as the family consumed the entire cow faster than a tribe of Utes. When the dessert had been cleared away, he rose to his feet and pounded on the table top for attention.

"When we first came to this valley there was less shade in one hundred miles than we have now in this back yard," he began. "We froze and starved and fought and built the city we wanted. These have been bold days and I'm damn proud to have seen them."

The family fell into a hushed silence. Not even a baby cried.

"We thought the Millenium was going to come, but it hasn't happened quite yet. We thought we were going to be wiped out, but they couldn't beat us. In spite of all the torment visited on us, the Saints are on the face of the earth for good. The world is a better place for it!"

A polite burst of applause followed this observation.

"Now it's time for me to take my leave of this city,"

Shadrach announced to the surprise of his guests. "I'm going to move to the wilderness to consecrate my life to my religion. I've never worn out the Tabernacle with my attendence but I'm going to spend the rest of my life making up for lost time."

Looks of apprehension showed on the faces of his descendants.

"I am giving up much of my property to the church. I never want to see another assembly hall padlocked for lack of money again. The rest of my property will be divided up among you although I hope you don't get rich from it. I came to this valley with nothing so you can't be much worse off."

Shadrach's wives all beamed proudly at him and he winked back at them.

"You younger people must get tired of us oldtimers telling about how hard we've had it. Just remember one thing. If the Millenium does come, it doesn't matter how big the house you live in. Prepare yourself for the end of the world, and you will enjoy yourself if it lasts."

The tears welled up in the old man's eyes.

"Most of all, I know you will be all right. Your are all of my blood, and that blood is strong."

The sidewalks of Salt Lake were crowded with people who had turned out to see the Pioneer Parade. Brass bands from Mormon colonies as far away as Manitoba, Canada, marched to the cheers of the crowd. Farmers from the Cache Valley and from St. George carried their crops in review.

The prancing horses pulled the gleaming steam boilers of the Salt Lake fire department pumpers. Even a regiment of soldiers in white pith helmets from Fort Douglas got a cheer as they marched by.

In the middle of the parade, a group of children had been costumed as the original pioneers.

The young boys wore floppy hats and horsehide beards over their freckled faces. The girls marched beside them keeping their long gingham dresses from dragging in the dust.

On the other end of town, a different procession was forming. Shadrach Tompkins had loaded his five wives and a few possessions into a train of wagons for the journey into the wilderness. The caravan lumbered away from the tree-lined street and paused on the hill overlooking the town.

"There it is, ladies. Take one last look," Shadrach said, squeezing Sarah who sat beside him.

The most visible landmark in the town was the spires of the Temple. The structure was almost complete. It had been forty years in the building. Two more years would see its completion.

The tall gray walls were as imposing as any cathedral in Europe. Four corner spires rose so high above the Temple block they could be seen for miles away. The building stood as a stern and quiet reminder of the Saints' granite faith. Both the religion and the Temple could endure ten thousand years without crumbling.

"My only regret in my life is that I was not able to do my church work in the completed Temple," Sarah said quietly. "This is the one deed left undone."

Shadrach nodded with understanding. Then he gave the reins of the wagon a brisk flick.

"We're going to a place that shares that glory," he called so all could hear him. "And when we find our Zion, we're never going to leave!"